MR. TERRITAFF
DARK MATTERS

A NOVEL

BY
GARY K. WALLACE

DEDICATION

For Brother Bruce, who introduced me to science fiction. For Brother Victor, who always knew how to make me laugh, and for my daughters, Amy and L.E., who are always by my side, supporting me in everything I do.

ACKNOWLEDGMENTS

My sincere thanks to my beta readers, Orest Zalopino, Walt Holmes, and Debbie Haas; their feedback was invaluable in writing the final draft. To my editor, Danny Sheiman, whose editing insights made the book more readable. Special gratitude to my writer groups, who encouraged me and helped hone my writing skills. A big shout-out to the community of friends in the Foothills of San Marcos; their support keeps me going.

And to my beautiful daughters, Amy and Lisa, for their unconditional love and honest critiques. Finally, my gratitude to my brother from another mother, Dr. Sandy Cohen, who suffered through reading many earlier drafts of both books. His critiques and suggestions showed me the way in my writer's journey.

TABLE OF CONTENTS

PART I

MR. TERRITAFF

CHAPTER 1

Territaff found her in an alley, propped upright against a dumpster. Her eyes opened, staring with a lifeless gaze, her face distorted by a ghastly smile, likely forced postmortem by her assailant.

He knelt on one knee and studied her with a coroner's detachment. Her high cheekbones and full mouth were swollen and blackened with bruises. Both of her extended hands had defensive wounds of thin cuts and blackened knuckles.

She must've fought a hell of a fight, Territaff thought, pulling a scanner from his black leather jacket. He set it for a humanoid bioscan mode, then ran it down her long and well-defined body. The scanner's small display put her time of death as 0934.23 hours.

He spoke into the scanner, "Cause of death?"

"Systemic shock due to intense electromagnetic discharge," the scanner's automated voice answered.

"Less than two minutes," Territaff said. "I could've prevented this. Dammit! How could this have happened?"

He gazed at her with regret and anger for not following his instincts. Territaff promised himself the next candidate would be one of his choosing, not from the military, someone he could trust to follow his orders and be dedicated to the mission, not their career.

"Cuz," Territaff telepathically transmitted to his friend, who monitored the situation from their cloaked ship orbiting Earth's moon.

"Yes, Terri."

"We've lost Tanya. I found her body. Get her back to the ship before she's discovered. Also, I want a complete area analysis, then sterilize it."

"Acknowledged. I'm sorry, Terri. I know you had your differences, but you seemed to like her spirit."

"Yeah." He let out a heavy breath. *"She didn't deserve this. She was bucking for promotion by trying to impress Cameron and got herself killed for her efforts. What a waste."*

"Tanya's death is an unfortunate loss. What are you going to do?"

Territaff thought for a moment as he studied Tanya's empty gaze before closing her eyes. Then he transmitted, *"Search for a new candidate."*

"Are we still meeting with Cameron?"

"Yes. I want to know why he had her following us."

"I've completed the analysis."

"Okay."

"Standard low-frequency pulse-phaser at point-blank range."

"No surprise there."

"However, there's also a faint trace of negative energy."

"Negative energy? Are you sure? How's that possible?"

"There is insufficient data for a cogent hypothesis."

"Make an educated guess."

"I'm sorry, Terri. The energy signature is unknown."

"Understood. Just thinking aloud."

"I see. You've been doing a lot of that lately. Is this related to being back on Earth?"

"Maybe."

"Could you be more specific?"

"Not now. I need a drink and time to rethink our situation."

* * *

Territaff walked for over an hour, searching for the right place. His mind whirled with memories as he passed familiar streets and establishments. He frowned when he came to the corner drugstore on Lincoln Road. After school, he would go there to buy the latest superhero comic and read it while enjoying a Cherry Coke. It has been remodeled into a super drugstore chain.

South Beach had long given up much of its seasonal allure

in favor of its glitzy 1990s makeover. Most of South Beach needed a facelift, but to Territaff's surprise, many old hotels and office buildings were renovated, retaining some of the city's original Art Déco charm.

He smiled when he saw the well-lit establishment at the end of a long block across from the beach. He sensed he was close to what he was seeking. The sign over the double wooden doors read, "Fat Jacks, Established 1918." *Is this the same Fat Jack's I frequented in Key West?*

He stopped outside the doors and listened to the sounds of people and music inside. The atmosphere sounded inviting, so he decided this was a good place to gather his thoughts and reflect on his circumstances.

Territaff paused inside the doors to observe. The lighting was soft and indistinct, lending the room gentle incandescence to escape the mounting tensions. Soft rock music played under the murmurs of voices talking and laughing.

The bar and grill had the same genuine Key West ambiance. Fish nets were strung on the walls. Opened parachutes covered the ceiling with hanging paddle fans, giving it a similar look to Sloppy Joes. It's just like Territaff remembered it. The restaurant was reminiscent of another time and place in his life. He recognized the old wooden bar. The owner must have moved it from the Keys, he thought. He recalled the owner telling him he salvaged it from a hundred-year-old yacht. Territaff ran his hand over its smooth surface. The wood had a marble-like finish, probably made by a century of oily, rubbing fingers.

Tanya's lifeless eyes lingered on Territaff as he sat on a stool in the middle of the bar. He spun slowly around a few times to absorb the room into his memory. As he completed his third round, he sensed a young server staring at him. He faced her and smiled at her pleasant features.

"May I help you, sir?" she asked, arching an eyebrow.

"Pernod, do you have any?" Territaff said.

"Yes, but we don't get many requests for it." The server gave Territaff a closer look. "Are you European?"

"No, just a tired traveler needing a short break from a tough day."

"And Pernod will do that for you? I can think of better things than that," she laughed.

Territaff liked her warm and friendly manner. He studied the curves of her young, slender body. Her soft, auburn hair and reddish-brown skin accentuated her cheerful brown eyes. He gazed into the server's large eyes. He sensed a strong inner strength within her. Could she be the one? He asked himself.

She felt Territaff's stare. She always had an answer for such looks, but this time, she searched under the counter for a bottle of Pernod.

"How do you like it?" she asked, holding a full bottle up to him.

"In a large glass," he answered, pointing at the oversized wine goblets hanging overhead on wooden racks.

She stretched her long, angular body for a goblet. Territaff caught a glimpse of her shapely buttocks peeking out of the bottom of her short pants, wondering if she was aware of the effect she was having on the male patrons, gathering around the bar.

"My name is Territaff," he introduced himself as she filled his goblet. "But my friends call me Terri."

"I'm Kathy," she replied, looking up into his eyes.

His eyes attracted her. She studied them with curiosity. They were like two dark orbs shining back at her. She avoided them to take in the rest of his face. She took pride in her keen ability to read people's faces. Her occupation had allowed her to develop the skill over several years of trial and error. Kathy looked closer. His features were subtle, almost indistinct. There were no age lines around his eyes and forehead to guide her. It wasn't a youthful-looking face. It looked mature but also ageless, perplexing her to near frustration.

Territaff waited for her to conclude her examination before draining his goblet in a few big swallows.

Kathy wrinkled her forehead and asked, "What do you do, Mr. Territaff?"

"Please, call me Terri," he said, pondering her lovely features. "What I do is a little hard to explain. I guess you could say I'm a diplomatic courier." He held his goblet up for a refill.

"Sounds fascinating." Kathy's puzzled expression changed to one of excited interest as she poured his Pernod. "You must travel a lot."

"Yes."

"You've traveled around the world, I bet."

"Oh yes. In a sense, you could say I've traveled to many worlds. He smiled and drank a long sip of his Pernod.

"I guess you've seen a lot of strange things."

"Strange and beautiful."

"I wish I could do that," Kathy said with a dreamy look.

"Be a diplomat?"

"No. Travel. Get out of this place and see the world."

"I understand."

Territaff looked out through the expansive window overlooking the beach. "I don't know. This doesn't seem so bad."

"You think so. Just wait until happy hour really gets going."

As Kathy was about to leave, Territaff said, "I can tell you a little about some of the places I've been if you're interested."

"Is that your best pick-up line?"

"You misjudged me. I'm most sincere about that."

She gave Territaff a sly grin before leaving to serve the ever-increasing number of impatient, thirsty people crowding around the bar.

He followed the homogeneous faces as they came and went. They would mingle and mix, then break into cavorting, intoxicated clusters. The room was filled with bodies pulsating and vibrating with rising sounds and emotions. Territaff had forgotten what an overwhelming aura of want and desire a cramped gathering of humanity generated. He reflected on them as they spoke, drank, and solicited for an evening full of promises never to be kept.

"Care for another?" Kathy asked as her rounds brought her back to Territaff.

"I thought you would never return, leaving me here to decay into a sober cloud of thirsty dust."

"Really? Oh, you poor soul, let me quench your thirst, but drink a little slower. It's happy hour." She refilled his goblet, then resumed her dance around the bar.

Territaff continued to observe with interest, remembering what it was like to be human. An odd-looking, diminutive man walked in and took a seat that opened across the bar from Territaff. Their eyes fixed on one another for a long moment until Kathy approached the man and asked what he was drinking. He ordered mineral water.

The man sat upright on his stool, staring outward through oversized, round-rimmed glasses. His watery blue eyes were cold and almost lifeless, except for the occasional blink. He gave Territaff a faint smile as Kathy served him his mineral water. He took a thirsty gulp and then turned his attention to Kathy.

Territaff sensed the small man's energy and became concerned for her. He finished his Pernod and held the empty goblet to get her attention.

She came right over to him and whispered, "There's something creepy about that guy."

"Yeah. I got the same vibe when he sat down. Do you know him?"

"No. I'd never seen him before, and I hope he leaves soon.

She cleared off empty beer bottles and glasses from the bar.

Territaff glanced at the man and caught him staring fixedly

at him. *Curious*, Territaff became intrigued with the odd little man and went to speak to him. As he approached, the customer sitting to the right of the small man got up and gave his seat to Territaff. The now-standing man gave Territaff a confused look. He was about to say something, but instead took a long swallow of his beer and resumed his conversation with his still-seated friend. He overheard the man's friend asking why he had left his seat. The confused customer shrugged as they looked at Territaff. Territaff gave him an appreciative nod as he took his stool, then leaned close to the man with the oversized glasses.

"Do I know you?" Territaff asked.

"Yes," the man whispered, narrowing his cold, probing eyes.

Territaff considered him, searching within his memory for who he was. When nothing came to mind, he telepathically transmitted to the ship, "*Cuz, do a quick scan of the man seated to my right.*"

Cuz responded with shock, "*It's Zohleemay.*"

Well, hello, old nemesis, Territaff thinks with a slow smile. "Nice cover, Zoh," he said as Kathy brought him another Pernod. She glances at the creepy guy and says to Territaff, "Here, you look like you need this."

After Kathy left, Zohleemay leaned closer to Territaff and said, "I guess the rumor of your resurrection was accurate." He turns his thin lips into a mocking smile and sips his mineral water. "I must admit that the Venubians are skillful engineers," he added, "but they're weak fools and will soon become part of the new order."

"You have developed some new morphing techniques and improved speech. Impressive."

"If you want to be impressed, ask your friend," he paused, "Cuz, to sweep the room."

Territaff transmitted the request to Cuz.

"*There are four morphed Zenti within the crowds around*

the bar. Transmitting their identities and locations." Cuz's transmission had a sense of concern and surprise. *"Terri, their ability to morph is far beyond anything we've encountered. Please use great care in executing your next move."*

"So, what now, Zoh?" Territaff asked.

Intense and unsettling emotions ran through Kathy. She looked up from the drinks she was mixing and glanced at the room. Territaff, seated next to the creepy little man, caught her eye. She focused on the spooky man for a moment. He had a disquieting aura about him. She glanced at Territaff and sensed that his energy was powerful and different.

I can feel you, she whispered, looking away from Territaff. The thought ran a shudder through her. She bit her lower lip in thought. Kathy gets two shot glasses and fills them with Tequila. She kept the shots low while walking to the two men, who looked like they were about to come to blows, and said, "We're having a special on Donatello Tequila." These are on the house." She placed the two large shot glasses in front of them.

Territaff welcomed her distraction and said, "Don't mind if I do. " He tilted it to Kathy, then downed the drink quickly and slapped the empty glass on the bar. Very good." He looked at Zoh, who appeared annoyed and said, "That's most impolite not taking a free round. You're insulting this attractive lady. Live a little and have a shot." Territaff slapped the stiffly seated man on the back and grinned.

Zohleemay gave him a glaring look and regarded the shot glass before taking it to his lips and allowing the clear liquid to flow down his gullet. He placed the glass down, gave Territaff a crooked grin, and said, "Not exactly Klaxon brandy wine, but not bad."

"Would you like another?" Territaff said, looking at the two morphed Zenti, watching their every move. "Your companions look nervous, Zoh. Why are they so antsy? I hope they're not expecting something stupid?"

Zohleemay glimpsed their way. "They'll do nothing unless I tell them to."

"So, if I were to pull out a gun and shoot you in the head, what would they do?"

With a mirthless grin, he said, "They'll kill you along with everybody else in this establishment."

"Why don't we go out to the beach and have a little chat?"

Zohleemay stood. The two Zenti closest to him also got up. He stopped them with a glaring look, then gestured for the other two morphed Zenti to stay put.

Kathy spied Territaff walking out of the beach entrance with the weird little man. They stopped at the water's edge and stared out into the distance. It was a clear night, and the full moon's silvery glow reflected on the smooth water, giving the scene ironic tranquility. The two men stood close to each other. Their faces reflected the soft glow of moonlight and the dull orange lights from the nearby pier.

Zohleemay took in a deep breath of salty ocean air. His slight frame stood upright as Territaff hovered over him like a giant.

"Beautiful, isn't it?" Territaff said.

"This planet has many wonderful resources. More than its inhabitants realize."

"They're learning and growing, and I'll do everything I can to protect them." Territaff's expression changed into an angry sneer as he stared into Zohleemay's smug face.

"You can do nothing to protect your people," Zohleemay said. "I suggest you run while you can. Because the next time we meet, I'll kill you. And this time, Phillip, it will be permanent."

"The name is Territaff. You killed Phillip Mann—remember?"

"What's in a name?" He paused before hissing out, "Territaff? Earthman." He arched a thin eyebrow and curled his mouth into an ironic smile. "How appropriate. They named you for what you are. A lowly Earthman."

"I wouldn't be so confident. These are resilient people who are not as helpless as you believe. But then, your overconfidence has always been your greatest weakness. They'll prevail. Like the Venubians, Klaxons, Kaydens, and most other worlds, you've tried to conquer and failed. Regardless of what you do. We'll prevail."

Zohleemay turned his bulbous eyes up at him and said, "You've no idea of the forces at work here. We're no longer alone, and you're unprepared for the reign of power, which is about to crush this isolated little pebble of a planet. Everything you know and love will soon be laid to waste, and I want you to see it happen before I kill you."

Territaff grabbed him by the throat, pulling him up close to his face. Their eyes became fixed. Territaff struggled to restrain the rising hatred he had for the gasping, wiry, grotesque within his grip.

"I should snap your neck like a twig and end you now—I want to...."

"Put 'im down," a scratchy-sounding voice shouted behind Territaff.

Territaff turned toward the nervous-looking man, who was holding a small, handheld pulse laser aimed at him. He smiled at seeing the Zenti from the bar joined by the other three.

"I admire your new morphing technology," Territaff said, studying the now-armed group of Zenti that had gathered around him. Reluctantly, he released his grip on Zohleemay, letting him fall hard to the sandy beach. He studied the anxious-looking group for a moment. None of them was taller than 1.5 meters. While there were distinct differences in their overall facial features, they all appeared similar in terms of size and appearance. Dressed in dark-colored suits, white shirts, and thin, solid-colored ties, they looked like throwbacks to 1970s business attire. Territaff realized that the weapon being held on him was the same type that killed Tanya.

"You killed her," he said in a low, angry growl as he faced

Zohleemay. "Why? She was no threat to you."

"She foolishly got in our way. So, we eliminated her. Besides, she served her purpose—she led us to you."

Territaff turned and studied the small group of morphed Zenti, who were all looking at him with the same wide-eyed stares.

"You're all so beautifully dressed that I almost hate to mess you up," he said, then grabbed two by their collars in each hand and held them tight.

"Now, drop your weapons like good little Zenti," Territaff ordered through clenched teeth. Their weapons fell to the sand as the aliens hissed and gasped. He pulled them up closer to his face before slamming their heads together, then flung them like rag dolls into the rushing surf.

Zohleemay regarded his struggling men for a moment before snarling at Territaff.

"Go. Run," he said in a throaty hiss. "Save yourself while you can, but you can't hide. I will have you and your homeworld. Your time is all but gone, Territaff."

A thick overcast of clouds blocked out the moon, creating a dismal, shadowy darkness. A sudden flash of intense, white light appeared for a moment, then dissipated in a thin veil that vanished. All the Zenti disappeared. Territaff stood still, almost mesmerized by the light, pondering the phenomenon in confusion.

"*Cuz,*" Territaff transmitted, "*do a quick scan of the area.*"

"*Interesting. I'm reading the same energy signature as before. The pattern is familiar, but I don't have enough data to identify it definitively.*"

"*Can you speculate?*"

"*I can say with some certainty that the phenomenon exhibits characteristics of a negative energy wave but of an unknown type and origin.*"

"*Are you implying that the Zenti somehow developed this energy?*"

"*At this juncture, I can't imply anything.*"

"*Good point, Cuz.*"

Territaff stared out at the moonlit sea, pondering the dark ramifications of the phenomenon he had witnessed. He looked up at the night sky and mumbled, "We're in some deep shit now."

He let out a long, heavy sigh before going back to the bar. Territaff saw Kathy walk in ahead of him. *Oh, Kathy, you saw something you shouldn't have,* Territaff frowned. *Now, what should I do about it?* It only took a moment, and he smiled inwardly at the thought. *Well, my dear, you've unwittingly enlisted in my private little army.*

CHAPTER 2

Territaff returned to his stool and continued to watch throughout the busy hours. He sat, sipping Pernod, until the bar had emptied to only a few couples in the early hours of the morning.

"You do your job well," Territaff said to Kathy.

She smiled at the compliment but didn't look at him as she cleared the bar of littered napkins, stirrers, and empty glasses. She returned clean goblets to the overhead racks but stopped and turned to Territaff. She leaned close to him and said with restrained excitement, "I saw what you did to those men." Her voice remained calm, but Territaff sensed her apprehension.

"I know," he said with regret. "We must talk."

"I should be afraid of you, but for some strange reason, I'm not. It's as though what I saw was more of an aberration. No one is that strong..." She turned away and went to the other side of the bar, mumbling to herself.

The last customers finally left, anxious and clumsy with inebriated passions. Territaff moved to where Kathy was working. She tried to avoid him by focusing on polishing the large brandy snifters. Her movements were jerky and full of nervous energy. He gazed at her, waiting for her to acknowledge him. Kathy lifted her large brown eyes and felt a chill run through her as she peered into Territaff's impassive face. His dark eyes shone back at her with an anticipatory expression.

"I don't know if you frighten or intrigue me," Kathy said in a low, controlled voice. But Territaff could feel her strong emotions pushing on her. "I know you're dangerous, and I should do everything in my power to avoid you." She held herself still as she noticed Territaff's intent stare. "So, why aren't I running?" she whispered.

She avoided Territaff's eyes while placing the rest of the

clean goblets into the overhead glass racks.

"It would be against your nature to run," Territaff answered her.

"What do you mean?" she said without turning.

"You're far too inquisitive to allow all you have seen to just go. No, my dear. You can't run because I intrigue and frighten you. That's my charm."

She squinted as if trying to see him in a different light.

He smiled broadly and added, "My great sense of urgency is compelling you to stay. You can feel me. I sensed you probing me..." His voice trailed off with a sudden revelation. "You're empathic." He looked closer at Kathy. "You are, but you don't have control over it yet. You will, though. In time. With my help.

Kathy's jaw dropped in astonishment. "How could you know that?" she whispered, her complexion blanching.

"Kathy, we must talk."

"Have we met before?"

"Unfortunately, no."

Kathy wrinkled her nose. "You're sure?"

"Quite sure. Why do you ask?"

"I don't know. I have this odd feeling I know you from somewhere."

"Why not just think of me as an admirer awaiting his last Pernod and the pleasure of getting to know you better?" He held his hand out to her.

She took his hand and began to study it. To her surprise, it wasn't soft and fleshy but felt hard and powerful. Kathy inspected his long fingers. His nails, as expected, were clean and perfectly trimmed.

"Does my hand interest you?"

"Everything about you interests me," she answered, staring closely at his palm.

"You fascinate me as well." He gave her hand a gentle squeeze.

Kathy considered Territaff's impassive face and said, "Okay," as if she had decided within herself. "Wait for me. I'll only be a few more minutes."

"*Cuz,*" Territaff transmitted. "*I think I found her.*"

"*Most attractive,*" Cuz said at seeing Kathy's transmitted image. "*She looks young,*" he added.

She's old enough, and I believe she's highly intuitive, with probable empathic abilities. Plus, she's smart. I need to conduct a closer examination of her capabilities. This was something I couldn't do with Tanya."

"*You're referring to having intercourse with her. Aren't you?*"

"*Well... yeah. I find it revealing and the most expedient method to discover her true nature and other qualities.*"

"*Really. I find that fascinating. Would you care to elaborate on what you mean by other qualities?*"

"*Not now, Cuz.*"

CHAPTER 3

"Good night, Jack," Kathy called back as she entered the street. Territaff watched her as she took in a deep breath of salty air. Kathy stretched out her tight back and walked up the street. She passed Territaff and pretended not to notice him, leaning against a wall of the restaurant.

"I understand the beach is beautiful right before dawn," Territaff said in a low voice.

Kathy smiled and said, "It's my favorite time of day."

"Would you like to watch the sunrise?" He extended his arm to her.

She narrowed her eyes into a penetrating stare as though examining his sincerity. "Now that I've stumbled into your sordid world, you're wondering what to do about me." She studied his face and asked, "Have I become an expendable liability you need to dump in some dark alley?"

"That would be one option," he said flatly.

"Oh?" Her face flushed in surprise. "What other options are you considering?"

Territaff scratched the back of his head in thought. He regarded her with probing eyes.

Kathy trembled with fear.

He stopped and placed his long hands on the sides of her face. He spread his fingertips across her brow, his thumbs resting under her cheekbones. Kathy's gaze became fixed on his dark eyes as he whispered something incoherent. The tension that had wrapped a smothering hold on her disappeared.

Kathy sighed with relief and said, "What did you do?"

"Dialed down your nerves a little. You have nothing to fear from me. You're right, however. You did stumble into my sordid world."

She gave Territaff a curious look and, in a timid voice, asked, "Are you going to kill me?"

Territaff shook his head, admiring the brazen question. He extended his hand to her. "Come, let's watch the sunrise."

She hesitated, chewing on her lower lip.

It was a familiar gesture from someone now lost to him. "I promise, you're in no danger from me, and I'll allow no harm to come to you." He started to smile, then frowned. "Unfortunately, you're no longer safe on your own."

"I'm not sure who's more dangerous," she said with a nervous laugh. "You or the strange little men I saw you with. What was that all about? And that white light. What was that?" She started walking toward the water, mumbling to herself. "I've always enjoyed a little danger. It spices things up a little." She stopped as she reached the water's edge, flopped down, took off her shoes, and curled her toes into the cool, moist sand.

Territaff sat beside her and listened.

"Why did you have to come into my life?" she shouted. She pondered the handsome face looking at her with a compelling smile. *Run, Kathy.* Her conscience yelled at her. *He's trouble, and he'll fuck up your life.*

She couldn't help herself. Her curiosity overrode her usual good common sense. Usually, she would've refused Territaff, but nothing was normal about him, which made him far too intriguing to let him go.

Territaff wrapped his long arm around Kathy's shoulders and moved her close to him. She looked at his face and said dreamily, "I don't know why I'm with you. You appeal to me in ways I can't figure out. What is it about you that worries and entices me?" She looked down and dug her big toe into the sand. "Even your name is strange. You're violent, yet I sense a strong, glowing spiritual light in you." She aimed a heavy stare and added, "And you have a hold on me that's frightening."

Her eyes welled, and a thin line of tears ran down her cheek.

"I'm sorry you had to see all of that. Look at me, Kathy."

She looked at him. He pulled a handkerchief from his back pocket and handed it to her. She dried her eyes and blew her nose. She gazed at the white handkerchief, then rubbed it between her fingers.

"What kind of material is this?" she said. "It's so soft, but it doesn't feel like cotton. Is it linen?"

"It's synthetic."

Kathy held the handkerchief out to him, then stopped and said, "Sorry. I'll have it dry-cleaned and returned to you. Thanks."

"Please. Keep it," Territaff said. "A small memento of our new friendship. Forget about dry cleaning. It'll clean itself. It's a prototype."

She took a second look at the handkerchief, which appeared dry and clean. "I don't know what to make of it or you, Territaff."

"As I've already told you. You have nothing to fear from me. However, you should fear what you saw. I admit I'm a walking contradiction." He looked up at the pale blue of the early dawn sky and smiled. "I'm a product of two worlds and belong to none. That's what's bothering you. You're empathic, and you're feeling my own strong emotions coming to the surface. Don't let your fear of the unknown prejudice your innate sensibilities, Kathy. Look into your heart. Can you sense my sincerity? You have a similar effect on me. If you knew the risk of talking to you—" Looking into Kathy's wide, brown eyes, he said, "I felt something special about you when you said, 'Can I help you' in the bar. As soon as I gazed into your beautiful eyes, I wanted to be with you. I know how this must sound, but—"

Kathy held a finger to his lips and said softly, almost timidly, "I think we're both going against our nature tonight." I never go out with customers. It's a bad practice, but I need to be with you for some compelling reason. Besides, most of the guys I meet are usually just after my body and couldn't care less about me. So, I spend much of my time alone. I prefer it that way."

"It's apparent that we feel the same about each other, Kathy. I'm no stranger to being alone. I've discovered that we all need to be with someone from time to time. It's essential to know someone other than ourselves who can appreciate who we are, if only to dispel the solitude, share our feelings, and compare life.

Kathy noticed a star-like twinkle in Territaff's eyes as he kissed her, first gently, then more passionately. A surge of energy ran through her. She had experienced nothing like it before. When he concluded, she felt numb and exhilarated at the same time.

The dawn broke the blue-gray into a visible orange glow as the first rays of the sun broke the horizon, then, with its subtle fluidity, into a glowing palette of bright oranges and blues. They silently watched until the morning air became heavy with humidity as the sun warmed the beach.

"It'll be a hot one today," Kathy said, standing and brushing the sand off the back of her legs with her hands. She looked down at Territaff and watched him for a moment in the clear light of day. His features appeared softer, and those mysterious eyes looked up at Kathy with a disarming quality that surprised her.

Kathy's conscience was nagging her to be careful as Territaff rose and wrapped her in a tight embrace. He felt her heart pounding with nervous excitement. He also sensed Kathy struggling with her emotions.

"Ahh, nuts!" Kathy blurted, stepping back from Territaff. "I hope I won't regret this." She blew out a long breath. "I don't live far from here," she paused, taking in Territaff's now expressive face. She sensed his anticipation, moved closer, and gave Territaff a long, passionate kiss. "Okay, Terri. Take me home."

CHAPTER 4

They entered Kathy's modest apartment, and Territaff roamed the three rooms, inspecting their contents with eager curiosity. He picked up items from her tables and shelves, studied them, and then returned them to their proper places. He smiled when he noticed several books on space and time while viewing her collection. Then he flipped through her CD and DVD albums.

"You like many things. That's good; variety is important," he said as Kathy took his hand and led him into the bedroom.

She sat on the edge of the bed and removed her T-shirt, revealing her round breasts. "Yes, variety is important in everything," she said, slowly undressing Territaff, then sliding herself under the sheets.

He paused and observed her for a moment before drawing the drapes to block out the intruding sunlight.

She's lovely and trusting. He hesitated before getting into bed. *I must complete what I've started. I'll test this one. Intercourse can be most revealing.*

"Is something wrong, Terri?" she said as she lifted the sheets and motioned with her eyes for him to join her.

"No." He smiled, then joined her under the sheets.

"Has anyone ever told you that you have a masterful touch?" she moaned as Territaff fondled her breasts and rubbed the inside of her thighs. She felt her whole body relax under his gentle, stroking touch. "I don't ever remember feeling so calm. It's... It's as though I were..."

"Don't talk," Territaff whispered, then kissed her. "I want you to close your eyes and concentrate on your feelings. Clear your mind of everything and let your senses become open."

"Concentrate," she repeated, closing her eyes.

An odd but soothing tinkling sensation ran through her body.

"Oh, that feels wonderful, Terri," she murmured.

A thin veil of vivid colors formed in Kathy's mind. The colors thickened and whirled into amorphous bright red, blue, and orange globs. The globules collided, then exploded into tiny clusters surrounded by a glowing white light, forming something that resembled a nebula.

Kathy jerked upright on the bed, almost knocking Territaff to the floor. The images were still whirling around her. She screamed while rubbing her eyes, then blinked several times. She stared outward for a moment until the room appeared normal again.

"What the fuck was that?" she yelled, punching him in the chest.

Territaff caught her fist as she was about to hit him again and kissed her knuckles.

"Don't be frightened," he said. "Nothing can harm you." He kissed her cheek, then held her face in his hands. "I promise. Just relax and let your inhibitions go."

"Relax!" she yelled in his face. "Are you crazy? I'm freaking out, and you want me to relax?" She narrowed her eyes at Territaff. "You're not all you appear to be? Are you? There's something about you that worries me, Terri."

"Freaking out? That's a term I haven't heard in a while," Territaff said, then went to kiss her, but she turned away.

"You're very weird." She flopped back and rubbed her eyes again. "I was hallucinating. The room... it was... I mean... I was seeing things."

She looked at Territaff, who stared at her with dark, attentive eyes. She thought his facial features had changed, and his face now had taken on a youthful glow.

She screwed her face up into a puzzled expression. Territaff sensed Kathy's uneasiness and allowed her a moment to calm herself. Their eyes became fixed in silence. A chilling clamminess seized Kathy. Her heart pounded hard in her chest.

The strange little men, Territaff's incredible strength, and the mysterious light flashed before her in a maze of confusion. Now, the sudden hallucinations. Kathy's complexion paled while chewing on her lower lip, and she trembled, tears welling.

Territaff wrapped his long arms around her and clutched her close to his massive chest.

"No need to be frightened, Kathy. I can't, nor would I ever harm you. She shuddered as he nestled her in his arms. "It's all right," he whispered, stroking her head. "I know we've only just met, but…" He lifted her chin so he could see her face. "I need your trust and friendship. I've no one else to turn to."

She calmed herself within Terri's warm embrace. Kathy ran her hand down his arm and over his chest. They felt solid and smooth, and she could sense their power and strength. She placed her ear to his chest and listened to his heart's slow, steady rhythm. It comforted her.

"Do you really need me?" she said. "Or are you just saying that?"

"Yes." He wiped a tear from Kathy's cheek with his thumb.

"No one has ever said that to me." More tears ran down her cheeks.

"I mean everything I tell you," he whispered. "Are you ready to trust me?"

"Yeah, but what do you have in mind?" she said, wiping her face with a corner of the bedsheet.

"Something that your mind and body can share and enjoy."

"I won't freak out again?"

"You mean hallucinate?"

She nodded.

"Kathy, study me as I'm studying you. Let your inhibitions go and set your mind free. Open your senses."

Kathy fluffed up a pillow and placed it behind her head. Territaff placed his fingertips on her temples. At first, Kathy felt uneasy with his engaging stare, but once she cleared her mind, she could sense Territaff. It surprised her, but she believed she could feel his mind touching hers.

"Close your eyes and breathe slowly through your nose, and out through your mouth." She started to breathe as instructed. "Good. Now, let go of all your thoughts and inhibitions. Relax your mind and body. Picture a large, white canvas in your mind."

He lifted his fingers from her head, raised her arm, and let it go. It fell freely. Territaff smiled and said, "I think you're getting the idea."

She opened her eyes for a second to peek at Territaff, then she closed them again and wiggled a little from side to side on the bed until she got comfortable. She took a deep breath, let it out slowly, and said, "Okay, do your thing." She let out a nervous giggle.

Kathy felt a gentle tingling in the soles of her feet, which gradually rose up her legs. As the tingling moved through her body, her muscles relaxed. It felt as if she were having a precision massage. She smiled, realizing all the stiffness and tension in her back and feet had waned.

The tingling sensation gave way to a feeling of weightlessness. It felt like her body was floating upward into a velvet darkness punctuated by radiant, iridescent colors. Her body tightened with this new sensation but relaxed, sensing Territaff's close presence. Now, she could allow herself the illusion of floating through space.

A part of Kathy was drifting in space, and another part was teeming with sexual ecstasy as Territaff gently penetrated her.

"It seems so real, Terri," she said dreamily. "It's like I'm out in space, and I'm here with you at the same time... How are you... I mean, what are you doing?"

"We're sharing and exchanging pleasure and thoughts. I'm lifting your consciousness to a threshold of another dimension. It's a little complicated. I'll explain it later," he said, then touched the sides of her head with his fingertips again.

"Terri, I feel so at peace and so bizarre," Kathy murmured,

her eyes closed. It's as if you can read my mind. No—it's more than that." She opened her eyes with a sudden realization, looking at Territaff in awe. "You're controlling my mind. These are illusions, and yet they feel so real," she said in a hushed tone as though she were thinking aloud. "How are you doing this? No ordinary man can do... whatever you're doing."

Territaff kissed her, then transmitted mentally, *"Stop thinking so much and focus."* She heard Territaff's voice within her mind. He gently touched her eyelids, allowing her to close her eyes. *"Breathe slowly and let your mind and body drift."*

Territaff's soothing voice calmed her uneasiness. He watched her for a moment until she surrendered to the dreamy, meditative state he had guided her into.

"Look," she heard Territaff in her mind.

Kathy watched the Earth shrink from sight. Jupiter swelled into view and passed Saturn in the blink of an eye. She looked back at the sun; it had become a bright star fading among the billions of stars in the Milky Way. She was traveling within her mind at unimaginable speed, but there was no feeling of movement or sense of direction. It appeared like a three-dimensional movie, with all the action coming at her as she lay transfixed and exhilarated.

Pressure. Kathy felt a slight tug of pressure pushing against her. The velvet blackness of space seemed to close around her until she could see nothing. The blackness made her nervous. She touched Territaff's shoulder to reassure her he was still there. She ran her hands up and down his back. It felt smooth and hard under her touch.

"Make the blackness go away," Kathy said.

A hazy yellow-white light burst into a full spectrum of colors and rushed past her in a tidal wave of luminosity. Thin, yellow clouds with white-hot centers emerged and approached her. Clusters upon clusters of stars, some so bright it hurt her eyes to look at them, flowed upward, forming into bright, colorful shapes. Kathy became excited, realizing she was moving through bizarre and beautiful nebulae and galaxies.

The sudden awareness of what she was experiencing almost overwhelmed her. Her mind revealed a panorama that no one on Earth had seen in such perfect detail. It astonished her.

"Terri, this is all too fantastic," she said breathlessly. "It's like my mind and body are surging with energy..."

Barely audible crackling sounds were heard as colors erupted from the blackness. Shimmering blues and reds vibrated as chords plucked at random on a harp. The colors and sounds mixed and pulsed, building a frenzy of visual, sensual music. Her mind's eye became fixed on streams of unimaginable colors. The colors were so intense that they would form white voids within the perpetual night surrounding them when they collided. Then the voids would explode, spewing rings of multicolored light that illuminated the darkness surrounding her. Kathy could feel a cycle of orgasmic pulses running through her body in concert with each exploding color.

She never felt so alive. The incredible beauty and the erotic pleasure her mind and body shared mesmerized her. She felt a heightened, rhythmic wave building in her loins, like ripples on the water, undulating outward through her body.

"Terri, you sneaky bastard," Kathy blurted. "Now I understand. I really understand... Oh, my God! Don't stop, Terri... please, don't stop!"

Kathy gripped the sheets tightly as erotic euphoria surged up her back and down her legs. She wished the sensation would last forever.

* * *

Kathy woke and stretched out, shaking the slumber from her body. She could still feel a fantastic sensation within her that reassured her that what she had experienced was not a dream. With a sudden urge to attack Terri, she turned to find only empty, wrinkled sheets. She checked the clock on her night table. A thin, gold disc lying beside the lamp caught her eye. She picked it up and examined it. It had a strange pattern of lines inscribed on it. She turned it over. The other side was blank. Kathy ran a finger across its smooth surface. She weighed it in her hand; it felt heavy for its size and appeared to glow. Something about its color and how it reflected her image made her uneasy. It was as perplexing as Territaff.

"Terri," she called out to the other room. She got out of bed holding the disc. "Terri, where are you?" The apartment felt empty. "Terri, you bastard. You promised to take me with you."

Kathy returned to bed. She held the disc and pondered it for a few minutes. She thought of Territaff and twisted her mouth into an angry snarl, throwing it across the room. It made an irritating ringing noise as it bounced off a wall. She thought she saw a flash of light when it hit the floor. At first, she thought she had broken the disc, but she let the thought pass as she lay on her back, staring at the ceiling.

"You promised. You promised to take me with you."

Her eyes grew sleepy as she repeated the words. With a heavy heart, she turned on her side and let out a long sigh. Her eyes grew heavier, and she gave in to sleep. She dreamed she was traveling through space to meet Territaff for a goblet of Pernod.

CHAPTER 5

A cold shower and two cups of black, sweet coffee helped revive Kathy. She sat at the small kitchen table, staring into her coffee mug, thinking about Territaff.

"Why did he take off like that?" she mumbled. "I thought he liked me. You're too trusting, Kathy. He was so incredible. God, I don't think I'll ever have sex like that again. Was it even sex, though? Or did he somehow play with my mind? What a bastard."

She got up and then tossed the mug into the sink. To her relief, it didn't break. She shook her head, realizing what she had almost done. It was her grandmother's favorite mug.

Kathy went into the living room and flopped onto the couch. She looked for the TV remote, which wasn't in its usual place. She searched under the sofa, then between the cushions.

"Where's the damn remote?"

After searching the living room in vain, she returned to the bedroom. When she entered the bedroom, the disc glistening on the floor caught her eye. She picked it up and held it to the light. Holding it, she thought of Territaff. His voice rose in her mind, and she placed the disc into her DVD player. Kathy flinched in surprise when the TV set turned on.

"Oh, my God," she mumbled as a pixelated picture filled the screen. The colored squares resolved into a crystal-clear image of Territaff's smiling face.

"Hello, Kathy," the image cheerfully greeted her. "I've made a few modifications to your DVD player so I can explain why I had to leave without a proper goodbye."

"You son of a bitch. You promised to take me with you," she yelled at the screen.

"I understand how you feel, Kathy. And yes, I'm a bastard. I used you in a way that, under normal circumstances, I'd never have considered, but the circumstances are extraordinary."

"You can hear me?" Kathy said, surprised by Territaff's reply. "How's that possible?"

"What you're hearing and seeing is a computerized image of me, capable of responding to your questions, but only in a limited context."

"I don't understand."

Kathy sat on the floor close to the TV with her legs crossed.

"The disc you're now playing is most important." The image continued. "I left it in your safekeeping. Please place it in the freezer portion of your refrigerator. I'll return for it soon. I trust you'll tell no one of its existence. You must do this."

"Why? What is it?"

"It's like one of your computer discs, only much more advanced. It contains vital information."

"Why have you given it to me?"

"Because I trust you." The image smiled.

"You trust me? You hardly know me and left me with this... heavy responsibility."

"I know you better than you realize, Kathy. You revealed a great deal about your true nature during our intimacy.

"You mean we had great sex, and now you know me? That's a lot of bullshit."

"It was more than sex."

Kathy blushed, recalling the experience. It was much more. He had given her a vivid glimpse into a world she could've never conceived.

"Why should I ever trust you again? You used me. Lied to me and left me with this thing to keep for you? You ask a hell of a lot for a one-night stand."

There was a pause before the image continued.

"Kathy, I know I'm asking a lot on faith, but you must believe me. I didn't lie. I'll return for you."

"And when will that be?"

"If all goes well, in a few days or less. Until then, tell no one about me or the disc."

"If all goes well? What must go well? What aren't you telling me, Terri?"

"I can say no more. Goodbye for now. See you soon." Territaff's image faded.

"Terri... Terri!"

Kathy stood and banged the top of the TV with her hand. She pushed buttons on the DVD, hoping to retrieve Territaff's image. After several tries, she gave up, ejected the disc, and held it tightly. She stared at the shiny object, cursing as she marched into the kitchen. She put it into a freezer bag and slid it under the ice cube bin.

"Goddamn you, Territaff," she yelled. "You're fucking up my whole damn life!"

* * *

Territaff found his way to Mumz's Hot Dogs at First and Ocean Drive. It was a 24-hour grill that was a favorite gathering place for the younger generation that had taken over South Beach. Their hot dogs were the size of thick sausages steamed in beer. During his long absence from Earth, Territaff often dreamed of eating a Mumz's Hot Dog.

The small grill was built into the wall of a quaint Spanish-style hotel. Its awning-covered bar stools overlooked the ocean on First Street. Territaff discovered his friend, Cuz, seated on the far side of the long counter.

It was four o'clock on an easy-going Saturday afternoon. The sky was a bright blue, and a thin veil of clouds lazily moved along with a soft sea breeze. Territaff smiled as he saw Cuz watching the lovely female bathers as they bent down to pick up their beach towels and belongings. Their tanned bodies still glistened with suntan oil as they wrapped themselves in sheer cotton beach dresses. Cuz's pale complexion was already beginning to take on a light tan in the short time under the intense Florida sun. He sat with his long frame and square shoulders upright on his stool. His large, dark brown eyes take in his surroundings with great interest.

It was a typical late April afternoon on South Beach. The air wasn't yet heavy with humidity, and a stiff, easterly breeze brought a pleasant current of coolness from the steamy beach. The ocean sparkled with reflected sunlight off the wave tops. Sailboats bobbed in the distance, and the Tiki bars filled with the promise of a lively Saturday night.

Territaff had grown up in the leisurely town of Surfside, located ten miles north of South Beach. In his youth, it was ten blocks of cheap, beachside, low-rise hotels with narrow streets lined with small, seasonal rentals. Its residents were mostly snowbirds and retirees living in retirement homes on the west side. Bright and vivid memories flooded in, filled with the sounds and scents of an earlier life, a distant one separated by space and time.

Territaff compared his surroundings with his memories of the area and frowned. South Beach had a little charm when he went to school. He thought it appeared like a glitzy few blocks of old and renovated hotels and bars. When I grew up here, he reminisced. It was more straightforward and a lot less crowded. South Beach had a certain allure and a slower lifestyle in the late 1960s until its decline in the 1980s. Space-time has a way of distorting everything. He grimaced at the thought.

He sat next to Cuz and took a deep breath. "There's no smell like ocean air." He followed Cuz's eyes to see what was holding his friend's attention. It didn't take long, but in an instant, Territaff became as mesmerized as his friend.

"Incredible," Territaff mumbled. "That's absolute perfection."

"I concur," Cuz said through a crooked smile.

The vision shattered for Cuz when she picked up a young child.

"Damn," Cuz snapped his long fingers. "I was just about to hit on her." He turned himself inward and faced an amused waiter.

"Have you had a dog yet?" Territaff asked.

Cuz shook his head. "I was waiting for your recommendation."

Territaff gestured to the waiter. He approached and gave them a broad smile. "What can I get you?" he said with a thick Cuban accent.

"Two Mumz's dogs. One with heavy everything and the other..." he glanced at Cuz and asked, "Do you like spicy?"

Cuz pondered the question for a moment, then replied, "Yes. I like sweets as well."

"Great. Make the other one with Mumz's hot sauce and sweet relish. Also, bring us two Guinness Blacks with bourbon shots."

"Primo choices, Señor." The waiter nodded, still grinning.

The waiter walked to the beer taps. He dispensed the two beers, poured the shots, and then placed them on the counter. "I'll bring the hot dogs when you're ready," he said, then walked to the end of the counter. He picked up a half-smoked cigar from an ashtray and relit it. Then, he continued to watch Cuz, his round face turned up in amusement.

"Cuz, I don't think you're ready for the ladies yet," he said, noticing how he was studying a young woman rinsing sand off her legs in one of the open public showers. Her well-endowed body was sparsely covered by a thong bikini, which left little to Cuz's imagination as she leaned forward to brush sand off the back of her thighs.

"What do you mean?" Cuz retorted defensively. His boyish features knotted in confusion.

"First off, you're not hitting on anybody. You will approach and talk with a lady, but you're not ready."

"How does one prepare to talk to a lady?"

Territaff knew Cuz had been reading romance, detective, and erotic novels since they arrived. This worried him.

"I got a great idea." Cuz noticed Territaff's face glowed with the thought. "I'm taking you to a special gentlemen's club."

"What's a Gentlemen's Club?" he asked, then thought for a moment and grinned. "A strip club?"

Territaff nodded.

"Let's go."

He had to hold Cuz in his seat.

"It's too early. First, we need to prepare." He dropped a shot glass of bourbon in Cuz's beer and the other in his. Lifting his mug high, he said, "Here's to beautiful women everywhere." He tapped his mug against Cuz's, then emptied it. He gestured to Cuz to drink.

Cuz regarded his mug for a moment, then drained it.

"Ahh," Cuz said, then banged his mug on the counter and proclaimed, "How about another round for the beautiful women?"

Territaff laughed and said to the waiter, "Another round, and bring us our dogs." The waiter acknowledged. Territaff leaned in a little closer to Cuz and said, "Trust me, you'll need the food and drink..." Cuz furrowed his brow. "Well, I do, anyway."

Cuz arched a thin eyebrow and said, "Okay, let the dogs out."

Territaff shook his head and beamed at his friend. "Oh man, the girls will love you at Passions."

"What about Kathy?"

He looked thoughtfully at Cuz and said, "I tested her last night. She's perfect for us. Intelligent, spirited, and, I suspect, empathetic as well. She has abilities she's unaware of. I trusted her to safeguard the disc, but I'm fearful the Zenti may already know of her."

"Aren't you concerned that they'll go after Kathy to get to you?"

"That's a real possibility—one I'm almost counting on. They'll stop at nothing to get to me. I'm waiting for them to make their move."

"I sure hope you know what you're doing, Terri. You've created a vulnerable situation for her."

"I know," he mumbled half aloud, then took a long draw of his beer. "We'll have to bring her into our confidence soon."

"May the Universe protect her," Cuz said softly, then took a large bite of his hot dog. "So, this is what animal flesh tastes like?"

Territaff nodded as he took a large bite of his hot dog. "Don't analyze its contents. Just enjoy it for its taste."

"Yes. Your advice is sound. However, I think I like the beer better."

CHAPTER 6

General Dickerson was a robust man in his mid-fifties. His broad, muscular frame reflected the wear and tear of the three tours of combat duty in the Middle East. Being assigned as Commander of Strategic Military Intelligence at Homestead Air Force Base was supposed to be a reward for his prior service. However, the general viewed the assignment in a different light. Besides the irritations of dealing with the day-to-day mundane administrative duties, he also found his adjutant, Colonel Cameron, to be a pretentious busybody vying for his job. As far as the general was concerned, Cameron could have it, gladly.

Dickerson was having another restless night when the phone rang. The call's late hour and the news of Tanya Ruiz's disappearance surprised and distressed him. He stared, unblinking, feeling a heavy numbness as he thought of Tanya. *She was so young and cocky with confidence.* She reminded him of one of his junior officers he'd lost during that senseless Iraq war. He slammed the phone onto the nightstand and jumped out of bed, cursing.

"I knew Cameron would fuck this up," he complained angrily. "Now I've got to clean up his mess along with all the other crap that has just dropped on my lap."

The general stretched out his aching back, hoping to relieve the sciatica running a sharp, stabbing pain down his left leg. He stood, staring at himself before his walk-in closet's large, mirrored doors. Shaking his head, he searched for his slippers. Finding them halfway under the bed, he sat heavily and put them on.

The news got the general to review the meeting in Cameron's office with Tanya the week before. "She was so eager to impress Cameron," he mumbled, pacing in a small circle between his desk and the closet. As he paced, he massaged his tight neck, pondering the disjointed events of the past month, hoping to get a coherent picture. Then he checked the time: 3:50 a.m.

"It's too damn early to go to the office, and there's no fucking way I'm going back to sleep," he barked, feeling the numbness of the initial shock resolving into anger and confusion.

"What the hell was she doing alone? What's Cameron not telling me?"

The general heaved a sigh as he went to his elegant, antique writing table in a corner of his spacious bedroom. It was one of the few things he had salvaged from his divorce. It was his late mother's. She had left him little else but many sordid memories.

The meeting in Cameron's office came to mind. Cameron's explanation of Tanya's disappearance could be summarized in a single word: *vague*. He took a long breath while staring at the phone, deciding who to call first. Then he remembered the meeting he had with the DARPA team. "Who were those consultants?" he murmured, his eyes closed, trying to recall what they said. *They were warning us about getting caught with our pants down.* He remembered that everybody laughed but him. *They were serious about a threat from sources with advanced technology.*

"We missed the point," he whispered.

The general was about to call Cameron but paused, decided against it, and looked up his contacts at DARPA.

* * *

Territaff and Cuz arrived at Passion's South around ten-thirty. A sparse crowd was scattered around the two main bars. The tables surrounding the polished dance floor were empty. Two angular, topless dancers moved in perfect syncopation to heavy dance music at the central bar. An attractive, petite young woman shadow-danced at the smaller rear bar. Cuz gravitated to the naked dancer closest to him. He sat center bar, never allowing his dumbfounded gaze to look away. The two dancers greeted Cuz with a quick circular gyration of their rounded buttocks. One of them finished her greeting with a sensual back-and-forth thrust of her hips. With his eyes fixed on the dancers, smiling ear-to-ear, Cuz appeared to be in Nirvana. Cuz noticed guys approaching the dancers, holding dollar bills and stuffing them into their garter belts. Occasionally, a dancer would lean close, her breast temptingly near, and take the dollars with her mouth. Cuz studied how the men and dancers reacted. Some men were brazen, getting close to the young lady, and then she'd back away, smiling, and resume her energetic movements to the loud music.

"Terri, I require one-dollar bills, please," he called out over the din of heavy rhythms and exciting conversations.

Territaff walked across the large dance floor toward a cashier's window. Even the cashier was topless. Her ample breasts bulged as she took Territaff's one-hundred-dollar bill. She gave him an indifferent glance as she held the bill under a blue light, then examined the back.

"How many?" she asked.

Territaff looked across the dance floor to check on his friend. He could see him talking between the dancer and the server.

"Fifty," he said, hoping it would finance his friend's new adventure.

"I'm waiting for the manager to come back with change. Will forty do for now?"

"Guess it'll have to." Territaff thought for a moment. "You'd better give the other sixty in fives and tens, okay?"

The cashier nodded, counted out the money, and handed it to him.

When he returned, he noticed heavy beads of perspiration on Cuz's forehead and upper lip. He looked worse than Nixon during the first Kennedy debate.

"Cuz, why are you sweating?" he said, handing him a thick

wad of bills.

Cuz wiped his forehead with a napkin. "Wow, I'm perspiring," he said, looking at the moist napkin. "Keep my seat, Terri. I'm going to the men's room and freshen up."

"Hurry back, honey," the server called to Cuz.

Cuz turned and blew her a kiss. The lovely woman pretended to catch the kiss, then ran her hand across her moist, full lips. Cuz grinned like a kid on Christmas morning, then dashed to the men's room.

"You have developed... uh... a rapport or something?" Territaff asked the server, uncertain about what he saw.

"Oh, please," she wrinkled her nose, looking insulted. I was just having some fun. What can I get you?"

"Bourbon on the rocks." He studied the young woman as she poured his drink into a large tumbler. Then he pondered on Cuz. He *was sweating. Remarkable.* He smiled at the thought. "My friend, Cuz, he's not very sophisticated when it comes to women."

She cocked an eyebrow.

"I can say one thing for sure." He sipped his bourbon. "You're a first-class server." He tipped his glass to her, then drained it. "I'll have another, please."

She smiled faintly at Territaff and refreshed his drink.

"What are you trying to tell me about your friend?" she asked, clearing the bar counter of trash and empty bottles.

"Just that he has no real experience with women. He views you as a new and exciting species he needs to explore on many levels..." Territaff noticed she was giving him a sideways look with a bemused grin.

"I think I get it," she said, wiping the counter with a clean towel. She narrowed a penetrating stare into Territaff, then placed her hands on her hips. "Are you trying to tell me that your friend's a virgin, and you want to get his cherry busted? You really expect me to believe that bullshit?"

"I know how it sounds, but yes. He's a genuine virgin."

"Oh, give me a break," she laughed.

Territaff was at a loss for how to sound sincere about Cuz. He watched the young woman as she worked the bar. He sighed to himself, thinking, Dummy, she's heard that line so many times... "Let me try this again," he resumed his plea when she returned.

She rested on her elbows on the counter and gazed at Territaff with her bright hazel eyes. Okay," she said with a dubious smirk. "Tell me your friend's story. The night's young, and I haven't been hit on yet."

"I think I need another." Territaff held up his empty glass.

She scrutinized him as she refilled his drink.

Territaff took a long swallow and said, "It's like this. Cuz, my friend, has lived a very sheltered life. I guess you can say he's a real," he paused in thought, "nerd. He's been driving me crazy to fix him up, and I was told this is the right place for him to... eh... You know..."

"Get laid," she finished his thought.

Territaff drained his drink.

"So, let me see if I understand," she said as she refreshed his drink. "You brought your friend here looking to get him laid by a warm and understanding whore, who will be both gentle and nurturing. How am I doing?"

"A hundred percent, my dear—your beauty only exceeds your wisdom." He raised his glass in a toast to her. She narrowed her eyes into slits that caused Territaff to swallow hard. "I'm screwing this up, aren't I?" He gave her his best imploring look, hoping she would soften.

"No, you're just being a typical guy," she smiled. "You're also a good friend, and he's kind of cute..." Her gaze lingered on Territaff before leaving to wait on two new patrons.

Territaff studied the server as she waited on the two young and anxious-looking men. While watching her, he thought of Kathy. She reminded him of her, not so much in her looks but more in her mannerisms. He liked what he saw and would entrust his friend to her, but he didn't even know her name.

"You kind of left me hanging," Territaff said when she returned.

"Sorry, I needed a little time to think about it. I just got over a four-year relationship and haven't been out for quite a while."

Territaff sensed an intense negative wave running through him. He looked away from the server and got up. Looking back at her, he said, "What's your name?"

"Natasha." She furrowed her brow. "You all right?"

"Yes, but I have to leave for a little while." He reached into his pocket and pulled out a wad of bills. He handed them to her without counting them. "Please take care of my friend while I'm away."

She counted the money. "There's over twelve hundred dollars here." She looked up in surprise, laughing. "For this type of dough, I'll marry him."

Just show him a great time." I owe him a lot. I'll be back shortly."

Cuz returned from the men's room feeling freshened up. He appeared somehow younger to Natasha.

"You clean up nice," she said with an approving smile.

Cuz looked around for Territaff before easing onto the barstool."

"If you're looking for your friend, he had to leave. He said he'd be right back."

Cuz frowned, unsure whether he should go after his friend, until he looked at Natasha, beaming at him. He gave his best charming smile and said, "While waiting, please, make me another of whatever that wonderful concoction was."

"Coming right up, sweetie," she said in a sultry voice. She leaned close to him and ran her hand down one side of his face, then ran a finger across his lips.

Cuz let out a little shudder as he felt the warm smoothness of her hand on his face.

"Wow," he whispered.

* * *

Territaff handed the cab driver a fifty-dollar bill for a twenty-seven-dollar fare and asked him to wait for him for a few minutes. The cabby nodded, then told his dispatcher he was still on the meter and would call back in ten minutes.

"Take your time. I need the break," the cabby called to him.

Territaff walked toward Kathy's first-floor apartment with heightened caution. He could see her living room from the front door. He peered through the transparent pane. A soft glow of light seeping from under the bedroom door lent the darkened hall a shadowy appearance. He tried the front door. To his surprise, it was unlocked. Territaff walked into the small foyer, then stopped and surveyed the surroundings with his eyes, while intently listening before moving into the hall. The apartment had an uneasy feeling to it. Kathy told him she loved listening to music when she got home from work. Then, it occurred to him that she should be at work. So, why was she home? he thought as he moved toward the bedroom.

He paused at the bedroom door for a moment and listened. Labored breathing came from inside the room, accompanied by the distinct odor of a man sweating profusely.

Territaff considered the man nervous and unprofessional. He gripped the doorknob. It was locked. With no effort, he forced the door open with incredible force. The impact of the swinging door knocked the large man off balance. Territaff followed with a decisive blow to the side of his head. The man fell unconscious onto Kathy's night table, smashing a small antique lamp on top.

Kathy's wrists and ankles were tied to the ends of the head and footboards. Territaff removed the duct tape from her mouth and then kissed her before she could utter a word.

"That was my grandmother's!" she cried angrily as Territaff untied her arms and legs. She wrapped her arms around his neck. He could feel her heart pounding in her chest. "My God, Terri," she wept, tightening her grip around him. "I thought he was going to kill me."

He held her close for a moment, then asked, "Was he alone?"

"No. There were two others," she said, holding back tears. She let out a heavy exhale to calm herself. "One spoke with a thick, indiscernible accent, almost like a wheezy brogue." The other was really big. I've never seen such a large head. I couldn't tell too much because, as you can see..." she pointed to the unconscious man, "they were wearing ski masks. What was strange was how awkward they seemed. Like they didn't know what they were doing. Terri, who are they? What do they want? How did they find me?" Looking closer into Territaff's face, she said, in a low, angry voice, "Were they trying to find you through me?"

"Take a breath, Kathy," he said as he stood over the unconscious man, then went through his pockets. "Can you describe the man with the accent for me?"

"I don't know what I could add. Everything happened so quickly. I... I thought he wanted to rape me at first." Her face tightened into an angry scowl as she stared at her attacker.

"Don't look at him. Look at me."

Territaff sat beside Kathy on the bed, wrapped his arm around her, and pulled her close. Kathy rested her head on his shoulder and let out a long, shivering sigh.

"Kathy, describe their awkwardness."

"The one with the strange accent was kind of short and walked as though his shoes were too tight. He moved as though he was, for lack of a better word, uncomfortable."

"And the big one?"

"His movements seemed almost mechanical, but not stiff, sort of jerky—if that makes any sense?"

"Unfortunately, it makes a great deal of sense." He frowned, then gave Kathy a reassuring smile. "There's a lot we need to do quickly."

"How did you know?" she asked, rubbing her bruised

wrists.

"How did I know what?"

"That I was in trouble."

She studied Territaff's face. His features had changed again. He had a hard, cold look about him, and his dark eyes were filled with a frightening intensity.

"Just lucky, I guess." He tried to relax the tension growing in her. He gave Kathy a warm smile. "I was coming over to apologize and pick up the disc. You still have it?"

She narrowed her eyes and grinned. "You must be the most artful bullshitter I've ever met."

Territaff grimaced, "Okay, the truth is I had a premonition you were in trouble. So here I am. Is the disc safe?" he asked again.

"I've no idea. Go look for yourself." She shrugged and pointed toward the kitchen.

Territaff glanced out the living room's sliding glass doors to ensure the cab was still waiting before heading to the kitchen. He opened the freezer door and looked under the ice cube bin. The disc was still there and sealed in the freezer bag. He held the bag up to the light. It appeared to be intact. He studied it closer, then smiled.

"I've got a cab waiting for us," he said, returning to Kathy's bedroom. "Get dressed. We need to get out of here."

He placed the disc in his rear pants pocket.

"And where are we going?" Kathy asked.

"To meet my friend at Passions." He grabbed a pair of jeans and a top from Kathy's closet. "Here, put these on."

"You don't wear this to Passions," she said, tossing the clothes on the bed.

"Grab something and hurry." Territaff looked down at the unconscious man sprawled backward across her night table. "His playmates will return to get him, and I don't want to be here when they do."

"Are you going to tell me what the hell's going on?" She

demanded as she emerged from her closet wearing a light blue top over a short, dark blue skirt that stressed her shapely body.

"Yes, when we're in the cab. We've got a lot to discuss, but we must go now."

He rushed Kathy toward the front door. Kathy looked around her apartment. She sensed that she would not return. Then she looked into Territaff's now impassive face. His expression filled her with apprehension and excitement. It was an incredible rush.

* * *

Kathy watched Territaff as he looked over his shoulder through the rear window. When their eyes met, he sensed her struggling with her stirring emotions. Her gaze fixed into a pensive stare, looking past Territaff.

"What the fuck is going on, Terri?" she blurted.

"What do you mean?"

"I'm not in the mood for any of your bullshit charms." She leaned in close as if daring him to kiss her. "Now be a good boy," she held her voice to a seductive whisper, "and tell me why people are trying to kill me while they're looking for you?"

"All in good time, my dear." He held a finger to his lips.

Kathy's face screwed up into an angry scowl, then she gave him an upward thrust of her middle finger and flopped back into the seat.

He ignored her belligerence, leaned toward the cab driver, and said, "Take us to Passions."

"The one on first or twentieth?" he asked.

"The one on First Street," Territaff answered, then thought for a moment, "What's the one on Twentieth Street like?"

"It's a little more upscale if you know what I mean," the cabbie said, glancing at Territaff through his rearview mirror.

"Interesting," Territaff pondered as he leaned back in the seat. He brought Kathy close and whispered into her ear. "You need to tell me everything you can remember. Everything is important; nothing is irrelevant.

Kathy nodded. "I'm really scared, Terri. This is all too weird."

"Why were you home?"

She took a deep breath and let it out slowly, turning it into a long sigh. Their eyes met, and Kathy's initially tension-filled gaze became calmer. She locked her hands behind Territaff's head, pulling his face up to hers for a passionate kiss.

"You're an incredible kisser," she said in a breathy voice. "That's the only rational explanation for me wanting to put up with all your abuse because I can't go more than a few hours without getting one of your kisses."

"You can wait a few hours?" He curled his lower lip in mock disappointment. "I must be slipping."

"Oh, you liar," she punched Territaff in his solid chest.

He grabbed her fist and kissed her knuckles. "Can you tell me now?"

"When I got home from my afternoon jog, they were waiting for me in my apartment. What was odd was that there were no signs of forced entry. Naturally, I first asked how they got in and what they wanted. The short one, with the strange accent, grunted something—it was nothing I'd ever heard before. It sounded like it slithered and hissed out of his throat. It was an awful, eerie, evil sound.

"Then the big guy threw me onto the bed and tied me down. They searched through my apartment. Then the little guy put something on my forehead, and the next thing I remember is waking up just as you found me, with that big goon hovering over me, holding a big knife. It was dark outside, and I'd no idea of the time."

"How'd you feel when you recovered?"

"What do you mean?"

"Did you have a headache? Did your stomach feel queasy or light-headed?"

"No. I felt rested and couldn't remember any side effects. Come to think of it, I wish I'd gotten more of whatever that was.

I got the best rest I've had in years." She wrinkled her nose and asked, "Do you know what they gave me?"

"I've got an idea, and if I'm correct, it's dangerous."

"Oh, you're no fun," Kathy pouted.

"Continue."

"There's not much more I can tell you. However, I'm sure they were looking for the disc. Before they put that thing on my forehead, the big guy came lumbering into the bedroom, looked through my nightstand, and went into the closet. Meanwhile, the smaller dude looked under my bed and behind the headboard. They seemed clueless and clumsy in their mannerisms and movements. They were neat, though. They left everything just the way they found it. If I weren't so scared, it would've been funny. At one point, the big guy bumped into the small one, knocking him to the floor. I laughed. It was like being invaded by the two Stooges."

"Could you see anything about their faces?"

"That was the strange part." Kathy closed her eyes for a moment. "There was something about the big guy's eyes. He must have been wearing special glasses because all I could see in the eyeholes were two green, shiny lenses."

"What about the smaller one?"

"His eyes were large, dark, and intense. He gave me the creeps." She shuddered at the memory.

Territaff leaned back in the seat, pulling on his chin in thought. He looked at his watch, leaned close to the cabbie, and asked, "What's your name?"

"Fred."

He studied Fred's face for a moment. Fred was staring back at him with tired eyes. His dark skin was smooth, giving him a younger appearance. His age was more revealed in his large and battered-looking hands. Fred had gentle features that suggested a kind and disarming personality. Territaff liked what he saw. Fred's large frame still looked firm but showed the beginnings of a small pouch around the midriff. He had all the signs of someone who had spent most of his time in a laborious occupation and only recently became a cab driver.

"Fred, there's an extra fifty for you if you can get us to Passions in fifteen minutes or less." He held up a crisp fifty-dollar bill in front of Fred so he could see it.

"You got it, pal." Fred grinned as he stepped on the accelerator.

"I hope Cuz is okay," Territaff mumbled.

"Who's Cuz?"

"My friend. I left him to get you."

"He's a big boy. I'm sure he can take care of himself."

"No, Kathy, he's as naïve as a newborn."

* * *

Territaff pulled Kathy by the arm as they rushed into Passions. "Hey, that's ten dollars, sir!" the cashier said to Territaff as he went to the bar where he had left Cuz.

"Take care of that for me," he told Kathy.

"Terri, wait up," she shouted, fumbling through her purse for money. "Hey Terri, I left my money at home," she said uneasily as a big, rotund man came too close to her. "You want to back off a little, big boy," she said, checking inside her bra for her emergency tip money.

"There's a ten-dollar cover charge, Missy, after ten o'clock," the large man said, his voice gravelly through the heavy cigar smoke. "That's ten dollars apiece."

"You want to back off a little," Kathy said in a firmer voice. "You are aware that smoking in public spaces is prohibited by state law?"

"Yeah, so arrest me." He gazed at Kathy in a way she was accustomed to, as if he were undressing her with his eyes. She sneered at him in resentment. "If you don't have the dough, babe. "I can maybe work something out with you," he said, removing the cigar from his lips, then gave Kathy a green-toothed smile.

"Not on your life, fatso."

Two bouncers watched their boss arguing with her in amusement.

"Need a little help, boss?" one of the bouncers asked.

"Nah, I can handle this little cutie. Okay, let's go." He grabbed Kathy's arm and then pulled her toward the door.

"Terri, I can use a little help here!" Kathy shouted over the throbbing rhythms of blasting rock, looking anxiously for Territaff. "Take your hands off me, you big, ugly gorilla."

She stomped her heel into his foot. He grabbed Kathy's other arm and lifted her close enough that she could smell the garlic lingering from his dinner. "That hurt," he said, grimacing and blowing smoke into her face.

"You want to put her down, please," Territaff said.

The big man released his grip on Kathy and gave Territaff an amused grin. "Coming to your girl's rescue?"

"No, actually, I was thinking more of you, my rotund friend," Territaff said.

"Really?" he snickered.

"Yeah, really." He noticed Kathy's fuming glare. "You don't want to mess with her. She has a mean streak when she is angered.

The man gave Kathy a careful look, then laughed. "I'm terrified."

"I wouldn't provoke her if I were you."

"Yeah, right—now pay up." He held out a beefy hand.

"I wouldn't give you two cents for this crummy joint," Kathy said as she straightened her blouse. Then, eyeing him, her anger rose.

"Well, now it's going to cost you forty for giving me such a hard time." He wiggled the fingers of his open hand for Territaff to pay.

"You know what," Territaff said. "I'm sorry for any inconvenience, and I think we'll just go."

"Nah, it don't work that way, pal. You entered, and now you has to pay."

Territaff scratched the back of his head and smiled. He wanted to avoid a scene and was about to pay. Then he noticed Kathy's fuming eyes and tight mouth and realized she wouldn't let things go that easily.

"Well, I tell you what. I'll forget about you roughing up my girl, and you'll forget about the forty." Territaff placed his arm around Kathy and walked toward the door. The big man put his hand heavily on Territaff's shoulder and pulled him back.

"Oh, I wish you hadn't done that," Territaff said, glaring into the man's dull blue eyes.

"Someone needs to teach you some manners," Kathy said through clenched teeth. "You know, I work at Fat Jack's, and we also use off-duty cops. Oh, I see one of our guys is working here. If I call one over and make a formal complaint of harassment—"

"Go ahead."

A tall, thickly built bouncer approached. He smiled at Kathy. "I thought that was you", he said and hugged her, then looked sternly at the club's manager. "Want to tell me what's going on?"

"Nothing's going on. Big misunderstanding." His round cheeks rolled up into a wide smile. "Right, missy?"

"You're an asshole," Kathy shouted in the man's face.

"Okay, tell you what." He reached into his baggy jeans and pulled out a roll of tickets. "Here. Have a few drinks on me."

Kathy threw the tickets at the manager, and his face turned beet red, realizing everyone was watching the action.

"Someone needs to teach you some manners," Kathy repeated, her jaw set with her mouth shut in a tight line. To the off-duty cop, she said, "It's good to see you again, Tomar. We miss you at Jack's."

Tomar eyed his boss. "I may be back soon." To the manager, he asked, "Are we through here?"

The sweating man nodded and returned to his office.

Territaff could feel the eyes of amused patrons, staring

with joy as they watched, with a certain sense of justice, the little gal protecting her man.

"You know he could have hurt me."

"I'd never let that happen. Besides, you handled him. And from what I saw, quite effectively."

"You did, huh?" She placed her hands on her hips. "So, you weren't worried at all?"

"He was no match for you," Territaff grinned.

When everyone at the bar clapped and cheered, Kathy blushed.

"Looks like you've made some new friends," Territaff said, pointing to the people giving her a standing ovation.

She nodded to the crowd, trying to hide her embarrassment. A tall, blonde-headed man handed her a shot glass of whiskey, which she held to the crowd. She threw back the drink, wiped her mouth with the back of her hand, and laughed.

"I hate to put a damper on your shining hour of triumph, my dear, but we need to get my friend."

"Do you know where he is?" Kathy asked.

"Yeah." He took Kathy out of the club. He saw a cab across the street. "Is that Fred?"

Kathy squinted. "I think it is," she said, then realized Territaff was already getting into the cab.

"What are you waiting for?" he called to her.

"I'm coming," she snapped. She sat next to him in the back of the cab. "Can you tell me what the hell is going on?"

"Fred, are you married?" Territaff asked as he unbuttoned his shirt, revealing a thick money belt. He pulled out a stack of hundred-dollar bills, counted twenty crisp ones, and re-buttoned his shirt.

"Yeah." Fred nodded and smiled. Married to my high school sweetheart. I had to wait six months for her eighteenth birthday so we could get married." His dark brown eyes lit up at the thought.

"How many kids do you have?"

"Three, two boys and a girl."

"Driving a cab is hard and dangerous work," Territaff said. "I'm sure you can use a little extra cash."

"You got that right," Fred said, looking at Territaff through the rear-view mirror.

"When does your shift end?"

"I just signed off."

"How much do you typically earn on a Saturday night?"

"Around six to eight hundred, give or take a dollar. Why do you ask?"

"Well, I need your services for the rest of the night." Fred's tired eyes briefly met Territaff's passive gaze in the rear-view mirror. In that brief exchange, Fred relaxed his guard as his curiosity rose. Territaff sensed Fred's character and liked what he saw.

"Okay." Fred's jaw tightened. "You're not planning anything that will get me in trouble? Ah... like anything funky?"

"There's nothing to worry about. I just don't want to chase down cabs the rest of the night, and I may need to make a few more stops. Are you up for it? I'll pay you well for your services."

Fred smiled. "How well?"

"How about two grand to start with?" He handed Fred the twenty crisp bills. Fred's eyes widened with excitement as he slowly counted the money. He snapped a few of the bills to ensure they were genuine.

"This isn't funny money, is it?"

"Funny money?" Territaff asked.

"Counterfeit," Kathy explained.

"No, they're the real thing."

He counted the money again. "Seems like you rented yourself a cab for the evening." Fred agreed, feeling like he had fallen into a strange dream. "You're not fucking with me?"

"Fred, can I count on you?" Territaff said, giving the cabby's shoulder a friendly pat.

Fred turned to face Territaff and said, "You can count on me. I won't let you down, especially if there's more of this comin'." Fred turned his attention to Kathy and smiled. "You sure are pretty. This is the first time I got a good look at you."

"Thank you, Fred." Kathy smiled, then gave his hand a friendly squeeze.

Fred carefully folded the money and placed it in his pants pocket. He patted his pocket as though to assure himself the bills were real. He turned his attention back to Territaff and asked, "Okay, where to, boss?"

"Passions North, Fred, and step on it," Territaff said, pointing a long finger for emphasis.

The cab lay rubber as it screeched off. Fred couldn't stop smiling as they sped up Collins Avenue. It was around 1:00 a.m., and the streets were all but deserted. The lights were blinking yellow, allowing Fred to drive fast with little concern about traffic or having to stop at lights.

Kathy opened the window and took in a few deep breaths of the cool night air. Her heart was beating hard in her chest, and Territaff noticed that her hands were shaking. He took her hands in his, then wrapped his arm around her shoulders and held her close.

"So, you're not as tough as you pretend," he whispered in her ear.

Kathy looked into his eyes, then leaned her head on his chest and sobbed.

"I'm so sorry, Kathy," Territaff said, stroking her head. "I never wanted you to get involved in all this... mess. Please believe me. I never wanted to involve you."

His heart ached for Kathy because he had involved her, and her life would never be the same.

"Don't you think I should know what the hell's going on?" she said.

"The less you know, the better all around."

"There you go again."

Kathy pulled Territaff's arm from her shoulders and sat upright. She looked closely into his eyes. She continued to gaze at him, a corner of her mouth raised in a dubious expression.

"Good old, Territaff, the cryptic bullshit artist." She spoke with a coolness that made him uneasy.

"Please, don't bail on me now, Kathy," Territaff said. He was in a dilemma and didn't know what to do. He reached into his rear pants pocket and pulled out the disc. Kathy, this disc contains information on an alien species that is plotting to take over the Earth. I know it sounds like a bad science fiction story, but it's true."

As usual, Kathy could read nothing in Territaff's impassive features. It was as though he could turn his expressions on and off with perfect control. She heaved a long sigh, then slumped back in the seat.

"What am I going to do with you?" she asked, staring out the cab window. She smiled sadly as she viewed the old estate homes along the Indian Creek waterway. They were all lit up, revealing their opulent beauty.

"I always dreamed of owning one of those someday," she said in a dreamy voice. "Now it seems that will remain a dream." She wiped tears from her face with her hand.

"Kathy, I've never lied to you and have always promised to tell you the truth. I've never broken that vow. But you have to—"

Kathy held her hand up to his mouth without looking at him.

"Save it, Terri. I don't want to hear anymore." She swallowed down the throb in her voice. "Fred, please take me home after you drop off Mr. Territaff."

"Is that okay with you, Boss?" Fred asked.

"No, proceed as instructed." He turned to her. "Listen carefully."

She continued to stare out the window, ignoring him.

"Kathy, please, you have to believe me. You can't go home."

"I don't want to hear any more of your lying bullshit!" Her bloodshot eyes narrowed with anger.

"Kathy, those men who met you in your apartment will kill you even if you give them the disc and tell them everything you know. You now present a risk, and taking a life holds no meaning to them. You can't reason with them, buy them off, or dissuade them from killing you. They're like automatons. They have no emotions beyond what is necessary to fulfill their mission.

Territaff turned Kathy by her shoulders. His features became full of emotion, unlike any she had seen from him. She could almost feel a powerful rush of angst flowing through him.

"They killed everyone I loved. I won't let them kill you. I wish I could tell you all you want to hear. I wish I could undo everything that has happened between us. I had repressed my emotions so deeply that I forgot their importance. Most of all, I used you to solve a problem. I convinced myself I was doing everything for the sake of the mission. I was wrong, and I beg your forgiveness."

Kathy's face paled, and her skin got cold and clammy. She looked as though she was on the verge of shock. He realized he had hurt her beyond words, beyond anything he thought he was capable of. Territaff felt her pain and rising fear. He knew anything he would say would sound empty and hollow, but he had to tell her the truth, no matter how it would affect her.

"Please, hear me out. For better or worse, your life is now in my hands."

She bowed her head into her hands and cried. Then she lifted her head, gasping for breath.

"I can't breathe," she cried through wheezing breaths.

"Fred, pull over," Territaff said, picking up a crumpled bag he found on the floor. "Here, breathe into this bag," he said as he unraveled it and held it to her face.

Kathy understood and breathed into the bag. "It smells like a whopper and fries," she said between deep breaths. "It's making me nauseous."

"Keep breathing into the bag. You're hyperventilating."

"I know that, goddammit!"

"Good, now slow down your breathing and listen," he said as he rubbed Kathy's back. "I know I hurt you, but I must tell you everything because it seems we'll be together for a long time, and we have an important mission ahead of us. Also, I should confess that you've awakened emotions I thought were dead in me."

"What did you say?"

She narrowed her eyes at him. Her burrowing expression was weakening Territaff's emotional restraint.

"I said we'll be together for a long time."

"No. After that."

"You've awakened emotions in me I thought were dead?"

"So, what does that mean—exactly?"

She studied his face, trying to determine his sincerity.

"You've become critical… and I can't continue the mission without you."

"Is this another one of your clever tactics?"

"Believe me. This is as real as it gets."

"What are you, some kind of covert agent?" Kathy said with a bite of sarcasm.

"Not exactly." Territaff scratched the back of his head in thought, feeling self-conscious. "I don't know where to begin. It's all so damn complicated." Then he realized Fred had turned around, looking at them with great interest. "Oh shit, now what am I going to do about you?" He shook his head and massaged his temples with his fingertips to relieve a mounting headache. His already complicated life became even more so as he looked at Fred's smiling face. "You've no idea how much trouble I just threw your way, my poor friend," Territaff said with a long sigh of regret.

"Did you really mean what you just said? That we'll be together?" Kathy's eyes lit up as she pulled Territaff's face closer to hers. "You mean you can't live without me? And you're taking me with you?"

"I've little choice now, do I?" He frowned, then turned his attention back to Fred. "Now, what do I do about you?" He pondered as he continued to massage his temples in thought.

"So, what's the problem?" Fred said.

"The problem is I'm a big-mouthed idiot and just put your life in jeopardy."

"What do you mean?" Beads of sweat rose on Fred's forehead and upper lip. His dark brown skin paled while he stared at Territaff's tense face.

"We need to devise a plan that will clear you of any suspicion of involvement."

"I've got an idea," Kathy said, "but Fred may not like it."

"Well, let's hear it," Territaff said.

"Let's rob him and steal his cab. That way, they'll ignore Fred, thinking he's just a victim, and chase after us."

A broad smile spread across Kathy's face until she caught the alarm in Fred's eyes.

Territaff pursed his lips as he regarded Fred while considering Kathy's plan. "Fred, write down your full name and address for me."

"Okay." He grabbed a pen and a pad from his sun visor. His hand shook a little as he wrote. "I don't mind telling you that this whole thing is scaring the crap out of me."

"Fred, everything will be okay," Territaff said. "Now, give me all your money and get out of the cab."

"You're serious about this?" he said, looking back at Kathy with widened eyes and opened mouth. I'm not sure this is the best plan. I mean, I got a wife and kids that are fond of me and—"

Territaff held his hand up and gestured for Fred to leave the cab.

"We know. That's why we're doing this. Fred, I'm truly sorry," Territaff said, pressing his thumb on Fred's neck. Fred's eyes rolled back, and he fell into Territaff's arms unconscious.

Territaff placed Fred's limp body on the grassy curb, then went through all his pockets, removing his money, his wedding ring, watch, gold chain, and crucifix.

"Shit," Territaff hissed. "I hated doing that."

He patted Fred on the shoulder, then jumped into the cab and sped off. Kathy sat in the back seat, her mouth gaping in shock at what she witnessed.

CHAPTER 7

Territaff parked Fred's cab in a municipal parking lot a few blocks from Passion's North. He filled the meter to its maximum, hoping Fred would come around in time. Fred seemed like a savvy guy, he thought. He'll call the police and report the robbery.

"Are you all right?" he asked Kathy, who became quiet.

"Yeah," she said, looking down. "It's just so much is happening so fast that my head is spinning. Do you think Fred's all right?

Territaff placed two fingers under Kathy's rounded chin and lifted her face.

"Fred will be well compensated, and he'll be okay. I'll make sure of that. They won't waste their time on him. They already know where we are and watch every move we make."

"You sound very sure of yourself, Terri. Are you going to tell me who they are?"

"Yes, but not now. There's no time, and it's complicated."

"Why do you always say that whenever I ask you for an explanation? Do you think I'm too stupid, or don't trust me? Terri, I'm trying hard to understand."

"Kathy, you don't understand how much I trust you. You also must understand that our intimacy was not only about sex. Believe me when I tell you I know about you. I know who you are as a person. You have a beautiful soul and don't easily give your trust. I'm begging you. Be patient and have faith. I'll explain everything. But first, we must get on our way."

She began a new objection, but Territaff kissed her. "Not now," he whispered, his hands cupping her face.

"You know the effect of your kisses will wear off on me," she said.

"We need to find my friend and get the hell out of here."

* * *

Live hard-rock music greeted them when they entered

Passion's North. A sparsely clad, all-female band was performing on the stage. Territaff couldn't help wondering how the base and rhythm guitarists kept their well-endowed bosoms from getting caught in the strings as they played their instruments with almost reckless abandonment. He also smiled in surprise at how good they sounded.

"I don't know about you," Territaff shouted over the pulsating din, "but this is a first for me."

Kathy smiled in surprise and shouted, "You've never heard of the Dixie-Pops?"

He shrugged and said, "Once your ears get used to the volume, they sound good."

"They just cut a three-record deal with Coastal Jam Records," Kathy explained. Then, noticing Territaff's bemused smile, she added, "But then they're not exactly your type, are they?"

"I don't know, I could get used to watching them in concert," Territaff mused, then roamed the room with his eyes.

There were three bars crowded with scores of loud patrons enjoying the spectacle of lovely, naked dancers gyrating up, down, and around tall brass poles. The crowds of young men drank, talked, and laughed to the harmony of flesh and music. Territaff regarded it as voyeurism at its finest.

"Who are we looking for?" Kathy said, then smiled at the congregation of sweaty, inebriated guys who appeared busy undressing her with their eyes.

It was a familiar scene for her, not unlike a typical Saturday night at Fat Jack's. She reflected on Jack, the colorful owner of her workplace, who often threatened to hire all nude servers. She viewed it as a hollow threat—one she answered with a cynical smile.

"I'm looking for my partner, Cuz," Territaff explained as he walked around the center bar.

"Can you give me a hint of what he looks like?" Kathy said, turning her back to Territaff.

"You can't miss him. He's a few centimeters taller than me and has dark brown hair, which he wears straight back. A fair complexion and bright, brown eyes—kind of nerdy-looking—stands out in a crowd.

Territaff turned and realized he was talking to himself. After a quick search of the room, he spied Kathy on the other side of the club, standing close to Cuz.

He joined her, and they listened to Cuz tell a joke to a small crowd of beautiful young women gathered around him.

"The bartender noticed a guy talking and laughing into his hand. After watching the man for a few minutes, he got closer to determine if the man was drunk or just crazy. When the bartender reached him, he heard him say, 'I'll talk to you a little later,' and then he put his hand down. 'What was that all about?' the bartender asked. 'Oh, you mean my handphone,' the man answered. 'What's a handphone?' the bartender asked, feeling like the man was playing a practical joke. 'No, really, it's the latest thing in cellular nanotechnology,' the man explained. 'You see, a miniaturized mic is implanted into the base of my palm, and the earpiece is inside my index finger.' He opened his hand and held it close to the bartender, who angrily pushed the hand away. 'Yeah, right. 'Very funny,' the bartender grumbled, convinced that the customer was playing a joke on him. The man appeared sober, so the bartender asked if he wanted another drink. He said, 'Yes. Thank you.' Just as the bartender was about to fix him another drink, he thought he heard a faint ringing coming from the customer's hand. 'Well, I'll be damned,' the bartender said in amazement as the man answered the call by saying, 'Hello' into his palm. The bartender brought him his drink, then laughed as he watched him talking into his hand with a finger stuck into his ear. The bartender got busy attending to other customers, then noticed out of the corner of his eye that the man had left to use the restroom. After some time had passed, the bartender checked on his unusual customer to ensure everything was all right. To his surprise, he found the man leaning against a stall with his hand up to an ear and a roll of toilet paper stuck up his ass. 'What the hell are you doing now?' the bartender yelled. The man smiled back and said, 'Waiting for a fax.'"

Everyone broke into hysterical laughter, even some of the guys sitting nearby. A server drinking bottled water sprayed a mouthful on the customer in front of her. And a bouncer laughed so hard, he said he almost pissed in his pants.

"That... that was," Natasha was having trouble catching her breath from laughter, "the best one yet, Cuz."

She gave Cuz a long, wet kiss as her hand rubbed the inside of his thigh.

Looking at the crowd he'd amassed, Territaff realized Cuz was a big hit. "Wow," he whispered, "They like him."

"And you were worried," Kathy said, beaming at Cuz. "He's adorable."

"Hi, Terri, come join us," Cuz said, drinking a colorful liquid from a large goblet. "Who's the delicious-looking brunette?" Cuz sounded as though each word was struggling to come out of his mouth. "Peggy," Cuz shouted to the server, who gave Territaff and Kathy a close look-over. "Nodder round for my friends." She relaxed her firm stare and nodded.

To Territaff's surprise, Cuz was slurring his words. He leaned close to him and said, "Cuz, if I didn't know better, I'd say you were plastered."

He squeezed himself between one of Cuz's admirers and the bar.

"You mean drunk?" Cuz asked, blinking at Territaff with bloodshot eyes.

"No, I think you passed drunk a while ago." He leaned closer, "You're shit-faced." He smiled at Cuz and thought, How's that possible?

"No," Cuz said, with sudden alarm, looking around him. "Who was the rotten bastard that shit on my face?" he shouted. Everyone looked at him and laughed, realizing how wasted he was. "You're wrong, Terri," Cuz poked him in the chest with a finger for emphasis, "Nobody shitted on my face."

"What are you drinking?" Territaff sniffed his breath.

"A cama… cama… mazzy," Cuz looked at his drink, then held it up to Peggy, who had finished placing a round of drinks across the bar. "What is this?" Cuz burped as he spoke.

"Kamikaze," she said. "What are you guys having?"

"The check," Territaff said to Peggy's obvious disappointment. "We need to go— right now," he told Cuz.

Cuz recognized the urgency in Territaff's face and became upright and sober-looking.

"Please give Peggy a generous gratuity," Cuz said. "She taught me how to French-kiss, then added with a sheepish grin, and she's a most proficient instructor."

"It was my pleasure," Peggy said with a sultry smile.

Natasha stood up and walked with Cuz as Territaff paid the bar tab.

"Twenty-eight hundred dollars," Territaff barked.

Cuz smiled at Natasha as he heard Territaff's objection.

"That includes the lap dances and two hours in the Champagne Room," Cuz explained to Territaff's annoyed expression. "Natasha insisted that my lessons in foreplay and sex needed a proper ambiance to be effective." He turned to Natasha, then took her hand and kissed it. "I must go now, but I'll never forget you and this wonderful evening. You have taught me so much, and it saddens me that I must leave you." They embraced and kissed.

"Wow is all I can say," Natasha said. "You're amazing on so many levels. I'll never forget you. I don't think I'll ever have that kind of passion and kindness from anyone else. It'll be something I'll cherish for the rest of my life." She wrapped her arms around Cuz's neck and kissed him again.

"Goodbye, Natasha," Cuz said softly.

As they left the club, Territaff turned to Cuz and said in a low voice, "I guess it was a good investment, my friend. You appeared to have acquired some insight into human emotions. Not to mention having a great time."

"Yes. Now, I can say I've experienced both pleasure and sadness. They're strong emotions and seem to permeate the fabric of human existence. Thank you, Terri, for the opportunity to experience them."

"You're most welcome, my friend," Territaff said, then wrapped his arm around Cuz's shoulders and pulled him into a sideways hug.

Kathy looked at the two men in total confusion. She didn't know what to make of what she had seen and heard. She thought, " Who was Cuz, and what was that emotional experience all about? Did Territaff get him laid? She smiled at the last thought.

She walked silently, feeling a little left out of the two men's personal equation, until Cuz said, "You must be Kathy. I'm sorry we haven't been properly introduced, but Terri sometimes has lapses in the amenities."

"Oh crap," Terri blurted. "I forgot that you two haven't met. That's odd." He pulled on his ear. "I thought you already knew each other."

CHAPTER 8

"We need to get out of here," Territaff said, looking up and down the street. "Kathy, see if you can find us a cab."

"At this hour? I'll have the club call us one."

"No, wait. I've got a better idea." He turned to Cuz and said, "Convertible or hardtop?"

Cuz smiled. "You know I'm a ragtop man."

"Okay, let's go find us a nice, speedy convertible," Territaff said, pointing towards the parking lot.

"Wait a sec," Kathy said. "First, we beat up and robbed our cabby, and now we're stealing a car?"

"Yeah?" Territaff gave her a puzzled look. "So, what's your point?"

"The point is, when the police catch up with us, they'll lock us up for a hundred years." She placed her hands on her hips, glaring. "I don't want to be some big mama's bitch for the next hundred years—that's the fuckin' point!"

"Who's big-mama?" Cuz asked.

"Go find us a nice convertible," Territaff said to him. He placed his hands on Kathy's shoulders. "What's wrong?"

"I'm scared. I don't know what's going on, and you keep telling me everything's going to be all right. But it isn't all right, and everything's happening so fast... and... I just don't know what you want from me."

"I know, Kathy. Please, I need you to be brave just a little longer. Cuz, and I won't allow anything to happen to you. I swear. I'll defend you with my life." He placed a crooked finger under her chin and lifted her face. He could feel her emotions rising, and her eyes welled with tears. "Look at me, Kathy." She looked directly into his dark eyes. "You must believe me."

"I've known you less than forty-eight hours, and yet... I think I'm in love with you," she said in a hushed voice. "It's the only logical explanation of why I'm so drawn to you." She lowered her eyes, adding, "I'm hopeful, in time, you will... or maybe I'll figure out what I'm feeling." She turned away, shaking her head, then blurted, "Shit! I don't know what I'm feeling other than confused and frightened."

"Kathy, I wish I could love you. If I were capable of such an emotion— Maybe I'd learn to love again... I'm sorry—"

She placed a finger across Territaff's mouth and said, "Please don't explain, Terri. The truth is the last thing I want to hear."

A bright red Ford Mustang came to a screeching halt. It was a high-performance, custom model dressed out with bright chrome wheels, low-profile tires, and a beefy engine. Kathy laughed at seeing Cuz wearing a large Panama hat and sitting upright behind the wheel. The top was down, and he was revving the powerful engine against the background of heavy Latin jazz.

"How's this?" Cuz asked.

"Nice. Let's go." Territaff said as he went around to the passenger side.

Territaff opened the passenger door. He moved the powered seat forward, gesturing for Kathy to get into the back.

"I'm not sitting in the back."

"What's wrong with the back seat?"

"Have you ever ridden in the back of a convertible with the top down?"

Territaff thought for a moment. "Oh, I see your point. I guess you'll have to sit on my lap up front."

He smiled slyly at her as he eased himself into the car, then patted his thigh for Kathy to sit. She gave him a crooked grin, then flopped on his lap and wiggled her full, round buttocks, making a statement with her body.

"Fasten your seatbelts, folks. We're going for a drive," Cuz said as he punched the accelerator.

The car roared, laying a long stretch of smoking rubber, pushing Kathy hard against Territaff.

"Do you always drive this fast?" she said with the wind

gushing against her.

"This is the first time I've ever driven a combustion-engine conveyance, so I've no comparable reference to answer your question."

"He's kidding, right?" Kathy said to Territaff.

"No, he's quite serious, I'm afraid."

"You've never driven a car before?"

"No need to be concerned, Kathy. I'm versed in all forms of terrestrial transportation." Cuz looked at her and attempted a reassuring smile.

Territaff rolled his eyes, grimacing.

"Cuz, please watch the road," Kathy said.

"You don't have to worry. Cuz is a quick learner. He also has fast reflexes and great eyesight." Territaff said.

"Is that supposed to make me feel better?"

"You mean it didn't?"

"Wouldn't you be a little concerned about the competence of a man who, just fifteen minutes ago, was wasted and is now driving a car for the first time," she glanced at the speedometer, "at, oh my God, over a hundred fifty miles per hour?"

"Not to mention, in an illegally obtained vehicle," Cuz added.

"That wasn't helpful, Cuz," Territaff said.

"Also, Terri, your friend Cuz looks and talks funny. No offense, Cuz."

"None taken."

Territaff looked at Cuz. "Well, he isn't from around here."

"Yah—think!" Kathy tilted her head to the side to get a better look at Cuz, then asked, "Cuz, where are you from?"

"Venubia," he answered to Territaff's dismay.

"Ah, Cuz, I think it would be better if we waited on telling Kathy your story until we get back to Biomei."

"Who the hell is Biomei?" Kathy snapped.

Territaff held up a finger to Kathy's face. "I want to stop you before you get a full head of steam and ask a lot of questions again. As I've been telling you all night, this is not the time or place for this discussion. Biomei is someone who'll be able to answer all your questions, fill you in on the details of our mission… and your new future home," he mumbled in a low voice. Territaff frowned, then closed his eyes, gathering his composure. "Jesus, Kathy, can't you wait a little longer and let us concentrate on safely getting you out of here?"

"Sorry, but I can't stand being constantly treated like a mushroom."

"A mushroom?" Territaff said, squinting his eyes.

"Yeah, a mushroom. Kept in the dark and fed nothing but bullshit." She grinned sarcastically.

"Query," Cuz said.

"Not now," Territaff cut him off.

"Terri, what route do you want me to take?" Cuz asked.

"Stay on US1 and take it to Homestead Air Force Base. That's where we came in."

Cuz nodded, then smiled at Kathy. "If it helps to know, our situation is also confusing and unsettling for me."

"Thanks, Cuz, it's nice to know I'm not the only one freaking out here." She said to Territaff, "Please tell me you know what the hell you're doing and that there's some plan you're executing."

He scratched his cheek. "I'm working on it… um… well, I don't have a clue. Making it up on the fly."

"Thanks, Terri. That's the first honest thing you've said to me."

She rested her head on his shoulder and resigned herself to the reality of her life being in the hands of two total nutcases. She let out a long sigh, then said a silent prayer.

The dawn was breaking the gray into a soft orange glow over the tall Royal Palms scattered throughout the open sawgrass fields. The air felt cooler in the strong currents blowing through the open car.

"There's an old dairy road to your right, Cuz. Take it. It'll lead us to an abandoned tree nursery," Territaff instructed.

"This is not the same route we used when we came in," Cuz said.

"I know, but we've been followed almost since we left the club."

Kathy sat more upright with the news. Territaff looked over his shoulder for the black SUV that had kept a safe distance behind them. "Cuz, ease us off the road a few meters ahead." He pointed to his left. "Pull into that patch of tall grass right over there." Cuz drove the car into a thick field of tall sawgrass that concealed it from the road. "Stop here and leave the car running. Kathy, I want you to lie across the back seat. Don't get up or leave the car for any reason."

"What are you going to do?" Her heart pounded harder in her tight chest. "You're not leaving me alone, are you?"

"Kathy, please do as I say and stay down."

He took Cuz off to the side and telepathically told him, "*Stay with her. If anything happens, don't come for me. Go directly to Biomei. Here, you'll need this.*"

He pulled a gold compact disc out from an inside pocket of his jacket and handed it to Cuz.

Cuz got back into the driver's seat, then took off the large hat and regarded it for a moment before tossing it like a Frisbee into the sawgrass.

"Kathy, I sense your uneasiness," Cuz said without looking back at her.

"What's going on?"

"Terri is trying to ascertain who has been following us. He should be right back."

"Cuz, tell me about yourself."

"What would you like to know?"

"Where's Venubia?"

"I can't give you that information right now."

"How did you meet, Terri?"

"Sorry, Kathy, I can't reveal that either."

"Jesus, what can you tell me?" She lifted her head and gave him an angry scowl. "Never mind."

She flopped back onto the seat, rubbing her temples with her fingertips to relieve a headache that had been brewing since she got into the car.

"I'm truly sorry, Kathy. I'm not being deliberately evasive. We're only trying to protect you." Cuz noticed Kathy rubbing her temples through the rear-view mirror. "I see you're in discomfort. May I relieve your headache?"

She nodded and sat up. Cuz placed his long, delicate-looking hands on both sides of her head. He closed his eyes as though he were in deep concentration. She felt a momentary pulse, and then her headache was gone.

"That's amazing. How'd you do that?"

"It's a simple technique. I'll teach it to you when we have time."

Their attention was drawn to an odd puffing sound followed by a loud concussion. The sounds were close, and in the direction Territaff had gone.

"What was that?" Kathy said as she craned her head up to see what was happening.

"Please, stay down on the seat as Territaff instructed," Cuz said, appearing undisturbed by the event.

Another puffing sound was heard, followed by an even louder impact. This time, a visible plume of dark-colored smoke also emerged.

Cuz had to restrain Kathy as she attempted to climb out of the back seat.

"Stay down. Territaff is unharmed and coming back to us."

"And how do you know that?"

"I can hear him," Cuz said, holding Kathy down on the seat. "I appreciate you wanting to assist Terri, but you'll only endanger him and yourself if you leave the car. Stay put, or I'll have to render you unconscious."

Cuz pulled the car around, then drove fast from the action.

"Cuz, what are you doing?" Kathy screamed. "You're leaving Terri behind." She wrapped her slender but firm arm around Cuz's neck in a futile attempt at a chokehold.

Cuz slammed on the brakes as another concussion exploded a few meters ahead of the car. He broke Kathy's hold, then reached out and gripped the front of her head with his free hand. She slumped back into the seat as Territaff emerged about thirty meters ahead of the car. Knowing he was out of position, Cuz stomped on the accelerator, causing the car to fishtail on the soft, damp dirt road. As the car picked up speed, two shadowy figures appeared a few meters behind the car. They aimed peculiar-looking weapons and fired. The weapons made an odd puffing noise. Territaff ran ahead of the car. As Cuz came alongside him, Territaff leaped into the front seat, and they ducked. They heard a whistling noise whiz over their heads, then a blinding explosion. The powerful concussion cracked the windshield and pushed the car sideways, almost into an old irrigation ditch.

"Their aim is improving. I don't think we'll survive another volley," Cuz said.

"They're shooting at the car, not us. If they wanted us dead, they would have blown us up. They're using concussion grenades to disable the car. Except they're missing the mark."

"I see." Cuz arched an eyebrow. "Zohleemay needs to know what we discovered. Doesn't he? Otherwise, they would have killed us."

"Precisely, my dear friend. What happened to Kathy?" Territaff asked, noticing her unconscious body, lying awkwardly with her feet on the seat and her head on the floor.

"May I explain later?" Another explosion rumbled just beyond the car. "We need to get some distance from them," Cuz said.

"You don't have to explain. Knowing Kathy, she probably gave you no choice."

"They most likely know where we're going," Cuz said, watching the two squat figures running back into a patch of tall sawgrass.

"I'm not so sure about that," Territaff said. "I think they've been keeping a close tail on us because they don't know. If they did, they would be waiting for us..."

"What makes you believe the tail wasn't a diversion to make us think what you inferred?"

"I think we're over-analyzing this. Let's stick to our plan and be ready for anything."

"As usual, your logic is sound. One other thing."

"Yes?"

"What do we do about her?" Cuz pursed his lips, looking thoughtfully at Territaff. "She's not part of the original plan."

"No, she's not." Territaff frowned as he looked at Kathy's unconscious body. "She'll have one hell of a headache," he mumbled, reaching out and lifting her head back onto the seat. "We need to get to the base. But it's Sunday."

"So, what do you propose we do?"

"First, let's eliminate our over-anxious friends, then visit Colonel Cameron. We need to find out what he knows and why he sent Tanya after us. I know she wasn't acting on her own."

Cuz glanced back over his shoulder. "They must've gone back to their vehicle."

"Let's give them a warm welcome up the road," Territaff said.

Cuz sped through the dirt road until it returned to the main highway. He positioned the car, blocking the road. Territaff reached into the inside pocket of his jacket and pulled out a .44 magnum revolver, then waited for the two menacing creatures to approach.

"Where did you obtain that?" Cuz asked, eyeing the gun.

"I borrowed it from a policeman."

"Borrowed?"

"Okay, I stole it from a parked police car."

"Have you ever fired a weapon of that caliber?"

Territaff looked at the gun and shrugged. "Not exactly."

"Under the circumstances, don't you think I should fire it? I'm familiar with all forms of Earth-based weaponry."

"And spoil all my fun?"

Cuz wrinkled his brow and was about to question Territaff, but a close impact stopped him, splintering palm trees and throwing a plume of earth and sawgrass into the air.

"There they are," Territaff said, aiming the large revolver at the black SUV rapidly approaching. "Come to poppa, fellas," Territaff whispered.

"I suggest you aim at the tires. It will cause them to lose control of their vehicle at their present speed."

"Thanks, I'll keep that in mind."

Another shattering explosion hit a few meters away, spewing a cloud of wet soil and sawgrass on the car.

"Territaff, I think now would be a good time to fire."

"Just a little closer," Territaff murmured as he braced his firing hand's wrist with his free hand.

The SUV was almost on top of them when Territaff finally fired three rapid shots. The first one took out the passenger leaning out of the window and firing the odd-looking weapon. The next one hit the front driver's-side tire. The SUV veered left, almost flipping onto its side. The third shot shattered the rear window. The SUV swerved back around. Right as the driver regained control of the vehicle, Territaff fired the last three rounds. One broke the windshield. One missed, and the third struck the driver in the head. The SUV sped past them and darted across the highway, smashing into a support column of the turnpike's overpass.

They walked to the car; its front end was crushed around the concrete column, with the rest of the twisted frame crumpled like a squeezebox. Both the driver and passenger were dead. Cuz gathered the weapons, threw them back inside, and then placed the passenger, hanging halfway out the window, back on the seat. They walked back to their car. Cuz aimed the weapon at the rear of the SUV, then fired. An intense fireball erupted, engulfing the vehicle in flames. They watched for a few minutes to ensure the blaze incinerated the two bodies into indistinguishable charred remains. They hoped an autopsy would only bewilder the coroner and might buy them a little time.

"We should go," Cuz said. "Police and fire trucks will be here soon. I'm sure the explosion caught someone's attention."

Territaff nodded, and they both got back into the car.

"Let's go to the base," Territaff said. "Colonel Cameron should be expecting us... or maybe not. I hope he has coffee."

CHAPTER 9

Captain Jayson felt an odd sensation as he rushed along State Road 84 on his way to the Fort Lauderdale Airport. He looked around, sensing he wasn't alone, but there was no one in the van. He felt like a dark presence had entered his body all at once. He shook his head and twisted in his seat, trying to fight off the surreal ghost-like presence taking him over. His van veered to the right, then swerved back across the highway. Another consciousness suddenly possessed Jayson's mind.

The captain screamed in agony, trying to rid himself of the excruciating ethereal presence that felt like it was devouring his mind and body. It only took a few seconds before Captain Jayson capitulated to the overwhelming force, just as his vehicle broke through the guardrail and plunged into the murky green waters of the Everglades.

* * *

The morning sun hovered above the horizon, giving the marshy plain an orange glow. A large crane took flight as their flat-bottom boat glided up to their favorite fishing hole. The young boy's dark eyes grew wide with excitement when he saw the thick, scaly body skim the water's surface.

"Look, Grandpa," he cried out, pointing at the alligator with half its head above the water's clear surface. Its bulbous eyes looked right at him.

"Oh, he's a big one," the grandfather said, holding his fishing pole.

The man's dark red, weather-worn face remained passive as he studied the mighty predator.

"What's he doing?" the young boy asked.

"He's waiting for his breakfast."

"Is someone going to feed him?"

The grandfather let out a warm laugh. "If we're not careful, one of us will be his breakfast."

The young boy jerked backward into his grandfather,

almost knocking him down. As the shallow boat rocked, they both nearly fell into the water. The elderly man grabbed his grandson as he recovered his balance.

"Grandson, be careful," the grandfather chided, holding the trembling child close with one arm while keeping his fishing pole in the water with the other.

They both closely studied the alligator. It seemed unperturbed by the boat's sudden movements.

"Let's go from here, Grandpa," the boy pleaded. "I'm scared."

The grandfather stroked the young boy's long, black hair as he spoke in a quiet voice, "Don't be frightened by nature. If you show fear to an animal, it will feel your fear, provoking it to come after you. Just respect them, and they'll often leave you alone. Remember, you look as big to him as he is big to you. Always put your fear aside until the moment of meeting has passed."

"He didn't move," the young boy said.

"He has probably already eaten and is waiting for the sun to warm him. I think we'll leave him be and go to our other favorite spot."

"That's a good idea, Grandpa," the young boy agreed, still looking at the unmoving beast. "He looks like he's sleeping."

"Then let's be very quiet and leave him to his rest; that way, he'll leave us alone."

As the grandfather reeled in his line, he felt it snag on something hard. At first, he thought he caught a rock, then jerked the line, but it held tight.

"Here, hold my pole," he said, handing his rod to his grandson. "Hold it up as I move forward, you reel in the slack."

"Okay," the young boy said, holding the rod almost over his head.

He pulled hard on the starter cord, and the small, outboard motor started with a rumble and a puff of gray smoke. The small boat stuttered forward until it bumped up against something hard. The grandfather looked over the boat into the murky, green water. He furrowed his windswept brow when another alligator moved under his boat. He felt a sudden surge of nervous energy followed by relief as the gator swam away from them. He found his line as he continued to peer into the dark water. It had caught on what looked like a large, flat piece of metal.

"What are you looking at, Grandpa?"

"I'm not sure," he said, straining to see through the cloudy water.

The water cleared enough to make out what looked like the roof of a dark green truck. The grandfather moved the boat forward a few feet and then circled.

"Reel in the slack," he called to the boy. The boy smiled brightly as the line went free, and he reeled it in.

The young boy put down the rod and knelt close to his grandfather.

"Grandpa, that's a car," the boy said in surprise. "Are there people in it?"

"I sure hope not," the grandfather said under a long breath.

He brought the boat to the driver's side of the sunken van, then peered into the water. He waited for the water to clear a little more. A moment later, the grandfather let out a shocked gasp. He could see the head and chest slumped forward over the steering wheel.

"We need to call the police," he said, revving the small motor.

"Grandpa, is that a man?"

The grandfather gripped the rudder, then pushed the throttle forward as far as it would go. "Sit down, grandson," he called over the loud whine of the small outboard's motor.

CHAPTER 10

The sergeant at the gate scrutinized the damaged convertible with a disapproving air. His eyes moved back and forth, taking in the ludicrous possibility that the unconscious female and the two disheveled occupants could be friends of the base deputy commander. He asked Cuz if he was sure he wanted to see Colonel Cameron.

"It's Sunday, gentlemen. The good colonel is probably at church," the sergeant scowled. "You're sure you want to disturb him?"

Cuz nodded, meeting the guard's disagreeable gaze with an unassuming smile. "Please, if it's no bother."

"What's her problem?" The guard asked gruffly.

"You mean the colonel's niece?" Territaff said.

"That's the colonel's niece?"

The guard stiffened as he regarded the unconscious female lying face down on the back seat.

"We had a rough night," Cuz interjected.

"Were you in the car when all this shit happened?" the sergeant asked as he walked around the dirty, battered Mustang, shaking his head. "You expect me to call the colonel's residence at 06:35 on a Sunday morning and tell him that two scruffy-looking men and an unconscious female, allegedly his niece, want to visit?"

"You could leave out the scruffy part, but you seem to have a grasp of the situation, Sergeant." Cuz looked at Territaff. "Is there anything you care to add?"

Territaff shrugged. "I think that covers it."

"Open the trunk, please, sir," the sergeant said.

A second guard with a restrained smile suddenly snapped to life and inspected the trunk.

"Oh, Sarge, you need to see this."

"*Did you check the trunk?*" Territaff transmitted to Cuz.

"*Didn't occur to me until now. What about the sonic?*"

"Great."

"You guys are big-time scuba divers? And what in the hell is this?" He held up the long, cylindrical weapon.

"I suggest you put that down, Sergeant," Territaff said firmly. "That's the colonel's. As for scuba diving. Oh yeah. Cuz, here, once speared a three-hundred-pound grouper just off the shore," he added with a broad smile.

"Sergeant, the colonel is expecting us for an important meeting," Cuz said, observing the other guard inspecting the car's underside with a large pole mirror.

"It's clean," the other guard called out.

The sergeant gave them a stern look as he handed them back their driver's licenses, then motioned to a corporal in the guardhouse. The young corporal leaned out the guardhouse door and asked, "What's up?"

"Bob, call Colonel Cameron's residence and tell him that Mr. Cuz Venubia and Mr. T. Territaff are bringing home his niece, as he instructed last night." The Sergeant gave Cuz and Territaff a cynical smile. "You realize if the good colonel says anything other than 'Send them right up,' I'll take great pleasure in throwing you in the stockade. You guys have trouble written all over you. I don't know what kind of bullshit you're up to, but you better keep it off my base."

"Terri, I feel the good Sargent, for some inexplicable reason, doesn't like us."

"Whatever gave you that idea, Cuz?"

"Maybe it's the way he's tapping his sidearm or something in the tone of his voice?" I'm not sure."

"He's only doing his job, aren't you, Sergeant Meyers?" Territaff said, reading the sergeant's name off his uniform.

"Hey, Sarge, the colonel said to have an escort take them to his office."

He looked back at the young corporal and growled, "He said what?"

"Have them escorted to his office," the corporal repeated.

"Yeah-yeah! I heard you." The sergeant looked back at the corporal, "So what are you waiting for? Call for an escort," he shouted. The corporal jumped to the phone and made the call. "Pull your car up over there," he pointed to a parking space in front of the guardhouse, "and wait for your escort."

They only had to wait a few minutes before a jeep arrived. It pulled next to their car, and the driver told them to follow close behind him.

"The colonel's office is in the HQ Building. It's only a few minutes up this street," he said with a cheery smile. "Can't miss it. It's the only three-story building on this side of the base."

Cuz nodded, then gazed at Kathy in the backseat and frowned.

"We need to wake her," Cuz said.

"You sure you want to do that?"

"We can't leave her in the back seat."

"Sure, we can. It'll be best to leave her right where she is now."

"Okay, Terri, if you think it's best."

Territaff had Cuz put the top up.

Cuz stared at Kathy's unmoving body and frowned. "Sorry," he whispered.

"Don't worry. She'll be fine." Territaff said, giving Cuz's shoulder a reassuring pat.

They followed the MP's jeep into the HQ's parking lot. The jeep stopped in front, and the driver jumped out and approached their car. He was young and lanky, dressed in green fatigues. Cuz recognized that he was an Army MP Corporal.

"Here's a permit that'll allow you to park in any of the visitor spaces to your right. Place the permit on the driver's side of your dashboard." He whistled as he looked over the car. "I'm sure there's a hell of a story about this torn-up Mustang. I bet the colonel will love hearing all about it." A broad smile spread across his face with a sudden thought, "By any chance, is this his car? 'Cause I happen to know Cameron is a ragtop man."

"It's not," Cuz answered, returning the young soldier's smile with a frown.

The MP's forehead furrowed into tight lines, noticing the unconscious woman in the back seat. "I'm sure there's a good explanation for her also," he said, looking attentively at Kathy's still form. "She looks dead. Is she okay?"

"We went clubbing on South Beach," Territaff explained.

"Oh," he nodded, his face breaking into a big grin. He turned his pale green eyes on Cuz and Territaff and said, "It looks like you had one hell of a night."

Cuz reflected on the evening and gave him his best interpretation of a bad-boy smile while Territaff looked annoyed with the corporal's insistent chattering.

"I'd love to tell you all about it, but we don't want to keep Cameron waiting," Territaff said.

Noticing Territaff's sudden change in demeanor, the MP stiffened. "Ah, no, sir." I'll only be a second. Wait for me at the entrance. It's those glass doors just ahead."

* * *

The Colonel's secretary had just arrived as they entered the reception area of his office. Cuz stopped to observe the secretary bent over, putting her lunch in the small refrigerator behind her desk. Cuz tilted his head as he mused over her shapely buttocks, which were prominent in her tight slacks.

"Good morning, gentleman," she said, moving items around on a small refrigerator shelf. "Take a seat. It's a coincidence that I'm here today. Came in to catch up on paperwork. The Colonel is on his way." She stood, giving them a warm smile. She was a pleasant-looking blonde with fiery blue eyes that seemed to take in everything around her. "Yes, Corporal," she addressed the young man who stood at attention.

"I was told to escort these men until Colonel Cameron arrived, ma'am."

"That's okay. They look harmless enough. You can go back to your duties now. I'll take it from here."

"But ma'am—"

"Thank you, corporal," the secretary said with a quiet authority that dismissed the MP.

"Thank you, ma'am. Have a good day," he said, then nodded to Cuz and Territaff as he left.

"What can I get you, gentleman?" she asked, sitting behind her large, meticulous desk.

"I could use a strong cup of coffee," Territaff said.

"How about you, sir?" she asked Cuz, looking at him with an uncertain smile.

"I'm fine. Thank you."

She tapped a few numbers on her phone. A man's voice answered, "Yes, Colleen."

"George, it's good you made it. Please bring in two coffees, one for the colonel and one with," she tilted her head toward Territaff.

"Black with heavy sugar," Territaff called out.

"Will do," George said.

"You both look as though you've seen a little action along the way," Colleen observed. "I should warn you, the Colonel is very formal and won't appreciate your appearance. So, I suggest you be extra polite," she warned in a hushed tone, making her point.

"Thanks for the heads-up," Territaff said, acerbically. "We've already met."

Collene's smooth brow creased with faint lines, looking a little unsettled, and forced a quick smile.

A Specialist First Class, wearing a well-fitted uniform, entered the office, carrying a tray with a pitcher of coffee, fresh pastries, napkins, and spoons, all nicely arranged. He placed the tray on a credenza in the rear of the office. He opened one of the credenza's double doors and retrieved an oversized dark blue mug. It was embossed with "U.S. Army 5ᵗʰ Calvary" in bright gold letters, along with a small, round silver tray. The Specialist placed the mug on the tray, poured coffee into it, picked up a tasty-looking pastry with a pair of plastic tongs, placed it onto a napkin, and put it next to the mug. The entire task was done with a practiced flair. Holding the tray up in one hand, he walked to Colonel Cameron's office door, then bumped his left rear pocket onto a proximity reader, the door clicked open, and he held it ajar with his butt.

"Good morning, sir," the specialists said.

"Good morning, George. I'm sorry to ruin your Sunday. I hope you didn't have any plans."

"No, sir." George let the door go, silencing the room to the outside.

"Gentlemen, you can help yourselves to coffee and pastries," Colleen said, pointing to the tray.

"Thank you," Territaff said, got up, and walked to the credenza.

He poured himself a coffee and looked over the selection of pastries. He picked up an apple turnover and took a hungry bite. To his delight, it tasted delicious. He took another one and sat down.

As he hungrily ate the second pastry, he looked at Cuz with a sudden thought. "You should eat something."

"I don't need—"

Territaff glowered irritably. Cuz stood and walked to the tray.

"This all looks... most appetizing," Cuz said, then looked at Colleen. "Can you suggest something? I rarely eat pastries."

"The cherry Danish is my personal favorite."

Cuz stared at the selection, unsure which was the cherry Danish, then looked back at Colleen.

"It's the square with powdered sugar on top," she said to

Cuz's puzzled expression.

"Ah. Thank you." Cuz placed the pastry on a napkin and returned to his seat, then ate it in slow, deliberate bites.

"Well?" Colleen asked.

Cuz was confused by her question until Territaff nudged him with an elbow to his ribs. "It's delicious," he blurted and ate a little faster.

"Will the Colonel be much longer?" Territaff asked, showing his growing impatience.

"He'll be with you as soon as George finishes the morning reports. It usually only takes about ten minutes or so, depending on the night's activity. But being here on a Sunday... Well, you can read between the lines," she said, flashing a sly smile before returning her attention to a neat stack of papers in the upper tray of her inbox.

"I think we'll be waiting for a while," Territaff transmitted.

* * *

Colonel Cameron was a short, imposing man in his late forties. His pepper-gray hair was cut in a clean, military style. His muscular frame highlighted the prominent bulges of his arms and chest beneath his athletically fitted uniform. A pair of stylish-looking half-lens glasses was perched on the end of his slightly bent nose. He pointed to the seats in front of his expansive desk for Territaff and Cuz to sit while he finished reading a lengthy report in his hands.

He laid the report on his desk and scratched the back of his head, his expression somber. He glanced at the two disheveled figures before him and shook his head slowly. He rubbed the area beneath his left eye, opened his mouth as if to speak, then clenched it shut. His forehead creased, and he squinted at them, the right corner of his mouth curling into a sarcastic smile.

"You don't look so good, Colonel. Is there something I can get you?" Territaff said, relishing Cameron's distress.

"Don't be so smug, Territaff. I have a good mind to throw

both of you into the stockade. You've got a lot of nerve coming in here, acting as if nothing has happened."

"Can't say we didn't warn you," Territaff interjected.

"You warned me of what? A possible invasion from an unknown source with advanced technology. I'm supposed to believe that crock of shit you presented to us as real. I don't know your game, but I'm not buying it. You're fucking consultants, for Christ's sake!"

"We're consultants vetted and cleared by every major security agency, including the CIA, NSA, and DARPA. Yet you still doubt our credibility? This is no game, Colonel. Tanya's dead. Is that real enough for you?"

The Colonel jumped up and walked around his desk to the large glass wall of windows that overlooked a small patio garden. He stared out in silence for a long moment before speaking. "I suspected something was wrong when she didn't report this morning," he said quietly.

Cuz's eyes darted between the colonel and Territaff, then frowned. "I don't understand—"

"Hold on, Cuz," Territaff interrupted, looking at the Colonel. "Can you tell me why she was following me?"

Colonel Cameron turned, narrowing his stare at Territaff. "Be careful. You may be civilians, but I still have rank over you," he said in a low, controlled tone. "You were supposed to report to me first. When you failed to report, I told her to check on you." The Colonel's voice was strained with regret. "Do you know how she..." He paused, closed his eyes for a beat, then returned to his seat. "Do you know what happened?"

"I found Tanya's dead body propped against a garbage bin in South Beach. As far as I can tell, she confronted her assailants, and they killed her. Beyond that, I can't say. As you're already aware, we were attacked on the way here. They knew our every move. Somebody is talking to them. This wasn't the first incident."

Territaff realized Cameron didn't know of Tanya's death

and appeared genuinely disturbed by it. He gave the colonel a moment to regain his composure. Cameron let out a long, heavy breath, then sat more upright in his chair.

"Do you know how she was… killed?" he asked in a firmer voice.

"She was shot at point-blank range. Beyond that, we don't have a clue."

"I see. I guess we'll learn more from the autopsy."

"We already took care of that. It revealed nothing."

Cameron's face reddened with anger as he stood, then leaned on both arms close to Territaff, looking like a great ape readying for a charge.

"Who the hell do you think you are?" he yelled in Territaff's face.

"The one in charge of this case," Territaff said calmly. "Now, sit down, Colonel, and let's talk."

Cameron was unaccustomed to being spoken to in that manner, but sat down. He stared back at Territaff with a confused scowl.

"What do you mean you're in charge? By whose authority?"

"Look, Colonel, I'm in no mood to get into a pissing contest with you. Let it suffice that we share the same interests in what's rapidly becoming a giant clusterfuck. I've neither the time nor the inclination for a bureaucratic tug-of-war with you. We both want justice for Tanya. But there are much bigger issues at risk than who's in charge of what."

"All right, Territaff," the colonel said, "let's talk. What were… those things in the SUV?"

Territaff hesitated, then blurted, "Zenti."

"What the fuck is Zenti?"

"The reason we're here."

"Can you be a little more explicit?"

"I'm sorry, sir, but I can't provide you with any details about the Zenti or our mission beyond what has been disclosed in your security briefing."

"I see. But you're asking for my complete cooperation and assistance with no clue what I'm committing my men and resources to. I've already lost one good soldier because of you. I'll not risk one more life out of ignorance."

"Ignorance," Territaff repeated. "That seems to be the way around here, Colonel."

Colonel Cameron removed his glasses and placed them into a leather case. He steepled his hands together on top of his desk and sat upright, his eyes fixed on the two men in front of him. A long, uncomfortable silence fell between them as though the colonel was pondering the situation.

"I don't have a damn clue what the situation is, nor who the hell you two are," the Colonel spoke, tension rising in his voice. "And if I don't get some answers to the what's and whys of your mission, the only thing you'll get from me is an escort to the stockade."

"We appreciate your position, Colonel, but any information we'd divulge now would only compromise our mission and place you in further danger," Territaff stated emphatically. "Believe me, sir, ignorance in this situation is for your protection. However, we tried to warn you that there was an imminent threat to national security."

"Ignorance is bliss. Is that what you're telling me? So, I'm supposed to stay happy and stupid? And accept everything you're telling me. Well, gentlemen, not on my base. I'm not letting you run unsupervised."

"Sir, with all due respect, we don't report to you. And yes. You'll let us do what we came here to do with or without your cooperation." Territaff folded his muscular arms across his chest, staring defiantly at Cameron.

Colonel Cameron glared, picked up the phone with a menacing smile, and pushed the intercom button.

"Colleen, call General Dickerson for me." He put the phone down and then looked closely at Cuz. "Where are you from, son?"

Cuz glanced at Territaff as though asking for guidance.

"Sir, Cuz's place of origin is classified," Territaff interjected before Cuz could answer.

"Really?" He arched an eyebrow. "You two are just full of secrets, aren't you?"

"I guess you could say that, sir."

"Well, we'll see about this—you cocky bastard. In the meantime, you can just relax in the outer office while I chat with General Dickerson about what to do with you."

"Eh, sir," Territaff remembered Kathy. "There's a young lady who's with us."

"You mean my alleged niece?" the colonel said. "I had her taken to the hospital for an examination when we couldn't wake her. What's wrong with her?"

"She was sedated for her protection," Territaff said.

Cuz frowned.

"You're quite a pair." Cameron narrowed his eyes with a disgusted look. "Wait in the outer office while I try to get a handle on the mess you created." He pointed toward the door as the phone rang. "Good morning, sir," Cameron answered.

Territaff and Cuz stopped to listen to the Colonel's conversation. Noticing them standing by the door, the colonel stopped talking and gave them a stern, dismissive look that sent them out of his office.

"*Cuz, listen to Cameron's conversation,*" Territaff transmitted.

Cuz nodded. Territaff started for the door.

"*Where are you going?*" Cuz transmitted.

"*I'll get Kathy. The last thing we need is for them to start all kinds of testing on her.*"

"*And what should I tell the Colonel?*"

"*I went to look on his niece.*"

That didn't go so well, Territaff thought. Colonel Cameron was not on board, which made him wonder what General Dickerson was up to. He regretted letting his guard down.

Trusting Cameron was a mistake. A mistake that has already cost one life.

CHAPTER 11

It took Territaff a while to locate Kathy because they had her tucked away in the psych ward. He entered Kathy's room and stood over her as she slept. She looked so peaceful that he considered leaving her there. After a moment's reflection, he couldn't abandon her to the military. Territaff viewed them as dangerous as the Zenti. He leaned in and kissed her gently on the forehead. She didn't stir. He listened to the rhythm of her breathing. She's so strong, loving, and vulnerable. What am I going to do with her?

Territaff's mind reflected on the Zenti. His heart was pounding so hard that he could barely breathe. Horrific images of decimated bodies and buildings being consumed in flames roared vividly in his mind. He closed his eyes, but the images stayed fixed. A sudden sensation of pain and horror got him to his knees. Holding his head with his hands. "No, not now," he sobbed, trying to regain his composure.

A hand stroked the back of his head. He looked up, and Kathy's eyes were smiling back at him. He stood, his eyes full of tears, and wrapped her up in his arms, holding her close and caressing the back of her head.

"Terri, what's wrong?" she said, sensing his intense emotions.

"Nothing now." He released his grip and smiled. "How do you feel?"

"Outside of a splitting headache, I'm fine."

"Good. We need to get out of here." He searched the small closet, pulling out Kathy's wrinkled clothes. "These are a mess and won't do." He poked his head into the next room. It was empty. He searched the closet and found a pair of jeans and a gray, long-sleeved top. He sized them briefly and decided they should fit her well enough. He went back into Kathy's room and tossed the clothes to her. "Here, get dressed."

"They're kind of big," Kathy said, pulling on the jeans. Where the hell am I? How did I get here?" she asked, sitting on the bed. "What kind of trouble did you get me into now?"

"No time to explain. Finish getting dressed. I'll be right back."

"Damn it, you're always doing that. Where're you going?" Kathy jumped out of bed and dressed quickly. "You crazy bastard. You won't be happy until you get me killed or something," Kathy mumbled under her breath.

Territaff went into the corridor in search of a wheelchair. He avoided the nurse's station and then found a wheelchair outside a bathroom. Realizing how bad he must have looked, he ducked into the back of the nurses' station and discovered a locker room. On one side of the room was a small shower and two sinks, each with a mirror. He knew a shower would press things, but looking at the blackened smoke stains and ground-in dirt covering most of his face and hands, he figured a good wash was in order. He stripped down to his briefs and attempted a sponge bath, substituting paper towels for a sponge. The soap and water were so refreshing that Territaff filled the sink with cold water, then stuck his head in as far as it would go.

In haste, he splashed soap and water all over the sink and floor. He got a wad of paper towels from the dispenser beside a hot-air hand dryer. He knelt under the dryer, wiping his underarms and chest with the paper towels. While on his knees, he tried to mop up some of the splashed water. He stood, feeling a little cleaner and refreshed. Then he looked for a change of clothes.

There was a row of six lockers. Two were empty, and the other four had standard padlocks. Three of the locks were keyed, and one was a cheap combination. Territaff spun the tumbler of the small lock and opened it. Unfortunately, there was only a small purse on the top shelf and a woman's thin coat on a wooden hanger. Territaff searched the purse for a pin or anything to pick the remaining locks. He saw nothing of use.

"What are you doing?"

He turned to find a young nurse standing inside the locker room. She was a plain-looking woman with reddish-brown hair tied into a tight bun. He grinned at her and asked, "May I borrow a pin from your lovely bun?"

The young nurse was both confused and shocked at finding an almost naked man going through her locker, asking for a hairpin.

"Are you serious?" she asked, her eyes wide and her legs visibly shaking. "You need to get back in your room, or I'll call security."

She was about to shout, but Territaff stopped her by holding his hand up and calmly said, "You don't need to call security. I won't harm you...." With an engaging stare, he slowly approached. The young woman's eyes widened, and her mouth fell open in surprise. Territaff touched the sides of her head with his fingertips. At first, she squirmed a little but became still and relaxed under his touch.

"You will not call for security or be frightened," he whispered. "You will reach into your hair and give me a bobby pin."

"Ooooh... kay," she said slowly in a low monotone, her eyes fixed on Territaff's engaging stare.

With her eyebrows arched, she reached up and retrieved a bobby pin, holding it out to him.

"That was most kind," Territaff said. "By any chance, does one of these lockers belong to a male nurse?"

"No. This is the women's locker room," she said.

Although the young woman appeared relaxed, her eyes stayed wide and unblinking. She knew she should call for security, but for some compelling reason, she didn't want to. Her gaze remained fixed on Territaff, and her expression took on the fascinated glow of youthful excitement. She had never been so close to such an attractive man.

"Damn," Territaff frowned, then re-engaged the nurse with a light touch of his hand on her right temple. "Would you be a real angel and find me some clothes? I can't go around in my undies."

With her eyes fixed on Territaff's perfect body, she smiled slyly. "With that body, I think nobody would mind. Would you take off your briefs?" Her face turned beet red, realizing what she had said, but it didn't stop her from gazing at him with dreamy eyes.

"I need something to wear as quickly as possible."

"Wait right here. I'll only be a moment."

He knew he was taking too long and paced around, anxious to return to Kathy.

"Territaff, they're taking me to the stockade," Cuz *transmitted. "The Colonel also issued an arrest warrant for you. The MPs are on their way."*

"Don't attempt to escape yet." Let them take you to the stockade, and I'll pick you up on the way."

"What's Kathy's condition?"

"She's fine."

"Please, hurry."

"We'll be right there."

The nurse returned, holding a set of blue scrubs. "This is the best I could do," she said.

"They're perfect," he said, giving her a grateful kiss.

When he was about to pull his head away, she wrapped her arms around Territaff's neck and gave him a long, hungry kiss on the mouth.

"Control yourself, young lady. I happened to be in a relationship with a very jealous partner. A beautiful and demanding one," he added.

"Figures," she moaned. "All the really good-looking ones are always taken."

"Trust me. I'm nothing but trouble." He smiled warmly and

patted her pale cheek. "The right guy will sweep you off your feet." He encouraged the frowning nurse, putting on the scrubs."

He retrieved the wheelchair he had stowed in the corridor and pushed it to Kathy's room. As he turned into her wing, he saw her running from the opposite direction.

"Kathy," he called to her.

"Where the hell have you been? "They're coming for me," she yelled, running into Territaff's arms. He gave her a reassuring hug.

"Quick, get into the wheelchair."

Two muscle-bound MPs and a male nurse greeted them as they entered the corridor.

"Hold it right there," one of the MPs called loudly, threateningly.

"Shit, just a few minutes quicker, and we would have made it," Territaff grumbled.

"I don't like the looks of this," Kathy said, looking up into his face.

"So, what do you suggest?"

"Let's run like hell for the exit."

"Are you up for it?"

"I'm not going to jail."

"Okay. Relax. Let them think we're giving up."

"I'm not going to jail, goddammit," she whispered as the MPs approached.

Territaff patted her shoulder and said, "I want you to hold on tight. Ready?"

She nodded. When the MPs approached within a few meters of them, Territaff pushed Kathy as fast as he could. They whizzed past them. He got the wheelchair moving so fast that her skin rippled against the friction.

He stopped abruptly by a stairwell, causing Kathy to fly out of the wheelchair. Territaff caught her right before her head hit the floor.

Kathy looked at him, startled. She glanced back at the MPs. Their sudden break stunned them both.

"Terri, give me a second to catch my breath," she gasped.

He scooped Kathy into his arms and pushed the exit door open with his back. He ran down the three flights of stairs, carrying Kathy. When they got outside, he put her down. She bent over and threw up.

"Better?" Territaff asked.

Kathy nodded.

"They must have taken the elevator," he said, then transmitted, *"Cuz, where are you?"*

"In a holding cell on the second floor of the stockade."

"I'll be there shortly."

"I overheard them. They intend to interrogate me. Terri, they seem most worried about us. General Dickerson instructed them to detain me until he could arrange a secure transfer."

"A secure transfer? To where?"

"I haven't been able to ascertain that information. However, their body language makes them look afraid of me, and I'm being closely guarded."

"How many guards?"

"Two, outside my cell, and I saw three more in the outer office. My cell appears to be a converted office. The window has high-impact glass and steel bars. The walls are constructed of standard cinder blocks.

"Well, that shouldn't pose a problem for you. I'll let you know when to take your break. Please injure no one."

"Acknowledged. I'll await your signal."

Territaff turned to Kathy, "Are you okay?"

She nodded, then turned when she heard the heavy footsteps of the two MPs running toward them.

"Let me handle this. You look for a car we can borrow."

"Jesus, Terri, they look pretty big and very pissed off."

"Just do what I said." He pulled her by the arm to his side.

"Go."

She hesitated, giving him an agitated glare before running off to the parking lot in front of the building. One of the MPs veered off after her.

Territaff cut him off. "No—no. You don't want her. You want me. She knows nothing."

The MP stopped and then pulled his nightstick out of its holster. "All right, we can do this easily or roughly. It's your choice," the MP said, slapping the club into the palm of his hand.

The other MP moved behind Territaff. Out of the corner of his eye, Territaff saw the MP nod as if to tell his partner he was ready.

"I know you're just doing your job. Following orders and all that, but unfortunately, I can't let you take me, fellas. So, I guess it will get a little rough."

"That's just fine with me." The MP with the club smiled grimly.

"Get on your knees, put your hands on your head, and there'll be no trouble," the MP behind Territaff commanded.

"Sorry, but I don't want to deprive your partner of all the fun he's expecting." He grinned at the soldier, holding his club in a ready position.

"I've had enough of your shit," he snarled, lifting his club and taking an aggressive step toward Territaff.

Just as he was about to swing at Territaff's head, Territaff dashed to the MP with almost blinding speed. He grabbed his arm, swung him around, and threw him into his partner, knocking them to the pavement.

"I'd stay down if I were you. You're no match for me, and I'd prefer to spare you the pain of engaging me further."

The MP on top got up wobbly. He reached for his sidearm. Territaff elevated his leg and swiftly kicked him in the midsection. He fell hard to the pavement. The other one recovered enough to stand and drew his sidearm.

"Don't," Territaff said firmly, causing him to pause. "I'll only hurt you. Attending to your friend would be smarter. He probably has internal injuries." Territaff eyed him as the MP seemed to be considering his options. He slowly placed his gun back into its holster, then pressed the radio mike attached to his uniform's epaulet and radioed for backup.

"That was very wise," Territaff said, trotting to find Kathy.

"You'll never make it out of here," the soldier called to Territaff's back.

Kathy pulled up to him in a military police jeep.

"Good choice. We can listen to their radio while we ride."

"I think that's the cop's Jeep," she said with a crafty smile. "They left the keys in." She glanced at Territaff. "Glad to see you in one piece. What did you do to them?"

"Just gave them a lesson in good judgment. At least, for one of them."

"Good, that means you didn't kill anybody."

"I'm not a violent man."

"Really," Kathy laughed.

"Find the stockade."

"I think I saw a base directory somewhere on the dashboard. Look to your right."

Territaff found a directory in an open compartment below the dash. The radio was full of chatter about them. He unfolded a map of the base layout inside the directory and located the stockade.

It's located in building 14, on the northwest corner. Go to your right, then look for a building with many MP vehicles in front."

"That must be it," Kathy said, pointing to a broad, two-story building with a chain-link fence topped with razor wire and tall pole lights with cameras surrounding it.

"That must be the place. Drive around it so I can survey their security."

As they made their way around to the stockade's side,

Territaff realized a subtle presence. He turned and took a long look behind. An unsettling feeling of being followed nagged at him, but he saw nothing behind them.

"What's wrong?" Kathy asked.

"I don't know."

"Why are you so jumpy?" She stomped on the brakes, causing Territaff to jerk forward.

"I have a weird feeling that we're being followed. But there's no one behind us. Did you ever have an unsettling sense that someone or something was..." his voice trailed off, noticing Kathy's puzzled expression. "Never mind, keep going around to the back." As they approached the rear gate, Territaff pointed and said, "Stop over there just beyond the gate."

"Got an idea?" Kathy asked.

"Yeah, but I need you to stay in the Jeep and be ready to move on my signal."

"And what signal would that be? And where do you want me to go?"

"I want you to come wherever you see me and don't stop for anything."

"Right. Just one more thing," she said as he started to get out of the Jeep. "What do I do if someone comes by while you're rescuing Cuz?"

"I don't know. That's up to you. Just make sure you're here when I signal."

"That's what I love about you."

"What's that?"

"You're just full of surprises."

He grinned at her, then jumped out.

A nervous flutter ran through her stomach as she watched him make his way to the rear fire exit of the building. He opened the door with little trouble and then slipped into the building.

Kathy was surprised that no one approached the Jeep or

even seemed to notice she was parked so close to the gate. She slumped down in the narrow seat, hoping to make herself unnoticeable to a passerby. Kathy worried about not knowing what was happening. Her mind wandered, and she talked to herself to ward off the sudden sleepiness pulling on her.

"What's taking him so long?" she mumbled half-aloud. "What's he doing? How did I get mixed up in this rotten mess?"

Her mind became full of horrible images and sounds as she drifted off into a vivid daydream. She was reliving the break-in at her apartment. Her heart pounded rapidly as the images of the two weird intruders came to mind. She couldn't make out the big one's face. She tried concentrating on his image, but nothing came to mind. He remained a featureless puzzle. The smaller one was wearing a ski mask covering his head, revealing only a distorted impression of some strange features. But his voice was full of hissing and wheezing. It was grotesque and frightening.

A sudden loud explosion shook Kathy. She realized that she had fallen asleep, and chaos surrounded her. She squinted her eyes to get a better look at two men jumping out of a large hole on the second floor of the building. Kathy gasped as she recognized the men. She watched with her heart thumping in her throat. How could they do that, she wondered, as she saw Cuz and Territaff running toward her, looking unimpaired by the 30-foot jump they had made.

She crunched the gearshift into first, then stomped on the accelerator. The Jeep lurched forward and stalled.

"Kathy, quickly," she heard Territaff call.

Her hand shook as she restarted the Jeep. The guards at the gate were almost up to her as she re-engaged the clutch and got the Jeep to peel out and away from them.

As she got close enough, Territaff and Cuz jumped into the back of the Jeep. They heard gunfire. The two guards were shooting at the tires.

"Turn hard, Kathy, then go right at them," Territaff calmly

instructed. She turned the wheel so hard she almost flipped the small Jeep onto its side. "Don't get crazy. Calm down and drive straight."

"Calm down!" she shouted in his face. "You want me to be calm? They're guards shooting at us. You stay calm. I'm scared shitless!"

"Shitless? That's an interesting term," Cuz said.

"Not now," Territaff snapped.

Kathy aimed the Jeep directly at the guards. She got the small vehicle almost to 50 mph, getting nearly on top of them. They dove out of the way before they could get another shot. "That's superb driving, Kathy," Cuz encouraged.

"Thanks. Now, can you give me a hint where in hell we're going?"

"Cuz, help the lady out."

Cuz's face became impassive, "Turn left in .045 miles. There'll be a dirt road that leads to a fuel depot 1.25 miles down the road. I'll give you more directions when we arrive at the depot."

Kathy found the road and followed Cuz's directions. To her surprise, the depot was exactly a mile and a quarter up the road.

"Okay, now what?"

"Do you see the fuel tanks to your left?" Cuz asked.

Kathy nodded.

To the right of the tanks is a small equipment shed. Pull around to the front and stop."

Kathy looked at Territaff, then at Cuz. She felt they were telling her only what she needed to know and nothing more. She resented always being kept in the dark. She wanted to know why they were being so cautious with her.

Kathy pulled the Jeep in front of the small shed, letting out a long sigh.

"Wait in the Jeep," Territaff said to her, following Cuz to the shed.

"Are you going to tell me what's going on or continue to keep me in the dark?"

"Work the lock, and let's get the hell out of here," Territaff said to Cuz.

Cuz glanced back at Kathy, then addressed the magnetic lock on the shed's door. He placed his long hand on the digital keypad; the lock clicked open.

"You have to teach me that technique," Territaff said.

They entered the shed as Kathy looked nervously on. Her anxiety got her stomach churning. "Oh no," Kathy whispered as she held her aching stomach.

Cuz noticed Kathy's tight face and rigid posture as he tossed two duffel bags on the back seat and then sat next to them. "Are you feeling ill, Kathy?" he asked.

"No, just really nervous."

"Move over," Territaff ordered. Kathy arched herself over the gear shifter as Territaff jumped into the driver's seat.

"God, what I wouldn't give for a bathroom," she cried.

"Now what?" Territaff snapped.

"You... sadistic bastard! I've got a nervous stomach and trying not to crap in my pants," she cried. "Get me to a fucking toilet—now!"

Just as Kathy's ire peaked, three Jeeps and a troop carrier approached them.

Territaff gave Kathy an annoyed glare. "You'll get us killed!" he shouted at her as he punched the Jeep into gear and took off.

"We can't outrun them, Terri," Cuz said.

"I know. We need to put a little distance between us. Then we can break out a few toys from the bag to discourage them a little."

"What do you have in mind?" Cuz asked.

Find one of the sonic rifles and set it to its minimum setting. That should do the trick."

Kathy cried out in pain, "Let them kill us. It will put me out of my misery."

"Allow me to relieve your distress," Cuz said.

"You can do that?"

"I believe so, but you must try to relax your mind for only a moment."

She gathered herself, then looked fixedly at Cuz. "Please do it quickly, Cuz. I can't hold back much longer."

"We don't have time for that now," Territaff growled, looking over his shoulder at the closing posse of troops.

"It will only take twenty seconds, and the risk-to-benefit ratio is most favorable," Cuz said.

"Okay, magic man. Do your trick." Territaff said, then drove erratically, hoping to keep the rapidly closing troops from locking on to them.

Cuz gave Kathy a reassuring smile. "Now, close your eyes, and try not to think about anything for just a moment."

"Work fast, Cuz. I think Territaff's driving is making me nauseated." She closed her eyes and let out a small burp. "See what I mean?"

"Okay, take a deep breath and hold still." Ready?"

She nodded, her eyes shut tight, swaying with Territaff's erratic movements.

"Okay, you'll feel a slight pressure in your head followed by a pleasant tingling down your spine, and then you should feel your muscles relax. You may feel a little sleepy, but don't fall asleep. Focus only on becoming tranquil."

Cuz placed his fingertips on the sides of Kathy's head.

She opened her eyes, grabbed his wrists, and gave him a stern look.

"The last time you did this, you knocked me out."

Yes, I understand your concern, but I promise this will be different. May I continue?"

"Should I let him?" Kathy asked Territaff.

"It's either that or crap in your pants. Personally, I'd trust Cuz."

"Hurry up. Go ahead."

Just as Cuz got his fingertips to the sides of her head, a spray of bullets whizzed by, one hitting the spare tire attached to the rear of the Jeep, another shattering the windshield. Kathy didn't move or react in any way as she became transfixed with a subtle but rising feeling of euphoria. It was miraculous how wonderful she felt. Her stomach ceased cramping and churning. Then, her entire body relaxed.

"Thank you, Cuz."

"You're welcome," he said, then pulled her down right as a bullet blew a hole in the passenger side door.

A burst of gunfire ripped through the Jeep, shattering the passenger's side-view mirror and tearing up the dashboard. Another volley tore through the rear of the Jeep and right through Territaff's seat, grazing his arm.

"That was too close for comfort," Territaff yelled at Cuz. "Will you please get out the baby sonic and stop those idiots before they do real damage!"

Cuz opened a duffel bag, now by his feet, and pulled out what looked like an air gun children used to shoot foam balls at Velcro targets.

"That looks like a toy," Kathy said as Cuz pushed a set of buttons on the side of the dull, gray weapon.

"This toy packs a big punch," Territaff said. "I'd suggest you get as far down in your seat as possible, Kathy."

Territaff turned the wheel sharply to the left while pulling up on the emergency brake. The Jeep swerved sideways. Cuz aimed at the lead Jeeps, then fired. A strong concussion followed a low puffing sound. The two leading Jeeps flipped onto their sides. The drivers, along with all the soldiers, were thrown from the vehicles. The trailing troop carrier came to a screeching halt as Cuz fired a second concussive wave. It struck the transport head-on, blowing its hood off and tearing the canvas roof away. The impact threw some of the troops out the rear and onto the short tarmac of the runway.

"Good shooting," Territaff said as Cuz returned the weapon to the duffel bag. He drove as fast as he could to the hangar at the far end of the airstrip, then followed along a narrow path far into a mangrove swamp. The sun was low in the sky, casting a reflective glow over the greenish waters of the swamp. The humidity thinned enough to make the air comfortable. Kathy was feeling sleepy from Cuz's mysterious tranquilizer.

"Do you know where you're going?" she asked, her voice dreamy.

"Almost there," Territaff said, reassuringly squeezing her hand.

"I don't know what you did, Cuz, but I'm feeling no pain," she moaned, slurring her words.

"The effect will wear off soon, and you should feel well-rested."

"I'd love to take a nap." Her head fell to the side, and she smirked at Territaff. "You really know how to entertain a gal."

"Close your eyes and take a nap. We still have a little way to go."

"Okay, if you insist." She let out a low yawn and then fell into a deep sleep.

He looked over his shoulder at Cuz and said, "I think it's best if she wakes aboard the shuttle."

Cuz nodded.

Territaff stopped the Jeep, got out, and then stood and listened.

"What is it?" Cuz asked, standing on the other side of the Jeep.

"I'm not sure. It's an odd impression that something is following us. No, it's more as if they're watching us. I've had this feeling for some time. Now, it seems as though it's closer."

Cuz walked to Territaff's side and surveyed the area with his eyes. His internal photoelectric sensors scrutinized the immediate area with high sensitivity.

"Can you feel it?"

"Yes, there's a definite presence, but nothing my sensors can detect."

"Zenti or stealth droid?"

"Neither, it's more like an energy signature," Cuz said, turning slowly to his left. However, it's unlike anything I've ever encountered. Stand by a moment." He stood and studied the nearby swamp. "I've also detected two biosignatures. I believe they're observing us from the cover of the mangroves."

"Get out a seeker."

"It will give away our position. They'll surely send more troops after us."

"We're not far from the shuttle. We could always make a quick break for it."

Cuz reached into his duffel bag and pulled out a hand-held device with a small display on top and a cone-shaped muzzle. Cuz reached into the pocket of his cargo pants and pulled out a low-profile headset. It was so small that, except for its eyepiece, it was almost indiscernible when placed on his head. He looked at Territaff. "Ready?"

Territaff pointed to his right. "Three o'clock."

Cuz held up the device, looked through the display for a few seconds, then depressed a button with his thumb. The seeker's broad-spectrum beam painted the mangrove swamp in a green glow. Two ghostly-looking forms came at them. Territaff reached inside one of the duffel bags and pulled out a large handgun. He fired, barely missing their heads. They stopped, reversed direction, and ran back into the swamp.

"That should keep them at bay for a while," Territaff said. "That energy wasn't coming from them."

"No," Cuz agreed. "But I know where I've seen it before."

"Oh?"

"That same residual negative energy was present when you found Tanya's body."

"Interesting." Territaff pulled on his chin in thought.

"Things are just getting better and better," he mumbled half-aloud.

They both jumped back in the jeep and drove off. Territaff looked at Kathy and smiled at her. "Lucky girl, you're dead to this world now, but when you wake, a whole new world beyond your dreams awaits."

The narrow path opened into a large sawgrass field. "How far, Cuz?"

"50 meters dead ahead."

Territaff relaxed a little, feeling they would make it until he heard the whooshing sounds of Helicopters whirling in the distance.

Cuz looked up through the small headset eyepiece and asked, "Are they for us?"

"Most likely."

"We'll expose the shuttle when we board. They'll see it." Cuz gave Territaff a concerned look.

"Yeah, but only until we're airborne. Then it will be too late."

"What if they try to engage us? They have well-armed aircraft."

"Cuz, you worry too much. We'll be gone in a flash. They'll report us as a UAP, make a report, and then go home, shaking their confused little heads. It'll be something to tell their grandchildren. That's if the government ever releases the report, which is doubtful."

Your voice is filled with disdain for these people. Why's that?"

"Because they're hypocrites and liars. They're charged with protecting the welfare of the people they serve, but most of them serve only what's in their best interest."

Cuz's expression became worried.

"What's wrong?"

My sensor has detected a vapor trail indicative of long-range rocket fire. I suggest you veer to the left, then make a sharp roundabout in... Three... two... one... now."

Territaff did as Cuz instructed. A rocket exploded a few meters to their right as he completed the sharp turn at the roundabout. The impact was close enough to flip the Jeep. Territaff hit the ground hard after being thrown clear.

"Cuz," he called out, uneasy about his friend. Then his heart raced a little, realizing Kathy was nowhere in sight. "Cuz," he called a little louder.

He could hear the whooshing roar of the approaching helicopters as they came to inspect the damage.

"I'm caught under the Jeep," Cuz called out.

Territaff came around to the sound of Cuz's voice and found him pinned under the Jeep. "What a mess," he mumbled, then asked. "Are you damaged?"

"I believe I'm undamaged but awkwardly pinned. Would you lend a hand to get this vehicle off us?"

"Us? Are you telling me Kathy's under there?"

"Yes. As it turned over, I positioned her in the back seat but didn't have time to avoid being pinned."

"So, she's okay?"

"I believe she's still asleep. I guess I misjudged her tolerance for mental induction. I've little experience with your species."

"Amazing. She slept through all of this. I think I'll join you on the ground for a few moments to throw our curious friends off."

Cuz looked puzzled as Territaff lay face down on the ground. He grasped his friend's meaning and closed his eyes as one helicopter did a close flyover. It made several low passes over their position, and Territaff was concerned that one might land to inspect. After several minutes of close passes, the helicopters flew away.

Territaff got up and lifted the Jeep off Cuz. He saw blue-tinted fluid coming from two large tears in Cuz's pants. "Are those serious wounds?"

"They're superficial. I'll attend to them aboard ship."

"Can you get to Kathy?"

"We need to upright the Jeep."

Cuz went to the opposite side as Territaff effortlessly flipped the jeep towards him and laid it down. Territaff looked at Kathy, lying on her back on the ground, shaking his head in disbelief. "She's still sound asleep. Unbelievable."

He cradled her in his arms and walked into the tall sawgrass.

Cuz pulled a small blue crystal from a large pocket in his cargo pants and whispered a few indistinguishable words into the device. The shuttle's silver hull glowed under the intense sun. Its stubby wings attached to its underbelly gave the ship a sleek appearance. A rounded, opaque dome covered most of the craft. A hatch glided open, equipped with built-in foot rails to facilitate easy entry into the vehicle. Cuz went ahead and then took Kathy from Territaff once they went inside.

The hatch closed silently. Soft lighting and a quiet electrical hum greeted them. Territaff strapped Kathy into one of the three rear seats. It adjusted to the contours of her body. He gazed at her for a moment before taking the copilot's seat beside Cuz.

Let's let her sleep until right before we engage the plasma drive. That's when we'll put her in an environmental suit," Territaff said.

"I agree. Once awakened, she'll be too excited to sleep," Cuz said, then told the onboard computer to power up as he ran a surgical knitter over the gashes in his thighs.

CHAPTER 12

Dr. DeZenti was not a man of great distinction but was a person of powerful connections. Under normal circumstances, he would never have been able to obtain the security clearances he received from the DOD and the other major security agencies. Given his personal and professional backgrounds, his connections must have extended far up the chain in Washington. According to one analyst, "His background can be summed up in a word: Vague." His unconventional vetting made the security agencies nervous and suspicious. Against both the CIA's and DHS's strong objections, the Defense Department insisted that his project was vital to national security.

Despite the best efforts of America's investigative agencies (both internal and external), they could only gather fragments of Dr. Zoh DeZenti's family and personal history. When the investigators pressed DeZenti on why there was such a lack of personal history, he claimed they were tragically lost, along with all the family records. "It was during that great tsunami," he told them in a dispassionate tone, "that decimated Sri Lanka in 2004," he sighed, cleaned his glasses, and added, "It was as though they were erased from existence." His story and demeanor only heightened some agencies' suspicions.

According to his academic records, he completed his undergraduate and post-graduate studies at the University of Sri Jayewardenepura. His undergraduate studies were in Computer Science and Mathematics. He received his Ph.D. in Biology. What was remarkable was that he completed all his degrees in an unprecedented six years. However, while not refuting his attendance and impressive achievements, the background investigation didn't get much substantiation from professors or students. No one seemed to remember him. When asked about his academic anonymity, Dr. DeZenti retorted, "I was at school for one purpose: to study, not to socialize." He further explained that he rarely attended classes outside of required attendance for presentations, labs, and testing. He did almost all his academic work off-campus.

In his vetting interview, DeZenti stated, "I knew what I wanted from college, and I found student life to be, for the most part, too immature, generally unappealing, and an unwarranted distraction from my studies."

His academic record appeared legitimate, impressive, and as hazy as the majority of his background, making it impossible to fully substantiate his personal history, frustrating all the investigator's efforts to vet him.

Only his more recent history could be qualified and confirmed. Following the death of DeZenti's parents, a substantial inheritance was left from their family's estate. Upon graduating from college, he used a significant portion of his inheritance to purchase a small biomedical company. It was on the cusp of developing a new method for growing artificial organs. DeZenti either had an exceptional eye or sheer luck in seeing the potential in that cash-strapped company and investing a substantial amount of capital in it. Under his management, the company went in a new direction with some intriguing and risky applications.

In only a few years, the company had perfected a process that combined nanotechnology with cyanobacteria and stem cells to create specialized cybernetic parts for novel medical procedures, cures for a wide range of diseases, and advanced apparatuses.

Shortly, DeZenti had the company start applying its patented biometric scaffolding directly to the patient. The procedure integrated the patient's stem cells with a programmable nano-virus. This method could replicate organs and is compatible with a wide variety of patients. Remarkably, over 94 percent of the new organ recipients didn't experience organ rejection or require antirejection medications. It was a remarkable breakthrough that would have catapulted the young company to the top.

Right before the company's CFO announced its new process to Wall Street as part of an IPO, De Zenti withdrew it from the market. He explained his sudden withdrawal to Wall Street: "My focus on the prototype shifted to something different, and I decided not to make a public offering."

Within six months, the company had developed and introduced a model of a bioengineered cyborg. He took the plans for his prototype to Washington, D.C., where he made an impressive presentation to the Department of Defense. The DOD presented its recommendations to the Chairman of the Joint Chiefs, who recommended it to the Armed Forces Committee. It took only seven months for the Department of Defense to receive the allocations. They awarded an unprecedented contract to Dr. DeZenti's company to research and develop the first fully independent, artificially intelligent cyborg soldier. Additionally, the government granted total access to whatever resources he required for the development of the perfect warrior. The project was classified under the name Cyber Sword.

General Dickerson's official assignment was to ensure that the Cyber Sword project progressed smoothly. His official title was Chief of Operations. His broad scope of duties included serving as the liaison officer for the DOD and as the official government's Project Oversight Officer. Additionally, he was assigned the unenviable task of keeping Dr. DeZenti satisfied. That meant the general had to ensure the doctor wasn't hindered by governmental minutiae and all the other inherent delays in performing government contracts. His personal and unofficial assignment was to keep a close eye on DeZenti.

General Dickerson was a distinguished and highly decorated officer. He was well-known and respected within the military community as a consummate professional. Dickerson viewed his new duty assignment as demeaning and misplaced. Not only did he despise his work, but he also regarded DeZenti with open skepticism and distrust. When asked why he was so suspicious of the doctor, he answered, without hesitation, "I simply don't like the wormy little bastard and trust him even less."

Their strained relationship came to a head after the puzzling incident at Homestead AFB. During the subsequent debriefing, General Dickerson questioned Dr. DeZenti on his knowledge of the alleged spies, Mr. T. Territaff and Mr. Cuz Venubia. DeZenti arrogantly proclaimed complete ignorance and questioned the general's competence in his response to the incident. This pinned the general's bullshit meter.

CHAPTER 13

"Wow! What in hell was that?"

"It just looked like it shot up from the ground. Then it was gone."

"Tower, this is Baker Charlie One-Niner-Seven."

"Go ahead, Baker-Charlie One-Nine-Seven."

"We would like to confirm a bogie at sector 125-zebra, over."

"Baker-Charlie-One-Niner-Seven, that's a negative on the bogie. Do you wish to make a formal sighting?"

"Negative tower."

"Affirmative. Return to base."

* * *

General Dickerson arrived early for the weekly ten o'clock briefing. He sat in the small, second-floor conference room in DeZenti's factory, sipping on weak coffee. He was watching the activity on the factory floor through a large window. As he observed the clusters of white-clad technicians doing more talking than working, he decided a revisit with Colonel Cameron was in order. Many loose ends were gnawing at him. He suspected Territaff and Cuz were most likely not spies. They were given security clearances that required detailed and thorough background investigations and vetting. Either their credentials were good forgeries, or current security procedures direly needed a complete overhaul. Neither scenario seemed to fit. The general's intuition was telling him that something was wrong. Dr. DeZenti was strange beyond belief. What about those two alleged spies? Cameron's handling of them was also disturbing. And why was Tanya killed?

The general's mind wheeled with questions. Why would they go to Cameron and ask for his assistance? Cameron knew they were contracted to monitor and verify the legitimacy of DeZenti's work. Who was chasing them? They used advanced weapons. Where did they come from? If they were spies, what was their mission?

Never in his career was he confronted with so many uncertainties going into a project. At the center of this evolving confluence of suspicions was Dr. DeZenti. That's not a coincidence, he told himself. *There's something terribly wrong with all of this. Dr. D, you're up to something, you—wormy little bastard, and I'm going to find out what you're really about.* He smiled at the thought, then made a call to Colonel Cameron.

He had left a message for Cameron when Dr. DeZenti joined him in the conference room.

"Good morning, General," Dr. DeZenti said with his irritating wheeze.

"Dr. DeZenti," the general greeted him with a polite nod.

Giving the doctor a narrowed stare, he took a sip of his now lukewarm coffee and winced disagreeably. "Somebody needs to learn how to make a decent cup of coffee around here." Noticing DeZenti looked more confused than upset, he suggested, "If you'd like, I can recommend the vendor we use on the base. He only uses the best coffees and has the advantage of already being cleared by us."

"That's most gracious of you, General. I apologize for the coffee. Few of us here drink it, but it would be nice to accommodate our guests." DeZenti nodded appreciatively, but a glimmer of suspicion remained in his thin smile.

"Where are you in resolving the neuro-interface problem?" the general asked, "The latest reports were, for lack of a better term, fuzzy."

"I believe we have several viable solutions. I prepared a report that outlines our approach and cost analysis for the change orders." He handed the general a thick, sealed folder.

Dickerson weighed the folder in his hand. "It feels expensive," he said, then placed it on the conference table. "I hate reading these things. They're so dry and full of technical jargon. Why don't you give me a quick overview of your proposed solutions? Particularly, why is there more than one? Multiple solutions make me a little nervous. They usually indicate an unclear understanding of the problem and the associated costs."

General Dickerson leaned back in his chair, preparing for a lengthy explanation.

"I appreciate your concern, but let me alleviate your apprehension." First, there are multiple solutions because there are multiple problems. The problems are interrelated and must be addressed in consideration of their interdependence. This is all explained in the report." He pursed his thin lips, and his large eyes became fixed. "Now, if nothing else, I must return to the floor."

He stood, then extended his hand to the general as if remembering the courtesy.

"One more thing, doctor," the general said, still sitting.

"Yes?"

"Why wasn't this discussed in the joint session last week?"

"We needed to review our findings before a cogent resolution course could be determined." His voice rose an octave, and his odd features betrayed his annoyance with the general's implication.

"No need to get testy, Doctor. I'm just doing my job," Dickerson said. He stood and stuck his hand out to Dr. DeZenti.

"Now, if you don't mind, I must do mine." He ignored the general's extended hand and left the room.

"Interesting," General Dickerson whispered to himself. He stood for a moment to watch the little man rapidly descend the rear stairs to the factory floor. "It appears I hit a nerve," he said, rubbing his chin in thought.

CHAPTER 14

"Cuz, you need to revive Kathy and get her into an environmental suit," Territaff said as he updated instructions into the navigational computer.

"Why are you doing that manually?" Cuz asked, retrieving three biogenic environmental suits from a small storage bin below deck. He tossed one to Territaff, then attended to Kathy. "You're being a little too cautious with our inquisitive guest." Cuz narrowed his eyes, looking annoyed at Territaff. "Why are you so adverse? She has earned the right to know the nature and intent of our mission."

"She has." Territaff glanced over his shoulder at her. "I just need a little more time to figure out how to explain it all."

"I'm sorry, Terri, but I don't understand what you mean by 'how to explain it.' Your statement implies that there is a method for conveying this information. This is most uncharacteristic of you. Or is there something else you need to tell me first?

Territaff regretted what he said. He opened his mouth to respond but found himself at a loss for words.

"Cuz, I'm sorry. I don't want to slap a transponder on Kathy and hope she can handle it. Trying to tell her anything..." He shook his head and frowned. "I remembered what I went through when Nicki slapped a transponder on me."

"That didn't turn out so bad."

"You weren't with us then. I thought I was going insane. It's wild having your brain suddenly filled with new knowledge dumped directly into your cerebral cortex. It can be traumatic."

Cuz did a final check of Kathy's environmental suit, then returned to his seat. He gave Territaff a thoughtful glance as he lowered and sealed the clear-domed headgear of his suit.

"Wait a second, Cuz," Territaff reached out, then grabbed his arm. "Do you understand my dilemma?"

"I'm running possible scenarios using all the variables

presented to Kathy over the past forty-five point two hours. Additionally, the events she has experienced since joining our mission. This should give us a range of probable reactions to using the neuro-transponder versus direct oral narration."

"So, what's your recommendation?"

"Use the transponder to calm her nerves first, then proceed with the data transfer. What I've observed of her is that she can handle anything you can throw at her. Kathy is resilient and trusts you."

"She trusts me?" Territaff laughed. "She thinks I'm an artful bullshitter."

"Earth idiom is so confounding." Cuz wrinkled his brow, shaking his head. "Terri, Kathy trusts you with her life. You recognize that most of her dubious retorts are a defense mechanism to hide behind. I'm surprised that it hasn't been obvious to you. She's afraid of being left behind and also of the unknown. Give her the transponder. I'll program it into sessions to make it less stressful for her."

"And that's your expert opinion? Give her bite-sized traumas."

"It's the most logical course of action."

"I'm curious. How much of that logical opinion is based on your probability analysis and emotional bias towards her?"

"Emotional bias?" Cuz's facial features became tight, and his eyes fixed on Territaff. "How dare you? I never thought you capable of such slander."

Territaff sealed his headgear on his suit, then enabled the intercom. "You're not serious... are you?"

"How could you insult me like that?" Cuz engaged the master system switch, and the onboard computer's voice became audible.

"Finally," the computer's emulated voice said.

"Hanc, can you believe what Terri said to me?" Cuz asked.

"Wait a second. Don't get Hanc involved in this."

"I was only asking him if he heard your insulting comment."

"I wasn't being derogatory. Simply attempting to find out how objective your analysis was."

"I'm a highly-evolved android and incapable of such emotional judgments."

"In fairness to Terri, Cuz, I don't believe he was being calumnious in his inquiry of your analysis. He was only being an insensitive human. He can't help being human any more than you can help being an over-sensitive android."

"That wasn't helpful, Hanc," Territaff said. "And now you're claiming to be an android. What happened to an enhanced, engineered life-form?"

"I think Hanc attempted humor. As for the other thing, it's easier to say ~~android~~Android." Cuz looked at Territaff, and they both laughed.

"What's so damn funny?" a muffled voice shouted.

Territaff looked over his shoulder at Kathy and smiled. "Turn on Kathy's intercom, Hanc." Territaff turned his couch to face her. "Welcome back."

Kathy looked around with her mouth slightly open. "Am I aboard your ship?"

"Not yet. This shuttle will transport us to Biomei. I have an idea of how nervous you must be. What you're about to experience can be awesome and nerve-racking. If your gastric distress acts up again, let it go. Your environmental suit will absorb any bodily waste. Trust me. I've soiled myself many times."

Kathy smirked at Territaff's joke, then asked, "Where're we going?"

"A little beyond the orbit of Europa."

"That will take years. Won't it?"

"No. It'll take a little over four days."

"What? How?"

"This little baby can travel really fast. And because we'll be traveling at such a high speed, the ship will be filled with a suspension liquid to protect us from the G-forces of acceleration and the increased mass as we approach a fraction of the speed of light. Space is vast, but when traveling within a solar system, there's an incredible number of high-energy particles from the sun, meteorites, and countless pieces of debris left over from the solar system's creation. However, the biggest killer is radiation, and there is much of it out here. Our environmental suits protect us from the hostile environment of space. The suspension fluid is for everything else."

Kathy nodded, but her eyes grew wide, and then her face lit up with a broad smile. "How close to light speed?" Kathy felt excited about traveling through space at incredible velocities. I read about this, but I can't believe it's happening. I'm really in space. Shit. I'm a goddam astronaut!"

"I know, it still astonishes me," Territaff said, reflecting on his first experience. It was different but just as exciting. "I'll never tire of it. You're in for quite an experience."

"So?"

"What?"

"How fast?"

"About 198 kilometers per second."

"That's almost three-quarters light speed."

"That's impressive. How do you know that?"

"I read a lot." Kathy looked at both sides of the ship. She frowned at the opaque dome. "Why can't I see anything?"

"We're in stealth mode. Once we get a little distance from all the orbiting spyware, I'll have Hanc clear the dome so you can sightsee. But you must be patient. Your eyes will take a little time to adjust. There's a complex array of instruments and sensors built into your helmet. They'll learn your capabilities, then adjust the images to something your brain can understand. It's amazing. So, are you ready for the ride of your life?"

"Yeah, let's get this thing moving."

* * *

General Dickerson's brown eyes reflected an authoritative intensity that could disarm someone with a stare. He looked at the shelling area with surprise and agitation. A short, wiry-framed man approached the general and stood beside him. The general didn't bother to greet the diminutive man, who wore a large, black felt hat low on his forehead and a dark, blue Armani suit, giving him an overdressed appearance.

"Why are you here?" the general asked gruffly.

I was understandably curious to know if you apprehended them. By the look of things, I assume they eluded you."

The general narrowed his gaze at him. "This doesn't concern you."

"On the contrary, General," the doctor retorted in a wheezy voice. "Anything that could jeopardize the project concerns me."

General Dickerson intently stared at the little man for a brief moment, then said, "Was this your idea or Cameron's?"

Dr. DeZenti turned up the corners of his thin mouth into a mock smile. "If this were up to me, I would've used more efficient means to apprehend them."

"Next time, Dr. DeZenti, you'll stay the hell out of it. I don't care about your congressional connections. This is my theater of operations, and you'll stay the hell out of the way. Are we clear?"

"Very well, General Dickerson, but if you're unsuccessful in apprehending them, I assure you this will not remain your theater of operations."

"Look, you little son-of-a-bitch, let's get one thing clear. Never threaten me again. You'll stay out of my business, or I'll prosecute you for obstruction. I don't tolerate insubordination from anyone, including stuffed-shirts like you."

DeZenti looked up at the general with an impassive gaze, pulled a handkerchief from his breast pocket, wiped his glasses, and got in the back of his limousine.

General Dickerson smiled, then shook his head at the

man's arrogance. I'll get rid of that smug little bastard as soon as I can locate the person responsible for allowing that little bug to infest my operations. Then I'm going to kick his stinking ass out.

* * *

Kathy became full of exhilaration as the dome cleared. Her wide, staring eyes barely blinked as she tried to comprehend the striking vividness of seeing the Earth, moon, and sun in such a breathtaking fashion. Is this real? She kept asking herself. Am I dreaming? She would look up and around the small confines of the shuttle's cabin to reassure herself that she was traveling through outer space.

Kathy became at ease after the shock of going from a dead stop to three-quarters of lightspeed.

I'm immersed in a liquid that doesn't impede my movements, dressed in a surprisingly comfortable environmental suit, and on my way to meet a ship named Biomei. Wow. This is weirder than Territaff's psychedelic head-fuck. God, I can't believe this is happening.

CHAPTER 15

"How's your stomach?" Territaff asked Kathy after the suspension liquid evaporated.

Kathy thought for a moment. "Good."

"Think you can eat?"

"I'm starving. But how can I eat in this get-up?"

"There's a display panel on your right forearm."

She looked down and saw a small rectangular pad with a dark display. "Okay, I see it."

"Tap it."

Kathy gave the pad a gentle tap. The display lit up, and then a pleasant, feminine voice asked over her intercom, "How may I assist you, Kathy Jordan?"

She smiled at the device and liked the voice's friendly tone. Then she realized what it had said. "How does it know my full name? Did you program it?"

"You did," Territaff said.

"I did? How?"

"Your environmental suit is intuitive. It reads your memory and gathers all the required information to serve and anticipate your needs."

"It read my mind! I don't think I like that."

He turned his couch to face her. "Kathy, there's nothing sinister about the device. It can't harm you, nor can it incite you to do anything against your will. You can erase any unwanted information by saying so." He leaned a little closer. "You'll experience a lot of new technology about seventy-five years ahead of what you're used to. Most of it is intuitive, but they're just tools and appliances. I promise that nothing I'll introduce can harm you in any way. If this were a perfect situation, I would have given you a comprehensive tutorial on all the new and wonderful things you'll experience. Unfortunately, we don't have that luxury. Use these seemingly miraculous tools, and I promise you'll have a hard time living without your new toys after a little exposure to them."

She gave Territaff a dreamy stare. "I'm in for lots of surprises, aren't I?"

"I can't describe what you'll experience over the next few days. All I can say is you'll adjust. Cuz and I will answer all your questions. And once we get aboard Biomei, I'll be able to provide you with answers to your questions along with all the information you'll need for the mission," his voice trailed off, then he regarded Kathy with an almost solemn gaze.

"Terri, what is it?" she asked.

"Some of this will be unpleasant."

Kathy wished she could reach out and comfort him.

"What are you struggling to tell me?"

She could almost feel the pain that became apparent on his face.

I wish I could have spared you some of the ugly details of this mission. But my options are limited, and time is precious." He laughed ironically. "Time is a cruel joke that the universe plays upon the ignorant. It's an illusion—a very real one. You'll soon discover time is arbitrary, yet we must dwell within its ironic limits."

"That sounded cynical," Cuz said.

"Sorry, Cuz. I didn't intend to sound cynical, only honest."

"Sometimes I have difficulty distinguishing the difference." Cuz looked at Kathy and said, "I think you should overlook Terri's current mood." This mission has compromised his objectivity, souring his typically amenable attitude."

"Are you trying to tell me he's moody?" She laughed.

Cuz nodded. "Precisely."

"Let's eat," Territaff said.

"Okay, how does this damn thing work?" Kathy asked.

"Think of what you would like to eat," Territaff said.

"Oh, I'd kill for some pancakes and bacon. You know, those really fluffy ones with gooey centers, chewy, thick bacon, and strong, sweet coffee with rich cream." She salivated, then frowned, realizing that her desires were impossible.

"Your order is ready," the friendly voice said.

"Huh?" Kathy's face screwed up in surprise as a tube appeared, then rose to her lips.

"Take a taste," Territaff encouraged.

Kathy took a careful draw on the tube. Her eyes lit up in surprise. "Oh my God," she cried, then took a long draw. "I can't believe this—it tastes exactly as I remember. It hits your taste buds like I took a forkful of pancakes. You... you can taste the syrup and butter, and on the second draw, I got a mouthful of bacon. I need coffee." She took another quick sip. "It's coffee! Rich, sweet coffee!"

Territaff and Cuz looked on in amusement.

Territaff smiled at Kathy, remembering his first synthesized meal, and was vicariously enjoying her new experience. "Are you still upset that the system can read your memories?"

"No. Not if it means I can eat like this. How's it doing it?" she asked excitedly between sucks on the tube.

"It's nothing more than a liquid protein suspension. The actual taste experience is created through a series of memory taps," Cuz explained.

"Wow. A girl can get fat with a device like this."

"You can eat to your heart's content and only retain what your body needs," Territaff said.

"What else can this contraption do?"

"Almost anything you can think of," Cuz said.

"Really? Anything?"

"Don't get carried away," Territaff said.

"Cuz," Kathy called over the intercom while gazing out the port side of the dome.

"Yes, Kathy."

"May I ask you a personal question?"

Cuz turned his couch to face her.

"You may ask anything you wish."

"I hope I won't offend you, but I need to know." She knitted her brow, thinking about what she was about to ask.

"I'm not capable of the emotional response you're expecting. Ask anything you like."

She pondered his face for a moment. Territaff knew what she was about to ask Cuz and decided not to turn his couch around.

Kathy opened her mouth, hesitated, and smiled. "I'm not sure how to frame the question." She frowned and looked down from the confines of her helmet.

"I believe what you want to ask me is, what am I?"

She gave Cuz a relieved smile.

"So, ask," Cuz said.

"Okay, what are you? You're not human, but you don't appear alien either. You're just different. Do you understand what I'm asking?"

"Yes." Cuz asked Territaff, "May I tell her?"

"I think it's time, but prepare for an endless stream of follow-up questions."

Kathy sneered at Territaff and then returned her attention to Cuz. "Okay, spill your guts. I want to know everything."

Cuz's brow rose into deep lines. "How does one spill their guts?"

"Sorry, that's just a saying. It means to tell everything."

His expression turned pensive for a second. Then, his eyes took on an alert glow. "I understand, but I can't relay everything to you. Biomei will better serve you in that regard. Nevertheless, I can satisfy your immediate curiosity."

"Okay, so tell me—what the hell are you?"

"I'm a genetically engineered life-form."

Kathy gawked at Cuz, and her eyes grew wider; then she said, "You mean... you're an AI... a real android or cyborg?"

Cuz considered her statement and said, "Kathy, I'm aware of the breadth and depth of the literature and various depictions of artificial life-forms in your culture. May I ask you to put all that aside and try to keep an open mind?"

She nodded vigorously within her helmet.

"I'm none of those technologies, but in a real sense, I have aspects of all of them within my construct."

"I don't understand. How can you be both none and all? What are you then?"

"In your understanding, I'm a genetically engineered android. However, it would be more precise to say I'm a different form of life. I'm sentient. While I was never an infant, I had a childhood of sorts and surrogate parents. Unlike synthetic life-forms, I can learn independently of my initial programming and grow through my experiences, as you do. I can eat and drink like you. And as you've observed, I have learned emotions. However, many aspects of me are not humanoid. I'll never grow old or get sick. Although I'm fully functional sexually, I can't procreate." Cuz's eyes reflected a sense of regret. "I hope, at some point, that will be made possible."

"You want to be a father. I can see that in your eyes." She pursed her lips into an approving smile. "I think you'll make a great dad, and I hope someday they'll find a way of making that possible."

"Thank you. It's my greatest desire. The engineers in my homeworld have been working on creating an adaptation for procreation for my species. However, there are concerns that this may have—"

"Cuz she's not ready for this," Territaff interrupted, turning his couch to face them. "She needs to be given an orientation beyond what we can share with her now."

"Damn it, Terri, what are you so worried about?" Kathy snapped.

"It's not that I don't want you to know. We're dealing with a tenuous situation, and the less you know, the safer you'll be."

"Terri, I appreciate your misguided belief that keeping me

in the dark will somehow protect you." They already must know I'm part of the team. What difference will it make to what I know? They'll assume I know everything, anyway. So, how does that protect me?"

Territaff and Kathy's eyes locked in a silent mental struggle.

"How do I tell her my real concern?" he transmitted to Cuz.

"She deserves to know the truth of the matter. You can't protect her in this. If she's captured, her knowledge will be irrelevant."

"You're right, but I'm so fearful for her safety and the mission's success."

"As am I."

"You know it's rude to exclude me from the conversation when I'm here," Kathy said.

"How did you know we were conversing?" Territaff asked.

"I can see it in your eyes."

"Really," Cuz said. "Interesting."

"Sorry. I'm trying to protect you, but I also must protect the mission. My fear is not about trusting you, but what if you're captured, and they can retrieve all you know? However, Cuz reminded me that if you're captured, it means the mission must already be compromised."

"Well, my two brave heroes—you're just going to make sure I'm never captured." She arched her eyebrows with a sarcastic grin.

Kathy returned her thoughts to Cuz. She realized how uniquely different he was. He was an artificial life-form, but she wasn't sure what that meant. Kathy only saw Cuz's humanistic qualities and found them beyond definition. While gazing at him, she understood why Terri felt so close to him.

"Your species?" she asked. Cuz was part of a race of androids. The thought was perplexing. "You mean you're not unique?"

Unlike the android population, I am unique because I was explicitly designed for Terri. There are over 128,743 general-purpose androids, and another 873 that are an independent, sentient species in Venubia's culture," Cuz explained.

"Venubia?" Kathy looked at Territaff and asked, "Is this on a need-to-know basis as well?"

Kathy could see a little condensation appear on Territaff's helmet as he let out a long, aspirated moan.

"You're incorrigible. I can't seem to make you understand that Biomei will answer all your questions."

"What's the harm in knowing where Cuz is from and his genealogy?"

"Because it's complicated, and in a real sense, it's part of what we're trying to protect." It will only invoke more questions. Trust me, there's an easier and safer way to do this." He turned his couch back to its forward position, feeling full of doubts and guilt.

Cuz gave Kathy a thoughtful gaze, then almost frowned. "Perhaps you're right," he said to Territaff. He regarded Kathy with a strange intensity that made her a little uneasy. "I can appreciate how consuming curiosity can be. Terri has a unique perspective on what you're going through, and I concur with his caution. Too much information can be dangerous for you and the mission. Biomei will serve your interests well. One of your proverbs is particularly apt now: "Patience is a virtue.""

Kathy tried to shrug in capitulation but could only manage a slight upward jerk. Cuz turned his couch forward. Kathy stuck her tongue out at them in frustration and defiance.

CHAPTER 16

Jupiter was breathtaking for Kathy. She stared, mesmerized by the Jovian world's colors and surreal beauty. Then she forced herself to take in Europa. Its radiant glow was so intense that her intuitive helmet darkened.

There was a preponderance of questions within Kathy, but she had resigned herself, at least for the time being, to wait for Biomei. When Territaff asked her if she had questions, she said, "By your admission, you can no longer answer my questions." Kathy repressed her enthusiasm and became quiet.

"I think you've misunderstood our intent when we suggested that Biomei could handle your questions," Territaff said, trying to placate her sober mood.

She tried to drown out Territaff's voice by sucking loudly on her feeding tube. Her sudden, chilly attitude made it clear she wanted nothing to do with them.

"Hanc, what's our ETA to Biomei?" Territaff asked.

"T-plus 1750," Hanc cheerfully answered.

"I'm going to shut down for a recharge, Hanc. Notify me at 17:00."

"Acknowledged. How about you, Captain Cody of Space Patrol?" Hanc said to Cuz.

"I'll recharge once aboard Biomei, Hanc. And Hanc, make a note to have your personality profile refitted."

"I thought that was pretty good."

"It wasn't funny," Cuz said. "It was inappropriate and demeaning."

"Are we being a little oversensitive today?"

"Hanc, knock it off," Territaff admonished the ship's computer.

"Sorry. I was trying out my new humor matrix."

"It needs work," Territaff said.

"How about you, Miss Kathy? Would you like to take a rest

period?"

"No, Hanc. I'm not tired."

"I am a shout away if you need me." Hanc happily offered.

Kathy smiled at the computer's animated mouth on the small display screen on her arm. She wiggled a little on her couch to get more comfortable. The environmental suit felt almost like an outer skin, light and flexible. Even the helmet didn't inhibit her movements. The only real restriction was the cabin's small interior. She slumped a little on the couch and found a comfortable spot. As she gazed, transfixed by the awe-inspiring view from the dome, her mind wandered. A sudden realization welled up in her. Her life would differ significantly from now on. How would she ever be able to adjust to an ordinary day after being exposed to such extraordinary events? The thought grew within her as she drifted into sleep.

* * *

A soft tone roused Kathy, and then a quiet voice said, "Your rest period has ended."

She was still tired, and her body felt heavy and lethargic. Then her eyes caught a view of Europa, which invigorated her.

She had read that Europa was a little smaller than Earth's moon, but at this close distance, it looked vast. At first, Europa's striking features glared up, causing her to squint. Then, she looked outward at the surface as the fluid motion of the ship's orbit took them across the moon.

As Kathy pondered Europa's vivid tans, browns, and grays, she wondered what form of life could exist beneath its forbidding surface. To Kathy, Europa looked like a frozen wasteland, curiously inviting and frightening at the same time.

Kathy overheard Territaff speaking to Biomei, "...Okay, we're on final approach to you now."

"So, I'll finally meet the mysterious Biomei?" Kathy said.

"Mysterious? What do you mean?" Territaff asked.

"Well, you've avoided telling me anything about her. But

you've been referring to her since I got mixed up in this incredible mess. Haven't you?"

"Hi, Kathy," a pleasant-sounding voice greeted her. She looked around to see if someone had suddenly appeared. "I'm Biomei, and I thought it would be helpful to introduce myself to you before we meet on board."

Kathy was startled at first. She heard Biomei in her mind and not over the ship's intercom.

"Where are you?" she said.

"Where's who?" Territaff asked.

"Terri, if you don't mind, I'd prefer to speak with Kathy privately," Biomei said, over the ship's intercom.

"As you wish," Territaff said, then turned his couch to face Kathy. "Don't be alarmed. Biomei can communicate telepathically. You may find it a little peculiar, but you'll quickly adjust. Your helmet has a built-in linguistic transponder—"

"That's quite all right, Terri. I can take over from here. Thank you." Biomei's tone sounded dismissive and protective to Kathy.

"What's with the attitude?" Territaff asked.

"You and Cuz have a lot to do to prepare for the continuation of the mission. We'll talk later. Kathy is my focus now, and we'll have a nice, long chat."

Kathy couldn't help smiling. "I like you already, Biomei," she mumbled to herself.

CHAPTER 17

Territaff and Cuz listened perplexedly to Kathy's laughter and ah-ha's over her open intercom while she was in a telepathic conversation with Biomei.

"What could they be discussing that's so damn funny?" Territaff transmitted to Cuz.

"I've got a feeling it involves us."

"What makes you say that?"

"Knowing Biomei, do you have to ask?"

"I see your point." Territaff nodded. *"I'm looking forward to getting aboard and having a private chat. I'm seeing a possible conspiracy between those two. Need to avert a sudden overwhelming tide of feminine logic."*

"I'm not sure I understand your meaning. Would you care to elaborate?"

"Not now, Cuz. Let's get aboard." Territaff asked the computer, "Hanc, give me our position."

"We are five hundred and thirty kilometers to the glide path," Hanc said, then asked, "What are Kathy and Biomei discussing?"

"Hanc, it doesn't concern you. Stay focused on our final approach."

"I can multi-task."

"Cuz, please make a note to have the techs perform a full diagnostic on Hanc's personality subroutine." He's becoming a real pain in the ass."

"Will do," Cuz said.

"You are not serious—are you?"

"As a heart attack," Territaff said.

"What has happened to your sense of humor?"

"What's happened to your sense of priority on this ship?"

"Okay. I am sorry. It will not happen again," Hanc said in his best conciliatory tone.

"That's better. Cuz, scratch the diagnostic note."

"Acknowledged."

"Autopilot is activated," Hanc reported. "Glide path is locked."

"Okay," Kathy said. Thanks, Biomei. That was most helpful. See you on board."

"Sounds like you ladies had a good talk," Territaff said, hoping to get some insight into their conversation.

"Oh, she's wonderful. I can't wait to meet her in person," Kathy said with a beaming smile.

"Well, if you look a little to your left, you'll get a look at her as we approach," Territaff said.

Kathy leaned to her left and stared out into the velvet darkness.

"I see nothing," she said.

"You will," Territaff said. "Biomei, disable stealth mode."

Biomei revealed herself.

Kathy's eyes widened, and her mouth dropped open as she viewed the mammoth ship.

"Oh my God," she muttered. "She really is a ship."

Biomei was enormous in both length and breadth. Her presence filled the velvet blackness with a golden radiance. She looked nothing like Kathy had imagined. Biomei had an extended, angular rear that tapered to a rounded nub, resembling almost a tail. She half expected it to wag at their approach. Beneath and slightly forward of her tail were the engines. Two massive, elongated cylinders, mounted to two V-shaped struts, taper into huge funnels at one end and form a rounded cone at the front.

As their small craft turned a few degrees to the port, Kathy got a close-up view of Biomei's forward sections. They were bow-shaped with a bulge in her midsection, giving her a well-endowed appearance. The upper forward sections widened into a three-quarter disk shape, featuring numerous large, curved windows interspersed above and between rows of portals. Then Kathy noticed something resembling a shark's fin on the dorsal section. As they got closer, she realized it was a complex array of antennas and strange-looking devices.

Biomei was beautiful to Kathy. She looked majestic and strikingly feminine. She appeared more like a living creature than a great ship. It was hard for her to reconcile Biomei's form. In one sense, she looked alive, yet she had all the apparent inanimate technology of an advanced starship.

"She's something to behold at first sight," Territaff said, sensing Kathy's awe.

"I find her both beautiful and incomprehensible," she said.

"I had a similar reaction the first time I saw her. Soon, you'll be aboard, and that's an entirely different experience altogether."

"I know this will sound kind of weird, but I already have a fondness for her."

"I feel the same way each time I board. She has a way of growing on you to the point you forget that she's a ship."

"She seems so alive."

"That's because she is. You'll soon come to appreciate her as another life-form. As we all are."

"I never would've dreamed that there could be so many unique life-forms and that they would become part of my life. Wow, Terri. You sure know how to enchant a girl."

PART II

TRANSFORMATIONS

CHAPTER 18

"Welcome aboard, Kathy," Biomei greeted her as she walked onto the shuttle bay deck. "Welcome home, Terri and Cuz. It's good to see you're both looking well."

Biomei's tone was warm and inviting. Kathy also noticed how different her voice sounded when spoken.

"Cuz, will you show Kathy to her quarters," Territaff said, "then join me in communications?" He waited for them to leave before addressing Biomei. *"Why are you engaging her now? She's not ready. She hasn't been mentally or physically adapted."*

"You've left me little choice," Biomei snapped. *"She can't be sent home, and you're correct; she's not ready. She must be biologically adapted, briefed, or have her memory erased, then placed in hibernation until the mission is completed. Unless you have a better alternative, those are the only viable options I can see."*

"Neither of those alternatives is right. She's a warm and caring soul, and I regret involving her. I'd never considered that she...." He let out a heavy breath. *"She's become dear to me."*

"You knew what you were doing. You understood the risk to her, and yet you seduced her without conscience or forethought. Your actions are reprehensible and beneath you."

"She has become important to me. I do care for her."

"But you don't love her."

"Why are you so angry?"

"Your actions have given me cause to doubt if your focus is still on the mission. You have lost your way, Terri, and it worries me."

"I understand your concern. Losing Tanya, the way we did, may have influenced me. You're right, though. I acted more on emotion than logic toward Kathy. But we've come too far already. She has the potential and the strength to be of value to the mission. Maybe she's here for a reason. All I can say in

my defense is that…" He frowned. *"I feel something different from her. I know you've sensed it, too. Not since Nicki have I felt such a strong force as hers. She has an inner light and strength that filled me with compassion and hopefulness."*

"Yes. She has some strong qualities," Biomei conceded. *"She reminds me of you when you first developed your inner strengths. She also has some of Nickada's qualities. Therein lies the problem. You allowed your grief for Nickada to cloud your better judgment. I hope you see that now, Phillip."*

"Phillip Mann doesn't exist!" he shouted, then caught himself.

"You can't deny who you are by changing your name. You are, and always will be, Phillip Mann. He's still who you are, and I'll always love you, regardless of who you try to be."

"Please, Biomei, things are complicated enough—let's not go over this again."

"As you wish, Territaff."

"Who's Phillip Mann?" Kathy said as she approached Territaff in the corridor.

"I thought Cuz was showing you to your quarters."

"He did, then left me. I felt strange and alone. I needed to be with you. It was as though you were somehow summoning me." She wrinkled her nose. "Does that make sense?"

"Yes." He smiled and glanced up for a moment, then wrapped his arm around Kathy's waist and pulled her closer to him. She leaned her head against his arm. "At first, this can feel like a large and empty ship. After a while, you'll become attuned to Biomei's presence, and that lost, and empty feeling fades away." He kissed her forehead.

Kathy smiled wryly, letting out a slight aww. "So, who's Phillip Mann?"

"I left out she's relentlessly curious," Territaff transmitted to Biomei. "An alias of mine," he said, hoping to satisfy her.

"Do you have many aliases?"

"A few, with a high likelihood of more to follow. They're part of the job."

"And what job would that be? Diplomatic courier or bumbling spy?"

Biomei laughed heartily, and Territaff couldn't help but laugh, too.

He escorted Kathy back to her quarters. As they entered the spacious room, he asked, "Did Cuz show you where everything is?"

"No. He seemed to be in a great hurry. He apologized and said he had to leave but promised to return and show me how everything worked."

"Did he say why he had to leave?"

"No. He looked distracted, like he received one of those mental transmissions or something, because he sure left in a hurry."

"That's odd. I wonder why he didn't alert me. I need to look into this. This bed is amazing." He patted it. "I suggest you try it out. You look like you can use some rest."

A wicked smile spread on Kathy's face. "Why don't you join me, and we can try it out together?"

Territaff's face lit up for a second as he led Kathy to the bed. They embraced and fell onto it, locked in passion.

Territaff stopped abruptly, stood, and straightened his jumpsuit. "As much as I want to make love to you, I need to look in on Cuz and see what all the urgency is about." He leaned in and kissed her. "Get some rest, and I promise to give you my undivided attention when I return."

"Is that before or after Cuz returns?"

Territaff shook his head, grinning.

"Okay," she said, preempting any clever response. "But I'm too excited to sleep. I'll be counting the minutes until your return." She let out a big yawn, then made herself comfortable on the bed. "Wow! I think it's alive." She jerked up and looked around. "What's it doing?"

"It's learning your biorhythms and conforming to your

body," he explained. "Relax. Give it a chance to learn your metabolic functions. It'll also respond to verbal commands, but after a while, you won't need to tell it anything."

"Is everything alive on this ship?"

"Yeah, pretty much."

"Isn't that a little creepy? I mean, all these devices know everything about you. Don't you ever worry about them taking over the ship or doing weird things to you while you sleep?"

"Kathy, you've been reading too many bad sci-fi stories. Those things don't happen. Lean back, relax, and rest. I'll be back as soon as I can."

"Okay, but please hurry. I'm really freaked out."

Territaff stood by the door for a moment and watched her as she timidly lay back on the bed. She looked so small, scared, and uncertain, reminding him of himself when he was adapting to this same strange new world.

"Look after her, Biomei," he transmitted.

"I'm always with her, just like you and Cuz. She'll be fine, but Cuz needs you in Communications. He's receiving an update from Venubia, and the news is disturbing."

CHAPTER 19

Kathy awoke from a deep, dark sleep with dread. She would have felt rested if not for the inexplicable, unsettling sense of alarm. Something was wrong.

"Biomei," she called.

"Yes, Kathy."

"There's something really bad happening—isn't there?"

"Why do you think that?"

"I just feel it. I can't tell you why, but I have this…" She jumped off the bed. "Where's Communications?" she asked, grabbing a fresh jumpsuit from the closet.

"Go to your left and follow the floor lights. They'll direct you."

"Do you know what's happening?"

"Yes."

"Will you tell me? I need to know."

"I think it'd be better if Terri tells you."

"And why's that?" Kathy's voice trembled a little.

"Go to them, and I'll be with you."

Kathy entered the expansive corridor and gazed down its length. "Oh, my god," she gasped. "This passageway looks like it goes on forever."

Her attention was drawn to a stream of lights flowing along both sides of the floor. She ran, trying to make sense of the almost overwhelming emotions rising within her. "What could it be that's making me feel this way?" Kathy wondered on her way to the turbo lift.

Standing before the open lift, her mind shifted for a moment. She realized this was the first time she had used this strange contraption on her own. The thought of riding a column of air seemed a precarious mode of travel, but she overcame her apprehension, stepped into the translucent tube, and said, "Communications."

* * *

"Have you confirmed this?" Territaff asked, Cuz.

"Yes."

"How can we stop them? They've got everything they need and all the resources of the US Government. That's incomprehensible. How did they infiltrate the government so quickly and high up the ladder?"

"Who did?" Kathy asked as she rushed into the Communications Center. She looked around the massive room filled with banks of tiny, blinking crystals.

Cuz greeted her with a warm smile that shone through his thoughtful expression. Unlike Cuz, Territaff looked annoyed by her sudden presence.

"I thought you were resting," he snapped at her.

"I was until I had a premonition that something terrible was happening."

Territaff looked keenly at her for a beat, then frowned. "Sorry, Kathy," he said. "What sort of premonition?"

"It's only a feeling, but now that I'm looking at the two of you, I believe I'm somehow feeling your emotions. So, tell me, what's going on?"

"One of the things we were going to brief you on seems to be coming to fruition. The men who broke into your apartment were agents of a group of intergalactic terrorists."

"You mean the Zenti," Kathy interjected.

"Precisely," Cuz answered with surprise.

"How did you know?" Territaff asked, feeling surprised and confused.

"You told me..." she thought for a moment. "No, Biomei did?" She paced in deep thought. "Biomei," she called out.

"Yes, Kathy, I did brief you while you were sleeping. I sensed your innate telepathic and empathic abilities. My intuitions about you are well-founded. Your unsettling premonition was due to your subconscious knowledge of my briefing. With some training, I believe we can fully develop those abilities. Gentleman, you'll regard Kathy as a full team member from this point forward."

Territaff and Cuz both nodded.

Territaff placed his hands on Kathy's shoulders, then turned her to face him closely. "I don't know whether to congratulate you or offer my deepest apologies, but you're now a member of our small force against an evil power."

"It's about time you recognized my talents." Kathy grinned, then turned to Cuz. She noticed how quiet he had become and was engaging her with a tense expression. "What's wrong, Cuz? You don't look pleased?"

"I'm pleased to have you join us, but I'm also concerned for your safety." Cuz's demeanor stiffened, and his gentle facial features became passive as he looked at her thoughtfully.

"Cuz, don't be concerned. For some reason, as long as I have you and Terri by my side, nothing can harm me." Kathy smiled warmly, hoping to break the stiff demeanor he had assumed.

Cuz tilted his head and arched an eyebrow, then said softly, "The problem is that we may not always be by your side."

Kathy went to Cuz, stared into his gentle face for a second, then hugged him. "Your job is to make sure you're always by my side," she whispered in his ear.

During their embrace, she heard Cuz's voice in her mind say, *"I'll always protect you with great devotion."*

The thought was full of an emotion that Kathy had never experienced before. She felt connected to Cuz in a way she couldn't articulate.

Kathy took a step back from him. His features had regained their familiar glow, which gave him his distinctive, humanistic quality. She recognized that the broad smile and the gleam in his eyes were for her alone. She leaned in and kissed his cheek. Then, turning to Territaff, she said, "It's none of your business."

"Okay." Territaff sighed, clapping his hands together, then rubbing them. "It's time to roll up our sleeves and get to work."

Cuz's forehead furrowed into tight lines. He looked back and forth between Kathy and Territaff, then lifted his arms to examine the sleeves of his jumpsuit.

"What does 'rolling up one's sleeves' have to do with preparing to work?" Cuz asked.

"Cuz, check under idiomatic Earth expressions," Territaff said.

He thought for a moment, then said, "Oh, I get it."

"You look almost relieved," Kathy said.

"I don't like working with my sleeves rolled up."

"Is he always like this?" Kathy asked Territaff.

"Like what?"

Her eyes darted between them, taking in their serious expressions. "Never mind."

* * *

"What are you so upset about?" Kathy asked Territaff, who typed on an odd-looking keyboard with strange symbols.

He held up a finger for her to wait a moment. She looked over his shoulder to see what he was working on. What she saw were lines full of those symbols. It neither resembled numbers nor words but rather some exotic-looking code.

"What's that?" she said, leaning over Territaff's shoulder.

"It's Venubian quantum encryption code," he answered.

"Okay, and you understand that?"

"Biomei understands it. I'll explain it in a minute."

Kathy rolled a chair over from another console and sat next to Territaff. She looked on, impressed with how fast he worked. It all looked incomprehensible to her. As she waited, she took in the vast room. It appeared to be designed for a much larger crew. Kathy's mind wandered: What was Biomei all about? Where's the rest of the crew? Then she refocused on what was innermost in her thoughts: Who are the Zenti, and why was she so frightened of them?

Cuz joined them and stood waiting to be acknowledged by Territaff. When he finished typing, he looked at Cuz, his gaze tight with concern.

"To use one of your colorful idioms, we screwed up," he said, letting out a heavy breath.

Kathy gasped. A wellspring of knowledge filled her mind. As she stared at the monitor, her heart raced with excitement and anxiety.

"I can read the code. How's that possible?" she mumbled.

The magnitude of their situation became apparent, and it overwhelmed her. Her head felt light, and the room took on a gray tunnel appearance. Territaff recognized the glassy look in her eyes, then held her head as she let out a long, heavy breath and slid off the chair.

CHAPTER 20

Kathy's head felt heavy, and it took an effort to open her eyes. She wanted to see where she was, because she seemed surrounded by white. After a few attempts to lift her head, she gave up.

"Hey, is there anyone here?" she called out.

She listened for a few moments for a response. The quiet was welcomed because it allowed her to mull over what had happened in the Communications Bay. Everything was vague, like trying to recall a dream.

"Hey, where's everybody?" Her voice echoed in the room.

She sensed Terri and Biomei were close, and she relaxed, waiting to be told what happened.

Kathy heard a subtle, melodic, low-pitched hum, like a sung chord. She could feel a slight vibration emanating from the bed. The hum and vibration were in sync and unwavering, having a tranquilizing effect on her.

"Kathy, dear," she heard Biomei's soft voice within her mind. It was a welcome sound.

"What's happening?" Hearing Biomei's voice in her mind surprised her.

"You're going through a transformation process to prepare you for the mission."

"Transformation? I don't understand. What kind of transformation?"

"It will become clear shortly. Relax your mind and allow yourself to drift, unencumbered by thoughts or emotions. It's also important that you breathe. Breathe in through your nose and exhale through your mouth with long, steady breaths."

Kathy concentrated on her breathing. It made her feel like she was back in her first Yoga class, learning to breathe again. She could hear each breath within her head, soothing her. Her eyes grew heavy. It wasn't long before she succumbed and fell into a perfect transcendental state.

* * *

Territaff sat in the observation room while Biomei prepared Kathy for the transformation procedure. He was uncertain about how to feel regarding her undergoing such a profound change.

"*Will she still be the same?*" he transmitted to Biomei.

"*It's hard to say. Think about your conversion. I don't believe you lost your basic personality. It's more of an addition than a subtraction for the individual. She's strong. I can't foresee any long-term side effects.*"

"*I hope you're right, Biomei, and she's ready.*"

"*What's your concern, Phillip?*"

Territaff's jaw clenched at hearing that name.

"*How many times do I have to remind you that Phillip is dead?*"

"*Why such emotion?*"

"*Phillip Mann died on Venubia, along with everything he loved.*"

"*So, what does that say about Mr. Territaff? Is he a hollowed enhanced human who's driven only by vengeance? Is that all you are now?*"

"*Stop it, Biomei! You know that's not what I meant!*"

He inhaled deeply, then blew it out. "Okay, you've made your point," he said out loud.

"*I'd prefer to put Phillip aside for now. Once the mission is over, we can get back to analyzing me. Territaff is the only identity I care to go by for reasons you know quite well.*"

"*As you wish, Phillip.*"

"*Great Universe, you're incorrigible.*"

"*You must prepare yourself for Kathy's curiosity about your persona change. She'll know everything about your former self, the Zenti wars, and Nickada. She'll be confused and seek your help in understanding some of your choices. The real question is, are you ready?*"

Biomei struck a deep chord that took Territaff by surprise. The sudden realization filled him with apprehension.

"I'm not prepared, but I'll be by the time she has completed the process. You brought many things to light. Thank you. With a little more time and a lot of patience on my part, I'll be ready for her."

"Time is a precious commodity these days. She has completed the first phase. You can see her now, but only for a few minutes. The second phase will begin shortly. Remember, Terri, this isn't about you. It's about her now."

"She looks so peaceful. It's almost a shame to wake her." Territaff said, looking down at Kathy.

"I know. Genetically engineering a perfectly healthy body for space travel may seem like a horrible thing, yet it's so necessary."

Territaff nodded, then pondered Kathy's stillness and asked, *"Are you going to implant a compiler too?"*

"Yes. She should be given as many advantages as possible. Don't you agree?"

"I do, but with reservations. It's such an invasive device to adjust to."

"We've got a little more experience now."

"Really? Who have you done this to?"

"You. Twice."

"I was assuming someone other than myself."

"You've given us much data. We're confident we've resolved most of the problems you experienced."

"I hope so for her sake." Territaff hesitated, *"She probably hates me by now."*

"Hate is too strong an emotion. I believe resentment would be more accurate."

"Thanks, but that was a rhetorical thought."

"Oh. But you don't know how she feels. She may be grateful."

"What do you mean?"

"She's living her dream."

He looked down at her and gently squeezed her hand. "Kathy?" She didn't stir, but he noticed her eyes moved under her closed lids. "Kathy," he said a little louder, squeezing her foot.

She jerked her eyes open, then stared at Territaff for a moment. She tried to lift her head, but he placed his hand on her shoulder to restrain her.

"Wha... ha... happened?" she slurred, looking disoriented.

"Take a moment and gather yourself," Territaff said.

Kathy lifted her eyes and focused on Territaff. Her sleepy gaze transformed into a dreamy smile as if she had suddenly recognized him.

"Terreee," she half-mouthed, speaking his name as though verbalizing was difficult.

"Don't speak," he transmitted, testing if she could respond telepathically. *"Concentrate for a moment and try to transmit your thoughts."*

She frowned, puzzled. After a moment, she closed her eyes, took a deep breath, and slowly exhaled through her mouth.

"Terri, can you hear me?" She was surprised at how easily she could communicate her thoughts to him.

"Yes. How do you feel?"

"I feel a bit strange, but good at the same time. Does that make sense?"

"It makes a lot of sense. Do you know what's going on?"

Biomei explained that I'm undergoing a transformation procedure that will become clearer once it's completed. So far, all I understand is that I went into a deep sleep and woke up feeling strange and full of new knowledge. To be honest, I don't understand any of it. I'm also a little afraid that I'll change somehow and won't be me anymore."

"Kathy, you lose yourself in the process," Territaff continued aloud, "but that's only for a short time while your mind and body sync up. What you're experiencing is normal. Believe me. We'd never change or harm the beautiful person you are. There will be events and things that will frighten you. Part of the procedure involves inducing strong emotions and then analyzing your reactions. At times, it'll be unpleasant, but it's all necessary for the computer to map your brain while protecting your core personality. Simply put, the system is rewiring your brain.

"Rewiring my brain? How?" Kathy's eyes widened; her complexion paled. Territaff squeezed her hand. It felt clammy, and her breathing increased.

Her reaction surprised Territaff. Seeing her become so anxious made him feel like an idiot for upsetting her. He wanted to relieve her anxiety, not exacerbate it. Then he realized there was more inside of Kathy than she was revealing.

"It sounds far worse than it is," he explained. "The process is called induced chemo-microscopy neural sublimation enhancement. It's a mouthful. It's a method of analyzing the brain through chemical stimulation and then creating new neural connections to enhance the way your brain reacts to different situations and stimuli. It's a way of suppressing unwanted emotions and enhancing the desired ones while creating new neural pathways.

"Additionally, a neural compiler will be implanted in the central prefrontal cortex of your brain. It will feel strange at first while it learns you. It will become your best friend once it's integrated and synchronized with your brain's rhythms and pathways. All your learning skills will become heightened and accelerated. You'll become more intuitive when dealing with new species and situations, as well as with general people skills. It merges the capabilities of a microprocessor with the human brain. It's pretty remarkable."

Kathy's face screwed up into a tight scowl as she listened to Territaff. "I don't think I like the sound of this. Is this necessary? You know, messing with my brain and all?"

"I promise it's not as bad as it sounds. Look how good I turned out." He grinned.

"Exactly, my point."

"Seriously, you've nothing to fear. The procedure will enhance your reactions and enable you to think on a much higher level." He let out a quiet sigh, seeing how apprehensive she looked. "We're here for you, Kathy. We'll help you through the process, and you know you can come to Cuz or me with whatever you need. You're not doing this alone. Never forget that Biomei is always your best choice for answers to all the questions you feel are too personal."

Kathy's expression relaxed. She smiled, feeling much better about the process, but she didn't understand why or how her apprehension and anxiety had faded.

"I'm glad you're here. I couldn't do this without you," she said.

Territaff wasn't sure but suspected Biomei had transmitted a Tal'ez, which was a Venubian tranquilizer.

"Was that necessary?" he transmitted to Biomei.

"It isn't what you think. I only brought her systems down a notch."

Kathy tried to lift her head with her shoulders pinned to the mattress. She barely managed to lift her head above the pillows. She lowered her head until her chin rested on the upper part of her chest. She surveyed as much of the room as she could see. Kathy frowned, looking disappointed. "I don't see Cuz. Where is he?"

"He's still in Communications. A lot is going on now. He'll be here by the time you complete the procedure."

"Let him know I missed him."

"He knows. He's monitoring the procedure but can't respond at the moment.

"Did he share our transmissions?"

"No. He can only monitor your biorhythms."

"I see."

"It's time, Terri," Biomei said.

Territaff leaned in and kissed Kathy. Her eyes were fixed on him. She still looked scared, trying to cover her fear by putting on a brave face before delving into the unknown.

"You'll be fine. Nothing bad can happen to you," he transmitted.

She forced a smile and closed her eyes. The second phase started, and Kathy was once more in a deep, transcendental state of consciousness.

CHAPTER 21

Kathy slept for over twelve hours after the procedure. When she opened her eyes, Cuz sat on a chair beside her bed. She smiled warmly, holding out her hand to him. Cuz gazed at it, hesitating, before taking it in his hand and giving it a gentle squeeze.

"Biomei said you did very well. Much better than Terri," Cuz said.

"That's not surprising." She laughed.

"Are you hungry?"

"Starving."

"That's good. If you think you can get up, we'll go to Biomei's Eatery, as Terri refers to it. When I inquired about the name, he replied, 'Mess Hall' sounds too military, and 'Galley' doesn't quite fit.' If you like, I'll give you a partial tour of the ship along the way."

"That sounds great, Cuz."

Kathy sat up on the edge of the bed, her head in her hands.

"What's wrong?"

"I'm a little dizzy."

"Take a moment and allow your head to clear. From what I understand of the procedure, your mind and body will need a little time to coordinate. You may also be slightly dehydrated."

Cuz walked over to a wall and said, "Water dispenser." Kathy looked on in amazement as a wall section formed into a familiar-looking, high-necked faucet and sink. "Point five liters of cool water," Cuz ordered.

A tall glass materialized in Cuz's hand, and water flowed through the faucet. Cuz held the glass under the running water, and the water stopped just a few centimeters from the brim.

"That was amazing," Kathy said, taking the glass from Cuz. She examined the water for a moment. "It has a slight blue tint to it."

"Yes. It's manufactured to Venubian standards. On the

shuttle, we were drinking purified water. I believe you'll find Venubian water to your satisfaction."

He watched Kathy as she emptied the glass in a few long swallows.

"This water is like nothing I've ever tasted." She pondered the empty glass. "Wow, that's Venubian water? It's incredibly refreshing. What's in it?"

"Hydrogen and oxygen are like any water molecule, but there are more heavy hydrogen molecules in Venubian water than in Earth's."

"And much fewer pollutants, I bet."

"There is only one billionth of one percent of contaminants per million decaliters from all planetary resources. Would you care for another?"

"Please." It took three refills of the miraculous liquid to quench her thirst. When she drank her final glassful, Kathy said, "I'll probably need to pee soon."

"You were pretty dehydrated. I believe we'll make it to the Eatery without a necessity break." He turned his thin lips up into a shy smile.

"You have such a pleasant way of speaking, Cuz."

"Thank you."

"You're welcome. Now, show me the way. I'm famished." Kathy narrowed her eyes slightly. "Are we going to have real food or more imaginary stuff?"

"By imaginary, do you mean what you had on the shuttle?" Kathy nodded.

"All the food is, as you put it, imaginary, but only in terms of taste and smell." The food synthesizers can replicate almost anything you can imagine in any form you desire. It will look and taste much like, as Terri says, 'the real thing.'"

"So, if I order bacon and eggs. I'd get a facsimile that looks and tastes like bacon and eggs?"

"Yes." He gave her a curious look.

"What?"

"I've often pondered food's strong social connection for humanoids. I've asked Terri about it, but he dismissed it as a primal human survival trait. I believe eating together is much more than that."

"It is, Cuz. It's a social event. Different cultures have various social gatherings that are part of the experience of eating together. Aboard the ship, it will become a welcome social event. Eating is a time for people to join and share their thoughts or discuss how their day is going. It can be anything from a quick gathering to eat to an elaborate and intimate exchange between people. It's much more than a primal survival trait. I think Terri has been eating alone for far too long."

"Interesting. I believe you're correct. You seem to have a much different experience with eating than Terri. I like your perspective on things. You're infusing much-needed positive energy into the team."

"Thanks, Cuz. I appreciate you saying that."

* * *

As Kathy walked with Cuz, she peered down the numerous empty intersecting corridors and marveled at their length. Biomei was impressive in both her length and breadth.

"Cuz, is it me, or do you sense how empty Biomei feels?"

"I'm not sure what you mean, Kathy."

"Walking through these long corridors, realizing how immense Biomei is, I get a strong melancholy about the ship. It feels like Biomei longs to be more occupied. Like an empty city, waiting to be filled with life."

"Interesting. I'm not capable of the emotion you ascribe to the ship. However, I agree that Biomei wants to be full of life and more utilized. I also believe it's a conversation you should have with her."

"Please continue telling me about Biomei."

Biomei absorbs all the raw essentials from the abundance of free particles within star systems. She sorts and processes the materials, then converts them into the energy needed to power ship-wide systems, including all living matter."

"Well, Biomei, you're truly alive," Kathy called out.

"Yes, Kathy. I am. It's sometimes difficult for humanoids to make the mental leap necessary to appreciate I'm not that different from them."

"I never doubted your existence. How I felt about it was giving me trouble," Kathy admitted. "Now it all seems so irrelevant. I believe the transformation process has given me new insights and a wealth of new knowledge. It's all so daunting yet exciting at the same time." She wrinkled her nose. "Does that make sense to you?"

"Yes," Biomei and Cuz answered together.

"Your mind and body will undergo many profound changes to prepare for the fascinating journey you're about to embark on," Biomei said. "It will be a more daunting and exciting journey than anything you could have imagined."

"My mind and body? More changes?" Kathy stared wide-eyed at Cuz with a dumbfounded smile. "You mean the procedure isn't finished? There will be more?"

"You've only completed the incipient phases. The actual transformation will happen most unexpectedly. Your mind will cue you when the changes are about to manifest."

Kathy looked up with her arms spread wide as though she were pleading with a higher power, "I don't want to change." I like who I am. Please, Biomei, is all of this necessary?"

"Kathy, why are you speaking as though I were a deity?"

I suppose it's because I view you with a sense of reverence. Maybe it's because you're a disembodied voice. I don't know. You just seem god-like to me."

"That's disturbing," Biomei said.

"Kathy, Biomei is only a different form of life—not a superior one," Cuz said, puzzled by her sudden change in attitude.

"I know." She looked down and said, "I'm sorry, Biomei.

It's... ~~it's~~ It's just that you seem miraculous. I... I can't explain what I'm feeling... guess I'm a little scared....” She walked to the side of the corridor and leaned against the wall, rubbing her forehead as her mind whirled in confusion.

“Kathy, I believe I understand,” Biomei said in a consoling tone. “Let me try to explain a few things to you.”

She looked up.

Cuz came to her side and said, “Biomei, sometimes can feel superior, but she's no deity.”

Kathy let out a quiet laugh.

“I believe what you're experiencing can be attributed to the transformation process.”

“Once your mind and body are in sync,” Biomei added, “you'll experience several dynamic forces emerging within you.” As I explained earlier, these forces will enhance you intellectually and physically. What they can't do is change you. To protect your psyche, I've suppressed much of the memory portion of the procedure. We wanted to allow your mind to initialize before incorporating the neural compiler. Soon, you'll go into a deep sleep. These changes will take shape. The memory streams will be released. Some of it will be unpleasant, and some of it will be enlightening. You'll wake up feeling different, but I assure you, everything that makes you who you are will remain unchanged.”

“But you said I'll feel different, and my brain will be altered. So, how am I the same?”

“Your personality and everything that makes you who you are will be untouched. Kathy, allow yourself to adapt,” Biomei cautioned. “Your initial instincts will fight the alterations out of fear. Don't fight it. Permit them to flow in you. They're all part of the process. Ask Terri. He has the best understanding of what you'll be experiencing. He also cares for you. Cuz and I are here for anything you need.”

“What kind of changes?” Kathy said. “I don't think I like the sound of that, Biomei. You're making me nervous.”

She felt her mouth go dry and broke out in a cold sweat.

Cuz recognized her distress. He wrapped a long arm around her slender shoulders and brought her closer. He spoke in a calm voice, "Don't be frightened, Kathy. The process is nothing to fear. Like many things in life, it'll be another change, but it's a change for the better. Come, we're at the Eatery, and I believe Terri is waiting for us."

"Do you think she needs a Tal'ez?" Biomei transmitted to Cuz.

"No. A good meal may be more effective."

"Are you two talking behind my back again?" She squinted at Cuz.

"No. We're transmitting privately," Cuz said.

She let out a long sigh and studied Cuz's face, taking in his dark eyes, reflecting a gentle, warm glow that calmed her. She gave Cuz a tight hug.

He looked at her curiously.

"Thank you," she said.

Cuz felt a rush of an unusual sensation that pleased and confused him. *I'm an enhanced artificial life-form. How can I be experiencing such intense sensations?* He didn't know what to make of these new and fascinating impressions. He also knew he never wanted them to stop.

CHAPTER 22

Territaff was already eating when Cuz and Kathy entered the small alcove tucked into a curved wall. Posters of baseball and football teams decorated the walls. A weather-worn football sat on a small shelf above the food dispenser.

"You kind of gave the joint a sports bar look. What, no soccer balls?" Kathy said, staring at the old football. She sat across from Territaff.

He looked closely at Kathy and smiled thinly, sensing her feelings. "The transformation process is driving you nuts, right?"

"It's that obvious?" Kathy frowned.

"It'll play with your emotions. And, by the way, you're handling it just fine."

"You can read my thoughts?"

"You'll learn to control your thoughts, but I didn't read them. It's considered a violation of privacy to read thoughts without permission. However, your body language told me enough."

Biomei said I would undergo many changes. How bad was it for you?"

"What would you like to eat?" Cuz interrupted, allowing Territaff to think of a response.

"Um?" Kathy thought for a moment. "Oatmeal," she blurted. Cuz started toward the food station, then Kathy called out, "Eggs, sunny side up on rye toast." He started again, and then Kathy added, "A side of hash browns and bacon, thick-sliced and chewy."

Cuz paused for a moment. "Anything else?"

"No, I think that covers it." She gave him a crooked grin, then, to Territaff, asked, "So, what was it like for you?"

"My circumstances were different.

"Different, how?"

I was," he paused, then mumbled, "rebuilt after a fatal car

accident."

Kathy's mouth fell open; her eyes grew wide. "You were brought back from the dead?"

"Hey, Cuz," Territaff called. " While you're there, could you bring me a refill of coffee?"

"Would you bring me some coffee, too? Please. Black with extra sugar." She turned her attention back to Territaff and said, "I can't believe it."

"That I was dead? Or rebuilt?"

"Well, yeah, that. But we have coffee and any food we want. This is so awesome; it seems almost too good to be true."

Territaff couldn't help smiling. He also feared for her, knowing the changes she would soon undergo.

"What's with the look?" she asked.

"What'd you mean?"

"You know what I mean. Your face always takes on a tight expression anytime you have bad news. I've been around you long enough to read you like a book."

Cuz returned carrying three trays of food along one arm and two cups of coffee in his hand.

"Careful. They may be a little hot," Cuz said as he leaned closer to Kathy so she could take the food trays.

"Wow," Territaff said, looking at the plates piled high with food. "You can eat all of that?"

"I'm starving," she said, diving into the oatmeal with a spoon and eating hungrily. After finishing the oatmeal in a few seconds, she broke the yolk of one egg, put a scoop of hash browns on top, then ate a heavy forkful of the mixture. "This is awesome. "It's just like breakfast at Jimmy's Diner," she said, her mouth full of food. Then she took a sip of coffee. "Oh man, I can't believe how good this coffee is. I'm not sure if this is good because I'm hungry or really good."

Cuz and Territaff both marveled at Kathy's ravenous appetite. They were surprised at how quickly she finished her food. She let out a large belch and then finished her coffee.

"God, I'm stuffed," she announced, patting the sides of her small, bulging stomach while beaming contentedly.

"Is there anything else you would like?" Cuz asked.

Kathy thought for a moment. "Yeah, do you have anything sweet, like chocolate?"

"Any particular type?"

"Get her some of my B'hav'la," Territaff interjected. After he said it, his taste buds triggered a craving, and he added, "Please bring me a piece also."

"Oh, that sounds like some wicked stuff," Kathy murmured, grinning.

"I think I'll partake as well," Cuz said, then turned toward the food station.

He returned with a tray of pastries covered in dark chocolate and more coffee. They all took a piece, then hummed their pleasure in unison as they ate the sweet pastry.

"This is delicious," Kathy said, taking another piece. "It's so light in texture and so rich in taste. Where did you find this?"

"I accidentally created it with a food synthesizer, but that's a story for another time." Territaff regarded Kathy with a brooding expression. "Is your tank full?" he asked.

"Stuffed to the gills," she replied. "You look full of thoughts. Care to share?"

He leaned back in his chair. His eyes took on a familiar darkness, giving him an emotional detachment that made Kathy uncomfortable.

"You never answered my question," she said, trying to break his sudden mood change.

"I forgot the question."

"Why are you being so evasive? And why do you look like the dark side has taken you over?"

"Sorry." His expression softened into a more affable look.

She sensed something was happening inside him and became increasingly agitated by his fluctuating moods and evasiveness.

If you don't want to answer, say so. But I'm either part of this team, or I'm not! I refuse to be kept in the dark and treated like added baggage."

She got up to leave, but Territaff grabbed her wrist.

"No. You're not extra baggage, and you're very much part of the team," he reassured. "It's hard for me to discuss what you want to know. I asked Biomei to suppress much of my history so I could share some of it with you myself. At least, that was my intention. Now, I can't find a good way to begin when I need to tell you. How can I express how important you've become to the mission and me without sounding patronizing or disingenuous? Only a moment ago, Biomei threatened that I would tell you, or she would do it herself.

"Start at the beginning and let it flow, Terri. Isn't that what you're always telling me? Isn't that how friends communicate with each other, with trust and honesty?"

"Come. Let's take a walk. I want to show you something." Territaff extended his hand to Kathy. She took it, came around, and warmly embraced him.

"Cuz, prepare to leave orbit," Territaff said.

"Any particular destination?"

"Celibran sector."

"We're going to Lunneziah? May I ask why we're going to that awful moon?"

"Picking up a special passenger."

"As you wish," Cuz said, arching his thin brows into a puzzled scowl. He watched them leave the Eatery, then transmitted to Biomei, *"Human emotions are so complicated. How will I ever be able to master them?"*

"Cuz, you already have a good grasp of the essentials. Now, you only have to learn to trust them."

"That's easier said than done."

"All you have to do is be you, and you'll never go wrong."

"Does he love her?"

"Yes, but not as you do. His love comes from obligation

and guilt."

"I don't understand."

"That's okay. Over time, you will."

* * *

They walked in silence into the arboretum. Kathy's mouth dropped open in astonishment. The colossal bay was filled from floor to ceiling with plants, trees, and flowers of every conceivable shape, size, and color. The stunning panorama was spread beneath a clear dome on Biomei's belly so that nature's diversity was in direct contrast with the grandeur of the cosmos.

Kathy walked up to a bright yellow blossom resembling a sunflower, but its petals were much broader and more colorful than anything she had ever seen. She touched and sniffed a petal. Its flesh was rough, but its scent was mild and pleasant.

"This is incredible," she said, walking in a small circle as she took in the entire room. "What a wonderful place."

"It was Nickada's favorite. This is her creation," Territaff said with pride. "It never ceases to amaze me. Each time I come here, it reminds me of her. She had an enchantment with nature and all living things. She could relate to every living thing on a personal level as though they were all conscious beings. I often caught her trying to communicate with the room." He smiled at the thought. He closed his eyes and reached out with his hands like a blind man trying to read a room. "Nickada believed some of the plants and trees understood her. That nature had its own language, and she could learn to understand it with time and patience.

"Who's Nickada?"

Kathy's attention swung away from the arboretum's beauty and back to her insistent need to know everything, which was driving Territaff's strong emotions.

He stiffened, and his jaw jutted outward with tension.

"She brought me back from the dead. She gave me a new body and a new life. I owe my existence to her...."

Kathy sensed a struggle brewing within him as he spoke. His bright, black eyes glazed over in a glassy stare as his emotions rose.

She took his hand and asked, "Tell me about her, Terri. You can't suppress these emotions any longer. They're eating you up from the inside out."

His mouth turned up into a sad smile. Then he looked down. "Where do I begin?" he thought aloud. "Nickada was extraordinary in every conceivable way. She was brilliant, full of energy and ideas. Loyal and honest almost to a fault, compassionate, and so loving." He looked into Kathy's eyes. "You would have liked her, and I believe you could have been friends."

"From what I've learned about her, I think we could've been good friends."

"I was a lost, miserable soul when I first met Nicki. She was trying to understand humanity and chose me as her teacher. What an irony. I'm unsure what she learned from me, but she taught me how to live."

He looked away from Kathy for a moment, then turned back as though trying to rein in his emotions.

"We've been over this already, Terri. You did what you had to, and I'll always be grateful, regardless of what happens. This was all meant to be."

"You shouldn't be here. This is not your fight."

Kathy scrutinized him with a burrowing look and said, "What happened?" She turned her own emotions off, then pried deeper into Territaff. "This is not the time for regrets, nor do you have the luxury of feeling sorry for yourself." Tell me what happened."

"A download of the war between the Zenti and Venubians will unfold during the next phase of your procedure," he said, staring outwardly. He exhaled a long, slow breath, and his voice softened into a quiet monotone. Territaff continued to stare outward as he spoke. "Nickada was my soul mate. She brought me to her homeworld, Venubia. At first, they needed me as a viable biological surrogate to help revitalize an impotent male population. The details of this are also in the download." He closed his eyes. "It was a hideous war—so much hate. There was so much waste. Too many innocents died needlessly. Isn't that always the price of war, the slaughter of the innocent?

"Nickada was taken by a vile creature called Zohleemay. He used her as a pawn. The Zenti implanted false memories into me that led me to believe she was dead. That I sacrificed her to save Biomei was the darkest and most painful experience I'd ever endured.

With Biomei's help, their dirty little plot was uncovered, and I learned that Nickada was not dead but had been taken by the Zenti. When I finally found her, she was barely alive. They tortured her and attempted to extract her knowledge of biogenetics. Biomei was Nicki's creation. Nicki was so brilliant." His eyes lit up as he spoke of her. "She created a new life-form with Biomei, and the Zenti wanted her knowledge at any cost. Once we uncovered their plan, I searched for her and never lost hope of finding her."

"Did you find her?"

"The war was over. The Zenti were defeated. Despite his defeat, Zohleemay couldn't let go of his hate. Nicki and I were finally reunited. During a long-awaited embrace, I saw him out of the corner of my eye. He stood, hissing with a grotesque sneer, holding a percussion grenade. He leered at us with eyes filled with burning hatred. Then, his face distorted in a dark, sinister smile as he released the detonator pin and let it fall to his side. There was no time to react. Nicki pushed me aside and fell on the grenade. The explosion was deafening. Everyone was killed."

He opened his tearful eyes and looked at Kathy. She could

feel and hear his pain as he spoke. "They were all killed, except for me. The Venubians used Nicki's logs and rebuilt me again. They believed I was a superhero. They call me Uzil. It means *deliverer or messiah*. Take your pick," he laughed. "That's the burden I carry. I'm the Venubian messiah."

Kathy pulled on her ear in thought. "So, what you're telling me is this whole thing is about your guilt and revenge. This is all about you?" Kathy got up close to Territaff, then regarded him with restrained anger. "Please tell me there's more going on here than your quest for revenge."

"Revenge is a big part of it," Territaff confessed. "It's also about saving Earth and the Venubian system from a madman who won't stop until he's destroyed all our worlds. He's your worst nightmare—a genetically engineered villain. He's neither humanoid nor machine. You can't reason with him because he lacks compassion, conscience, and remorse. The Zenti is a genetic mistake that their designers discarded. They've become the scourge of the galaxy, killing and pillaging for technology. The Venubians thought they had rid themselves of them, but they only delayed the Zenti for a while. As long as Zohleemay lives, he's a threat to everything that comes in his path. He's a vicious predator that kills for both the thrill and resources that his prey can provide, then leaves a trail of putrefied carcasses in his wake. He's pure evil, and I must destroy him."

Kathy shook her head in disbelief. "Your motives are very clouded, Terri. I pray for all our sakes that we're not on a fool's errand." She narrowed her eyes. "You do have a rational plan?"

"We do, and before Biomei releases the download into your memory, you have a choice."

"And that is?"

"Biomei can erase all your memories and knowledge of everything that has happened since we've met. I can return you to Earth, and you'll awake in a hospital as though you have recovered from a bad fall that will account for the loss of time and memory. We can alter your appearance and DNA and give you a new identity. We'll provide you with sufficient funds to live well anywhere you choose. Zohleemay wouldn't need you. You'd no longer pose any threat to him. Therefore, I don't believe he'd risk exposure by going after you. Or..." he paused for a moment to read Kathy's body language. Her demeanor stiffened, looking stoic. Her control impressed him.

"Or?" she prompted.

"Or you can complete the transformation and become a permanent member of the team. It would be an awful waste of valuable resources to send you back. However, once you complete the procedure, you'll never be able to go home again. You'll never be able to return as Kathy Jordan of Miami Beach. That person will no longer exist."

"Are you trying to scare me?"

"No. Just giving you a true picture of the situation."

"I never really knew, Kathy Jordan, but I'm beginning to understand who I am now," she said with a sly smile.

"Oh yeah? So, who are you?"

"The team member who'll keep you focused because you're really screwed up."

He drew her close, and they hugged.

"You sound pretty sure of yourself," he said, gently caressing her cheek. *She's so different from Nicki. Yet she possesses many of her qualities.* "I need your strength and honesty."

"You've done for me almost what Nickada did for you. You gave me a new life. My life felt like a trap, living a dull and meaningless existence. I had no passion, no desire, and no direction. I only knew I was meant for something better, something with purpose. You've given me all that and so much more. Now, I know the universe put me here for this very reason." She smiled and patted Territaff's face. "Thank you. I have finally found something important and have a direction. My job is to make sure you keep your eye on the ball."

Territaff's face lit up with joy and relief. He looked as though a great weight had been lifted from him.

"It's funny, but I never appreciated what Nickada had done for me until now. You're right. The universe did put you here." Territaff looked into Kathy's face, placed his hand behind her head, and moved her close for a kiss. At first, they kissed gently, then more passionately. When they finished, they stared at each other for a long moment before Territaff pointed to a corner of the arboretum and said, "Let's sit over there and listen to the trees for a while."

CHAPTER 23

"Terri, it's time," Kathy said, rising from the wooden bench under a large oak tree. "I understand why you love this place. It's like a little slice of home."

"It's also a slice of your future home."

"Venubia?"

He nodded. "Actually, there's life from over twenty planets here."

Kathy looked around. "I only dreamed what life would be like on different planets, and now I'm among alien life and don't even recognize it. Is all alien life so much like ours?"

"Only what's represented in this arboretum. Everything here comes from planets with atmospheres and gravity similar to those of Earth and Venubia. There are countless weird and wondrous worlds out there. The Venubians and their neighbors, the Kaydens and Klaxons, have only explored their immediate systems. There's so much out there, Kathy, but it's still far from our reach. The distances remain beyond our ability to traverse."

"But you have the corridors. Why can't you create more of them?"

"The technologies that make up the corridors were created by a long-extinct species known as the Ezdenian. Even after millennia of analysis and experimentation, the Venubians have only uncovered the primary elements that comprise the corridors.

"They're artificial portals that require large quantities of antigravitons combined with entangled energy. It's an exotic mix of energy and matter that we haven't been able to duplicate. Some believed it to be a new form of energy. Like so many things about the corridors, it's another mystery. Anyway, it's a rare combination of elements. These elements only exist near massive gravitational forces like those found near black holes and neutron stars. Creating the corridors is limited to where these forces exist. Folding spacetime is not only a delicate matter; it's also dangerous. So far, the corridors have remained stable for over two hundred millennia. But they can collapse without warning."

"Wow, there's so much I need to learn. I can't wait to complete the transformation procedure." Kathy's eyes grew wide at the thought.

Territaff regarded her enthusiasm with guarded concern. He stood, took her hand, and looked into her alluring green eyes.

"Remember, your basic personality will always be part of you, but you'll feel and think differently."

"Different? How?"

"I can't explain that to you, but you'll know soon enough."

"There you go again, being cryptic as usual," Kathy said. "Jesus, can't you even give me a hint?"

He gave her a thoughtful smile and pointed to the exit, "Well, you won't be such a persistent pain-in-the-ass about having to know every little thing."

"Oh yeah. Why's that?"

"Because you'll already know everything, and your mind will need time to assimilate it all."

"So, how'll that change me?"

"You'll be a lot like Cuz was when we first met. He was a clueless nerd with a head full of knowledge and no idea what to do with it all."

"Well, I could do worse. He hasn't turned out so bad. He's the nicest guy on this ship."

Biomei asked, "Are you ready?"

"Yes," Kathy said. "I can't explain what I'm feeling right now. I believe that, somehow, I was meant to do this. It feels like I'm fulfilling my destiny or some higher spiritual purpose. I know how this sounds. It probably makes little sense or may even sound a little hokey, but I know the universe has delivered you for this reason."

"I know from experience that things happen for specific reasons," Territaff said. "The Venubians believe the universe is a living entity unto itself. I've come to believe that as well; it must be. To paraphrase an old Earth religious proverb: The universe moves in mysterious ways. So, my dear Kathy, we have all come together under the most extraordinary circumstances. For better or worse, we're inexorably connected."

Kathy went into the med lab and hopped onto the table like an excited child. Territaff watched her through the clear observation window with guarded happiness. *She has a beautiful innocence, and I know she will be lost.* The thought lingered with him as he went to join Cuz on the bridge.

* * *

Territaff found Cuz busy at the holographic communications console. "What is it, Cuz?" Territaff asked as he looked over Cuz's shoulder.

"We need to go back to Earth."

"What have you heard?"

"Zohleemay has made a copy of the Ezdenian Disc."

Territaff looked at Cuz with a whimsical smile.

"You seemed pleased, Terri. Are you not concerned that the Zenti now have plans to build an autonomous android with a biogenetic neocortical net?"

"What have you learned?" he asked, looking more curious than concerned.

"Zohleemay has convinced the US Defense Department that we were industrial spies posing as cybernetic specialists. He also accused and somehow convinced the Pentagon that DARPA was incompetent in its background investigation, allowing established spies to consult on the project. He produced uncontroversial evidence of our alleged subterfuge. Now, the Defense Department has pulled the project from DARPA. Additionally, they have initiated a thorough investigation and issued subpoenas for us to appear before a congressional committee. Zohleemay has successfully discredited us while gaining complete control over the project. General Dickerson is now the government liaison, responsible for project management and oversight. Zohleemay has positioned himself as the sole developer of what appears to be a Venubian Android prototype. The Pentagon believes it'll be the first military to possess a programmable, genetically engineered cyber-soldier.

"We have also confirmed that Zohleemay has gained long-term morphing capabilities and humanoid personality matrices. How he has managed all of this remains unknown."

"Interesting," Territaff said.

"What's remarkable, Terri, is that he's somehow gained the trust of the highest echelon of the US Government, awarded a well-funded contract with total autonomy to build the ultimate automated soldier. This is most distressing. How could they have been so easily deceived? He gave Territaff a careful look. "Why do you appear so unconcerned?"

"How will Zohleemay pass off a Venubian Service Android as a genetically engineered cyber-soldier when the plans for its brain won't work?"

Cuz furrowed his brow, confused. "I believe I'm missing something?"

"As is Zohleemay," Territaff said, looking pleased. "Tell me what you heard from Venubia."

"Venubian security has uncovered a detailed record that Zohleemay had created to establish his cover. It has family records, birth certificates, and several academic degrees from a legitimate university. He's left no, as you like to say, holes in his profile. For all intents and purposes, Zohleemay is Doctor Zoh DeZenti."

Territaff pulled on his right earlobe in thought. "He couldn't have accomplished this elaborate impersonation without a lot of inside help."

"Biomei and I have reached the same conclusion. The question is, from whom and why?"

"Whoever they are, they will only last as long as they're useful to Zohleemay. We're all aware of Zohleemay's dislike of partners. Now, who could be low enough, or desperate enough, to get in bed with the devil?"

"Should we compile a list of possible suspects?" Biomei asked.

"I was being rhetorical, Biomei," Territaff said, then considered her suggestion. "However, it might be helpful at that. At least it's a place to start. Biomei, trace all Zohleemay's contacts and anyone high enough up the government food chain to be a viable partner. I'd include both public and private sectors in your search parameters.

"Cuz, Kathy will need a little time to recover from the final phase of the transformation. I need you to watch the situation on Earth. At some point, Zohleemay will slip up, and that's when we'll make our move. I'm going to Lunneziah and get Karoft. He has all the expertise we need. Nobody knows Zohleemay and the Zenti better than he. He also possesses the military and governmental expertise to help us secure the assistance from the Department of Defense."

"Do you think it's wise to leave now?"

"Do you have a better plan?"

Cuz thought for a moment, then shrugged and said, "This fucks up our original plan."

Territaff arched an eyebrow in surprise. "What's up with your language?"

"I've been reading some American detective novels from the mid-1970s. I found their use of idioms to be the most colorful. Don't you agree?"

"I think you need to work on the timing a little. Cuz that was profanity, not an idiom."

"I don't understand."

"We'll discuss that later. In the meantime, continue

updating our situation with Venubian security. I also need you to contact Karoft to arrange a transit permit for me through the corridor. Don't get into details about our situation or my reason for coming. Karoft is sharp and knows something's up. It wouldn't surprise me if he knew our current situation.

"Are you sure about going to Lunneziah? If Zohleemay is already executing what appears to be an elaborate plan, he'll have associates placed on all the major Venubian and Kayden territories."

"I'm counting on it. I hope my going to Lunneziah will confuse Zohleemay and make him send some of his associates after me. He's clever but lacks the sophistication to see a plan like this through. His people are slow-witted and easily fooled. If we can provide them with some disinformation, it may force Zohleemay to reveal at least part of his plan to us. It's a good idea if for no other reason than to make him expend resources, he's already short on.

"He's getting help, and whoever's behind the scenes is the real problem and, most likely, the real brains of the operation. If we can throw enough distractions at them, we may get them to come out into the open."

"I see the merits of your plan, Terri," Biomei interjected. "Yet, is it wise to go to such a dangerous place alone?"

Cuz said, "Taking the shuttle through the corridor could also be dangerous. We haven't had a chance to install an environmental medium. You'll also be exposed to high radiation levels and powerful gravimetric forces."

"I appreciate your concern, but I think I'll be fine. Remember, we reinforced the hull with altirium."

"My concern was not for you," Cuz smirked. "It would be a shame to lose the shuttle after spending so much time and resources on its retrofit."

"Very funny, Cuz. I'll take good care of it and keep in constant contact with you. If, by some chance, Zohleemay makes a move before my return, try to enlist General

Dickerson's help. I think we can convince him that Zoh is not who and what he appears to be. I got the impression that the good General knows Zoh is full of crap and wants to prove it. When Kathy is up for it, see if you two can contact the general. Don't give him any information about who we are. Only give him enough info to look more closely at Dr. DeZenti. Unless you have no other choice, stay out of Zohleemay's way. Sooner or later, he's bound to screw up. Biomei, I'm leaving everything in your capable hands. Watch over them, and don't let them do anything stupid."

Cuz gave Territaff a puzzled frown and said, "That was an inaccurate and unwarranted statement. I don't recall ever doing anything stupid."

Territaff patted his cheek and said, "There's a first time for everything, my friend."

Cuz pondered his statement for a moment, then realized something and asked, "Terri, if Zohleemay has the plans for biogenetic androids... he can build a new army—"

"He can't," Territaff interrupted. "The disc in Kathy's refrigerator was a decoy. It's full of disinformation."

"Won't he figure that out?"

"Most likely, but hopefully not for some time. Zohleemay is clever but lacks the expertise to recognize the missing information. It won't be long before the military figures out that his 'Cyber-Soldier' is another billion-dollar failure and cuts off his funding.

"So, you used Kathy as a decoy. You knowingly put her life in danger. Why?"

"It seemed like a good plan at the time. I underestimated Zohleemay, which I won't let happen again."

"Your methods seem questionable at times."

"I agree, Cuz. There's an old Earth saying: All is fair in love and war."

"I don't understand."

"I hope you never do, my friend."

CHAPTER 24

"Computer on," Territaff said, waving his hand over rows of sensors.

A spectrum of colored lights glowed on throughout the shuttle's compact interior. The aft bay doors opened, revealing the great expanse of space ahead and the gray and white frozen world of Europa beneath. Territaff pondered Europa's bright surface for a moment, regretting that he didn't have time to explore the moon's hidden oceans. *There's life underneath that frozen surface waiting to be discovered. One day, I will visit your depths and uncover your secrets...* He smiled.

For Territaff, space was still a place of fascination and adventure. It was also an unforgiving environment fraught with danger and death. The simplest of mistakes could cost you your life. Surviving in space took exceptional courage. Even genetically engineering one's body could not protect against the deadly tapestry of deep space, primarily from unknown phenomena.

A view screen lit up above the central console. He magnified a tiny blue and white orb in the lower right corner of the screen. He gazed at it and smiled. "My lovely and troubled little world." Then he reflected on Kathy, "Good luck, Kathy," he whispered, then commanded the computer, "Tie-in."

"Tie-in completed. Welcome back, Territaff," the ship's emulated voice cheerfully greeted him.

"Thank you, Hanc. It's good to have you aboard."

"Systems status?"

"All systems are nominal," Hanc reported.

"Prepare inertial guidance for departure."

Territaff glanced over the navigational charts as they scrolled on his built-in optical sensors.

"Territaff."

"Yes, Hanc."

"I have been monitoring the Earth's various communication transmissions. I must admit, they are among the most colorful and disturbing things I have ever inputted. They seem to be a diverse and imaginative species. I also noticed how immature they act and appear so violent at times."

"What's the basis of your uneasiness?"

"Are you intending to initiate 'First Contact' with them?"

"It seems that the Zenti situation will make that almost unavoidable. However, I believe we'll be able to contain our contact with only a few essential individuals."

"Is there not a risk of exposing them to advanced technology?"

"I think I understand, Hanc. We've taken what humans would call a calculated risk."

There was a pause as Hanc pondered Territaff's answer.

"Ah," he emulated. "A risk that has a low probability of occurrence."

"Yes, something like that."

"Query?"

"Yes, Hanc."

"I am curious about humans. Are they as emotionally inconsistent as their transmissions suggest? Could they be more developed than they appear? Like our late Brother Phillip?"

Hanc's reference to Phillip Mann took Territaff aback. Then he remembered Hanc did not know of his transformation. He insisted those chapters of his life be withheld from the official Venubian record. Territaff argued that it would have been in the best interest of national security for his reboot, as he referred to it, to remain sealed. He was tempted to ask Hanc to explain the reference, but decided against it.

"Humanity is showing signs of becoming more mature and civilized over the next millennium, Territaff said. "And remember, Brother Phillip was a human before he came to

Venubia."

"I know," Hanc blurted. "After downloading his biography from the central record, I often wondered why Nickada had taken such a risk."

"I'm not sure I'm following you, Hanc. "What would you like to know?"

"Was it not dangerous for her to be among them so long?"

Territaff smiled inwardly and said, "She limited herself to minimal contact with the humans."

"That was prudent. Earth women seem complicated. How do you manage a meaningful relationship with them?"

"Hanc, is there something specific you wish to know?"

"I will now come to the central point of my query. Do you love her?"

"You mean... Kathy?" He was surprised by Hanc's inquiry, then realized the source of his curiosity. "You've been picking up some of my random thought patterns again."

"Please forgive the intrusion, Terri. I do inadvertently sense any strong emotional patterns when you tie in. They are most intriguing, and I was curious about your feelings for her."

"That could be dangerous to your mental health, Hanc," Territaff teased, recalling a paranoid computer in one book he scanned in Kathy's apartment.

"I did not understand your last statement. Would you care to elaborate?"

"Not now."

"One last query?"

"What?"

"At this point, would you consider the mission a success?"

Territaff thought for a moment, then let out a low sigh. "Only time will tell if we're successful, Hanc." He looked directly into the computer's optical sensor as he spoke. "Biomei is safe." He reflected on the decoy disc and thought, at least, I hope so.

"I gather by your tone you still have reservations about the mission's success."

"I've reservations about everything."

He reached down to the right side of his command chair and pressed his thumb on a security lock concealed in a small compartment in the lower half of the chair. The lock oscillated open, revealing a thin, clear crystal. He removed the crystal and inserted it into a small, implanted sinus cavity at the base of his head.

His large, intense eyes glowed as the crystal initialized his autonomic systems. He could sense his humanoid personality being overtaken. In a few seconds, he would become a living machine, interfacing and interacting with the other machines that comprised his ship. The conversion was subtle. His humanoid persona would be repressed, creating a highly ordered, precise, logical thinking process.

He was now half-humanoid and half-machine, but the combination didn't form a complete being. There was always a part of him in transition, ever eluding a state of completeness. However, he was still considered a sentient being; a part of him sought what Phillip Mann once possessed. A true spiritual consciousness and a state of inner peace were always within his grasp, yet, for reasons unknown, he consciously avoided them.

The absorption process was completed. Territaff was integrated with his ship.

"Prepare to leave orbit," Territaff transmitted.

An infrared starfield blinked on his internal view-screen.

"Venubian Corridor-44 coordinates."

There was a brief pause as the computer fixed the position. A white cursor flashed briefly, indicating that the coordinates were locked into the navigation computer.

"Enable inertial guidance system."

"Enable neutrino deflector field."

"Enabled."

"Prepare for muon impulse drive."

"Ready."

"Stealth field."

"Field activated.

"Prepare 12-G acceleration."

"Caution, internal suspension medium is unavailable," the environmental system transmitted.

"Override," Territaff transmitted.

"Ready."

Territaff braced himself and transmitted, *"Engage."*

The tritium engines fired, catapulting the compact ship out of the solar system. Hanc prompted Territaff for a complete power-up burn. He acknowledged. The ship's two main plasma engines ignited, increasing velocity to almost one-quarter lightspeed. The ship's velocity will approach three-quarters of lightspeed within a few Earth days.

Territaff's autonomic half could not question this, but his humanoid half pondered the necessity to tell Karoft anything in advance.

"Shut down mode," Territaff instructed the computer.

He went into stasis mode to conserve energy. His eyes regained their onyx luster momentarily as his autonomic system gave way to his humanoid manifestations. A beat later, he was suspended into a dark, dreamless state.

CHAPTER 25

The ship's auto-alert signal brought Territaff back to consciousness. He checked the forward and aft views, then reviewed the ship's systems. Everything was in an alert condition.

"Report?" he said.

"Unidentified object," the computer responded.

"Type?"

"Unknown."

"We're close to the corridor. Does it conform to any possible Kayden or Klaxon configurations?"

"Negative. It has a unique configuration with a high-energy signature."

"Do you have a fix on it?"

"Its signature is elusive to our telemetry. I have been attempting to obtain a fix using both wide and narrow-range tracking sensors, but I have been unable to establish a lock. It is as though it has no definitive locality other than its power signature."

"Try a gamma burst and attempt to lock on to the reflected particles."

"I have already attempted that without a definitive reflection. I am compensating by transferring more energy to the sensor array. Stand by while I attempt another burst." Hanc briefly paused. "I have identified an approximate location of the secondary gamma burst. It now appears to be maintaining a position outside of our long-range telemetry. I have extrapolated that its trajectory would come out of sector J-2-0-3-7."

"Very curious, Hanc, that would place its origin outside Earth's system. Now, who could've sent such a sophisticated device from that sector? Certainly not the Zenti or the humans. It's beyond both of their capabilities."

"I pondered that myself, Terri. That is why I brought you back online. I have been tracking its movements for some time now. It is pursuing our course through our plasma signature."

"Is it close enough for a visual?"

"It has a curious cloaking capability. The dynamics of the masking field are created by a strange non-locality phenomenon rather than through meta-lensing. I must admit that it is an intriguing technology. It suggests that some form of negative energy is generating it."

"What you're describing, Hanc, is remarkable. How were you tracking it?"

By realigning our long-range sensors to encompass any esoteric matter. I have traced its movements through its interaction with the surrounding high-energy particles in its wake. The problem is that the residual energy signature fluctuates, making it difficult to determine its exact location. It appears to be oscillating on multidimensional levels. Its power signature appears one moment, and the next, it is gone."

"So, you can only tell me where it's been, not where it is?"

"Affirmative."

"Send an alert message to Venubian control and Biomei. Maybe they can—"

"Alert, an unidentified object is on an intercept course," the ship's auto-defense system advised.

Transfer the data stream from the sensor tracks to the unidentified device. Prepare for evasive maneuvers."

"Terri, telemetry has updated me. It's jamming us on all frequencies."

"Warning," the auto-defense system announced. "The unidentified device has locked on. Its power signature has increased by 47 percent."

"It has taken a hostile posture, Terri," Hanc reported with emulated concern.

Interesting, Territaff thought, gazing at the blinking red light on the navigation monitor.

Territaff switched himself back into his autonomic state, into a full military construct. The ship's propulsion and navigation systems were running through him again.

"The unidentified device is in range and locked," the auto defense updated. "Data confirms that it has taken an attack vector and is closing."

"Evasive maneuver Alpha-one-seven," Territaff transmitted to navigation.

The ship engines engaged, thrusting the craft into high acceleration. Then it made an abrupt starboard bank into a wide arc and pulled its nose into a ninety-degree, full-powered, upward burst from its relative position.

"The unidentified device is still locked on," the auto-defense system advised.

Territaff had the ship make several quick turns, pushing it to the limits of its capabilities. However, his efforts were ineffective in freeing his ship from the closing unidentified object.

"If we can't outmaneuver it, let's see if we can outrun it," Territaff transmitted.

Hanc transmitted, *"Full power-up in five... four... three... two... one... Full power engaged."*

The small ship vibrated under the strain of being pushed so hard.

"I have visual," Hanc advised.

"Let's see it." Territaff stared at the streamlined device closing in on him. "It's a surprisingly simple design. Do you recognize it?"

"It is so generic I cannot ascertain a specific design feature that would associate it with any known group."

"How about its subspace turbulence?"

"The particle-wave dispersion exhibits a familiar pattern, but it's akin to trying to identify a rock from the ripples it creates when it hits the water. Without the benefit of closer analysis, I cannot ascertain anything definitive."

"The unidentified object is now 1052.5 kilometers and closing," the auto-defense system updated.

"We don't seem to be outrunning it, Hanc."

"I have been able to establish a sensor read on its payload. It is a deuterium, iridennium compound suspended in a magnetic bottle. I could not detect any mechanical or electronic detonation mechanism."

"That's an odd mix."

"Impact imminent in 400 kilometers," the auto-defense system announced.

"Hanc, wouldn't an unstable combination of deuterium and iridennium have a built-in safety mechanism to prevent premature detonation?"

"We need to be much closer to make such an assertion."

"It will be close enough in a few clicks. Hypothesize."

"I have identified the device's configuration. It is a form of a ramjet plasma-drive missile. It scoops up, converts the surrounding hydrogen into tritium, heats the mixture into plasma for propulsion, and exposes the iridennium to the plasma stream for detonation. It is a remarkable device. Mechanisms of similar configurations track their targets and detonate on impact by breaking the magnetic containment field. However, this one is different. Systems of this type are used in short-range deployments. This one could track its target indefinitely. There is one additional element that seems to be missing."

"What's that?"

"How could it track us through all those high-energy particle fields? I detect no telemetry. Up to this point, it has locked onto our power signature, even though we have changed it several times during our evasive maneuvers."

"How's that possible?"

"There is only one workable conclusion. It must be guided by some outside means."

"Impact imminent in 7.55 microns," the auto-defense

system updated.

"Are you suggesting the device is being manually guided?"

"That would be the most logical conclusion."

"That's most illuminating, Hanc, but we don't have time to discuss its guidance system.

"Impact imminent in 5.50 microns."

"Hanc, postulate what would occur if we flew through an area that lies between the powerful gravitational fields of the corridor and the event horizon of a black hole?" Is it possible that the high concentration of positron radiation from the black hole and the strong gravitational waves from the corridor's mouth confuse whatever controls the device's tracking?"

"I believe I follow your line of thought. If the missile has sensor tracking, it will lock on to the stronger radiation output of the black hole. Manual tracking would make the same decision or back off until it has a better read."

"Precisely, Hanc. Where's the black hole's strongest concentration in this quadrant?"

"Sector 183. I should caution that it would bring us dangerously close to the event horizon."

"Acknowledged."

Territaff gave the nav com the new heading, then calculated the small ship's combined thrust.

"It'll be close," Territaff transmitted while engaging the engines.

If the compact star cruiser were an animate creature, it would have screamed in pain as it burst into three-quarters light speed in 85 milliseconds with 33Gs of thrust power. Even in his autonomic state, Territaff was impressed with how well his ship performed.

"Territaff, the device has disengaged and is now on a new heading."

"Give me the new heading."

"180.23. It is heading for the corridor."

The revelation struck Territaff with a heavy jolt. Even in his present condition, his small human part was in a state of painful disbelief about the folly of his actions.

I led it right to the corridor. The thought was like a dagger in his mind. Territaff reflected for a moment. The Zenti couldn't be so diabolically clever to pull off such a maneuver. They have made a pact with the devil for sure.

Then a thought came to mind. "Hanc, we must position ourselves between the device and the corridor. If we override the plasma containment, then we can eject a stream of high-energy particles and ignite it with the muon thrusters. "

"It would, Terri. However, the shock wave from such an explosion will release high-energy positrons and gamma radiation. A possible matter-antimatter eruption so close to the corridor will spew a cascade of tachyons and antineutrinos sufficient to collapse the corridor and annihilate everything in this quadrant."

"I've considered that," Territaff said, thinking that a matter-antimatter event of that magnitude could also cause a temporal rift, momentarily displacing the local spacetime by 0.27 picrons. Enough time to go through the corridor before it closes. "While I can't believe the Zenti is capable of such a sophisticated mechanism, I'm hoping its designers didn't consider the countermeasure we're attempting."

"Your plan has a point twenty—"

"Forget about that?"

"I sure hope you're right," Hanc said with an emulated sigh. "Collapsing the corridor could have long-term ramifications, but then we will most likely not be around to know if it worked."

"Do you have a better alternative?"

"I will begin the override of the magnetic containment field. On my mark, you will engage the muon-thrusters. " Mark in... three... two... one..."

CHAPTER 26

Kathy's mind was filled with vague images. She struggled to focus on flashing strands of distorted forms, colors, and sounds. Although initially disconcerting, she relaxed when she heard Biomei's quiet voice reassuring her that what she was experiencing was normal.

"The bioscanner is reading and adjusting to your body's biochemical and electromagnetic configurations," Biomei explained. *"The images you're seeing are random bioelectric feedback strings. Try to ignore them. They'll soon dissipate, and the procedure will become apparent."*

"I understand," Kathy transmitted. *"Thanks, Biomei. I don't know what I'd do without you."*

"I must leave now. Stay calm; remember that what you're experiencing is not real and can't harm you. Some of it will be unpleasant, and some will be wonderful."

"Wait, why do you have to leave?"

Biomei noticed that Kathy's heart rate and blood pressure were rising.

"Calm down, my child. There's no need for anxiety. I can't interject myself into the procedure because it would distort the process. Cuz and I'll be monitoring your progress. Trust your instincts. They serve you well."

While Biomei's words reassured Kathy, her enthusiasm waned a bit, as she knew she had to face the unknown alone.

She wiggled on the couch until it readjusted to her comfort. Then, she took a deep breath, closed her eyes, and anticipated the start of the procedure. She listened to the scanner's low-pitched whine as its soft, blue light progressed over her body. The whine stopped, and the light turned off. Kathy was immersed in dark silence. It was a void so dark and quiet that she could hear her heart beating under the ragged rhythm of her breathing.

I've felt this before, Kathy thought. This is from my

childhood. The first night in foster care. After her grandparents were killed in that terrible car accident, she cried at the memory. They left her in a dark and empty room, anxiously waiting for anyone to come and take her away from the horrifying emptiness.

Her mind was fixed on how alone and frightened she felt. Therefore, she resorted to what had saved her in the past: talking to herself.

"Okay, this is only temporary," she whispered. "Nothing can harm me. Biomei said some of this would be unpleasant. You were right, Biomei!" she shouted, "This is unpleasant. In fact, it's downright shitty. When's the good stuff starting?"

The sounds of indiscernible voices abated her fear. They were talking rapidly in a melodic flow of strange clicks and sounds. The voices changed, becoming clear. They adopted a familiar intonation, and their rhythms made her feel more at ease. She felt herself falling into a gentle lull from the melodic stream of the soft voices.

Kathy listened. The sounds took form. Although their language was not English, she understood a word here and there as though she were learning the language of the voices as they spoke.

"Uzil came from Earth to save us." She heard a voice say.

"Uzil is different now. Someone new takes his place," another voice said.

"Now, you must learn what Uzil learned," the first voice demanded.

"I must learn what?" Kathy said.

"Everything," the two voices said in unison.

"The universe will speak to you now. Each element has its sound to blend into the concerts of harmonies of creation," a chorus of voices sang out.

A new voice sounded as if it were speaking from a distance. "Prepare. The learning begins."

A burst of colors flashed before Kathy. It dissipated like

fireworks on a clear night's sky.

Kathy found herself seated in a comfortable chair. She looked around and saw only the chair beneath her. She was sitting in a vast white void.

"I'm Venubia," a warm, feminine voice said, sounding beside her.

"Where are you? I can't see you," Kathy said.

"I'm here beside you."

Kathy was startled by the sudden appearance of a woman standing by her. She looked as Biomei had described a typical Venubian. She was short, only about one and a quarter meters. Her slender, angular body was covered by a long, flowing white dress reminiscent of ancient Greek attire. It was low-cut with a gold rope belt around her midriff, accentuating her narrow hips and small, rounded breasts. Her skin and hair were as white as her dress. Her high forehead and oval face ended in a square chin. The woman's large, oval eyes shone with an intelligent glow above her small, button nose. Kathy studied her as she stood, her round red lips upturned into a pleasant smile. Her features looked alien, but Kathy felt at ease in her presence.

Kathy looked at the woman closer and said, "I think I know you, but I don't know how."

The Venubian's large eyes studied Kathy for a moment, "You know me on an instinctive level from the first phase of your transformation procedure."

After a moment's thought, she recalled the woman's image. "You were my guide through the first procedure."

"Yes, you remember. That's good. I'm here in the same capacity with you now."

"Do you exist outside of this mental construct?"

"That's an interesting question. However, I believe you already know the answer. Look inside your consciousness, Kathy."

"How do I do that?"

"Give yourself a moment. It will come to you." Her guide placed her delicate hand on Kathy's head. "Close your eyes and concentrate on my image. The data stream should appear to you as a clear memory."

Kathy closed her eyes, took a deep breath, and slowly exhaled. "Oh, I understand. There's no difference between conscious and unconscious reality. They're the same because it's all conscious energy in different states of perception."

"Excellent," she nodded approvingly. "A sub-neural processor will be inserted into the right quadrant of your cerebral cortex. A sub-processor will be connected to your hypothalamus. It's a painless procedure, but necessary."

"What's it for?"

"It will facilitate the storing and processing of data streams into your long-term memory. All humanoid brains are limited to how much data they can hold without neuron signal reduction. The human brain is miraculous on many levels and efficient in processing data, but it has a finite memory capacity. The processor is similar to a digital computer compiler, as it takes code in the form of electrical impulses and translates it into usable data. Once the device is initialized, it will enhance your memory, all your body's senses, and various functions. Would you care to watch the procedure?"

"I can watch it being inserted into my brain?"

She nodded.

Kathy thought for a moment and said, "Sure," excited by the prospect of seeing herself in such a unique way. "What do I need to do?"

"Look straight ahead. The images will appear in a moment."

Kathy stared outward and then stood, seeing a three-dimensional image of herself lying on the couch in the Med Lab. It seemed as though she was standing outside her own body, looking in. The image looked close enough to touch.

"How's this possible?" she asked, mesmerized and odd at seeing herself that way.

"It's a holographic construct created from the entangled particles inside your eyes, then transmitted through the optic nerves."

"Are you telling me I'm seeing this with my own eyes, in my mind, on an imaginary, three-dimensional construct?"

"Very good, and you did that all on your own."

Kathy watched dumbfounded as an automated arm swung over her image's head, then stopped within centimeters of her forehead. The instrument slid out a long, thin arm from a sleeve. A tiny dot of amber light became visible a few centimeters above her right eye. Then, a high-pitched whine was heard. Kathy felt a pinprick on her forehead as the narrow device burrowed into her skull.

"This is so weird," Kathy said. "I can feel the device working as I'm watching it."

"You're not in any discomfort, are you?"

She screwed up her face into a puzzled expression. "No, it doesn't hurt, but I feel something on my forehead. It's a strange sensation."

"That's a normal reaction. The procedure is almost complete."

Kathy could see a real-time image of her brain on a monitor above the couch. She noticed a faint dot centered on the right lobe of her cerebral cortex.

"Is that it? It's almost microscopic. I thought such a complex device would be bigger. You guys have miniaturization down."

"Yours is slightly larger than the one we inserted in Territaff, but his brain had already been configured."

"Configured?" Kathy looked closely at her guide's face. "What do you mean?"

"I'm sorry. I thought you knew of Territaff's retrofit."

"Are you telling me that Terri is an android like Cuz?"

"No, Territaff is not an android. He's considered a hybrid humanoid."

Kathy's mouth became dry, and her head throbbed. She wasn't sure if the jolting news or the stress of the procedure had caused the pain.

The guide looked at Kathy's flushed complexion, bewildered by her sudden physical changes.

"Kathy, you must calm yourself, or we won't be able to continue." The guide reached out and placed her hand over Kathy's left eye, her fingers spreading across her forehead and upper cheek. The guide concentrated on Kathy and then removed her hand.

"I did not understand that this information would affect you in this manner. Please forgive me," the guide said.

"I'm sorry," Kathy said, feeling self-conscious. "It just took me by surprise. I guess everything around here will be full of surprises. I'm better now. Thank you." Kathy forced a smile to reassure her guide that she was okay.

The guide came closer to her and said, "I must inform you that once the memory integration begins, you'll be experiencing some intense data streams. I'm concerned about your emotional stability. Kathy, once the process begins, it can't be stopped. Are you certain you want to proceed?"

Her Venubian guide looked at her with the detached demeanor of an automaton awaiting instructions.

Kathy was taken aback by her guide's sudden change in attitude. She pondered her situation with growing apprehension. For the first time, she realized the magnitude of her decision. She recalled both Terri's and Biomei's cautions about the procedure. It was all coming to full fruition, and the reality of it became heavy upon her.

Am I ready for such a profound change? The thought made her pause and search for her true feelings. "There's no turning back, girl," she mumbled.

She looked at the strange woman standing before her with

an impassive expression. Her alabaster skin and cold, dark eyes reminded Kathy of a statue of a Greek goddess. Then Biomei's voice chimed in her head: *Nothing is real. It's all like a dream, and nothing can harm you.* Those words were like a life raft for her mind.

She gave the stoic woman a glowing smile and exclaimed, "Let's get this fucking thing over with."

The guide seemed to come alive again, giving Kathy a bemused grin.

"Does that mean you're ready?"

"Oh yes, I've been waiting for this my entire life."

The Venubian guide gave her an impassive look, then faded away.

"Wait, did you say your name is Venubia?" Kathy called out.

"Yes," the woman's disembodied voice answered.

"Like the planet."

"I am the planet."

She's the planet? Kathy thought. What the hell does that mean?

She was still pondering on her guide when she found herself reclining on the couch, immersed in darkness again.

CHAPTER 27

Territaff regained consciousness, floating in the shuttle's tiny life pod. He was back in his humanoid form, but was vague about how he had entered the pod or what had happened to his ship. He didn't know his location because the pod had no navigation systems. It was a little more than his ship's couch wrapped in life support. Communications were limited to a short-range lingual transmitter, a medium-range beacon, and a ship-to-ship intercom. Territaff hoped he was not too far from the corridor so his distress calls would be picked up quickly.

The chatter of voices soon became audible on the pod's comm system. The voices were speaking in Tungzi, a mishmash of several spacer languages. He regretted never taking the time to download the language's basic lexicon. Between his built-in universal translator and the ship's linguistic library, he never thought he would need to learn it. So much for planning for all contingencies, he chided himself.

The voices were reassuring, though. Territaff listened closely to discover if they were a search and rescue patrol or the usual chatter between ships in the area. After listening briefly, he recognized the speech patterns on one of the ships. Some of the words were Venubian. A broad smile grew as he picked up enough to recognize a familiar conversation. Ship captains exchanging stories is as ancient as ships themselves. It's a long-held custom that marks the welcome breaking of the monotony and solitude of deep-space travel. What was encouraging to Territaff was that the dialect of Tungzi they used had Venubian words commonly spoken on Lunneziah, which meant the ships must be close to the moon.

Then his spirit lightened, hearing Venubian being spoken to him.

"Unidentified pod," a synthetic voice spoke. "This is Bylar freighter coming to assist you." The message repeats in

Kayden and Klaxon. "Going to bring you aboard. Transporting to Lunnezian Central Control. Do you understand?"

"Understood," Territaff acknowledged. "Did you say Bylar freighter?"

"Affirmative. Locked onto your position and bringing you aboard soon," the emulated voice said.

"Acknowledged."

Territaff felt a sharp jolt as a towing tether attached to the small hull. He could already sense the intense emotions of the Bylars aboard the unseen ship as it lifted the pod into its cargo bay's belly.

"Crap," he muttered under his breath. "Why did it have to be Bylars?"

Territaff's limited experiences with Bylars could be summed up as eventful. They were not only freakish in appearance but also irascible by nature and almost impossible to reason with. For some inexplicable reason, they loved humans, but not in a flattering way. They viewed humans as wonderful pets and treated them accordingly.

Territaff's first exposure to Bylars was on Jo'vah, an industrial moon in the Venubian system. He recalled spending most of his time fending off the unwanted affections of a particular Bylar's wife. Their concept of affection for their pets included being cradled, stroked, and tucked in at bedtime, much like a mother would her newborn child. All this sounds innocent until you realize the bed was inside a cage.

The Bylar's wife would try to hand-feed Territaff raw meat and potatoes. They were general herbivores, but they thought the human diet somehow consisted of raw meat and potatoes. This misguided understanding of the human diet was most likely due to a conversation in which Territaff told a Bylar he craved a good steak and potato dinner. This offhand remark got misinterpreted in translation.

Also, it was customary for Bylar women to bathe their men. To Territaff's great dismay, this custom also included their pets.

He discovered it was difficult to convince a Bylar female that privacy was essential to humans, especially regarding washing and other toiletry matters.

It's believed their evolutionary path to dominance evolved from an avian species. Somewhere in their evolutionary development, a large bird evolved into a mammal. This odd mix gave rise to a two-and-a-half-meter-tall, four-hundred-kilogram creature with a bizarre combination of features, including an elongated, bird-like head adorned with colorful, peacock-like feathers, large hawkish eyes, and a long, thick neck.

Bylars are powerful, with muscular, broad torsos covered in soft, furry scales. The most menacing feature is their two thick arms, ending in hands that, besides having tool-grasping, opposable thumbs, also possess three long fingers with retractable, ten-inch, razor-sharp talons. This genetic oddity is supported on two thick predator-like legs. They can move quickly when needed, but usually they lumber around like elephants.

As Territaff was lifted into the cargo bay, he recalled his last encounter with a female Bylar. She was the mate of a Bylar with whom Territaff had been working during the previous Zenti Venubian war. Once she got a good look and a snootful of his pheromones, she seized him in her enormous, taloned hands and began stroking his head while making a cat-like purr. Territaff remembered how helpless he felt in her powerful grip and how demeaning it was to be handled that way.

At first, his Bylar acquaintance appeared amused but recognized Territaff's distress and came to his rescue. The ensuing disagreement between the couple was violent. If it weren't for his durable, reinforced skeletal structure and musculature, the incensed wife would have crushed him. Her grip on Territaff increased with her rising anger. She squawked and hissed, shaking Territaff with vicious indignation. It wasn't until her husband slashed her midriff with a swift slice from a talon, drawing blood, that she finally relented, putting Territaff down to the floor, then stormed out of the room. Territaff remembered the husband nonchalantly telling him not to worry; she heals quickly, seemingly unconcerned for his wife and him.

He was relieved when the hatch to his pod opened, and a male Bylar greeted him. Territaff made a fist, tapped his left shoulder, and then nodded in a typical Venubian greeting of gratitude and solicitation. He waited for the Bylar to acknowledge the greeting with the closing of his large eyes while nodding. Bylars are skeptical during first meetings with other species, and this one was no exception. Territaff got a modest nod, but his large eyes remained fixed on him.

The Bylar language is incomprehensible without the aid of a universal translator. They have no written language and communicate with various body and head movements, intermixed with loud clicks, squawks, and squeals that sound much like the raucous noise of Earth's crows when congregating in trees.

The Klaxons recognized the Bylars as distant avian cousins. They initially viewed them as great, heavy-duty laborers. Over time, they realized that the Bylar were intelligent and wanted to explore space like any other curious species. A historic agreement was reached between the Bylars and Klaxons. It was a simple agreement. The Klaxons would provide the Bylars with ships, technology, and training in exchange for their labor and protection when needed. It turned into an equitable agreement that had lasted for over three millennia.

"Where are we?" Territaff asked in Venubian, hoping the Bylar would understand. He pointed toward a wide ramp in a corner of the massive cargo bay. Bylars were too large and bulky to use lifts. Their ships were designed to spread things out instead of up. Territaff nodded, then looked around the bay. It was empty. He hoped it was empty because they were en route to pick up a shipment on Lunneziah rather than returning to their point of origin: Bylaria.

Territaff cringed at the deep-throated clicks, clacks, and shrieks of Bylars talking. He followed up the ramp, meeting Bylars along the way. Some would give him a curious look. Others seemed annoyed by his presence, but most made way for him. When he reached the main bridge, he was warmly greeted by its female captain.

Territaff looked on with mounting apprehension as he watched the captain take in a deep snoot full of his scent. Her great, hawkish eyes closed, and she inhaled, then let out a long exhale as though she was savoring each molecule of his pheromones. She approached Territaff cautiously as though he were a stray animal. Her eyes grew wide, looking as though she recognized Territaff.

"Ah, you Uzil?" she asked in a strange, high-pitched squeak, as if she inhaled helium before speaking.

Her eyes glowed, and Territaff noticed her neck feathers fanned outward in a beautiful display of Bylar excitement.

"Yes, I am," Territaff said. "How can I understand you?"

"Ship has speak-talk for 'ooman. It is new. You like?"

"Very much. Also surprised. How did you get such a new and upgraded linguistic program? And how do you know who I am?"

"Venubian do."

Territaff found this quite puzzling. He became suspicious of this incredible coincidence: being rescued by a Bylar ship with a brand-new linguistics program for humanoid languages, and how she knew who he was.

"When did Venubian do?" Territaff asked, trying to mimic Bylar's syntax.

"Just now, for your convenience," a familiar voice said from outside the hatchway of the main corridor.

Territaff turned, and to his surprise, Administrator Karoft was standing in the hatchway, trying to maintain a serious demeanor.

"You know how to get everybody's attention, old friend."

The two shook hands, then hugged, patting each other's shoulders.

"I'm so glad to see you," Territaff said.

"I wish I could say the same. I would've preferred different circumstances." Karoft's expression became apprehensive.

"Tell me what's going on. What happened to my shuttle?"

"Not here." He clutched Territaff's arm and led him to a remote corner of the massive bridge. "The situation on Earth has become more serious," he spoke in a low, urgent voice. "The Bylars will dock in their sector on the far side of the moon as a precaution. They're assisting us with our mutual problem, but don't have all the details."

"How much do you know?"

"A lot has happened since you left Biomei." Karoft turned and spoke to the Bylar captain in Tungzi. She closed her eyes in acknowledgment. "I told her where to dock and to ensure you're escorted to a prearranged, secure location."

"Meet you at Larzz's," Territaff said.

Karoft frowned and said, "I had something a little more secure in mind."

"I can't come to Lunneziah without seeing Larzz. Besides, his place is as safe as it gets."

Karoft nodded, then managed a thin smile. "Trouble always seems to follow you, Terri." He shook his head and started for the hatchway, then turned. "By the way, you were not in the shuttle that exploded outside the corridor. You were taken here from Venubia on this Bylar transport. Understood?"

"So, what you're telling me is that everyone knows about the explosion, but no details as to who or what was in the shuttle."

"That's close enough." He shrugged and left, mumbling in Venubian.

CHAPTER 28

Kathy was bathed in light that gave her an angelic glow. Her heart raced, and her blood pressure had climbed dangerously high. She wasn't aware of her metabolic condition because she was transfixed by the horror being downloaded into her implanted compiler.

"Her biorhythms appear to be erratic," Cuz said. "Is she in as much distress as these readings suggest?"

"Venubian and human brains have similar morphologies but differ in physiological processing. Human intelligence is limited by their brain's capacity to create new neural connections through a complex interaction of physics and chemistry. The physical limitations of entropy could be overcome by altering the design of the neurons and axons. The Venubian brain evolved a more streamlined physiology through gradual genetic engineering."

"You're referring to the Android Epoch."

"Yes. After the technological singularity, Kathy discovered that androids have made many enhancements to Venubian physiology," Biomei explained. "Neurons were miniaturized, and axons shortened to enable greater capacity. This permitted the development of new, more layered folds and lobes within the cerebral cortex. The increased capacity enabled specialized glands for memory and data storage. Besides developing greater intelligence, these new adaptations also had unanticipated benefits, providing Venubians with telepathic and empathic abilities that altered them as a species. Kathy is now learning the high price the Venubians paid for these alterations and enhancements."

"She's struggling," Cuz said.

"This is always the most difficult part." Biomei scanned Kathy's neural pathways to ensure the download wasn't overloading her newly implanted compiler. "One thing in Kathy's favor is her human physiology. It's more resilient than

Venubian. There's a lot we can learn from her."

"Phillip was different?"

"Yes. Nickada had prepared him well. But I'm not sure she'd approve of what we're doing now."

"Why?"

"She told me she had always been uncertain about the possible changes in Phillip's personality." She loved his insecurities and his constant inner battle to improve. She feared she'd lose him."

"Do you think Nickada would still feel the same way about Terri now?"

"I don't know."

"I recognize the changes you're referring to in Terri. Yet, I found he's still mostly human and conflicted."

Biomei noticed a sudden change in Kathy's biorhythms.

"She's now entering the final phase of the Zenti war. It's the most stressful part of the history download. I believe I'll give her a slight buffer and hope this will reduce her anxiety to a tolerable level."

"I wish there were a better way," Cuz whispered, then returned his attention to his mission directives.

* * *

Flashes of high-intensity light obscured Kathy's vision. She heard thunderous sounds all around her. When her eyes adjusted, she could see scores of heavily armed troops flooding into a surrealistic-looking debris-strewn area. She became aware that the soldiers were both androids and Venubians.

The androids looked nothing like Cuz. While humanoid in form, they still possessed a mechanical appearance. The Venubians were strikingly different in both form and appearance. They were small despite all the equipment and battle armaments they wore. She couldn't get a good sense of their physical attributes and features because they were so heavily covered in protective gear.

There was death and destruction everywhere she looked. The air felt heavy and full of putrid smells, turning her stomach in revulsion.

The androids were systematically surrounding horrid-looking creatures. Large, well-armored tank-like vehicles floated just inches above the ground and took positions behind them. Kathy could hear the creatures making hissing and incoherent sounds at the androids. A few of the creatures ran from them. One android made a high-pitched noise, lifted its weapon, and fired at the fleeing creatures. The weapon discharged a burst of yellowish light. The beings cried out a searing wail as their bodies contorted in pain, then fell to the ground.

Several of the androids surrounded them, closing into a tight pack. One of them pointed its weapon at the tight group and made a low-pitched grunt. All the creatures dropped their weapons. The automaton, pointing its particle weapon, made several more grunts. The captives were made to sit on their hands, back-to-back, on the ground. Kathy could sense strong emotions within the captives. Their feelings became apparent. They were full of hate, resentment, and not even a hint of fear.

Several deafening explosions erupted near the tanks. The tank's guns rose, then fired at the unseen targets. A familiar puffing sound went off all around her. She turned to a puffing sound near her. Kathy spied one of the horrid-looking humanoids, lying on the ground, firing what appeared to be a familiar weapon. Kathy looked closer and realized it was like the sonic weapons that Cuz and Territaff used at the Air Force base. She didn't realize the full power of the firearms until she saw them in action up close. A hollow puff was heard nearby. She turned and watched the weapon's discharge hit the intended target. A strong concussion nearly knocked her off her feet. A bright plume of fiery smoke came from a floating tank. The smoldering tank slammed to the ground, and three

Venubians crawled out from a rear hatch. They got to their feet, and a second concussion thundered, and they were all gone.

"No!" Kathy screamed.

She felt helpless and distraught about the horrific scene that was being played out before her. She knew none of it was real, but it seemed real enough to her. A throaty, whining sound of a powerful engine came over her head. She looked up and saw a colossal ship approaching. The ship glided to a soft landing a few hundred meters from her field of view. Multiple hatches opened on each side of the ship, and scores of androids marched out. They were large, and their metallic bodies reflected the glaring brightness of the clear day's sun. They reminded Kathy of knights in shining armor rushing to the aid of their kingdom. She wished she were watching one of her childhood dream narratives instead of the carnage unfolding before her. The astonishing reality was too real, though. She understood what she was seeing. The androids were there to annihilate the Zenti.

Kathy looked out at the rolling landscape that reflected glimmers of its beauty before the slaughter. Bombed-out buildings were still smoldering, revealing that the battle was young. Then she got a close-up view of one of the horrid-looking humanoids as the androids rounded up a group. What she saw astonished her. She didn't know what to make of them.

Most of them appeared to be around 1.5 meters tall. They had a humanoid form and symmetry, with reptilian-shaped, lipless mouths and large, bug-like eyes that protruded under prominent brow ridges, and long, pointed ears. Kathy looked closely as they passed. The Zenti didn't appear like frail beings. They had broad, well-defined thoraxes with prominent pectoral muscle bulges and slender waists, giving them a fit appearance. Yet, their arms and legs appeared lanky within their form-fitted battle suits. Kathy found them sinister-looking, like archetypal gremlins, covered in smooth, pale green flesh. She finally saw the enemy, and they horrified her.

* * *

"Cuz, why are you so upset?" Biomei asked.

"I didn't want to trouble you while you were involved with Kathy's transformation, but I've received a disturbing communique from Lunneziah. First, he mouthed it as if he couldn't articulate the horrible news. He took a breath and said, "Terri is dead.""

"Terri's not dead. I would've felt it."

"The message was from Karoft," Cuz explained. "Karoft's communique was certain. A high-energy plasma implosion from an unidentified missile vaporized Territaff's shuttle. They conducted a full sensor sweep of the immediate area. It identified Territaff's DNA and some of the shuttle's material signature. Karoft stated nothing could have survived such an intense discharge. He's gone, Biomei."

Cuz could feel a tightening in his throat and chest as he repeated the report summary to Biomei. A sharp pain shuddered through him like an overwhelming force. Cuz was surprised as he felt an uncontrollable urge to do something he believed he was incapable of, crying. He stared, bewildered, at his reflection on the shiny, black communication console. His eyes were full of tears, and his body shook as his mind filled with confused and conflicted thoughts. He could not understand why his emotions had become so out of control.

If it weren't for the fact that he was so distraught, Biomei would have been overjoyed by his sudden display of real emotions.

"Cuz, believe me, Terri's not dead. I'd know. Terri's entangled photons are still being transmitted back over the great distance between us. I can feel his life force within my mind."

"You sound most sure," Cuz said, trying to rein in the strong emotions that have overtaken him. He let out a long sigh of relief with Biomei's reassurance.

"This communique was sent for specific reasons," Biomei continued. The most logical conclusion is that Karoft and Terri have devised a new plan in response to updated intelligence. We'll continue monitoring the situation with Venubian intelligence. That we haven't heard from Chancellor Verubeal is also a sign that the communique is disinformation intended for the Zenti monitoring our activities. As one of your favorite detectives would proclaim, 'It's Elementary, my dear, Cuz.'"

"Yes, that makes sense." Mimicking his best English accent, Cuz said, "It's elementary, my dear Biomei; the game is afoot!"

"Cuz, your display of strong emotions is remarkable. You're becoming more humanoid with each passing day. And, by the way, Doyle never wrote that famous refrain for Holmes. Basil Rathbone, playing Holmes, coined it in one of the many movie versions. Cuz smiled at the revelation.

"While it's apparent I have emotions, I wish I could be more in control of them at times. They're taking me by surprise more often than I care to admit. To be humanoid, there is a constant struggle between pleasure and pain. It's often disconcerting to find the proper balance."

"That's all part of being humanoid, my young friend. As Terri has often pointed out, emotions define humans and characterize their personalities. As you discover, a humanoid personality is a lifelong dynamic force constantly evolving. All sentient beings share this commonality. Give yourself time to learn, as humans do, through experience."

CHAPTER 29

Kathy saw Nickada emerge from the remains of the administration complex, looking weary and dazed from the long ordeal that the Zenti had put her through. She walked awkwardly as though she could barely stand. An enhanced-humanoid that Kathy knew as Tezabouh came to her aid.

Tezabouh and Phillip had just saved a group of important Venubians, along with Nickada and Verubeal, from the Zenti. Nickada appeared different from what Kathy had imagined. She was a little taller than the other Venubians and had large, alluring eyes. Kathy was viewing her from a distance, but discovered that if she concentrated on Nickada, her image would enlarge enough for Kathy to get a close-up view of her.

Phillip Mann also seemed different from Terri. However, she could identify Terri as Phillip; the differences, although subtle, were distinct enough for Kathy to notice. His facial features were less intense, giving him a younger look with soft, alert eyes.

As soon as Nickada saw Phillip, Kathy noticed a surge of energy in her, restoring a vivacious glow. They embraced and kissed as long-separated lovers do. The scene was endearing; part of Kathy grew jealous, while another part understood. They had all endured the mental and physical anguish that victims of war suffer. She now clearly understood Territaff's deep emotional scars and his often inconsistent behavior. He was a man struggling to live two different lives. Kathy also knew he would have to let Phillip Mann die so Territaff could live.

She recognized Verubeal helping one of the injured as they made their way out of the building. Their eyes squinted under the glare of the daylight. Kathy knew Verubeal was Nickada's mother. Territaff had often spoken of her and the close relationship they had forged during the long ordeal they had both shared. Even after all Verubeal had been through, she still moved in a stately manner, her head held upright with a look of unflinching confidence. The resemblances between Nickada and Verubeal were striking. They looked more like sisters than mother and daughter. Although Kathy was given a detailed description of the entire harrowing ordeal, this was Kathy's first close-up view of Nickada and Verubeal together.

Kathy felt as depleted and anxious as the survivors she was viewing in what had become a transformation nightmare. Even though she knew what she was witnessing was a mental manipulation of her senses, it did little to help her overcome the strong empathy running through her. It felt almost as real to her as it was for the Venubians who had lived through it.

The battle had finally ended, but its lingering aura of shock and despair remained. There was a gathering of Venubians, looking like they were trying to come to terms with their new and sudden reality. Kathy could see a look of stunning bewilderment on their faces. Some were hugging each other in a guarded celebration of surviving the desolation. Others walked among the multitude of bodies strewn across what was once a beautiful courtyard and gardens, seeking to give aid to the wounded and what little comfort they could provide for the dying, Zenti and Venubians alike. Kathy realized that humans and Venubians shared a common characteristic: They're at their best when circumstances are at their worst.

Kathy was surprised by a Zenti who burst out of a side door. His face contorted with seething vehemence as he tossed a small, round object at Territaff and Nickada during their loving embrace. Tezabouh was the first to notice the concussion grenade. He started to push Nickada away as Territaff went for it. When Nickada saw Territaff going for the grenade, she pushed Tezabouh to the side right as it exploded. The intensity and devastation of the blast left Kathy stunned. Body parts flew into the air. The cruel blast killed everything within a nine-meter area.

Cuz came from around the other side of the building with

several other androids. The androids stopped for a moment, impassively inspecting the destruction. Cuz stood with his mouth open and eyes wide, staring in disbelief.

Her heart was heavy with the shock and awe of the Zenti's cold, ruthless acts, and she cried, "No more. Please. No more. Biomei, make it stop."

The scene shifted, and she found herself in a peaceful setting. As she looked around, the panorama became familiar. She was sitting on a rock ledge that jutted from a shallow grotto along the Pacific Ocean. Kathy let out a long sigh as she soaked in the tranquil setting's aura. All the good memories of this place flowed into her mind like a soothing sedative upon her raw and jagged nerves. She was a few blocks from her grandparents' house in southern California, north of La Hoya Beach. Her grandparents raised Kathy. She never knew her parents. They died when she was two. Even though she had only nine good years with her grandparents, they were the best years of her life. The grotto had become her favorite place whenever she wanted to be alone. She often went there and dreamily watched the seals playing on the rocks below. Kathy's pounding heart and throbbing head subsided as she breathed in the cool sea air.

"Is this better?" she heard Venubia's voice behind her.

"Yes," Kathy answered without looking up.

"I can understand why you like this place. It's peaceful and full of life. A direct contrast to that atrocious war."

"Was it really necessary to put me through the horror of your nasty war?" Kathy snapped.

"We believed it necessary for you to understand our present fears," Venubia explained. "There's a war, far worse than the virtual war you experienced. It's imminent unless we act to prevent it."

Venubia's form appeared beside Kathy. She could feel her strong presence, but didn't turn to greet her. Her mind was still whirling with the images of the explosion and the intense pain and sorrow she felt for Terri.

"I don't understand," Kathy snapped.

"Take a moment to calm your emotions. Things will become clearer once you do," Venubia said in a patient voice.

Kathy took in a deep breath and tried to clear her head of the atrocities she had just witnessed.

"They're worse than the Nazis," she mumbled.

"The Nazis had a plan and were driven by human ambitions. As bad as you believe they were, they were still human and could be handled on human terms. The Zenti share no humanoid characteristics. They have no sense of morality or any thread of compassion you could appeal to. They were genetically engineered to survive any environment and adapt to any situation. They were also given no moral prerogatives beyond protecting their species against any perceivable threat. The androids created them to help rejuvenate a nearly extinct race. Regardless of how benign the intentions behind their development, they're a perfect example of the worst possible outcome when tampering with the natural course of evolution."

"The Technological Singularity," Kathy uttered with a sudden realization. "That's what this is all about? Isn't it?" She stood and paced in a tight circle. "They were the horrible mistake that the Venubians didn't want to speak of. The androids wanted to use them to rectify their mistake, but this only worsened things."

"Precisely," Venubia said, looking pleased. "We left out that portion of the history lesson, hoping you could make the connection."

Kathy shook her head in disbelief. "This is all so wrong. How could the androids not see the folly of what they were creating?"

Androids don't possess the discretionary emotional insights that humanoids do. They only examined a problem using logic born out of their immense intellect. They believed the Zenti to be the perfect solution. Develop a robust and adaptable line of genetically superior males. Cross-mate them, using engineered in-vitro insemination with the strongest and most adaptive females, and believe that an ideal male offspring will result.

"The sentient Androids were certain the subsequent progeny would develop into the most genetically perfect babies. Ironically, they shared a common goal with the Nazis. They both used artificial means in seeking a race pure of all genetic and intellectual defects.

"Like the Nazis, the Androids failed to realize until it was too late that evolution can't be hurried. Racial and collective memories must be developed over millennia of shared experiences. The Zenti are perfect genetic specimens. However, they lack an essential characteristic that makes humanoids humane: the ability to love. This was beyond the Android's realm of understanding. Therefore, when they realized how wrong their genetic experiment was, they exiled the Zenti to a hostile world, hoping they would die off. They didn't know how adaptive and resourceful the Zenti had become in perpetuating themselves as a species.

"You have been given the details of the first Venubian Zenti War and the Technological Singularity, which was the inception of everything that followed. The final piece of this complex puzzle is what the androids never gave the Zenti."

Venubia paused, closely studying Kathy's face. Kathy was surprised. She looked remorseful and almost reluctant to speak.

"What haven't you told me?" Kathy glared at her. "Tell me."

"Through all the terror and killing that the Zenti have been inflicting upon the worlds in our quadrant, no one has understood what was driving them so fiercely. Time after time, we've attempted to negotiate peace with them. The Klaxons and Kaydens have willingly offered perfect planets in the best habitable zones around ideal stars, yet they were still dissatisfied.

"Each time we would negotiate a peace, they would break it and start the violence all over again. They would go from system to system, raiding unsuspecting ships of their resources, stripping them of their technologies, usurping colonies, and enslaving the populace with no reason or provocation. It was not until Phillip Mann delivered us from the last Zenti conflict that we learned their true secret. The androids gave them no gender or means of natural procreation. They were all clones and dying from a phenomenon known as the Fade of Replication. It's a degenerative decay of their DNA. Cloning without renewed genetic material, allowing for natural mutations, is analogous to making copies of copies until the copy becomes illegible. They had exhausted their entire source of viable DNA and are desperate to find a new and compatible one."

Kathy gasped at the sudden revelation and said, "We're the compatible source." She turned away from her guide and walked along the narrow edge of the cliff. She stopped, turned towards the woman, and said, "I know all I need to know. End this now."

CHAPTER 30

Lunneziah is a large, frozen rock with a mean temperature of -225 degrees Celsius. It orbits a ringed gas giant, Celibran. Celibran is a spectacular planet with a mass twice that of Jupiter's and a massive magnetic field stretching hundreds of millions of kilometers outward from the planet.

Celibran's enormous presence filled the sky, reflecting an eerie yellow-white light upon the moon's tundra. Summer on Lunneziah gave the moon an inviting look, and the temperature had risen to a balmy -77 degrees.

Territaff gazed in wonder at the ring system's magnificence, creating an aurora of blue and green lights that danced atop the inner rings. Fountains of light would shoot up for hundreds of thousands of kilometers due to the interaction between Celibran's high-energy particles and the atoms of the gases trapped within the rings. This was the first time Territaff saw the aurora at its fullest. His last visit to Lunneziah was in its winter cycle, and the aurora activity was much lower and dimmer.

The system's sun was a massive blue star that appeared like a large, bright blue-white, distant ball. Territaff gazed in fascination at the spectacle through the clear dome of the transit shuttle while trying to piece together his fragmented memory. Under normal conditions, his memory was virtual and infallible. What happened? He asked himself over and over. I recall everything that happened just before entering the corridor. Why can't I remember what happened to the shuttle? How did I wind up in a life pod? Someone must have messed with my memory. But who? And Why? He also wondered if his memory loss had anything to do with the buzzing in his head.

Territaff pushed all of those thoughts aside and turned to his two Bylar companions, who didn't seem to share his fascination with Lunneziah.

"What are your names?" Territaff said, hoping their new

universal transponders were working.

The Bylar beside Territaff said, "I am Nozuulitaazara, but you can call me Noz. He is my younger brother. We call him Sahvuul." He made a low, guttural sound as he said the name. "It means slow-witted."

"My brother tries to be funny but is too stupid to make good jokes," Sahvuul retorted.

Territaff smiled at the brotherly banter and said, "I think I'll call you Sol. No way I can say your name without hurting my throat. Were you here during the Zenti occupation?"

They both nodded their large heads and blinked.

"Two planetary cycles on this frozen wasteland before freed," Noz said. "We called it Fazulol, 'The Frozen Heart', not only because of the terrible cold but also of how the Zenti brutalized us as slave labor. All you see down there, we transformed into a network of big domes, intersecting tunnels, and transportation tubes."

"We built those," Sol said, pointing down at a complex of interconnected domes on the surface. "We, along with captive Kayden engineers and Venubian architects."

"They made us build our encampment. Many died there," Noz said, closing his eyes.

Territaff looked down as they passed over a large complex of buildings and said, "At least all your labors weren't built in vain. Now, they make up an interconnected network that houses many businesses, residences, and official government and military facilities. You should be proud of those great accomplishments under such unthinkable conditions and circumstances."

Territaff sensed his companions' strong emotions as they passed over the former labor camps.

"Lunneziah's atmosphere is barely breathable for Bylars," Noz said in a reflective voice. "The Zenti took advantage of our resilient bodies. They forced us to work in a hostile atmosphere and climate with minimal protection. Zenti could not design suits to protect us against the cold and prolonged exposure to radiation. Environmental suits proved to be no good. They provided us with makeshift housing, but it only offered protection against the cold, not against radiation."

"Those of us who were forced to work on the surface constructing those buildings and all the other infrastructures for their mining operations had to endure many illnesses," Sol said, leaning closer to Territaff. "Hypothermia and frostbite were the most common problems for workers. The Zenti often treated it by cutting off the limb and replacing it with a prosthetic. Then those who didn't recover enough to do hard labor were given menial work."

"The worst disease, though," Noz added, "was radiation sickness. Many became incurably sick, others suffered mental disorders, and most died. The only thing that saved us from complete elimination was our spirit." He made a faint smile, and Sol nodded in agreement.

"You are a noble species and should take great pride in all your service during that hideous war. Venubia owes you a great debt and eternal gratitude for your sacrifices," Territaff said, reflecting on his experience with a Bylar who gave up his life to save others.

Both Bylars nodded, then turned forward and closed their eyes.

* * *

Territaff dismissed his Bylar companions to enjoy themselves. They objected initially but relented after he assured them he was in no real danger. He asked if they would convey his sincere gratitude to their captain for his rescue and sent them on their way. Bylars don't make good travel companions when one is trying to keep a low profile.

It was the close of business for most of Lunneziah's commercial enterprises when Territaff arrived at Larzz's Pub.

Territaff smiled at the towering arch that glowed with its larger-than-life hologram of Larzz. His arms stretched wide, welcoming all who crossed his threshold. According to its proprietor, Larzz's Pub was considered the only one of its kind in the galaxy. Larzz drew inspiration from an ancient design in his ancestry for the pub's design, stating, "Venubian architecture was devoid of character." Territaff could sense from the outside that the establishment was already teeming with business.

The sounds and smells of a hundred different species washed over Territaff like a tremendous tidal wave on his senses. However, a singular and unmistakable presence was among this strange brew of sounds and smells: Larzz himself. Larzz's dark features were accentuated by his fierce red eyes, large, flat nose, colossal frame, bushy dark red beard, and hair like a lion's mane, all conspiring to give him a menacing appearance. Yet, beneath his severe demeanor beat a gentle heart, a jocular personality, and a sharp mind. The old master was busy directing his service droids from table to table from his command post behind the great expanse of his bar. Klaxon music, sounding more like scratchy notes without a melody, played under a current of intersecting conversations from the intergalactic mix of diplomats, government officials, business executives, travelers, and locals.

The Venubian Corridor allowed commerce to establish itself like plants on a newly terraformed planet. Over the past fifty planetary cycles, Lunneziah had inadvertently established itself as an intergalactic haven for commerce and politics. Larzz seized the opportunity and created the pub. He developed it into a singular intergalactic meeting place where one could get the food or drink they desired while discussing anything without risk. Privacy in such an establishment became essential—Larzz based privacy on a strict honor system. If anything of interest is overheard, it's forgotten, or the offending individual mysteriously disappears.

Larzz's Pub became known throughout the local system as the unofficial dispute resolution center. Officially, the governing body was the new Alliance or Intergalactic Council of Aligned Worlds, created after the last Venubian-Zenti war. It deliberated final decrees on all disagreements, conflicts, and various legal matters. It's something like a Supreme Court without the politics. It supposedly was above politics and only used the law and common sense. Despite this widely accepted claim, some judgments ruffled many feathers, but it was a respected and mostly functional body.

The price of peace seems to be endless bureaucracy. Many disagreements were resolved in one inebriated session at Larzz's than in the two to three annual cycles it takes to sue before the Council, not to mention the additional two to three planetary cycles before the Council logs its final decree.

Many have discovered that it's much more civilized and expedient to argue differences of opinion under Larzz's hospitality.

The brief history of this intergalactic bar and grill already filled an entire bank in the Venubian central record.

Larzz's ancestry was of the great Boravahrian House of Vejar-Alpurses, an old planet located two hundred light-years from Venubian. His family is notorious within the Vejar system. They were among the first to venture out and bring commerce to all the rising colonies and civilizations within Vejar-Alpurses. The discovery of a corridor connecting Vejar to the Venubian sector sparked a boom in commerce. Over time, his family established itself as a powerful landlord and merchant. It's believed his father was killed during one of the many territorial conflicts on Vejar when Larzz was young. Some thought a jealous rival murdered him.

Larzz was left in the care of his paternal grandparents. His grandfather made his fortune in trading goods and services for any purpose or need. There are some persistent but unfounded rumors that Larzz's grandfather didn't discriminate in what he sold or to whom. There are also rumors that when Larzz was younger, he carried on his grandfather's business similarly. Larzz, of course, dismisses all the rumors with a deep belly laugh. His family's seal of honor is proudly displayed on the wall behind Larzz's central console.

Territaff approached his favorite stool on the left side of the console. He removed the reserved display on the order reader and punched in for Pido. A droid made its way over to Territaff. Larzz's thick, muscular arm pushed it aside as he spied Territaff from the corner of his dark red eye.

"Zu flu ventil aq tot-uvut." Larzz said the ancient Boravahrian greeting of friendship. Then he reached over the bar's counter and wrapped his bulky arms around Territaff, lifting him out of his seat and into a great bear hug.

"Ze a tot-uvut, old friend," Territaff said, patting Larzz's broad shoulder.

"You, son of genetic slime," he bellowed as he dropped Territaff back on his stool. "Never a goodbye, farewell for your friend, Larzz. Just leaves like a Cudrong cat in the dark of time and space. I should break a couple of your bones for such an insult."

"I think you already did in that hug. I guess I deserve that. Sorry, Larzz. They never gave me enough time to say goodbye."

"Yes, but it's good to see you're still in one piece, old friend." He turned his face up into a smile.

Territaff scrutinized the smile and asked, "What do you mean by 'in one piece'?"

"I thought you got blown up in the great explosion right outside the corridor." He leaned a little closer to Territaff and said in a low voice, "You're supposed to be dead."

"You heard wrong. I'm still here and don't have a clue about what happened."

Larzz squinted an eye and gave him a close look. "Are you telling me you don't know? Or are you being secretive?"

"I was unconscious. Don't remember a thing."

"Ah, Terri, you're always good for a laugh, but one of these days you're gonna meet with more trouble than your quick-tinking apparatus can get you out of." He snorted, then, noticing Territaff's confused expression, sighed and patted him on the top of his head. "What's wrong?"

"My shuttle didn't blow up. It was attacked and destroyed by a missile with interesting technology. You need to be discreet with this knowledge and check with your many sources for information."

Territaff studied the faces close to him for a tell-tale reaction. No one showed any signs of interest. Larzz's patrons were well-versed in the establishment's policy of discretion.

Larzz's expression narrowed into a serious scowl and, in a low voice, asked, "You were attacked that close to the corridor? That's very serious... very serious indeed." He stroked his bushy, red beard. "You need a drink. What are you drinking these days?"

"Pido," he said, surveying the bar. He wasn't sure what he was looking for, but he had a strong notion that a skillful tracker was closely watching him.

"Pido eh, Venubian pisswater, you mean."

Larzz let out a great laugh that shook his massive frame. Territaff turned and smiled. He relaxed a little in his friend's company.

"Here," Larzz said as he pulled out a tall crystal container from under the bar, "an ancient and very potent measure saved just for you."

He placed an oversized goblet in front of Territaff and poured a generous helping of the clear, thick liquid into it.

Territaff took a sip and nodded approvingly. "Just the way I remembered it. This resembles an Earth drink called Pernod, but Pido is much smoother and has a stronger kick. And Larzz, it's not a Venubian drink. It's Klaxon in origin. Venubians would sooner drink pisswater than anything that has that much alcohol."

"Okay, Pido is Klaxon, not Venubian, and you're the only one who drinks this shit. Now, tell me something interesting." Larzz raised his thick, red eyebrows, expecting to be told something exciting and extraordinary as Territaff drained the goblet of Pido. "So?" he said.

Territaff handed the empty goblet to him for a refill.

"This better be good, Terri, or I'm charging you double for everything."

"So, this one is on the house?" he said as Larzz grabbed the goblet from him and poured him a refill.

Larzz placed the glass in front of him. He narrowed his large eyes, wrinkled his massive brow, and leaned on an elbow to get closer to Territaff.

"Talk," he squinted one eye.

Territaff took a slug of Pido.

"A lot is going on in my homeworld, Larzz."

"Nah, that's not what I want to hear," he growled.

"The truth is, I remember nothing. I suddenly woke in a life pod on the other side of the event horizon."

Larzz shook his head in disbelief. "That's lame-ass womp shit, Terri. You should be ashamed of yourself. You want info, but you don't give me nothing to go on." Larzz swiped the crystal container from the counter, then walked over to a group of diplomats sitting at the bar's far end.

"How about another Pido?" Territaff called to him.

"I'll send a droid," he said without turning.

A droid promptly came over to Territaff and took his order. He spun himself around on the stool to survey the room. He studied the crowded room, trying to match up any familiar face with his internal databank of known operatives. There were humanoids of all kinds within the growing masses. He knew it would be a long shot to match up a face. Having spent most of his time between Earth and Venubia, Territaff was almost overwhelmed by the diversity of species, all of which were having a good time. The scene was reminiscent of a typical Friday night in a bar on Earth. They were conversing, drinking, and cavorting, their voices getting louder by the hour.

"See anyone you like?" a sensual-sounding voice asked.

Territaff spun himself around to see if the face matched her voice. He wasn't disappointed.

"It seems I just did," he said, smiling approvingly. "Vultaran beauty is not overstated."

She was a young and lovely Vultaran looking at Territaff in a way he had not seen from a woman in many years. She was taller than the average female, around two meters. Her long, lean body was athletic and proportional.

Vultaria was the newest member of the Alliance. Territaff was familiar with the Vultaran morphology, physiology, and the limited history Hanc had updated into his internal databank.

Her intensity softened into a refreshing curiosity. He also sensed an intense emotional wave emanating from her. He found himself drawn to it and had to rein in an impulse to kiss her. This unexpected reaction made Territaff suspicious.

She smiled at the compliment, then asked, "You are Terran—yes?"

"My name is Territaff."

"I am called," she paused, then said, "Celesta."

"That's a beautiful Earth name. Did you make it up or translate it?"

He studied her face. She had striking humanoid features, brown, cat-like eyes, rimmed in yellow, and small openings for ears partially hidden by her medium-length, silky, light brown hair with black streaks. Her dark complexion accentuated her deep, bright eyes above a full mouth and subtle chin. Her expression reflected a bright and cheerful glow that was pleasing and disarming.

"I translated it," she answered carefully, looking like she had done something wrong.

Something is compelling about this young alien, Territaff thought as he asked, "How do you say your name in Vultaran?"

"Tehrarra," she said in a heavy, breathy voice, emphasizing the r's and a's. "May I join you?"

Territaff motioned for her to take the stool to his right as a Klaxon was about to sit. The Klaxon gave Territaff an annoyed glare but politely nodded to the Vultaran.

"Do you know him?" she asked, sitting on the stool.

"Administer Ez? All too well," Territaff said with relief. "You not only graced me with your lovely presence, but you've also saved me from a long and boring dissertation on why my planet is not ready for admittance to the Alliance."

"So, is he right?"

"His argument has merit, but the Earth has as much right as any other civilized world to—" Territaff's voice trailed off as he considered the young Vultaran's face, realizing she had been leading the conversation with the skill of a seasoned politician. "But how foolish of me. Only a naïve fool would waste time discussing politics with a beautiful woman."

She smiled with her eyes and said, "What are you drinking?"

"Pido."

"I am not familiar with Pido. Is it strong?"

I suppose that's a matter of what you're accustomed to. Let me suggest a tasty Earth drink." Territaff motioned to Larzz. Larzz turned and gave Territaff a broad grin, seeing the lovely Vultaran beside him.

"What can I do for you, Terri?" Larzz asked, gazing at the young alien.

"Would you have one of your droids prepare a Champagne cocktail for my new friend?"

"What's a Champagne cocktail?" Larzz said.

"I thought you said you would update your drink recipes with Earth mixes?"

"I did?" He pulled on his long earlobe, eyeing the Vultaran.

"I must've forgotten. Besides, you're the only Earthman I know, and you only drink Pido." Larzz narrowed his eyes at Territaff, then regarded the Vultaran with a crooked grin as he motioned for a droid.

"How may I serve you, sir?" the droid asked.

Territaff had to think of a close approximation for the Champaign, then input the carbonated white Venjah recipe, a light Klaxon berry wine, into the order terminal.

"Very good, sir," the droid said, then left.

"Thanks, Larzz," Territaff said dismissively.

"You're not going to introduce me to this intriguing Vultaran?"

"I'm sorry. I thought you knew every female species that graces your establishment." Larzz frowned at him, then smiled graciously at her. "Tehrarra, may I have the great pleasure of introducing my friend, Larzz?" Territaff said.

"I am familiar with Larzz," she said, with an amused upturn of her lips.

"Have we met?" Larzz asked, furrowing his large, bushy brow.

"Not exactly, more by reputation," she explained, unsure of her words. "But it is my honor to meet you in person," she added.

"The honor is mine," he said with a slight nod.

"See, Larzz. Your reputation precedes you even on Vultaria." Territaff patted his thick, muscular arm.

Larzz stood upright, took a thoughtful pose, and then creased his forehead. "Is that a good thing?"

The Vultaran blinked her bright eyes, smiling broadly at Larzz. She revealed her pointed-tipped teeth with long, needle-like canines, a disconcerting look incongruous with her lovely mouth.

"Being famous is not a bad thing," she said.

Larzz sighed heavily and said, "The first drink is always on the house." He leaned closer to Tehrarra and, in a lower voice, added, "Especially for ladies as beautiful as you."

Larzz took her delicate, long hand into his beefy mitt and kissed her knuckles. Tehrarra regarded Larzz's gesture with an uncertain look.

"That's an old Earth custom of greeting and flattery I taught Larzz," Territaff explained.

The droid came in perfect timing to relieve the awkward situation, then presented her drink in a frosted martini glass. She held it up as if to study it, then took a careful sniff. "It tickles," she said, rubbing her small nose with her finger. "It is very colorful and has a pleasant aroma," she said, downing the drink.

"Would you care for another?"

She briefly considered it, then said, "I would like to try what you are drinking."

Territaff offered her his goblet.

Her expression tightened as she took the goblet from his hand.

"It's all right. I hadn't drunk from it yet," he reassured her.

"You are not offended, yes? Cross-species microbes and all."

"I understand. You've nothing to fear from me. I'm biologically neutral. No horrible little organisms that can harm you."

"How is that possible? You are an Earthman?"

"Venubian biological engineering," Territaff explained, then gestured for her to taste.

She brought the goblet up close to her nose and took a deep whiff of the clear liquid. "It has an interesting scent," she said, holding the goblet up as though she were inspecting it for clarity.

"You're treating my Pido like many examine a fine wine on my planet."

"Wine? That sounds intriguing. Is it also a drink?"

"Yes, but different from Pido. It's similar to the drink you just tried."

She took a sip. "I like this," she said, turning the corners of her mouth upward, then drained the goblet in one long swallow.

"Slow down until you see how these drinks affect you."

"Why?"

"I'm not sure how alcohol works on your metabolism. It has deleterious effects on many species—take a look around."

She tilted her head, pondering Territaff's words. He studied her. There was something about her that was pulling on his emotional center to a point that was confusing and unsettling.

"Ah." Her expression brightened. "I think I understand your concern." She let out a slight laugh. "Do not worry. Alcohol metabolizes too quickly for it to accumulate enough to be... what is the word?" She wrinkled her upper lip, then arched her thin eyebrows into a puzzled look.

"Intoxicated" is the word you're searching for."

"Yes, intoxicated," she agreed, tilting the empty goblet towards him.

"Would you like another?"

"Please." Territaff studied her while contemplating his rising emotions. "Are you aware of the effect you're having on me?"

"I am not sure I understand your meaning." Her dark cheeks flushed with a rosy hue.

"It's hard to explain." How could she understand something I'm unsure of myself, he thought? He tried to engage her empathetically but found that he couldn't. He struggled to know what to make of her as she gazed at him. Was she being defensive with her emotions, or was that her natural emotional state? He was tempted to take a chance on a telepathic intrusion, but knew it could be a grave mistake if detected.

"You look lost in thought," she said.

Could she be empathic or even telepathic? "I'm sorry... It's just that I'm trying to think of a delicate way to express my feelings, realizing I should be honest and open with you."

She sat a little more upright. He went to take a sip of his drink and realized the goblet was empty. He looked at the empty goblet, then at Tehrarra's expectant gaze.

"I forgot to order us another round," he said, buying a brief reprieve to gather his thoughts. He input for two Pidos. He stared at her for a moment, then said, "Are you empathic or telepathic?"

"We are empathic," she answered meekly.

"Were you reading me all this time?"

She looked down and then up at Territaff like a child caught in the act.

"I apologize," she sighed. "It's impolite to read your feelings, but I can only read you empathetically. I cannot hear your thoughts. Please forgive me. I was curious as you are... to know me, yes?"

"I see. That explains a lot." It became apparent that her species engaged in empathy superficially but effectively. "You're forgiven, but now you must tell me your impressions of me."

"You are complex," she arched an eyebrow. "I was having trouble getting a good read on you because you must be telepathic and were feeling me. But you said nothing—why?"

Territaff placed his elbow on the counter to support his chin in thought. He gazed at her with a hard stare, then deadened his feelings.

"You are upset with me?" She squirmed a little on her stool.

Territaff continued his intense gaze until a droid delivered their drinks. He sat upright on his stool and softened his look.

"I am complicated," he agreed. "All humans have conflicted emotions, but our emotions define us, and I'm discovering that while we aren't unique in that respect, we are special in how we use them."

Tehrarra was startled by his sudden openness. Her expression took on a curious pose. She appeared surprised and confounded.

"With all your conflicted emotions, how do you communicate with each other on a meaningful level?"

"We just do." Territaff gave her a glancing smile. "Not to suggest we do it well, but we're a work in progress."

"Are you a typical Earthman?"

Territaff laughed heartily. "I'm not a typical anything. As you said, I'm complex."

Territaff took a large swig of his Pido, then watched her as she took a more modest sip. He felt Karoft approaching.

"We need to talk in private," Karoft transmitted with urgency.

"I'll meet you in one of the private meeting rooms," Territaff replied.

"Is something wrong?" Tehrarra asked.

"No," Territaff said. "But I must go. I have a meeting that's about to begin. Please forgive me for leaving so abruptly. I was enjoying our conversation. I don't know how long the meeting will last, but it shouldn't take too long. Will you wait for me? I want to continue getting to know you better.

"I also have to leave... if you will be here tomorrow... around the same time?"

"Then, I'll see you tomorrow," he said, and took her hand, turning it palm up, and kissed it. "That's a special goodbye on Earth." Then he touched his forehead to hers. "And that's goodbye in Venubian."

As he was about to leave, she placed her arms around his neck, pulled him close, and kissed him passionately. Her kiss almost made him want to cancel his meeting with Karoft.

"That is—until tomorrow in Vultaran," she said, then finished her Pido before leaving.

He watched her gracefully move through the bar. She nodded respectfully to Larzz as she passed him on her way out, then stopped to talk with a Kayden military officer sitting at the end of the bar.

Larzz looked at Territaff with a shocked expression, as if to say, ' Why are you letting that lovely female go? '

"I need a private room," Territaff called out to Larzz.

He grinned slyly and said, "PR-4 is available." His glee dissolved into puzzlement when he spied Karoft entering the room ahead of Territaff.

"It's not what you think," he said, responding to Larzz's look.

Larzz shrugged, then turned his attention to a noisy diplomat with too much to drink.

* * *

As Territaff approached the private room, a droid came up and handed him a magnetically sealed envelope with the stamp of the Pro-Council embossed on it. It was marked in bright red print: 'OFFICIAL BUSINESS-CRYPTO LEVEL.'

Karoft sat at the small table, looking preoccupied in thought. The dim lighting and soft music made the room more suitable for intimacy than discussion. Karoft's short, curly blonde head and milky complexion reflected the soft lighting, giving him a ghostly appearance.

Territaff sat opposite him and smiled. "You really know how to charm a guy," he said, hoping to break Karoft's dour mood.

Karoft regarded him with weary eyes, looking like he had endured a stressful experience.

"Do you have any idea what this is?" Territaff asked, sliding the envelope over to Karoft.

"It's probably the debris analysis."

"Why do you look so grim?"

"Read the report."

"Now you're being cryptic."

"Just read the damn report," Karoft snapped, with his large, hazel eyes glaring.

"What's wrong?"

He pushed out a long breath and said, "I'm sorry, Terri, but you're in real danger here. Why did you leave Biomei when so much was happening in your world?"

"I left to get you," he said, pressing his thumb on the identification chip to release the envelope's seal. "I need both your expertise in integrated systems and linguistics. Also, you're someone I can trust." He scanned the data, then looked at Karoft in surprise. "Can this be right?" He scanned it again. "This makes little sense. According to this, my shuttle just blew itself up. That's not what happened?"

"I didn't have time to come up with a better cover story. They'll request that you appear before a board of inquiry within a standard quarter cycle. Under the circumstances, that's the least of your worries. Biomei sent me an update on the Zenti problem. It seems they have a new ally, and we haven't gotten any information on them. We've exhausted all our known sources and came up empty."

"That's not new. We've already concluded that they've a silent partner—one who has organized them and provided them with advanced technology. We haven't learned anything about them as well, which is why I'm here for you. We need to pull our efforts and not be so transparent about it. I require your skillful and devious mind."

He half-grinned, then frowned, and said, "There's something you need to know, but I'm not sure I should tell you here." He surveyed the room with a sense of unease.

"Would you prefer talking telepathically?"

"No, I think English is best—only what I need to tell you will be upsetting."

"I don't understand. Since when have you become concerned about my feelings?" He narrowed his gaze into a hard stare. "What's up with you, grandfather?"

"That report is inaccurate. And for a good reason."

"Damn it, Karoft." Territaff banged his fist on the table. "Stop beating around the bush and tell me what in hell's going on. What did you leave out of this lame report?"

"I downloaded a pseudo-destruct signal to Hanc with instructions to ignite the shuttle's particle discharge and had you ejected as you entered the corridor."

"You blew up my brand-new shuttle. Why did you take such a chance so close to the corridor?"

"Hanc had enough time to transmit most of your log. We wanted to retrieve the device and make the incident appear accidental. I only had 13.25 seconds. It seemed the only way I could save you from the crazy scheme you were attempting." He paused, blowing out a long breath. "I need a drink."

"That's another first. A Venubian needing a drink."

"A bad habit I picked up from you," he said and inputted for a Pido and a Klaxon Brandy. "That's not all." He sprang up from his chair and walked around, inspecting the room.

"What are you doing?"

"Is this room secured?"

"Well, only one door, and my internal sensors would have detected any surveillance devices. But look for yourself."

"I guess this is as good as anywhere on this crummy rock." Karoft sat heavily on his chair and looked at Territaff with his mouth clenched.

"Okay, out with the rest of it."

"We were tracking a strange energy source outside of the corridor. We could only read it as the corridor opened and closed. As you know, the corridor can only be manually opened briefly when ships pass through. We determined the signal's frequency to be a few hundred milliseconds below that of cosmic rays, but on a negative bandwidth. Initially, we believed it was of natural origin. It appeared, for lack of a better description, as a ghost signature. After eliminating all naturally occurring signals, we realized they must have been artificially generated. No known particle or phenomenon oscillates at that frequency.

"When your shuttle approached, Navcom and Control recognized that the device coming toward the corridor generated it. When your shuttle took an intercept approach, we understood your intentions. I hate to tell you this, but your heroics would have only made the explosion bigger. We would've lost you, the device, and your shuttle. Nothing, thankfully, would've happened to the corridor."

"Oh? I thought it could've collapsed."

"The payload consisted mostly of antimatter."

"You're referring to the iridennium."

"Yes. It would've caused a spectacular matter-antimatter explosion, but the corridor's event horizon would have absorbed the energy. What's of interest, iridennium is an unstable particle and will only attract its symmetrical partner, siridennium. These rare particles are part of a class of matter still new to us. Even more mystifying is that the device had no discernible guidance system, meaning it had to be navigated manually."

Territaff's jaw dropped in dumbfounded surprise. He had trouble wrapping his head around what Karoft described.

"That's a first. Territaff speechless. There should be a record of this occasion," Karoft said.

"Oh, shut up," Territaff barked. "I forbid you to gloat."

"You're right. These are serious times. In all fairness, you took the right actions. If I were in a similar situation, with the data you had, I'm not sure I wouldn't have attempted the same thing. The missile's configuration conformed to a standard hydrogen-fueled ramjet drive. Spectrometry of the actual debris analysis detected small traces of deuterium. There was sufficient iridennium to have vaporized your shuttle, but it didn't detonate as expected for some unknown reason. It was sealed in a type of magnetic containment bottle unknown to us. If it had detonated, the energy would've been absorbed as described earlier."

"What you're suggesting makes little sense. They only wanted to see how I'd react. It was all a ruse to study me. Why? Why would they go to such great lengths? It doesn't add up. The Zenti already knows me well enough." Territaff reflected for a moment, then shifted his eyes to Karoft. "No. On second thought, it does make sense. Their new partners must be curious about me. They were studying every move and decision I made. I find that interesting and a sound tactic." He murmured, "Know thy enemy as thyself."

Karoft nodded. "I concur with your hypothesis. Up to this point, everything they've done suggests they're studying us. We're dealing with intelligence far greater and more mysterious than the Zenti."

"Now you understand why I've come for you. We need your expertise and contacts."

"You've anticipated me, Terri. I had arranged to join you."

"I hope you've packed a bag, because we must leave immediately."

"There's another problem that deserves our attention."

"Oh? What would that be?"

"Sub-Pro Councilman Muravh."

"Muravh? What happened to Kursha?"

"He left under clouded circumstances that everyone is avoiding talking about. With the Zenti on the move and Kursha's sudden dismissal, paranoia has become even more rampant. Things are getting ugly around here. Everyone has become suspicious of everything, and nothing's getting done. Some disturbing talk has suggested that the Earth is being portrayed as a silent partner with the Zenti. It's only an unfounded rumor, but it's getting traction. At least around here, but if it persists, it will dampen Earth's admission to the Alliance.

"It's looking like a well-conceived conspiracy plan being played out. I suspect Zohleemay's influence behind the rumor, but it could also be our mysterious foes," Territaff said, pulling on his earlobe in thought. "Where's Kursha now?"

"He was recalled home without explanation."

"Is anyone from his staff still here?"

"Yeah. Kursha's personal assistant's retention has added more fuel to a growing confluence of suspicions."

"His personal assistant." Territaff arched an eyebrow. "It appears there is some political wrangling going on."

"It was an unprecedented appointment. Kaden's pick their Personal Assistants carefully. Rumor had him having more than a professional relationship with his young, beautiful aide. His selection of a young female was bad enough and raised many eyebrows among the council members. When it was revealed she's Vultaran—"

"Vultaran?" Territaff reflected on the young and probing female he left at the bar.

"Yeah."

"Do you know her?"

"Kursha and I often had lunch, and I met his aide a few times. Why?"

"Just a minute." Territaff held up his hand, "Security monitor." A holographic image of the bar appeared above the small table. "Pan left." They watched the dozens of faces pass as the holographic scanner panned to the end of the bar.

"I don't see her," Karoft said.

"Pan from central control right," Territaff said. The image paused momentarily, then focused on Larzz, busy coordinating dozens of droids while entertaining a small gathering of diplomats and regulars seated and standing around his central console. "He's a master of his craft," Territaff mumbled. "Stop," he blurted. "Is that her?" He pointed at Tehrarra, who was to the right of the small gathering, talking with Administrator Ez.

"That's not her." Karoft smiled slyly at Tehrarra, "But, she knows, Le'nez."

"Who's that?"

"She's the Vultaran liaison to the Alliance. Be careful of this one, Territaff. She's not the innocent and naïve little Vultaran she portrays. She has an agenda. And so far, she has shown no loyalty to any group or individual. However, she has kept our security personnel occupied, and the Kayden officials worried."

"Oh? Why's everybody so nervous? We've met, and she's... really good." Territaff mused as he watched her working on Administer Ez. "I had to catch myself several times with her. She's empathic and, despite her denial, telepathic as well?"

Karoft jumped up at hearing the door buzzer. Territaff pressed the door release on the table to let the droid enter. The service droid entered, carrying a large tray that, in addition to their drinks, featured an attractive selection of fresh Venubian vegetables and a variety of cheeses and meats from across the galaxy.

"Did you order this?" Karoft said, stuffing a vegetable into his mouth.

"Compliments of the Vultaran Embassy," the droid said.

"Thank her for us, and bring another round of drinks."

"Very good, sir," the droid bowed stiffly from its hinged waist and left.

"You have to admit. She has a sense of style, making her even more dangerous than I first believed," Territaff said, noticing Karoft taking another large chunk of vegetable from the tray.

Karoft furrowed his brow in sudden bewilderment as he swallowed hard. "You don't think someone tampered with our..."

"No. You don't have to worry about the food or drink; it's good." He motioned at the plate. *"It's the garnish we should inspect,"* he transmitted as he picked up the food plates and inspected the colorful leaves and flower petal garnish. "Ah, there you are," he said, picking up a miniature audio transmitter. "Here's your drink, Karoft." He placed a finger over the transmitter and whispered, "We need to get out of here."

Karoft nodded. "I don't know about you, but I'm starving. What'd you say about getting out of here and trying Zoomah's for a change? I can get a Venubian Salad, and you can order one of your favorite choices of dead animal meat."

"Good idea," Territaff said, pointing to the door.

"Is there nowhere safe anymore?" Karoft complained as they walked to his vehicle. "Larzz should be told about what happened."

"I agree, but not now. He's better off not knowing, or there's always the possibility he already knows." Territaff frowned at the implication.

"You can't believe Larzz would have anything to do with this? We know him all too well. He's not capable of being involved with the Zenti..." He scratched his cheek, "But he loves information."

"It's not Larzz that I'm worried about, nor his employees. It's a particular, lovely Vultaran that concerns me."

"Interesting. I'll have security run another check on her. This whole new regime thing has gotten me off course. Okay, what's next on your agenda?"

"I don't believe whoever arranged Kursha's ouster wants him dead. They could've as easily arranged for a fatal accident rather than establishing the subterfuge to get him packing. There's much more to Kursha's removal than pretty aides and politics. The farce played out using that strange missile device or whatever the hell it was. Everything that has happened since I left Biomei is far too complicated for the Zenti. "We're missing a lot, which makes me nervous."

"I see your point," Karoft said with a heavy sigh. "The most recent reports from Earth are disturbing. Are you aware that the Zenti is gaining more traction within the American government on your planet? And what they're attempting is scary. If they have the specifications for—"

"They don't. You're returning with me to ensure this mess doesn't escalate into a full-blown intergalactic war. I need your expertise to coordinate possible scenarios and counterplans for the Zenti problem with Biomei. I thought Zohleemay was acting alone, but now I know he's working with some shrewd and well-connected associates."

"What about Muravh?"

"He's a decoy. I'm through with being played. We'll take the fight to them before they become any stronger. Leave all your tracking and identification devices in the vehicle."

"Great," Karoft said as they got into his compact hovercraft. "Getting me fired from my job wasn't enough. Now you want to get me killed."

CHAPTER 31

The inner city of Lunneziah was shrouded in perpetual darkness by a system of solar shutters that also served as photoelectric collectors, which Larzz had installed at his own expense. He recouped the cost in three planetary cycles and gets additional income from the hundreds of other businesses and government buildings that pay Larzz for the energy. When asked about the arrangement, Larzz answered, "My grandfather had always posited, 'Never do a public service that's unprofitable."

Outside the dome, Celibran's massive waves of highly charged particles bounced against the moon's powerful magnetic fields, scattering them into spectacular sheets of shimmering, yellow, blue, and green lights in the moon's sky.

Karoft had transmitted two travel orders and an arrest warrant for an unspecified suspect as they traveled outside the dome in his private shuttle.

"I've never been to this side of the moon," Territaff said.

"It's the Bylar section," Karoft explained. "Knowing their history on this moon, it's not surprising that they chose the most isolated area."

"They're a strange species. Have you ever had one of their females come after you?"

Karoft raised an eyebrow.

"By your expression, you don't know what I'm talking about."

"We're almost there, and I believe there's a familiar shuttle waiting for us in docking bay four."

Territaff craned his neck to see around Karoft as he banked into a landing posture. A small portal opened in a massive bubble-domed hangar. When the shuttle straightened, Territaff grinned. His beautiful shuttle was bathed in lights on the launching spur of the docking bay.

"How...? I was in a life pod... You have a lot of explaining to do," Territaff said, jabbing a finger for emphasis.

"That will have to wait," Karoft said, looking around as they stepped onto the small landing pad. "I want to place these restraints on your wrists and ankles," he said, kneeling and snapping the ankle locks. "We only need them to clear docking control and receive our departure clearance. I hope my guy got my message, or we're both going to be in shackles."

"How do these things work?" Territaff said, admiring the lightweight restraints on his ankles.

"Try running."

Territaff made a forward motion, and his legs locked. No matter how hard he tried, he couldn't lift or move his legs.

"That's impressive. Muscle induction?"

Karoft nodded as he locked the wrist restraints on him. "You need to relax to move. Any sudden change in muscle tension will cause them to lock. They're not too tight?"

"No, they're fine." Territaff frowned at the restraints.

"Okay, relax and look criminal." Karoft glanced at Territaff's deadpan expression and mumbled, "Never mind."

"Well, we're about to find out if our little pretense will play out," Territaff said, seeing a small security detail approaching them. "Are these your guys?"

"No. They're not even from my department. They're Alliance security. We've been uncovered."

Karoft swallowed down an anxious lump that rose from his chest. He stiffened into a military bearing, jutting out his chin.

"Administer Karoft," the largest of the three guards, addressed him. "We have orders to detain your prisoner, pending proper clearance from Venubian Control."

"There must be a mistake, officer..." Karoft glanced at the officer's nametag, "Behz."

Behz handed Karoft a copy of his orders.

"Officer Behz, these orders are not from Venubian Control nor signed by an Alliance official. Who's Elmer Fudd?"

Karoft looked at the officer, who was now holding a stun

gun on him. "Sir, I was instructed to bring this prisoner, willing or not."

"I see," Karoft said, looking at Territaff, who had the familiar look of a man contemplating a plan. So, who do you work for?"

"That will become apparent if you follow me, sir."

The officer gestured with his gun for them to walk. The other two guards pulled their guns out and filed in behind them.

"There's something screwy about this," Territaff transmitted to Karoft. *"Elmer Fudd is a code name known only to one person."*

"Well, at least they only have stun guns. What do you want to do?"

"Let's see what happens. I got a feeling we're caught up in someone else's deception."

"We don't have time for this, Terri. Let's make a break for your shuttle."

"Minor detail. I'm shackled."

"Think of something."

"I've a hunch this will be all right. I sense a strong and familiar presence."

Karoft's demeanor relaxed, sensing the same strong signature. Territaff's heart raced with joy and apprehension as they approached a figure covered in a long, red hooded cape.

"Verubeal!" Karoft shouted in surprise as the figure removed the large hood from her head. She gave him a warm hug. "I thought you would meet us on board," Karoft said, but her joy soured when she saw worry lines around Verubeal's eyes and mouth.

A tide of emotions washed over Territaff as he gazed at her ageless, beautiful face.

"Why are you here?" Territaff said.

"Is that the best hello you can give me?" she chided him.

"I'm a little handicapped." He held up his wrists.

"Based on my reports, I think shackles may be best for you."

"Sorry," Karoft said, releasing Territaff's wrist and ankle restraints.

Verubeal walked up close to Territaff and kissed him gently on the cheek. She ran a hand through his long, wavy black hair. "You need a haircut," she said with a sad smile. They wrapped their arms around each other in a long, tight hug.

"I've missed you," Territaff said, "but why have you come here? It's not safe. He sensed her apprehension through their hug. "We're not just dealing with the Zenti. A new and mysterious faction has eluded our efforts to uncover its identity. They're organized and have a well-conceived plan. Zohleemay now has assets everywhere."

Verubeal nodded. "We are aware of this additional participant in the Zenti's cause. That is why I'm here. We thought we saw an opportunity to make it seem like you were out of the way for a while. Venubian Control detected the missile as you approached the corridor and would have it destroyed. Karoft realized the missile was not a threat in time to capture it. His quick thinking may allow us to learn more about the Zenti's mysterious ally. It's also apparent we need you back aboard Biomei instead of sitting in a comfortable detention cell here in the Bylar sector."

"Do we know who fired the damn thing?" Territaff asked. "The missile's technology was too advanced to be of Zenti design."

"Yes," Verubeal looked at the guards. "Thank you," she dismissed them, then regarded Karoft and Territaff solemnly. The missile used a type of antimatter that we believed was of Vultaran design, and it was fired from the Earth's moon. The Vultarans deny any knowledge of the device or its material design. We've no reason not to believe them. The Zenti stole enough technology from their system to create the missile, but it was not such a sophisticated device without help."

"Earth's moon?" Territaff's face screwed up into a tight, puzzled expression as he recalled all the events since his departure from Biomei. "Then it wasn't the Zenti who were pursuing us." He stiffened and said, "Do we have any ideas on what we're dealing with?"

"What we know is Zohleemay has made some strong connections on Earth," Verubeal said. "We're more interested in how he has accomplished such a rapid rise within the U.S. Defense Department's industrial complex. The Americans are being manipulated and are unaware of anything beyond what Zohleemay has presented. There are those within the military who suspect him but aren't in a strong enough position to expose him. We need to help them expose Zohleemay. You must find out who he's aligned with and stop them. The Alliance is new and is in a fragile state. All we've worked for is about to be lost if we're unsuccessful. No one can afford another war."

A Bylar came lumbering down the long gangplank, stopping at the bottom, then chirped something to Verubeal.

"Uh, Karoft, is that the same freighter that rescued me?" Territaff asked with a sudden uneasiness as he observed the Bylar gawking at them.

"Yeah. Why?"

The Bylar took a few paces closer to them, then blinked her large, engaging eyes, recognizing Territaff. She arched her head up, took a deep breath, and let out a long, shrill-laden squawk.

Verubeal said, "It seems the captain knows you, Terri." She noticed the Bylar's extended neck feathers and wanting gaze. Then she lowered her head close to Verubeal. "Oh my, Terri," Verubeal gave him an amused smile. She wants you to join her at her table for an intimate dinner."

"Verubeal, you know damn well what she wants," Territaff snapped. He said to the Bylar, "I must refuse your generous offer. I'm preparing to leave on urgent business, maybe some other time?" He spoke quickly, then gave Verubeal a pleading look to enlist her help with this anxious Bylar captain.

"He's very disappointed that he'll not be able to share your generous hospitality," Verubeal transmitted to the Bylar.

The Bylar made another horrible screech, then swung her large frame around and into her ship.

Territaff let out a long breath. "Thank you. I had visions of being squeezed and stroked all night."

Karoft and Verubeal both smiled at him.

"It will be tight, but we can all go together."

"No. As much as I would like to...." She eyed Territaff for a moment, then ran her hand down his cheek. "You know I can't go. The Bylars have agreed to take me back to Venubia. I only wanted to see you before you returned to Biomei and share this information with you. A retrofit for an upgraded weapon's design has been integrated into Biomei's defense matrix. She promised me not to reveal its existence until its installation became necessary. Regrettably, that time has come. There are specifications for the droids to install the new stealth shielding and a defensive navigation system." She handed Territaff a Thailion crystal, then spoke in a low voice. "Download this information into your internal compiler, then destroy the crystal. Upload the information into Biomei upon your return.

"We've detected strange energy signatures from sectors above and below the Earth's surface. There also appears to be much activity on the Earth's moon. You need to pin this down. That's what Karoft does best. It could be what we're looking for. We'll be trailing you through the corridor. Be safe." She patted his cheek in a motherly way. "Don't look so worried, my dear, Phillip. I'll be fine. These dark matters will pass."

She turned and walked up the long gangplank with all the grace and majesty of her office.

"She came especially to see you, Terri," Karoft said.

Territaff nodded as he watched Verubeal for a moment.

"She's an amazing woman," he whispered, then said to Karoft, "Okay, my friend, we got our orders. Let's get the hell out of here."

CHAPTER 32

"Dr. DeZenti, you seem distracted," General Dickerson said, looking into the doctor's large, pale eyes, which somehow seemed incongruous with his tiny face and broad chin.

DeZenti was an oddity for General Dickerson, both in appearance and behavior. The general always took pride in being a good judge of character, an essential trait for his leadership position. The little man sitting opposite him was unreadable, adding to Dickerson's growing suspicions.

"General, I must apologize. We've reached a critical juncture in the project. This meeting, while necessary, comes at a bad time."

"I see. Well, we should reschedule then and allow you to get back to the project. After all, we share a common goal." He forced a smile.

Dr. DeZenti looked down as if in thought and then lifted his head. "Yes. That's fine. Let's reschedule at your convenience."

DeZenti stood and started for the door. He stopped and turned, then respectfully nodded to the general, as though reminding himself of the courtesy before leaving the small conference room.

General Dickerson stood and walked to the expansive windowed wall to observe the activities below on the manufacturing floor. He sipped hot coffee from a new company mug and looked curiously at the logo embossed in bright gold detail on the dark blue mug. It comprised interwoven circular lines surrounding a hydrogen atom.

"At least DeZenti listened to me, and now they have decent coffee," he mumbled.

He finished his coffee and placed the mug on the conference table. The general noticed Dr. DeZenti had left his laptop on. At first, he gave the screen a passing glance. He was about to leave when something on the screen caught his attention.

There were odd-looking symbols on the bottom of the page. He quickly looked around while pulling out his cell phone and took a picture of the screen. He pressed the page-down button, and a whole page of symbols appeared. He was unsure if he had stumbled upon simple scientific shorthand or a cipher as he studied the wavy lines and overlapping patterns. In either case, it aroused the general's internal alert system, and he decided it warranted further study.

He lost himself for a moment, scrolling and taking pictures. After reviewing a few pages, he glanced at the count in the left-hand corner of the screen. "Two thousand and seventeen pages," he mumbled under his breath.

The document was too large, and he knew it was impractical to photograph the entire thing. *What I wouldn't give for a Flash Drive right now.*

With a sigh, he returned to the large window and looked around the facility. From his vantage point, he could see large presses stamping out what appeared to be the shell of the mechanized soldier's torso. He stared at the cleanroom on the far side of the plant, where a small group of white-clad workers was inspecting circuit boards under a microscope. As he pondered the activities below him, he realized he had never seen a completed cyborg or a constructed portion. He wondered if DeZenti was hiding the other parts. The general took in the rest of the expansive floor. He noticed a group of overhead doors at the rear of the enormous bay.

"Where's the receiving office?" he wondered aloud.

He saw separate men's and women's bathrooms, but no breakroom. He estimated there had to be at least two hundred workers on the floor, all looking busy. None of them appeared to be interacting with each other as they had on his earlier visits.

"Very odd," the general shook his head, realizing it. He was witnessing the most disciplined workforce he had ever seen.

"Ah, you're still here." DeZenti surprised the general.

"Yes, doctor. I was impressed by the dedication of your employees. I haven't observed any of them leaving their workstations to converse, use the bathroom, or even drink water. They just work. You must tell me your secret, doctor."

"Eh, my secret?" His face flushed. "Yes. It all begins with good breeding," the doctor said, slightly flustered.

"Breeding?" The general questioned with a raised eyebrow.

"I'm sorry. I... I mean good attitude and training," DeZenti said, giving the general an uncertain look.

Dickerson smiled inwardly at catching the doctor by surprise. His curiosity was piqued, thinking This is most interesting. "Well, whatever you do in your selection process would greatly interest me. Perhaps we could meet for lunch and discuss this further. It would be good to get you out of here for a couple of hours. You look like you could use the break." The general picked up his hat, squared it on his head, and regarded the doctor with a friendly smile. "I'll have my administrative assistant call you to arrange a convenient time."

"That's most gracious of you, General, but I never take lunch. And leaving the facility until this project phase is completed would be most difficult," DeZenti said, with his composure and aloof attitude regained.

"Very well, but we still need to have our weekly briefing. How about early tomorrow morning, say around 07:00?"

"As you wish," he said, nodding slightly, then retrieved his laptop.

He eyed the general, noticing it was on a different page, but said nothing.

"Good day, doctor. See you tomorrow." General Dickerson felt good as he watched the doctor's expression flush up again. Interesting. Very interesting," he thought as he bounced down the stairs.

When he was about to go through the large glass door that led back to the reception room, he caught a strange sight out of the corner of his eye. He turned to look closer, but whatever it was had gone. He thought he had seen something that was neither human nor animal.

"What the hell was that?" he mumbled.

There was a large metal press to his right. His curiosity was heightened before he spied the oddity, and now it was compelling him to discover what it was. He thought it went behind the machine. Right as he went behind the press, it went into operation. The sudden hissing of the machine's hydraulic press startled the general. Once he regained his composure, a worker stood in front of him.

"Is there something I can help you with, sir?" the worker said.

"Was there someone else here just a moment ago?"

"Just me, sir," he said, puzzled. "Is everything okay?"

The general nodded, then turned for the exit. He gave the area another glance before leaning into the door and leaving.

"That was too close," the young worker shouted over the heavy sounds of the press.

A small, wiry creature, partially hidden within the shadow of the large machine, made a clicking sound. Then, scurrying close to the wall, it ducked into a concealed door behind a high stack of boxed parts.

* * *

"You're back early," General Dickerson's administrative assistant said.

"Fran, get me that nerdy specialist from cryptology and Captain Jason up here on the double."

General Dickerson tossed his hat onto a hook on his antique coat rack in the corner of his spacious office. He flopped into his plush, leather executive chair and rifled through the drawers of his expansive desk.

Despite his military discipline, the general was a hands-on, multi-tasking workaholic with a tendency toward clutter. His desktop was always neat, but his drawers were a different matter. He constantly needed help locating items of "timely necessity," as the general would refer to any item he couldn't find.

"General Dickerson," Fran called over the intercom.

"Yes, Fran."

"Specialist Crenshaw is meeting with Colonel Cameron, and Captain Jason was ordered on a TDA to Los Alamos."

"Shit," Dickerson exclaimed, leaning back in his chair, considering his next move. He pressed the intercom button again and said, "Fran, find out who sent Jason to Los Alamos?"

"I would need to look that up. Sir, come to think of it, I don't recall ever seeing those orders."

"He was reassigned without my approval?"

"It appears so."

"How did that happen?"

"I have it here. The orders came directly from DOD."

"Really? That's interesting. Since when does the DOD reassign someone from my base without notifying me? I want you to drop everything you're doing, find out who signed off on those orders, and get Crenshaw here. Also, please find me a flash drive."

General Dickerson reflected on the two escaped detainees and wondered if they had any connection to the events unfolding. He recalled what the two consultants had told Cameron and began to believe they might have some credence after all. *They were trying to warn us about something. I had a feeling about those two. Now, how do I go about finding them?* "Shit! What the hell is going on here?"

He lifted his feet onto a corner of his desk and locked his hands behind his head. He reviewed all the disjointed events of the past few months. *DeZenti and the strange disappearance of those two consultants seemed to be somehow related. Why did Cameron want them out of the way when they were brought in to assist us? Why was Cameron talking with Crenshaw? He doesn't report to him. He's assigned to Jason, but Jason reports to Cameron.*

"Shit!" he snapped, not realizing Fran had walked into his office.

"Is everything all right, sir?"

The general dropped his feet back onto the floor and sat upright in his chair.

"No, everything is fucked up, my dear."

Fran was an army brat, and Dickerson's rough language was nothing new to her. Despite her height (almost six feet), her movements were remarkably graceful for a woman of her size. Her perfect posture and long frame gave her round body a fit appearance. She wore her luxurious, light brown hair up, and, with her probing green eyes, gave her an authoritative appearance that was subdued by her soft Southern accent and warm smile.

"I've located the orders, sir," Fran said. She handed a copy to him.

He looked at Fran in surprise, which quickly turned to anger. "I never signed these orders."

"Is it possible that you just forgot to sign them? You have been very busy the past few weeks. Maybe you signed them perfunctorily along with the hundred other items that cross your desk daily."

"Don't do that," he objected.

"Do what, sir?"

"Try to cover for me. I look at every piece of paper that comes across this oversized desk, and I'd remember reading any goddamn orders," he slapped his fist into his hand, "that reassigned someone from my goddamn command." Dickerson noticed Fran's puzzled expression and, in a calmer voice, said, "You don't remember seeing them either, do you?"

"Sorry. I thought because you have been—"

"I appreciate it." He cut her off. The last thing he wanted to hear was excuses. "Fran, these orders are two days old. If you recall, I was out of the office all day on Wednesday. There was no way I could've signed these orders."

"Could they have been sent to your phone for expediting?"

The general got out his phone and scrolled through the e-mails from the past few days.

"They're not here." He frowned.

"May I see the orders, sir?" He handed them to her. Her eyebrows arched upward as she scrutinized the signature.

"That's not your signature."

"What?" he grabbed the orders from her and gave them a closer look. "I hate to admit this, but I can't tell the difference."

"Your signature varies depending on the time of day and the document you're signing. If you compare this D…," she looked closer at the signature and added, "and the r in the morning report, it's different from the d and r later in the day."

She returned to her desk with a copy of another order he had signed earlier and handed it to him.

"You tend to print your D's when you sign orders, and you use a more stylized D when you sign other things."

She picked up a copy of a receipt he had signed earlier from his outbox on the corner of his desk and handed it to him.

"I never thought about that," the general said, rubbing his chin. "Whoever did this would have known it would be discovered. So why would they do it? Fran, get me, Major Oliver. You'll find his number in my defense department contacts. Call Cameron and tell him that Specialist Crenshaw is needed now. If Cameron says anything, put him on with me."

"Yes, sir. Oh, by the way, Dr. DeZenti called while you were en route and asked if he could postpone the weekly briefing until the beginning of next week. He said he'd e-mailed a summary report he'd gladly review with you next week."

"Oh, really. Well, that won't do. Tell him we need to—" He had a sudden thought. "No… tell him…. next week will be fine. I suspect the doctor and I'll be discussing a lot more than what's in his cryptic report when we meet. Fran, don't call.

Send him an e-mail using my signature block."

"You look like you could use a good cup of coffee and a cheese Danish." Fran smiled warmly.

"You know, that sounds like a good idea." As she started to leave, the general added, "Oh, Fran...."

"Yes?"

"Thank you."

A few minutes later, Fran walked back in, carrying a cup of coffee covered by a paper plate with a large cheese Danish on it. She handed him a flash drive.

"Specialist Crenshaw is waiting for you," she informed him, placing the coffee and plate on his desk.

"That was quick," Dickerson remarked, taking a large bite of the Danish.

"Specialist Crenshaw showed up before I could call Colonel Cameron. Should I send him in?"

"Ahh," he sighed with a mouthful of Danish, "you went to Patsy's, my favorite." He took a big swallow of coffee. "Make Crenshaw comfortable. I'll be with him in a few minutes. Also, could you please get that flash drive for me?"

"Right away, sir."

The general finished his Danish and coffee while reviewing his e-mails. He looked back a few days to ensure he didn't miss Jason's TDA. There were the usual scores of chatter and clutter, and then he came across an e-mail sent at 03:34 hours. It was from Captain Jason, who requested assistance from the general, that Jason preferred not to put it in writing. Dickerson's internal red flag went up. He picked up his secure phone and called Captain Jason's cell phone. He got the captain's voicemail and left a message to call him on his secure line. Things are getting interesting, the general thought. He pushed the intercom button on his phone and told Fran to send in Crenshaw.

Specialist Robert Crenshaw was your quintessential nerd. His uniform always looked like he slept in it, and his appearance could be summed up as disheveled. General Dickerson always had to restrain himself whenever he saw Crenshaw, but forgave his untidiness because of his remarkable talents. The general found him to be a brilliant young man. Also, one of the most reliable soldiers the general had ever worked with. Crenshaw had been asked to do some complicated and a few dicey operations for Dickerson. What he was about to ask the young man now could be a real challenge and possibly illegal.

"Good morning, sir," Crenshaw greeted him while standing at attention in front of the general's desk.

"Good morning, Crenshaw," Dickerson motioned for him to sit. You're aware that the post laundry will clean and press your uniform," the general reminded, giving the young specialist a stern look. Then, noticing his tight demeanor, he said, "Relax, Crenshaw. I'm not beating you up on your appearance, but if you're going to work under my command, I insist on proper military attire and appearance."

"Sir, are you reassigning me?" Crenshaw tried not to smile. "That would be a great honor, sir."

"Well, you might think differently after I give you your first assignment." Dickerson scrolled through the pictures he had taken from Dr. DeZenti's laptop and handed the phone to Crenshaw.

Crenshaw's forehead furrowed as he studied the pictures. "What am I looking at, sir?"

"That, my young friend, is your first assignment. Consider these pictures classified. First, transfer the pictures to this drive, then upload them to your computer, and see if you can determine what they are, such as a language, a code, or anything else. I need this right away. Please take my phone, transfer the pictures, and return it promptly. Make sure no one sees you transferring these pictures, and do not discuss this with anyone. Any questions?"

Crenshaw nodded without looking up from the general's

phone. He stood, paced around the room with the phone in hand, then looked up in surprise.

"Sir, this is unlike anything I've ever seen. Where did you take these?"

"Stop pacing and sit," Dickerson snapped. "Give me your eyes." Crenshaw looked attentively at him. "Analyze these pictures and try to decipher their meaning. I'll have more for you to analyze tomorrow. From where I took these, it is on a need-to-know basis."

The general leaned back in his chair and studied the young man. Crenshaw returned his attention to the phone, turning it around and viewing the pictures from different angles.

"Tell me about yourself."

Crenshaw lifted his eyes, giving the general a quizzical look as though he had to think about the question for a moment. "Well... sir, what would you like to know?"

General Dickerson smiled at his innocence. "You really are a nerd, Crenshaw. You probably don't get out of your cubicle very much—do you?"

"Captain Jason keeps me pretty busy."

"Do you have any hobbies? A girlfriend? Are you married? Do you have a life outside of work? Tell me about yourself."

Crenshaw's face blushed, feeling embarrassed by Dickerson's inquiry. In his fourteen years of service, he has never been asked anything more personal than How was your weekend?

"Well, sir, I'm not in any kind of relationship," he said timidly. "I love building model boats, cars, and starships," he blurted. I have quite a collection of different Enterprises, including aircraft carriers and a couple from the Star Trek series. I love science fiction." His eyes lit up as he talked about his hobby.

"Are you a Trekkie?" the general asked, trying not to sound condescending.

Crenshaw shook his head and smiled. "No, I'm a nerd, not

a Trekkie. I enjoy building futuristic things. My dad was a big fan of both Star Trek and Star Wars. I'm more of a reader than a movie watcher, though."

"Tell me about your dad?"

"He was an Army pilot... killed in Iraq by a roadside IED."

"When was he killed?"

"About eleven months ago. We were just getting close again, and he was looking forward to his discharge from active duty." Crenshaw hung his head, trying to hold back the emotions welling up in him.

"I'm truly sorry, son." He shook his head and sighed. "I never agreed with our involvement in those wasteful wars. What made you join the Army?"

"I didn't know what I wanted to do after high school. I was only fifteen. Skipped a few grades by going to summer school. Then, I traveled with a friend across the country for a few years, doing various odd jobs, including fixing computers, removing viruses, and locating lost documents. You know, nerdy stuff." He chuckled. "When my dad was assigned to San Diego, he invited me to live there. My parents were divorced. Mom remarried and moved to France. My stepdad owned a manufacturing company and was pretty well off. I didn't get along with him, so I took my dad up on his offer. That led me to apply to San Diego State, where I majored in mathematics and computer science. When my dad was killed, I moved back to South Florida, then, for some inexplicable reason, thought the Army would be the best option for a career, and the GI Bill is now paying my tuition. It helped me attain several degrees in Computer Science and Mathematics, and I'm currently collaborating with a few post-grads on my doctoral thesis in Theoretical Physics. We were given a government grant to construct a quantum-based computer. It's a very exciting project."

"Really? Where do you find the time? Those are challenging subjects."

"There's a lot of crossovers between the disciplines. Once you get the basics down, everything becomes rather simple.

"Well, there's no doubt about your smarts, Crenshaw... Crenshaw, what's your first name again?"

"Robert, sir."

"So, do your friends call you Rob or Robert?"

"I have no friends, and everybody calls me Crenshaw, but I would appreciate being called Rob, sir."

"What's your current security clearance?"

"Top Secret, sir."

"Well, it'll be bumped up to Crypto, so expect NSA, CIA, and FBI background checks over the next few days." Is there anything I should know before they begin?"

"Nothing I'm aware of."

"Very good. I'll also need to kick you up two grades to get your rank aligned with your duties. I'll have your reassignment orders by the close of business today. Captain Jason will handle the details when he gets back from Los Alamos. Go wait in the outer office and send Fran in for me." General Dickerson stood and held his hand out to Crenshaw. "Welcome aboard, son." Rob jumped to his feet and extended a firm handshake to the general.

"Thank you, General Dickerson. I'm honored to be serving with you. I promise always to give you my very best." When he reached the door, Crenshaw turned and said, "Did you say Captain Jason was returning from Los Alamos?"

"Yes. Why?"

"Well, sir, I distinctly heard Captain Jason say he was going to DC."

"You're sure about that?"

"Yessir. I overheard him telling his wife he would be gone for a few weeks. Captain Jason also always emails his itinerary and contact information in case I need to reach him." Crenshaw pulled out his cell phone and looked up the e-mail. "He had a flight scheduled at 0:500 hours out of Miami to arrive at Andrews at 08:47 with no return info.”

"Thank you, Rob.” The general sat down and thought for a moment. “Oh, Rob, what did Colonel Cameron want?”

"I'm not sure. He asked me if I knew anything about a project, *Rail Gunner*. I told him I didn't.”

"Was that true?”

Crenshaw's face reddened as he looked at the general with a nervous smile. Then, he looked down for a moment as though pondering his thoughts. “No,” he answered timidly, looking uncomfortable. “I thought you already knew about this, sir. After all, it's your project.”

"Project *Rail Gunner?* You mean project *CyborSword*?”

"No, sir, CyborSword is with Doctor DeZenti's team at DARPA. Rail Gunner is a separate project developing a weapon prototype to track and destroy space-based threats, such as asteroids or missile attacks. Captain Jason was to brief me on it when he returned. He told me he was attending a conference with DARPA's coordinator and project leads.”

Dickerson stared, lost in thought, making Crenshaw uneasy before he spoke in a low, measured tone, “From this point forward, you'll report directly to me. I'm arranging for you to take over the empty office next to mine. You'll not engage in or discuss anything with anyone, including Captain Jason, and especially not with Colonel Cameron. I want to be notified if anyone approaches you about these projects. You'll not return to your office or speak to anyone unless I say so. Are we clear?”

"Crystal, sir.”

"Thank you, Rob. That will be all.”

"Yessir,” Crenshaw snapped to attention, then made a neat military about-face out of the office.

General Dickerson sat upright in his chair in thought. Railguns and cyborgs. “What's that weird little bastard up to now?” he muttered, dialing Fran's extension. “Fran, get me, Captain Jason. Get him on the phone, no excuses.”

* * *

General Dickerson's frustration was seeping through in his voice, which was gruff and sharp as he spoke with Major Oliver. "Somebody issued those orders," the general snapped. "They're properly formatted and have a valid order number."

"General Dickerson, I've checked and rechecked. There's no record of those orders ever being cut, at least from here," Major Oliver explained in an exasperated tone for the third time.

"Well, if you didn't cut those orders, then who did?" Dickerson said, thinking aloud.

"Sir, for lack of a better explanation, those orders must be bogus."

"So, what you're telling me, Major, is that someone with access to your department is issuing bogus orders right under your nose?"

"With all due respect, sir, those orders could have been written from any headquarters, including yours. Whoever issued them had knowledge and probable access to the DOD's system, which is cause for concern."

"Major, I need you to do a thorough investigation on your end and report back to me by the close of business today." He banged the phone down, cursing under his breath.

Major Oliver had confirmed what he already believed. Either Captain Jason or someone else created counterfeit orders. But for what purpose? The events mounting over the past several months were increasing his frustration. He didn't want to believe what he suspected because it would involve people he knew and had trusted for decades.

It was almost six o'clock in the evening when Fran knocked on the general's door and walked into the office with a ghostly, pale complexion. The general stood, gently took her arm, and led her to the couch. "What's wrong?" he said.

A line of tears ran down her cheek. She licked her dry lips

and then asked for water. He went into the small refrigerator in the corner of his office and got a bottle of water. Her hands shook so badly she couldn't open it. The general took the bottle from her, removed the cap, and handed it back. She took a large swallow, then coughed.

He waited while Fran composed herself. She took another swallow of water, then let out a long, shuddering sigh. She handed him a copy of an email she had received. Dickerson had to read it twice to make sure he understood.

"That good man," Fran sobbed. "He had a lovely wife and two small children. It makes little sense." She stared outward as she spoke.

Dickerson sat beside her, wrapped his arm around her shoulders, and said solemnly, "No, it never makes sense, especially when it hits so close to home. Do you know if his family has been contacted?"

She shook her head, inhaled deeply, and looked into the general's eyes. "I'm sorry, Bill, for all the emotion. His wife, Joyce, and I had gotten close over the past few months, and… and…" Her voice cracked, and her body trembled as she cried. The general turned on the couch and embraced her as she wept.

"I'm afraid, Fran, that this will only be the first of many shocks to come," he said as he looked once more at the e-mail and thought, car accident, my ass.

CHAPTER 33

Kathy jerked awake from a disturbing dream. She wiped the sweat from her face and chest with a corner of her bedsheet. "What's wrong?" Biomei asked.

"Just a bad dream," she said.

Kathy called for a sink and washed her hands and face, hoping to wash away the horrors of her dream. The transformation process had cut some deep emotional scars. She kept their lingering darkness at bay while awake, only to have it seep into her sleep. They would return to her, haunt her dreams for days, then disappear. There were days when the images of mangled and dismembered bodies would appear every time she closed her eyes. This was one of those days.

"You should reconsider removing those awful memories. It's a simple process, Kathy. Why do you refuse?"

In hindsight, Biomei regretted giving Kathy the full experience of the last Zenti conflict. Territaff also had reservations but thought it would give her a clear understanding of the evil they faced. Neither of them anticipated she would suffer such a profound side effect. Territaff was Biomei's only guide. She had never considered the emotional cushion Territaff had through his enhancements before his transformation process. Nickada was careful and deliberate with him during his procedure. If only she were here, Biomei thought, surprised by such a human reaction.

"My brain has been messed with enough. Thank you," Kathy said. "Where's Cuz?"

"Did you forget? Concentrate on him for a moment, and he'll respond to you."

Kathy closed her eyes and visualized Cuz's image in her mind. He responded as soon as she had him fixed in her mind's eye. Even though it has been almost two months since she completed the transformation, her new abilities still surprised her. Biomei always encouraged her to use and explore the full range and depth of all her new skills. Her human nature still dominated her thinking, especially in incorporating her telepathic and empathic abilities.

"What's wrong?" Cuz transmitted to her.

"Could use some company."

"Come to the bridge. I can use your help."

"On my way," she transmitted.

She grabbed a jumpsuit from her closet, put it on, and then jogged out of her quarters.

Cuz was busy monitoring the activities on Earth when Kathy joined him on the bridge.

"Received a communications brief from Verubeal," he said to her as she came up behind him, wrapped her arms around his waist, and rested her head on his broad shoulders. Cuz turned in the cradle of her arms and kissed her. "You had another dream, didn't you?" he said, picking up her intense, lingering emotions.

She nodded, regarded Cuz warmly, and then kissed him back. "It's nothing you need to worry about. I'm just a little worn out, but otherwise okay."

"You must practice your breathing exercises. They'll help you when you're having those disturbing dreams."

She looked down and said, "I know."

"They'll pass."

"You keep telling me that, but it's been almost two months." She frowned. "I'm sorry. It's just the dreams. They make me crazy."

"Keep in mind they're only dreams, and the breathing helps to clear your mind of their effects."

"I'll try to remember for the next time. What's going on down there?" she said, looking at the forward-view monitor. It had only been a few months since Kathy had left home, but it felt like a lifetime ago as she gazed at the tiny, bluish-green distant orb. She missed the warm, humid air and the gentle, salty breeze always present during her morning jogs. She missed Fat Jack and some of her favorite regulars at the bar. Living aboard Biomei was like living on a remote island. She was so far from home and so far from who she was that everything down there, on Earth, seemed like a distant dream.

"Territaff and Administer Karoft are already past Europa and will be here soon," Cuz said. "Karoft believes he recognizes those energy signatures we're analyzing. The strongest signals emanate from a subterranean cavern off the Yucatan peninsula at Chicxulub. The latest updates indicate that the signals have become stronger."

"That doesn't sound good," Kathy said, pinching her lower lip in thought.

"I'm concerned the Zenti is close to gearing up for something. I've transmitted the coordinates to Terri. He wants to investigate the location as soon as possible."

"Tell him to hurry. I miss him."

"Tell him yourself. He's in range now."

"He's that close?" Kathy said, her eyes widened with excitement.

Cuz nodded, then gestured for her to contact him.

"Welcome back," she transmitted.

"Hello, love. It's good to hear from *you. Your transmission is strong."*

"Biomei said I'll develop many new abilities, but I think telepathy is becoming my favorite."

"Just remember, it's a dual-edged gift."

"Oh, I've already discovered how the empathic half causes communication problems. Pure honesty is sometimes difficult for a former lying bitch like me."

Kathy could feel Territaff's smile within his transmission. It was a pleasant surprise to feel him in this new emotional light. She had never felt a human emotion in that way. Kathy could also sense a difference in Territaff's transmissions from Cuz's. Cuz's were warm and sometimes erratic, whereas Territaff's were even and controlled.

"Well, welcome to the honesty club."

"What's your ETA?"

"Twelve hours, fourteen minutes, Earth-time," Territaff transmitted, then to Cuz, "I need you to arm Biomei with the following defensive weapon modules."

"How can we implement those modules?" Cuz questioned. "Biomei has no true weapons, or do you, Biomei?"

"After our first encounter with the Zenti, Verubeal and Nickada convinced me to be retrofitted with defensive weapons," Biomei explained. Cuz and Kathy could sense Biomei's apprehension within her transmission. "However, I insisted that their existence be kept secret. We agreed that my weapons would only be enabled if no other recourse existed. Verubeal has convinced me that our present situation makes their employment necessary."

"I'm sorry, Biomei," Territaff transmitted. "I understand your feelings toward violence of any kind, but this is necessary. Okay, Cuz, standby for download."

"Hold that download," Biomei interjected.

"What's wrong?" Kathy transmitted.

"I've detected a carrier frequency piggybacked on one of my sub-bands. Stand by while I confirm."

"Hanc has also picked it up," Territaff transmitted.

"It's narrow and powerful," Cuz observed. "Biomei has a power signature similar to the subterranean energy wave. The technology generating these frequencies is unknown to me, but there's something familiar within certain segments of the pattern."

"Hanc informed me they may be Vultaran design," Territaff transmitted.

"Vultaran?" Kathy eyed Cuz with a puzzled look. "I'm not familiar with Vultarans. Who are they?"

"A new piece of the puzzle," Territaff transmitted. "I'm unhappy to admit, but I think one of them did a read on me. I'm *increasing speed. Our new ETA is now four hours and eighteen minutes. Hold everything until we get there."*

"Is that wise, Terri?" Biomei cautioned. *"At that speed, you'll be close to critical mass."*

"I understand, but the shuttle has been upgraded with many new toys, and Hanc assures me we'll be well within our updated threshold parameters."

Territaff sounded confident to everyone but Kathy.

"What do you mean by a read?" Kathy questioned, still curious about the Vultaran.

"One thing at a time, guys," Territaff transmitted, avoiding Kathy's question.

"Territaff, my immediate concern is you'll appear as a large gamma burst, which may cause a great deal of unwarranted attention and blow our cover," Cuz transmitted with uneasiness.

"I understand your concern. But if I'm right, our cover has already been blown," Territaff responded. *"I strongly suggest you relocate to Alpha-Two and await our arrival. We'll do a quick flyover of the Chicxulub site, then conduct a neutrino-read and x-ray scan."*

"What's Alpha-Two?" Kathy asked Cuz.

"The asteroid belt," Cuz said. "You heard what he said, Biomei, let's move."

"I sure hope he knows what he's doing," Biomei said with a heavy sigh.

Cuz curled his lower lip and said, "I have a bad feeling things are getting dicey."

* * *

Hanc barely had time to react as the missile missed striking the shuttle's midsection by less than fifteen meters.

"That was too damn close," Territaff barked at Hanc.

"Sorry, Terri, there was no warning. It seemed to appear out of nowhere," Hanc said with emulated concern. "What is confounding me is how they got a lock on us at this velocity?"

"They didn't. It must have been an intuitive guess," Territaff said. "Was that what I think it was?" he mumbled, then scanned the high-speed video tracking and his internal visual log. "It was, damn it. Did you guys get a read on that thing?" Territaff said over his intercom.

"We did. Now I know why the power signatures from the Yucatan site were so familiar," Cuz transmitted, with the corners of his mouth curled into a bemused smile.

"Okay, guys," Kathy said with her hands on her hips. "Would you care to bring me up to speed?"

"Shame on you, Cuz," Territaff scolded.

Cuz regarded Kathy with a passive expression, then said, "I was about to explain everything to you and Terri as soon as I confirmed my data."

"Well, grandfather, what did you come up with?" Territaff asked. Cuz paused for a long moment until Territaff broke the uneasy silence with, "We're turning blue in anticipation, Cuz."

"Yes, the data confirms it," Cuz resumed, as though pulled from deep thought. "They both have the same power signatures. The energy waves emanating from the Yucatan site and the missile... Ah, guys, brace for evasive maneuvers," Cuz blurted, transmitting the plasma drive's firing sequence to Biomei.

Biomei made an abrupt twelve-G nosedive into a hard bank to port, sending Kathy and Cuz flying into the forward bulkhead. As they got to their feet, Biomei made another sharp maneuver, sending them tumbling into the starboard midsection hatchway.

"Are you all right?" Cuz asked Kathy.

"Fine, just a little bruised in areas that will remain unmentioned."

"Understood."

She frowned and said, "We're in trouble again, aren't we?"

Cuz nodded, stood, helped Kathy to her feet, and returned

to the communications station.

"Is everyone all right?" Biomei asked.

"Just fine," they answered.

"At least, now we know what their internal carrier wave looks like," Cuz said, then wrinkled his forehead in thought as he transmitted, *"Hanc, send me the data from the missile that engaged you outside the corridor."*

"Cuz, you'll find they are both similar in design, and there is a 90.579 percent probability they are Vultaran, in design, but not in origin," Hanc transmitted along with the requested data.

"Vultaran. Why haven't we known about this species before now?" Cuz stated what everybody was thinking.

"If a quantum generator is transmitting its carrier wave, how will we be able to decipher it?" Kathy's question surprised everyone.

Cuz nodded in approval. "You've been doing your homework, young lady," he whispered. "Although hacking into a quantum signature is impossible, knowing what it looks like will let us emulate it. We'll generate a duplicate five megahertz apart. That'll let us track the origin and reception points. We'll also get some idea of the data configuration, provided we can keep our carrier in sync with theirs. If we can, it'll give us precise locations and a general idea of the transmission's structure, but unfortunately, no actual information."

"Won't they know we're eavesdropping on their signals?" Kathy asked.

"That's the beautiful thing about one quantum computer copying another's data patterns. It all looks the same to the end-user. I should also note that this is a unique feature of Biomei's quantum processor. It's biogenetic and can mimic any natural or artificial signal without detection," Cuz proudly stated.

"Wow, Biomei, you never cease to impress me," Kathy said.

"I've intercepted the secondary carrier wave," Biomei informed them. "It was a clumsy attempt to do to us what we're about to do to them. *It's now safe to download, Terri.*"

"So that confirms my earlier assertion," Cuz said as he inputted a set of commands into the linguistic computer.

"What assertion was that?" Territaff asked.

"The missiles are guided remotely, and once within a certain range, they lock onto their target's power signature, then power up to engage. The Universe only knows what we'll face from the strange brew served up to us next."

"Biomei," Hanc's synthesized voice called.

"Yes, Hanc."

"Stand by for download on this frequency." Hanc then transmitted a compressed data stream into Biomei's primary memory node.

"Biomei, decompress the files and be ready with a firing solution on their next pass," Territaff transmitted.

"Standing by," Biomei acknowledged. "I have you on visual, Terri." The forward and aft view screens revealed Territaff's shuttle approach. Kathy's mouth dropped open, watching a small dot of light get bigger as the missile closed on his shuttle.

"How fast is that thing going?" she said, wincing.

"Terri, you're aware that the missile is gaining on you," Cuz said, his emotions rising.

Cuz's sudden passions took him by surprise once again. Will peace ever prevail? he thought, then pushed the thought aside, along with his heightening emotions, and regained his android-like detachment.

"Oh yeah, I'm counting on it," Territaff said excitedly. "How're you doing on that firing solution, Biomei?"

"It's a program created in haste and looks it," she said sharply. "Terri, I need more time to decompress and convert it into a compatible sequence. May I suggest a few evasive maneuvers in the meantime?"

"Just hurry, or we'll both be converted into large debris fields."

"Understood," Biomei said.

"Biomei, there is an embedded sequence code that must be followed to decompress the navigation and tactical modules," Hanc interjected. You are experiencing a higher-order conflict because the operation sequencing is syntactical. We did not have time to embed an auto-quantum computation operative narrative to sequence the upload, so you must do it manually. Install the navigation routine first; the other modules will automatically populate their required sectors. I know that sounds counterintuitive, but the source software is designed for operations that utilize multidimensional algorithms. This is how they can track us over long distances using superposition qubits for their tracking data and ramjet, plasma propulsion, which increases the missile's range almost infinitely."

"A second missile has been detected," Biomei cautioned. It has been launched from a different location. Stand by..."

The silence was unnerving as Kathy watched, holding her breath through clenched teeth as the second speck of light enlarged at an alarming rate.

"Jeeezzzus, the first one has reacquired and locked onto us. It's almost on top of us, guys!" Kathy cried out nervously.

"Firing solution is locked," Biomei said, as the first missile got close enough to read its manufacturer's label: U.S. Army XRJM 1475.

A bright flash filled the aft screen, and then a violent shudder ran through Biomei as an intense shock wave washed over them. A second flash of white light lit up the forward view screen a few seconds later.

"Both targets have been destroyed," Biomei said remorsefully. "I never thought I'd see the day when I'd become a harbinger of war rather than a protector of the peace."

"Defending yourself from evil oppression doesn't make you an aggressor," Territaff said. "These are bad times all around."

"They are," Cuz said with his head bowed. "Did you

happen to make note of the missile's label?"

"Yeah, Cuz, but it shouldn't be a surprise considering the intelligence updates we've been receiving over the past few days," Karoft said. The US government believes Zohleemay is developing a cyborg soldier for military and exploration operations. It's most likely that these new weapons are being manufactured right under the government's nose, and they appear to be unaware of their existence."

"The problem is that we don't have enough intelligence to expose Zohleemay's true intentions. Based on what we've put together, he has a new silent partner providing him with advanced technology. We're dealing with a new dynamic in our problem, and as you can see," he proclaimed, pointing at the debris field of the destroyed missiles, "they're making their intentions known."

"I believe they just made us expose our hand," Territaff added.

"What do you mean, Terri?" Kathy asked.

"It's brilliant," Territaff said, wincing as if suddenly bitten by an invisible force. "By firing on us, they now know Biomei has weapons. They must have moles placed in strategic positions, keeping Zohleemay one step ahead of us. We must infiltrate their network and feed them disinformation, or all our efforts will be in vain.

"It's obvious that Zohleemay has made a powerful ally. The Zenti's tactics differ from what we've seen from them in the past," Cuz observed.

"What's on your mind, Cuz?" Territaff asked.

Cuz's expression turned passive. After a long pause, he said, "Dr. DeZenti does not behave as Zohleemay, which begs the question: is he still Zohleemay?"

"That's interesting," Territaff said. "I've been asking myself that same question for the past hundred million kilometers. Biomei, permission to board?"

"Permission granted," Biomei said and added, "Welcome

home. Go to decontamination."

* * *

Kathy waited anxiously as Territaff completed decontamination. "What should I tell him?" she asked Cuz, chewing on her lower lip.

"You won't have to say a thing. Trust me, he'll know."

Kathy ran up to Territaff as soon as he entered the main bridge. They fell into a warm embrace. He felt the difference in her at once. She had changed, except for a few beautiful traits that remained intact. It was a wondrous joy for him to hold her so close again. For him, just a few days had passed, but for Kathy, more than two months had gone by. She now understood what he meant about time being an illusion. Under normal relativity, Territaff would have been gone for over two hundred years. However, time and space both cease to exist inside the corridor. What would have been thousands of light-years in spacetime are suspended by the miraculous dynamics of the corridor.

The transformation procedure had dug up some painful memories he experienced vicariously through her. Territaff and Kathy's minds were inexorably joined like entangled particles through the transformation procedure. Time and distance were irrelevant to the joining that occurred in the process.

Looking back, he regretted the decision to have her experience the full brunt of the horrors of the Zenti War and the pain and anguish of friends losing loved ones. He was proud of the courage and strength she displayed during the procedure. However, seeing and feeling her in this new light made all the difference, and he concluded it was the best decision for her and the mission.

They remained closely pressed against one another, gazing into each other's eyes. Territaff realized Cuz's presence, shining within Kathy. At first, he was taken aback. He realized Cuz had been the singular stabilizing force in her life since they met. Territaff was happy for her, but even more thrilled with Cuz's incredible emotional leap in his development. Kathy and Cuz were in love, and Territaff felt delighted and relieved by this new development. Also, he had concerns about their compatibility. Reflecting on Kathy for a moment, he wondered if a genetically engineered android and a hybrid humanoid could make a viable couple. He smiled inwardly and concluded that love would prevail.

Cuz watched passively with his alert eyes, analyzing and appreciating every movement. He studied them with a childlike curiosity, taking in every emotion and experiencing them as a brand-new discovery. Cuz couldn't know how much Territaff and Kathy admired his childlike innocence.

Territaff, in a soft voice, asked, "When did you know?" He moved Kathy to arm's length and gazed into her face.

"Know what?" Her brow wrinkled, and she tilted her head back, grinning at Cuz.

"Kathy, you don't have to be coy with me. I'm interested in sharing your joy." Territaff pulled her close again, studying her. "Tell me," he said, his voice stronger, holding his smile. "So, when did you fall in love with Cuz?"

She turned from Territaff in thought. "Looking back on things, I think he had me when he told me he was a biogenetically enhanced android." She looked back at Territaff with glowing eyes. "That did it!" she cried out in joy. "I knew he was perfect for me at that moment because I would be genetically altered and programmed like him. He's a perfect mate." She turned and gave Cuz a loving look. "He's also an amazing guy with an unassuming quality, which I find charming and compelling."

Territaff smiled at Kathy's sincerity. He could feel her joy. *"She really loves him,"* he transmitted to Biomei.

"Am I interrupting?" Karoft asked, feeling a little self-conscious around such strong displays of emotion.

"Sorry," Territaff said, then grabbed Karoft's arm. He led him into the center of the small group. "Kathy, Cuz, it's my pleasure to introduce a good friend and comrade, Renginarri Karoft of Venubia."

Cuz and Kathy placed their left arms across their chests and made a shallow bow from their hips in a formal Venubian greeting.

"I thank you for that kind welcome." He gave everybody a toothy grin and said to Territaff, "You omitted my Administer rank, but I rarely use it anyway."

"Sorry, grandfather, I forgot. But who cares?"

Karoft shrugged and asked, "Where are my quarters?"

"I've sent for one of our droids to show you to your quarters, Administrator Karoft," Biomei said.

Karoft said, "Is that you, Biomei?"

"Yes."

"So pleased to hear from you again. It's good to be aboard."

"It's a pleasure to have you here. I believe this is your first time aboard since my retrofit."

"Yes. I look forward to a tour after a little rest."

"Wait a minute," Kathy said. "Did you say a droid will show him?"

"Yes, Kathy," Biomei said.

"We have droids?"

"Yes."

"Cool." She asked Territaff, "When were you going to tell me about them?"

"I was hoping to keep them in storage as long as possible," Territaff said. "Biomei has seen the need to activate them to finish the defensive retrofit. He transmitted to Biomei, *"I thought you would wait until I got back?"*

"I only activated Shorty. And I didn't know I needed your permission to activate anything on my ship."

"Okay, but you should have warned me so I could've

prepared Kathy."

"Concentrate on the mission, and let me handle everything else."

The bay doors whooshed open, and a humanoid-like machine walked in. It stood on two flexible, multi-hinged legs and moved with a distinct bounce. Kathy marveled at its beautiful design. She was surprised at how proportional its limbs were to its body and how lifelike it appeared for a mechanical device.

It walked up to Kathy and looked at her, its glowing optical sensor blinking. She studied it for a moment, taking in its features. Its body resembled a typical Venubian, with an oval-shaped body and head.

"Hello, Kathy. I'm Shorty," the droid said in a clear voice, then extended one arm with its hand reaching out to her. It's a pleasure to meet you."

Kathy's mouth fell open as she stared wide-eyed at the incredible-looking machine. At first, she didn't know what to make of the droid's actions, then realized it requested a handshake.

"It's a real pleasure to meet you," she said, shaking the droid's hand with a broad smile. Its hand felt warm and soft in her firm grip. "He's adorable," she laughed. "Can I keep him?"

The droid's optical sensor flashed, then said, "No. But I'm at your service anytime you wish."

Shorty turned to Territaff and said, "It's pleasing to see you are all right, Terri. Welcome back."

"Thanks, Shorty," Territaff said, patting its head.

"If you will all excuse me, I need to freshen up a little and take a short nap. Let's regroup in a ship's hour," Karoft said.

"Shorty, please show Administrator Karoft to his quarters," Biomei said.

The droid turned on its heels and said, "This way, Administer."

Noticing the slight bounce in Shorty's gait, Kathy asked

Territaff, " Is there something wrong with his leg?"

"No," Territaff answered. "He has a minor deviation in his left leg's servo. Nickada wanted to correct it, but I stopped her. I thought it would give his character a distinction from the other droids."

Karoft smiled at Kathy's excitement at seeing the droid and knew he would find her interesting. He also realized how different she was from Territaff. He was encouraged by what he sensed in her. She's emotional but has a strong inner strength, and I sense other fine qualities. I think we'll like each other, he thought as he made his way out of the bay, following close behind Shorty.

Karoft was impressed with his quarters. The spacious room was a welcome surprise after the cramped seating in the shuttle and his small apartment on Lunneziah. He removed his boots and stockings and walked around the room, curling his toes into the plush carpeting. Biomei ensured Karoft's every comfort. His presence gave her hope of uncovering the Zenti's plan.

"That's a relaxing exercise," Biomei said.

"Terri introduced it to me when we worked together on the Klaxon treaty. I remembered how pleased we were with our accommodations. Speaking of him, I have concerns."

"Concerns? Please elaborate."

"He's carrying a lot of guilt, and it's showing. He needs to decompress, or he'll have a high-order breakdown."

"That's his human half seeping through. Terri occasionally allows his emotions to run a little unchecked. Despite all his changes, Phillip Mann is still apparent in him. While your concern is justified, he's quite resilient and disciplined. He'll rein in his emotions and act accordingly when needed."

"I hope you're right, Biomei. We all need to be at our best, or we'll lose everything we've accomplished. What worries me is the Zenti's new ally. They must know the Zenti can't be trusted. Who would be so daring or so foolish?"

"I believe you may be looking at this all wrong, my dear friend."

"What'd you mean?"

"You're assuming the Zenti are running things. I've said nothing about the Zenti question because I'm seeking a missing piece for this complex puzzle. Now, I may have discovered it. We all know the Zenti are incapable of such a well-organized and executed plan. They never retrieved the information they sought from the Ezdenian disc. What's even more apparent, they no longer appear to need its information."

"Who's helping them with their cyborg?" Karoft asked as he reclined on the bed.

"The new player is far more advanced than any known world. At first, I thought it might have been the Vultarans. They're an old and mysterious race. After communicating my concerns to Verubeal, she assured me the Vultarans were not involved. Like every other civilization that has dealt with the Zenti, they were duped and taken advantage of. While not admitting it, the Vultarans have intimated that they have covert operatives working, but wouldn't divulge any information about their operations. Under the circumstances, I believe that's prudent of them."

"Have you discussed this with the rest of the team?"

"Not yet. I was awaiting your arrival. I'll wake you in a few hours. You look as though you could use the rest."
"Thanks, Biomei," he yawned. "I'm exhausted. Vultarans, we know so little about them. We must learn more." He pulled back the bed covers and got under them. "Vultarans, very interesting," he mumbled, propping a pillow under his head and drifting off to sleep.

CHAPTER 34

General Dickerson jumped out of his plush leather chair, angrily mumbling. He punched in Crenshaw's extension and said, "Get in here."

Crenshaw looked like a made-over soldier. His wavy brown hair was cut short military-style, and his Class-B uniform was sharply pressed, with all the brass buffed to a mirror shine. He stood inside the door and regarded the general with a clear, attentive gaze from his dark blue eyes, patiently awaiting his orders.

General Dickerson paced around the room, cursing under his breath. Crenshaw could see from his reddened face and puckered brow that he was about to explode.

"Sir, you look upset," Crenshaw said timidly, "Does it have something to do with the strange phenomenon happening on the moon?"

Dickerson stopped pacing and regarded Crenshaw with a frustrated expression. He returned to his desk, sat hard in his plush chair, and hissed. "I just got off the phone with Colonel Ramsey, my man at NORAD. I asked him about the flash report. He told me the events weren't from the moon. They claim it was a solar hiccup." He slowly shook his head. "Nothing I was told makes any sense, yet they're sticking to their ridiculous story."

"I don't understand how they could be so wrong. Or... are they distracting with disinformation?"

"I must be losing it. Nothing makes sense anymore. My people are lying to me. And I suspect DeZenti is somehow behind all of it. The strange energy readings from the Yucatan and the moon are somehow related... but how and why? DeZenti has been holding back information, and when I pressed him about the production delays, he told me they were all part of the development process. I'm tired of being played, Rob." He leaned back and steepled his fingers, his gaze contemplative.

Crenshaw was concerned that the government was engaging in another one of its infamous cover-ups. "But, sir, there must be someone we can alert at command?"

"And tell them what?"

"I don't know, but we should do something." Crenshaw's face flushed as he thought about all the strange events piling on top of one another into chaos, waiting to spill over on everyone he knew. "And, sir, what about Captain Jason? Do you believe he died in a car accident? How did his car get that far from the road?"

"All good questions. He looked at Crenshaw with a sly grin and added, "And we're going to find the answers."

"Sir, I know that look. You have something in mind. I have only one question."

"Yes."

"What are you thinking, and will it get me killed?"

Dickerson's brow rose in surprise. Then, he considered it and nodded. "Better go to the armory and check out a sidearm just in case. Afterward, go home and get some rest. Meet me here at 0100 hours." He wrote the address on a piece of paper and handed it to Crenshaw."

Crenshaw checked the address and looked closely at the general. "This is Dr. DeZenti's facility." He narrowed his eyes slightly. "You really are going after him." A slow smile spread. "It's about time."

CHAPTER 35

"The Homestead site's energy readings have changed," Karoft alerted Cuz. "There's something familiar about this pattern."

"I was thinking the same thing about the Yucatan readings," Cuz said, switching on the holographic display.

"Cuz, bring up the Yucatan site to compare them."

Cuz brought up the display as Karoft suggested to compare both outputs simultaneously.

"Interesting. Except for the magnitude, they're almost identical," Cuz said. "However, a significant power source is required to sustain a fusion reaction of this scale. The level of radioactive decay is low at both locations. What could they be using for a power source?"

"Fascinating," Karoft said, waving his hand over the Homestead holographic projection and superimposing it over the Yucatan site. "You're right, Cuz. They have the same frequency but different amplitudes. If the power source isn't coming from Yucatan or Homestead, where's the point of origin?"

"I suggest we conduct both a vector and a spectral analysis. That should give us direction and more data on its quantum chromodynamics," Cuz said.

Karoft continued pondering the holographic display as Cuz set up the interferometer. The power signatures had a pattern he recognized but couldn't quite put his finger on until Cuz brought up the spectral analysis.

"Cuz, that's it," he blurted. "I thought it looked familiar. That's an Ezdenian signature. I'm certain of it. Look at the sign wave. It's litinnium," Karoft thought aloud, reviewing the spectral analysis.

"Litinnium does not exist in this quadrant. Therefore, it must be produced artificially. Whoever is creating these high quantities of litinnium particles would need an extensive mining and processing operation to get the raw materials,"

Cuz's voice trailed off as the thought became apparent. He looked at Karoft and said, "It could only be one place."

"The Earth's moon," Karoft finished Cuz's thought for him.

They looked at one another with concern.

"That must be one powerful generator to produce such an intense energy field," Cuz said.

"One thing is for sure," Karoft said, continuing to analyze the holographic telemetry. "Whoever designed that generator and communications array has access to ancient data. If this is what it appears to be—we're in trouble."

"What's that?" Kathy asked as she joined them and curiously looked at the intricate holographic images.

"The stuff that nightmares are made of," Cuz murmured.

* * *

(14:50 hours Homestead AFB Post Indoor Firing Range# 4)
Master Sergeant James reviewed the release order, then looked closely at Crenshaw and said, "Fired one of these recently?"

Crenshaw weighed the semiautomatic in his hand and said, "It's been a while."

"From your expression, it's been quite a while."

Crenshaw nodded.

"You should go into the firing range and get reacquainted. Don't want to be in an uneasy situation holding that cannon and wondering how you'll fire it."

Crenshaw took the sergeant's advice and walked to the firing range. He thought, I've plenty of time, so why not learn how to fire the damn thing? "It's a big gun," he whispered, looking down at the SIG M17 semiautomatic sidearm. Crenshaw was no stranger to guns, having grown up in a military family.

The range instructor's words went through his mind as he put on the sound-eliminating headphones and protective eyewear. He held up the gun and squeezed the trigger.

Crenshaw cringed at the muffled, ringing explosion and powerful kick. It was such an unnerving experience that it took him by surprise. *Damn, this isn't like my old Glock.*

Crenshaw put the gun back in its holster, removed the protective gear from his head and eyes, and turned to leave.

Master Sergeant James called to him strongly, "You can do better than that, Sergeant. " His voice was strong with irritation at Crenshaw's timidity. "Fire a full clip at one of those targets," he ordered.

Crenshaw looked at the line of targets. "Which one?" he asked, shrugging his shoulders in confusion. His nerves were rising, and he wanted to get out of there.

"I don't give a shit! Just point and shoot. See if you hit anything." The instructor's tone softened, noticing Crenshaw's body stiffen with his hands shaking. "What're you so afraid of?" he said in a softer voice as he walked closer to him.

"Me, having to use this hideous thing on someone," Crenshaw said, looking down at the holstered gun.

"I see." The instructor scratched his dark chin stubble. "I'll tell you what," he glanced at Crenshaw's nametag, "Staff Sergeant Crenshaw. I promise you won't ever use it unnecessarily. But if you find yourself in a situation where you have to, make sure you know how to defend yourself."

The instructor's argument made sense to Crenshaw. "I should be logical about this," he mumbled, unclipping the holster strap and pulling the gun out. He held it flat in the palm of his hand. Then, he looked at the tall army sergeant, who was staring at him. He gave the sergeant an ironic smile, then turned and fired off a quick clip at the farthest target from him.

While waiting for the target to be retrieved, he studied the gun before placing it on the firing line shelf. The target ran to him on its wire rails, then stopped just inches from his face. He reviewed his target with the detachment that caught the instructor's steely blue eyes.

"Not a bad grouping for a nerd," he said, nodding his approval. "Trust your instincts. They may keep you alive. Good luck with your mission." The tall sergeant glanced at Crenshaw as though he knew something about him.

"Mission? What mission?" Crenshaw knew his act was unconvincing.

"Exactly," the instructor said, then returned to his office. "Shoot another clip before you leave," he called back to Crenshaw. "You need the practice. Get a feel for your weapon. Sometimes, it's the only thing you can trust."

Crenshaw considered the instructor's advice and reloaded the semiautomatic. This time, he replaced the clip, reloading it smoothly. His original fear was gone. He could also hear his father's voice, telling him to relax. Taking careful aim at the center target, he held his breath and fired a tightly grouped pattern at the head area of the target. Crenshaw smiled, feeling pleased with himself, and then loaded another clip.

Good job, son, his father's voice praised. *Take another deep breath, let it out slowly, and squeeze off another clip.*

For some inexplicable reason, his father's presence felt close to Rob. He hadn't thought about his father in some time. Lately, he came to mind often, mostly in his dreams. It made Rob realize how much he missed him.

* * *

(0300 hours, Dr. DeZenti's Main Facility)

Crenshaw nearly jumped out of his car seat when the general tapped on the driver's side window. He realized he had nodded off while listening to his favorite R&B CD. The general motioned for him to get out of the car. Crenshaw had never seen the general dressed in fatigues and wearing a sidearm.

"You look nervous," he said.

"That's because I am. Is this necessary?" Crenshaw said,

holding up his gun.

"Yes. Now, put it back in its holster and follow me."

He watched the general thoughtfully as he walked to the main entrance.

"Sir," Crenshaw whispered loudly, quickening his pace to catch up with Dickerson.

"Yes, Rob," he said.

"What's the plan? I mean, do you have a plan? Or are you, as you're fond of saying, just winging it?"

"Well, I know where I want to go. It's the getting there that may prove interesting."

He winked at Crenshaw, waving his pass card over the proximity reader beside the door. The large glass door clicked open, and the general motioned for him to enter.

"I guess this is where the interesting stuff happens," Crenshaw muttered as he headed for the elevator. "You're aware that cameras are everywhere, recording everything we do?"

"Yes," Dickerson said, sounding unconcerned. "No, not the elevator; use the stairs." He pointed to the stairway entry. Crenshaw wondered why he seemed unconcerned with the cameras.

"Where are all the guards?" Crenshaw wondered aloud.

He went to the door and pulled it. It was locked. He saw no locking mechanism on the door or a proximity device on the wall, so he gave the general a puzzled glance.

General Dickerson looked around the room for another stairway and smiled when he spied the rear stairs to the second-floor conference room.

"This way," he called.

Crenshaw approached the glass wall, partitioning the small reception area from the rear stairway. He couldn't help admiring the door's design—it looked like it was part of the wall.

"What incredible workmanship," he said under his breath,

appreciating the precision of the tiny seam that formed the edge of the door. It appeared to have been cut right inside the thick glass wall. There were no noticeable hinges. "They must've used lasers to cut this door," Crenshaw said, running his hand over the smooth seam. "I can't fathom how this door opens. There are no noticeable hinges or mechanisms."

Dickerson glared impatiently from the upper part of the stairs. "It slides open on an embedded magnetic release built into the track. Now, if that satisfies your curiosity, would you move your ass? Stay close and be quiet," he ordered in a low voice as Crenshaw approached. "I'm surprised security hasn't greeted us," he added, surveying the lower level closely. "Come to think of it, I haven't seen any security personnel."

"That's kind of odd. I mean, this is supposed to be a high-security facility, right?"

Crenshaw got up close behind the general. They stopped when they reached the entrance to the conference room. Dickerson pulled on the tall, metal door and frowned. "It's locked." He briefly examined the lock, then looked at Crenshaw. "Did you bring your toolkit?"

Crenshaw reached into an inside pocket of his lightweight military jacket and pulled out a thin wallet. The general moved to the side and allowed him to examine the lock.

"Well?" he asked impatiently.

"I never thought my brief job as a locksmith would ever come in handy. "It's a conventional lock, and it should just take a moment," Crenshaw said as he inserted a long, thin probe and a conventional lock pick. The lock tumbler moved, and Crenshaw opened the door a few inches, then got out of the general's way. "Eighteen seconds," Crenshaw mumbled while glancing at his watch.

"Is that a record?"

"No, it shows how out of practice I am." He blushed, realizing what he had said.

"I don't think we should pursue this conversation any

further."

Crenshaw nodded and followed Dickerson into the office.

"What are we looking for?" he asked as he watched the general go through all the drawers in the credenza, which was centered on the only solid wall in the room.

"Look for anything out of the ordinary. For some uncanny reason, I suspect a hidden entry up here."

"An entry to where, sir?"

"Look at the factory floor below." He waited for Crenshaw to look. "What do you see?"

"Machinery."

"Do you see any product in any stage of completion?"

Crenshaw looked back in surprise. "Oh, I see what you mean, sir, but could it be that they moved all the completed devices into another area?"

"Precisely, my astute friend, over the past eight months, I've yet to see anything on that floor other than what you're seeing now. Yet, according to the progress reports, at least a hundred working cyborg soldiers should be ready for final testing. Either DeZenti is full of shit, or he's storing his product somewhere in here. That's probably where all the security is. He's been skillfully keeping me out of the loop. I want to see what the slippery little bastard is really up to."

"So, you believe he's saying one thing and doing something else? I'm not sure I follow that, sir."

"I know. It's just that there's been a lot of weird shit happening, and it all seems to be connected with DeZenti. It's a feeling that's been gnawing at me. The recent strange and unidentified phenomenon was the final straw. My weird conversation with Ramsay at NORAD this morning got me thinking about many things—Captain Jason's unexplained temporary duty assignment. Then, there was the car accident and the sudden classification of the autopsy report. Jason wasn't an isolated incident. Shortly before you joined the team, we also lost an investigator under mysterious circumstances. Colonel Cameron's handling of the two consultants was unusual, even for him. There are too many coincidences, all pointing to DeZenti. He's too well-connected for me to open an investigation. So, we're on our own for the time being. We need some hard evidence I can nail him with, or we're both going to be spending a lot of time in Leavenworth."

"I think I'm seeing your point, sir," Crenshaw agreed. "Saying I was just following orders won't be a good legal defense. Will it?"

"Sorry, Rob. I got you more involved than I intended. You should leave. I insist that you leave." He patted him on the shoulder. "You've done above and beyond anything I could have asked of anyone. You're a good man. Now get the fuck out of here!"

"Thanks, sir, but I've gone too far to turn back now. So, I'll ignore that last order and carry on."

General Dickerson nodded approvingly, then continued to look around the conference room.

"There has to be something like a release button or remote device," the general said as he ran his hand under the conference table. "I know there's another area. Every time I've been here, DeZenti is waiting for me, sitting in this chair at the back end of the table. I've never seen him on that floor. I've even made excuses to stay here and see where he goes after our meetings. He seems to disappear once he gets downstairs."

As Crenshaw watched Dickerson, he noticed something odd about the wall where the credenza stood. It appeared a little further into the room than the adjacent walls. He ran his hand over the smooth surface, but something about it seemed odd to Crenshaw's eye. He moved closer and pushed on different spots. Then he placed an ear against the wall, running his hand up and down its surface.

"What are you doing?" the general asked.

"There's something about this wall," he said, pushing against small sections.

When he got to the credenza, he motioned for the general to help him move it away from the wall. Then he stood back and studied it for a long moment. He looked up and saw what appeared to be a small lens in one of the ceiling tiles. The lens looked centered above the credenza's location. Crenshaw stood fixed, staring intently.

"Is this some transcendental thing you're doing?" Dickerson said acerbically.

"No, sir, it's just good old-fashioned observation," he said with a sudden smile. He moved his fingertips slowly across a central area of the wall.

"Do you want to let me know what you're doing?"

Crenshaw stopped at the center point of the wall and pushed against it. He heard a faint click, like a switch being thrown. The surface became icy cold. He gasped as part of a section dissolved, creating an arched opening with a shallow landing. He walked onto the landing and noticed a metal ladder with handrails leading down to a lower level.

"Does that answer your question, sir?" He smiled smugly.

General Dickerson looked at Crenshaw, dumbfounded, appearing awestruck. His expression was reserved for children when struck by amazement.

"That's impossible," he exclaimed, examining the opening on both sides for a concealed slot where the missing wall portion must have gone.

I must admit that the technology used to create this portal is beyond anything we have. But it's possible because we both saw it." Crenshaw said, giddy with excitement, wishing he knew what he had done so he could do it again to see the miraculous made possible once more.

Crenshaw looked up and noticed a pale blue light glowing out of the lens. Contemplating the light, he believed it was the mechanism he tripped to open the portal. He furrowed his brow, clueless about how it worked with the portal. He continued to ponder the light until he felt General Dickerson grab his arm and lead him to the landing of the steep stairwell.

When he cleared the threshold, the portal closed in the same incredible way it had opened. A soft light came on, revealing how far down the stairwell went. There was no intermediate landing; it was a steep, narrow, continuous ladder.

"This stairway doesn't appear for normal-sized people," Crenshaw observed.

"It looks like something off a ship." The general said, looking down the deep stairwell. "Let's go," he gestured for Crenshaw to lead.

Crenshaw removed his gun from its holster. Dickerson touched his shoulder and said, "You don't need that yet."

Crenshaw was having difficulty with the steepness of the narrow steps. Glancing at the general, he said, "I want to try something."

"Try what?"

As the general uttered his question, Crenshaw faced the steps, straddled them with his feet and hands on the outside of the low handrails, and slid down. He landed a little harder than he wanted. He looked up and saw the general already on his way down.

"Good idea," Dickerson said. "It's just like a ship's ladder."

"What's over there?" Crenshaw said, searching inside his jacket pocket for his LED flashlight. He found the small light and switched it on. It put out a wide, bright beam. "Are those feet?" he said, moving the light around the area.

The general stiffened at seeing feet sticking out from behind a tall stack of boxes along a wall.

"Bring the light over here," he called to Crenshaw.

"Jesus, there must be a dozen bodies here." Crenshaw gasped at seeing a row of unconscious security guards resting upright along a wall. He scanned them with his light.

"They're alive but appear to be in a deep, unconscious state," Dickerson said after checking a few of them for a pulse. "I've seen nothing like this. Look at their expressions. They all appear to have the same surprised look."

"Well, that answers where all the security is, but who the hell could do this? There are no signs of a struggle. It appears they were knocked out all at once."

"We may find a few answers in there," the general said, pointing to the next room. He pulled out his weapon and walked toward the lighted opening. Crenshaw copied the general, drew his weapon, and followed close behind, his gun held upward.

"Good morning, General Dickerson." Territaff surprised them. "You won't need your weapons." He gave them a friendly smile.

"You two," he mumbled, seeing Cuz appear behind Territaff. He recognized them from the base's security video. "I'd hoped we'd meet."

"We've been watching you ever since you arrived. Good work, Crenshaw," Territaff complimented. "That portal wasn't an easy find."

"What type of technology is that?" Crenshaw asked.

"I'll be happy to explain it to you at another time," Territaff said.

The general asked, "You knocked out all those guards?"

"It appears we're looking for the same thing," Territaff said, avoiding the general's question.

"And what would that be?"

"Come, I'll show you."

They followed Territaff into a cavernous room that appeared to have been carved out of the area's bedrock. The lighting was as bright and clear as daylight, but there was no visible light source.

Crenshaw walked wide-eyed, taking in his surroundings like a little boy in Wonderland.

"What's lighting this room?" he said.

Cuz looked at Territaff as if he should answer. Territaff gave a slight nod.

Cuz went to Crenshaw and looked at him thoughtfully. "Mr. Crenshaw," he addressed him in a formal tone.

"Please, call me Rob," he said with eager friendliness.

Cuz's demeanor softened. "Rob, the lighting is generated by the same principle as the sun's nuclear fusion, only on a much smaller scale. As we proceed, you'll see technologies ahead of you, some of which seem miraculous but are all real. No illusions. No magic."

"You mean like the portal upstairs?"

"The portal was the simplest of the technologies you're about to see." Cuz turned to the general. "General Dickerson, we're here to assist you in apprehending Dr. DeZenti and foiling his plan. However, the technology being developed here must be destroyed, along with any information about the designs and implementations of the completed devices and any subsequent developments. We need your assurance you'll not interfere with our mission."

"Assurance?" Dickerson arched his brows in a puzzled look. "Assurance to what? I have seen nothing I can confirm or deny. Your concern is unfounded and unwarranted. However, we share a common interest. We both want DeZenti."

Cuz glanced at Territaff, who had been closely observing.

"General Dickerson," Territaff said, "I believe what Cuz is trying to say is that what you're about to see here will stay here." We prefer to work together, but we can also make alternative arrangements that may not be as agreeable to you.

Crenshaw swallowed down a nervous lump and said, "I don't like the sound of that, sir."

Dickerson narrowed his gaze at Territaff, "Are you threatening me?"

"Yes," Territaff said. "You can cooperate with us, or we'll eliminate you."

The general cocked an eyebrow, then forced a brave smile.

"Under the circumstances, I guess we'll cooperate with you as long as it's in the best interests of my country."

"Your cooperation is not only in the best interests of your country, but also in the best interests of your planet," Territaff said.

"That's a wise choice, General Dickerson, because Dr. DeZenti has arranged for both of you to be eliminated later today," Cuz flatly informed them.

"How'd you know that?" the general asked.

"We've been monitoring Dr. DeZenti's communications," Cuz said with certitude.

Dickerson asked, "Do you know how?"

"I believe you were to have a fatal car accident on your way home, and Rob was killed in a gas explosion in his apartment," Cuz bluntly stated.

"Dr. DeZenti has a proclivity for fatal accidents." General Dickerson reflected for a moment, then asked, "Is that what happened to Captain Jason and Lieutenant Rojas?"

Captain Jason's death remains a mystery and appears to be one that will likely remain so. We're unsure what happened to his body, and that's a concern. From what we've gathered, the body retrieved from the Everglades was too decomposed and dismembered for a positive ID. Adding to already mysterious circumstances, the decomposition described in the coroner's report was inconsistent with the time the body was submerged. Additionally, the DNA analysis was inconclusive due to the presence of an unknown contaminant. Before we could get to his corpse to perform our analysis, Captain Jason's alleged remains were cremated."

"How could that have happened?" the general said. "An autopsy is mandatory in suspicious deaths."

"That's right. The local coroner's office was erroneously informed that Jason's family insisted that no autopsy be performed and wanted the remains to be immediately cremated. This was done before the military coroner's office could get a release to claim the remains. Now, due to these strange circumstances, we don't have anything to substantiate the actual cause of death, and we'll be unable to confirm our suspicions. As for Lieutenant Rojas, she was killed by one of DeZenti's henchmen. Her death was both unfortunate and unnecessary. She got too close to this evolving and volatile situation."

"None of this sounds right. Do you realize what you're saying?" Crenshaw said, feeling unsettled about what was being described. "This all sounds like a convoluted conspiracy story."

Cuz could tell from the general's tightened expression and Crenshaw's stiff body language how contrived all this information sounded to them, yet he felt compelled to tell all he knew, hoping to gain their trust.

"We suspect Captain Jason may have been taken over by an alien life-form working with Dr. DeZenti. You should also know Dr. DeZenti is an extraterrestrial life-form known as Zenti."

Cuz was not surprised by the shock on Crenshaw's face and Dickerson's incredulous sneer.

"What the hell are Zenti?" Crenshaw said.

"The enemy," Cuz stated emphatically. "And they have aligned themselves with a powerful partner with highly advanced technology. At this juncture, we're still gathering information on them. Up to this point, they remain a mystery, who and what they are."

"That's bullshit," Dickerson shouted. "Jason had a wife and daughter. His wife would've known if something was different about him. Additionally, she was friendly with my secretary. They talked all the time. She would've told her if her husband acted strangely. I don't buy the alien crap. It makes little sense."

General Dickerson became suspicious of Cuz's honesty.

Was he being played here by a bunch of high-tech con artists? The uncertainty of the situation was unsettling. Not being in control irritated him. His bullshit meter shot up and pegged. He wanted something tangible, some actual proof. He gave Crenshaw a sharp look that put him on guard.

Dickerson was transparent to Cuz. He could sense all the doubt and uneasiness through his stiffening manner. He wanted to ease the general's mistrust but was uncertain how to reach him without exacerbating his growing irritability.

"General, Rob, I believe the proof you're looking for is in here," Cuz said, swinging his arm to signal them to proceed to the next area.

"Where are you from?" Crenshaw asked, moving closer to Cuz's side.

"Not from here," Territaff answered.

Cuz frowned at Territaff and said, "Under the circumstances, Terri, I can't see the logic in not being open with them. After all, we're asking for their trust. Why not let us start by trusting them?"

"You're right as usual, my friend, but by the look on Crenshaw's face, he may hyperventilate when he hears what you're about to disclose."

"Oh, don't worry, Cuz. I'm more than ready to hear what you have to say. I know you must be extraterrestrials."

Territaff couldn't help smiling at Crenshaw's naivety.

"What's so amusing?" Crenshaw asked Territaff.

"Crenshaw—"

"Please call me Rob," he interrupted.

"Rob, I'm from right here. Grew up on Miami Beach and got my BA at FAU."

"No kidding. I got my first BA there. But you seem somehow different."

"Different, how?" Territaff was impressed with Rob's obvious intelligence and curiosity. He liked his energy and amenable personality.

"Well, I'm not sure how to explain it, but I get a sense of you possessing an inner strength on both intellectual and physical levels. Am I right?"

"Your instincts are sharp. And you're on track with your perceptions, but we don't have time for this discussion. Maybe after we finish this mission, I'll tell you everything you want to know and more."

"I look forward to that."

"You never answered his question," the general said. "Where are you from, Cuz?"

"As Rob has observed, I'm not from Earth. I'm from a system called Venubia. It's approximately eleven-point-two-thousand-light-years from your system." Cuz observed Rob with his eager curiosity.

"How do you travel such astronomical distances? You must have FTL capabilities," Crenshaw speculated.

Rob's assumption amused Cuz, but Territaff arched an eyebrow and transmitted to him, *"You're going to get yourself too engaged in a protracted conversation we don't have time for now. And by the way, the general is grinding his teeth; he'll pop at any minute."*

"Rob reminds me of Kathy in his curiosity. I'll try to give him the short version. As for General Dickerson, he'll settle down once he gets something tangible to gnaw on." Cuz gave the general a passing glance, then returned his attention to Rob.

Cuz eyed Rob with the line of his mouth curled into a faint smile. "Faster-than-light travel is physically impractical and too slow for conveying vast distances. Even at two or three hundred times the speed of light, it would still take lifetimes for most species to travel between star systems. However, the universe provides many other methods to traverse the immediate galactic neighborhoods. We've discovered strategically located corridors that shorten the distances between systems. There are naturally occurring shortcuts within the fabric of spacetime that permit, for lack of a better term, a hop through space."

"Wormholes?" Crenshaw said, looking unsure.

"Not as you envision them. While there are wormholes, they're far too small and unstable for practical applications, but there's something we call a corridor. It's more of a bubble of antigravitons generated to keep a tunnel that uses negative energy to stay open. If you can imagine creating a bubble that fits into a tube that bridges a fold in the fabric of spacetime, you have a close approximation of how we travel."

Crenshaw's lower jaw dropped as he stared wide-eyed at Cuz, "That's amazing."

"Also, we discovered there are non-locality formations similar to the corridors that cause splits in spacetime," Cuz continued. "When these two-dimensional splits are aligned with high-energy photons, they can be manipulated to broadcast radio waves over vast distances of subspace. This is the method we use for bridging vast distances without data degradation, permitting instantaneous communications between star systems."

General Dickerson looked on; his jaw muscles tightened, and his mouth closed into a crooked line, showing his growing impatience with his subordinate.

"Holy shit!" Crenshaw shouted. "How do you know where the corridors are?"

"They generate a unique energy signature we can decode, then manipulate when needed."

"And they're stable and permanent?"

"As far as we know."

"You mean you guys didn't create them?"

"No. We discovered them by accident. An expedition on one of our moons uncovered information left by an advanced and extinct civilization that was believed to have created them long ago. It took our best minds eons to translate their language and decipher the code that revealed the corridor's locations and a little information about their basic operation.

But to this day, we still don't have the technology or skills to create one of our own."

"Wow. But that means you can only travel to areas with corridors." Crenshaw said.

"Yes. Rob," Territaff said, deciding to end the conversation. "There's a lot we're unsure of regarding the corridors, and right now, our focus is on the people who want to control them. Our immediate concern is that they created an army of cyborg combatants to decimate your planet for its resources. We can't allow that to happen."

"So, your mission is to blow this place up?" Crenshaw said.

"Yep, and get DeZenti, dead or alive." Territaff pointed ahead, "If you'll follow me, gentleman." He led them into the next section.

"It's about fucking time!" Kathy yelled at Territaff as they entered the cavernous area.

General Dickerson's face screwed up into a disappointed sneer, seeing nothing of interest. There were boxes of all shapes and sizes along a long wall to his right. Directly ahead was a row of large machines whose purpose was unclear. He noticed an operations center on the left side of the closest machine. Outside of the odd machines and boxes, nothing related to manufacturing. As he continued to survey the floor, he thought that at least the upper floor had actual manufacturing, but what the hell was this?

Crenshaw's mouth fell open as he gazed at Kathy. She was still in her form-fitted biosuit that revealed the shapely curves of her beautiful body. Little was left to the imagination for Crenshaw as he studied her. He slowly lifted his eyes to her face and gawked at her glowing auburn hair and warm brown eyes. He was in love and didn't even know her name.

"Hi, I'm Rob," he said, extending his hand to her.

Kathy regarded his hand, looking confused and annoyed. "Hi," she said, then went past him and up to Territaff. *"Who the hell are they?"* she transmitted.

"You're talking somehow, aren't you?" Rob said.

Kathy looked back at him, mouth open in surprise. She recognized a familiar, inquisitive glow within his piercing stare and realized that the nerdy-looking guy was sharp.

"Yes. How'd you know?"

"Your body language seemed to be in a conversational posture."

Cuz came to Rob and wrapped his long arm around his shoulders. "I think Rob may be of some value to this mission. Let's welcome him and General Dickerson as new team members."

Kathy looked at Territaff, then back at Cuz. "Welcome aboard," she said and extended her hand to Rob. "I'm Kathy," she introduced herself, gathering all the congeniality of an annoyed host trying to be friendly to unexpected guests.

Rob held her hand with both of his like a priceless piece of porcelain.

"You're so beautiful. Are you an alien?"

She laughed at his unassuming curiosity and understood it.

"You're quite a charmer there, kid. And no—I'm not an alien," she paused. "Well, I might be considered an alien," she stopped herself, then grinned. "I'm from Key West. Some people might consider me an alien from the Conch Republic."

Rob laughed. He was hopelessly enchanted by Kathy's beauty and wanted to engage her in conversation. Territaff could sense his growing infatuation and took control.

"Crenshaw, er, Rob," Territaff said in a low, patient voice to distract him from Kathy's obvious allure. "Rob, you have to tone down your driving emotions and focus. And Rob, you should know Kathy's already in a relationship."

"Sorry," he said, releasing Kathy's hand and stepping back to the general's side, his face flush and his eyes looking down, feeling crushed and stupid. *It never seems to fail. I always screw up around beautiful women.*

"All right, I've had enough of this bullshit," Dickerson blurted as he drew his weapon and pointed it at Territaff. He caught Cuz coming toward him. He stepped back, waved his gun at him, and said, "Get over there with your friends."

Cuz hesitated for a moment. The general's sudden aggression surprised him. He considered taking the general's gun away, but reconsidered and moved next to Territaff.

"I want some damn answers from you, and I want none of your techno-babbling bullshit," he spoke in a controlled voice full of hostility.

"Sir, please, this is not the way," Crenshaw nervously objected.

"Shut up, Crenshaw," Dickerson snapped. "Just who the hell are you, and what are you after?"

Cuz arched his brow into tight lines and said, "I thought it was made clear. We're here to dismantle this facility and apprehend Dr. DeZenti."

"You expect me to believe that crock of shit. I see no cyborgs, or any staging area for them, or any other goddamn thing that suggests a threat of any kind. The only threatening things I see are you. Now, talk, or I'll shoot you one at a time until somebody talks."

He leveled his gun at Territaff and pulled back the hammer.

"Okay, if you don't believe our story, I guess you'll just have to shoot us," Territaff said, glaring at the general, daring him to shoot.

"Oh, I've had just about enough of this shit," Kathy growled, then gave Dickerson an intense look that sent him flying backward. He hit hard against a wall and fell winded on the smooth concrete floor.

Rob quickly went to the general's side. "Are you all right, sir?"

He let out a painful groan as he tried to stand back up while still holding his gun, then pushed Rob aside and said, through clenched teeth, "I still want answers."

He shot at Kathy's leg. She avoided the bullet with a quick turn, then ran up to him. Her movements were so fast that she appeared to pop from one point to the next. She was on the general in an instant and took his weapon in one fluid move, grabbed him by the collar, and lifted him several feet.

"I can break you like a twig, so cut the crap," she shouted, then let him drop to the floor.

Rob looked back at them with anger and disappointment. "You didn't have to be so rough with him. He was just doing his job."

"I don't like being threatened or shot at," Kathy said.

Territaff sighed and said to Cuz, "Tend to the general." He looked at Crenshaw and frowned. "Sorry, Rob, but your boss must be more patient. Everything will become clear shortly. Now, let's see if we all can remain calm and try to work together." Territaff turned to Kathy and transmitted, *"Jesus, where did that come from?"*

"It was part of my transformation process. I need to work on my control."

"I got no telekinesis training. That was impressive."

"Biomei told me that my guide saw I had powerful empathic abilities; one of its characteristics is telekinesis. The only problem is that it takes a lot of energy out of you. Now, I'm starving for junk food. We've got to make a quick run to a drive-through."

"I'll see what we can do. In the meantime, have Karoft send down the micro-fusion charges. We want to make sure we only destroy the subterranean levels. We'll leave the surface facility intact and hopefully avoid any investigation by the local authorities. The last thing we need is more bureaucrats and police running around here."

Cuz was kneeling beside General Dickerson, evaluating his injuries with a hand-held scanner.

"That's right out of Star Trek," Rob said, staring at the device.

Cuz smiled at the reference. "I purchased this at one of your medical supply stores, but I've made a few modifications."

"Is he going to be okay?"

General Dickerson was groggy but conscious. He moved and tried to get to his feet, but slumped back down in pain. He looked up at Cuz with resentment and pushed his hand away. His complexion was pale and sweaty. His face was distorted with the writhing pain shooting through his body.

"General Dickerson, I suggest you remain still for the moment," Cuz said. "You have two fractured ribs and herniated discs in both the thoracic and lumbar sections of your spine. The back injuries appear to be older but have been exacerbated by the impact with the wall. The ribs are from the altercation with Kathy. If you permit me, I can heal these injuries so you can continue the mission, or we can take you back to your car."

"What the fuck did that bitch hit me with?" The general groused, sounding woozy, and his head slumped.

"That, sir, would be difficult to explain," Cuz said as he continued to run the scanner over the general's body.

"You mean you don't know." Dickerson looked sharply into his face.

"I know, but I am uncertain how she did it. May I attend to your injuries?"

The general nodded and watched Cuz closely as he pulled out a small, square cube from his utility belt, then placed it on Dickerson's forehead.

"What's that thing?"

"It's a neural interface," Cuz explained as he held the scanner next to the box.

"Now, what are you doing?"

"I'm transferring the data from the scanner to the interface. The interface will analyze the data and send neuro impulses to the injured areas to promote rapid cellular regeneration and heal your injuries. Sir, I should also caution you that the scanner has revealed plaque in both the anterior and posterior arterial walls and possible damage to your right ventricular valve. I can't tend to those conditions now, but would happily attend to them after we finish here."

Dickerson appeared dumbfounded. He had been experiencing chest pains but thought it was indigestion brought on by all the stress he'd been dealing with over the past few months. He scrutinized Cuz with his dulled eyes. What he saw in Cuz's dark, shining gaze and almost impassive facial features presented a quandary for the general as he studied Cuz. "What are you?"

Rob's eyes became wide in anticipation of Cuz's answer.

Cuz stiffened and said, "I'm a genetically engineered life-form."

"Holy shit," Rob blurted. "You're an android. I thought so. You're so perfect, you could pass for human."

"Thank you," Cuz said. "I've been attempting to alter my facial features to appear more human, but there are limitations to what I can articulate. Human emotions are as diverse as they are confounding."

"How much longer, Cuz?" Territaff said.

"Three minutes, fourteen seconds. The lower lumbar disc is slightly displaced and undergoing a temporary fusing, but will require a more permanent corrective procedure at some point."

"Well, hurry it up. We need to get out of here."

Kathy came to Cuz, stroked the back of his head, turned her eyes on Rob, and smiled.

"You got a lot going for you, Rob," she said sincerely. "Being a nerd can be sexy if you show confidence in yourself. The right woman is out there looking for you. You have to put yourself out there to find each other."

Rob nodded, then walked away in thought. Kathy looked down at General Dickerson, her expression full of regret. Their eyes met, and they stared at one another for a long moment before Kathy spoke, "Sorry for the rough treatment. Didn't know I could exert such a strong blow. I regret inflicting any injuries. I only—"

"You did exactly as I would have done in the same situation," the general said, dismissing Kathy's apology. "Besides, Cuz here discovered an imminent heart attack on its way. So, some good came out of this. However, you still haven't shown me anything to change my mind about your intentions. If I could, I'd run you all in for interrogation."

Kathy asked Cuz, "Can he get up?"

Cuz glanced at the scanner, then at the general, and said, "Try to stand up, sir."

General Dickerson stood shakily, but once upright, he noticed he felt different. He ran his hand over his ribs while rocking side to side on his hips. Feeling no pain or discomfort, he stretched out his back and rolled his thick shoulders. He grinned, realizing he could move freely and without discomfort for the first time in years. A broad smile spread across his face as he realized how good his body felt.

"I feel reborn. Healed. It's miraculous," Dickerson said with sudden confusion and delight. He walked to Cuz and said, "It's been a long time since I've been able to move like this. Thank you."

He extended his hand out to Cuz. Cuz took it and gave it a firm shake. The general glanced at Cuz's grip for a moment, impressed with the sense of power within his hand. It felt like there was more than flesh and bone, giving Dickerson an inkling of his potential power.

"Now, general, let me show you the proof you've been seeking," Territaff said as he pulled out a small crystalline device from his utility belt and pointed it at a central point in front of the machines.

A line of armored robots appeared. The general and Crenshaw walked to Territaff and looked wide-eyed in amazement at the menacing-looking, mechanized warriors.

Only half a dozen of the completed cyborgs were in front of them.

"I assume they're more of these?" the general said.

Territaff motioned with his hand for them to follow him. They walked deeper into the enormous, manufactured cavern. As they walked, more lighting came on, revealing vast numbers of the heavily armored cyborgs. Columns of twenty cyborgs stood shoulder to shoulder, a few inches apart. They stood row upon row for as long as the eye could see.

"There must be thousands," Rob said.

"Tens of thousands," Territaff added. "And thousands more in various stages of completion in three other locations we know of. Besides these, General, there are thousands of mechanized combat machines. Only a few of these cyborgs and a couple of machines can take out a city like Miami in a few hours. Imagine the devastation that a number of these machines could cause. Your defenses would be no match against these cyborgs."

"We need to destroy them before they're activated," Dickerson said.

"I agree, but we must also apprehend the man behind all this."

"That slimy little bastard, DeZenti," the general said through clenched teeth. "Somehow, I suspected him from the beginning. He's been using our resources to wage war against us." He shook his head in disgust at the arrogance and stupidity of his government. "Somehow, I knew this whole project was corrupt, but now..." He threw his hand up, then turned away, feeling ashamed.

"Your instincts were right," Territaff said. "However, DeZenti had been getting outside help. He could not have done all of this on his own. We must be careful not to expose ourselves too early. We plan to weed out the rest of the group, and we could use some inside help of our own. That's where you come in. Will you help us?"

The general looked at Crenshaw, who was walking around a cyborg. "Rob," he called to him. "Sir." He gave Dickerson an absent look.

"I can't ask you to risk anymore—"

"All due respect, sir," he interrupted, "we're both into so much shit now, I believe the only thing we can do is to work with them. As I see it, it's our only option."

General Dickerson aimed his gaze at Territaff and said, "He's right. I guess we have little choice."

"Now, you both must get out of here before we proceed. You need plausible deniability with your people. You're also, unfortunately, our best bait for seeing how DeZenti will come after us. He'll want to find out what you know before he eliminates you. With your permission, I'd like to implant a neural tracer unit in each of you."

"That sounds invasive." The general eyed Territaff.

"It sounds worse than it is," Cuz said. "Are you familiar with nanotechnology?"

"Yes. I've got a basic understanding of some of their applications."

Crenshaw came to Dickerson's side, looking intrigued. "Are you intending to inject biobots into us?"

"Precisely, Rob. This nanorobotics monitors neurological activity within the cerebral cortex and the amygdala. Consider them an early warning signal if any of DeZenti's agents confronts you."

"That sounds invasive, son. I'm not too keen on having miniature robots in my brain," the general objected.

"I assure you, they won't interfere or influence you in any way. However, it will alert us if your stress levels increase, allowing us to react promptly. It's our best means of protecting both of you. We don't have the luxury of a workforce or time."

"Listen," Territaff said. "DeZenti knows we're on to him, and he will come after you. This is our best and only way to monitor the situation."

"What do you want us to do?" Rob asked.

"Allow us to implant the nanobots and then stay sharp. Don't let your guard down for a second."

"Okay, implant away," Rob said, rolling up his sleeve and holding his arm out to Cuz.

"They're implanted through the eyes," Cuz said as he held a small vial with an eyedropper filled with a clear liquid.

"Oh," Crenshaw said, then tilted his head back so Cuz could administer the nanobots with a few drops of solution into both eyes.

"General," Cuz addressed him, holding up the eyedropper.

"I just hope you guys know what the fuck you're doing," he said gruffly, then tilted his head back for Cuz to administer the drops.

"Thank you, gentleman. I know that was a big leap of faith. I assure you, it was not done in vain. Now, go home. Return to work, as usual, tomorrow morning. We'll be in touch. Oh, one more thing you should know, General Dickerson."

"Yes."

"Dr. DeZenti is an alien named Zohleemay. His species is called Zenti. They're a genetically engineered humanoid class, unlike anything you'll ever encounter. Zohleemay is extremely dangerous and capable of killing you with no conscience or forethought. He can also assume any shape or form, but can't assume anything greater than his total mass. He could pose as anyone from a secretary to an officer. You must be vigilant in screening anyone you have been working with or who has access to you."

"If he can assume any identity, how do we expose him?" Rob asked.

"It takes a great deal of energy to maintain a morphed state. We've discovered he can't maintain the morphed state for more than a few hours."

The general's eyes narrowed. "Did you say only a few hours?"

"Yes. Why?" Territaff asked.

"I've been in all-day meetings with him on several occasions. Come to think of it, I don't ever remember him taking a bathroom break."

"Interesting," Cuz said. "You're certain you've been with him for over two or three hours."

"Yes." He nodded. "Our weekly briefings have gone over two hours on more than a few occasions."

"It appears Zohleemay has gained some new technology," Cuz said pensively.

"Apparently," Territaff said. "Here, take this scanner." He handed the general a small device resembling a cell phone.

He examined it. "How does this thing work?"

"Flip up the cover," Territaff said.

The general did.

"Look at the two displays. The top is a positioning scanner, and the bottom is a general-purpose display. It is voice-activated and intuitive. Tell it what you want, and it will give data on both screens. Put it anywhere in the room and instruct it to scan and identify for Zenti. It will alert you to any method you choose. Take it with you, but whatever you do, don't lose it. It has technology that's way beyond your current capabilities, and in the wrong hands, it can be easily corrupted."

Dickerson studied the device momentarily, then realized Crenshaw was standing close to his side, looking at the scanner. The general remembered the pictures he had taken from Zohleemay's laptop.

"Does this mean anything to you?" he asked, scrolling up the picture on his cell phone screen.

Territaff took the phone from him and looked in surprise at the familiar pictograms.

"Where did you get these?" he said, handing the phone to Cuz.

"I took them off DeZenti's laptop."

"This explains much," Cuz said, staring at the phone. "These are Zenti pictograms. It's the closest thing they have to a written language. They're instructions on how to construct the cyborgs. They retrieved this information from a disc Territaff had planted. The information was intended to misdirect and delay their efforts. It seems someone has been supplying the Zenti with the correct information and, from the looks of those cyborgs, also additional technology."

"Guess we're not the only ones being played by Zohleemay," the general grimaced.

Territaff nodded thoughtfully.

"Here, this is more up your alley than mine," Dickerson said, handing the scanning device to Crenshaw.

He took it, looking like he had just gotten the Christmas gift of his dreams.

"Oh, thank you, sir," he said, flipping open the device to get familiar with its displays. "Wow, it's remarkable. The top display shows all of us on a grid of the room, and the bottom identifies our basic compositions. That's interesting." His brow wrinkled as he held the scanner up to Cuz. "You're coming up as an amber dot, and everyone else is red."

"That's because my physiology is silicon-based," Cuz said. "The scanner is based on chemical composition, the most accurate setting for detecting specific life-forms. You'll note that the lower screen is reading out our chemical signatures. Zenti will appear as a blue dot. Their copper-based organisms."

"I see. That's remarkable. Look, sir, it's showing all our chemical makeups by atomic number and mass. So, to change a setting, I tell it what I want?"

"Yes," Cuz said.

"So, I should say, 'scan for Zenti'?" Crenshaw looked at the scanner. "The screen is blank. I guess they're no Zenti present." He looked pleased with the simplicity of the device.

Cuz grinned approvingly.

"See, he's an expert already," the general said.

CHAPTER 36

Crenshaw followed closely behind the general as they made their way out of the complex. He held the scanning device before him, moving it back and forth as he walked. Then he stopped and slowly turned full circle.

"What the hell are you doing?" Dickerson snapped.

"Trying to get a feel for the device's range," he said, extending his arm.

"Put that damn thing away." The general almost regretted giving him the apparatus. "It's not a new toy. Please treat it with the same regard as you would any classified device. Luckily, it can pass for a cell phone. Be discreet with it."

Dickerson sighed at Crenshaw's youthful excitement. He realized not all of this seemed strange or frightening to his young subordinate. Most of all, he lamented that he was in a dangerous situation. He liked Crenshaw and feared for his safety.

"Sorry, sir. You're right," Crenshaw said, putting the advanced instrument into his coat pocket.

"I'm going to the office. I want you to go home and get some sleep. Meet me at the office at 14:00. I don't have to remind you not to discuss anything with anybody. Alert me if anyone approaches or contacts you."

"Understood, sir."

* * *

Crenshaw arrived at his condo in Homestead at almost 0600. His new rank allowed him to live off base. He hated the old, dingy, enlisted bachelor apartments with smelly carpets, lousy plumbing, and often nosy neighbors. He purchased the condo as a builder's close-out. It was a spacious unit overlooking a natural lake. He usually sat on his small terrace and watched the ducks feeding and paddling across the smooth green water. The lake was connected to a natural waterway stocked with freshwater fish. Crenshaw didn't like freshwater fishing. It seemed to lack something that saltwater fishing had, an intangible feeling he couldn't explain.

Crenshaw intended to take a quick nap before showering, but fell into a deep sleep as soon as he got comfortable.

A sharp clicking sound roused him from sleep. Sitting upright on the bed, he looked around the room, listening intently. He sniffed at an odd smell that put his senses on alert. Crenshaw slowly got out of bed, walked over to the window, and opened the blackout drapes. The room was flooded with brilliant sunlight. Shit, what time is it? He thought, then checked the time: 14:05.

"Damn," he shouted, upset about oversleeping. Seeing no one in the room, he went to the bathroom to relieve his almost bursting bladder. He showered and dressed quickly.

He was about to call the general to apologize for running late, but froze when he saw a man sitting in his favorite living room chair.

"Good morning, Sergeant Crenshaw," the man said in a wheezy tone.

The small man gave him a thin smile. His well-tailored suit looked as though he slept in it. Crenshaw realized the odd odor was from him. The man gazed at Crenshaw with pale, watery eyes. His oval face, oddly shaped head, and round-rimmed glasses perched on the end of his thin nose gave the diminutive man a weird appearance, as if he were put together by poorly fitting parts.

"How'd you get in?" Crenshaw said, trying to remain calm.

"Through the front door." The odd-looking man grinned smugly as though Crenshaw had asked a stupid question. "I believe you have technology that you shouldn't possess," he said, narrowing his beady eyes into a burrowing stare that made Crenshaw uncomfortable.

"I don't know what you're talking about. If you don't leave

this instant, I'm calling the police." He started for the kitchen but stopped, thinking of entering the bedroom to get his gun and scanner.

"I don't think you want to call the police," the man said, seemingly undisturbed by Crenshaw's threat. "We both know it will take them far too long to get here, and you'll be dead by the time they arrive."

Crenshaw considered what the man said. He was right. The average police response was slow and varied depending on your location. Crenshaw went with his instincts. He ran to his bedroom, slamming the door behind him and locking it. He opened the small safe in his closet and grabbed his gun, snapping a full clip into it. With a gun in hand, he turned to find the little man standing inside his bedroom.

"You got one second to leave before I shoot," Crenshaw said, trying hard to hold the gun steady. It felt heavy.

The man regarded Crenshaw with an overconfident grin. "Go ahead. Shoot."

Enraged by the intruder's arrogance, he squeezed off two rounds. The gun made a horrific sound that startled Crenshaw. He didn't realize that he had closed his eyes when he fired. He opened them and frowned at seeing the man standing before him with a mocking sneer.

"No, that can't be." He looked at the gun.

"Give me what I came for, and I'll let you live, for now," the man said, holding his hand out to Crenshaw.

"Fuck you!" he shouted and fired three more rounds, point-blank, at the man's head and chest.

The diminutive intruder laughed. Crenshaw noticed five flattened bullets on the floor. He stared in disbelief at them, then at the uninjured man. Crenshaw heard the scanner beeping inside his night table. He opened the small drawer, grabbed the scanner, and flipped it open.

Crenshaw's hand shook as he spoke into the device, "Display life type."

One word appeared: Zenti. He looked at the invader and cringed. The pint-sized man had transformed into a grotesque creature. What stood before Crenshaw stared at him with bulging eyes set wide apart in an oval, hairless head. From what he could see of the hideous humanoid, it looked insect-like. Crenshaw couldn't get a feel for whatever it was because it looked incongruent, still dressed in that tailored suit.

Crenshaw's head felt light as he stumbled backward on the edge of the bed. He looked on, horrified by the insidious-looking being, as it slowly walked to him and grabbed the scanner from his hand.

"I'll take that, thank you," Territaff said, snatching the scanner from the surprised Zenti, then punched it in the head, knocking it hard to the floor.

The dazed Zenti reached inside his pants pocket. Territaff stomped on its arm. It let out a chilling, hissing wail that sounded like a cat's cry. Territaff kneeled on one knee, jerked out a small device from the Zenti's pocket, and then punched it again in the head. This time, the horrible creature looked unconscious.

"That's... that's... uh... uh... Zenti." Crenshaw's complexion turned ghostly white as though all the blood had drained from his head.

"Take it easy," Territaff said.

Crenshaw could feel Territaff's tremendous power as he cradled him in his arms like a baby and placed him on the bed. He unbuckled Crenshaw's belt, then put two pillows under his feet. His color returned to his face.

"What the fuck just happened?" Crenshaw asked, holding his now throbbing head between his hands.

"You handled yourself well, my young friend," Territaff said. He sat next to him on the bed. "How are you feeling?"

"Better. I felt lightheaded for a moment." He sat up a little and gave Territaff a confused stare. "I shot that son of a bitch five times, and the bullets just bounced off." He looked down at the unconscious Zenti. "All you did was hit him. I don't get it."

"It appears the Zenti developed a dampening field while morphing. This complicates things, though." Territaff frowned, scratching the back of his head in thought.

"Complicates how?" Crenshaw said, glancing at the Zenti to ensure he was still unconscious.

"For one thing, until this Zenti showed up, we thought only a select few of Zohleemay's group could morph. Morphing is not something that anyone can do. It must be genetically engineered for the user. It also has many side effects. If given to the wrong genotype, it can be lethal."

"Okay, that explains the morphing. What about the bullets at point-blank range?"

"Well, it looks like the Zenti had modified their morphing technology. Mutating works on a subatomic level. I would guess that if the field were dense enough, it would act as a shield. That's also why it's so dangerous. To maintain the energy state, the individual must rearrange their physiology into the desired pattern and then hold it. It requires a great deal of discipline in both concentration and muscle memory. It's kind of like maintaining a pose while holding your breath. You can do it until you need to breathe. In maintaining a morphed-field state, an individual can sustain it as long as their energy holds out. Once the mutated individual becomes fatigued, the state collapses. But what the Zenti are doing. Creating an impervious field from a mutated state is beyond anything I have seen.

"That's incredible," Crenshaw said as he rolled off the bed. "What you're describing is the ability to control physiology on a subatomic level." He shook his head as he tried to comprehend the concept. "How far ahead of us are they?"

About seventy-five years, but the Venubians don't even have this morphing level. Few of them can morph at all. And the ones that can only maintain it for a short time. That's what makes the Zenti's ability so baffling. Just think of the ramifications. They can assume any physical shape if they maintain the same mass."

Crenshaw sighed heavily, his face tight with a disconcerted scowl, then noticed the time. "Oh shit, I never called the general."

"Relax, Rob. The general knows everything."

"What do you mean?"

"Did you forget about your neuro tracer? We've been monitoring both of you. Dickerson was greeted by another Zenti when he arrived at the base. Cuz picked it up and notified me at the same instant I picked yours up. Cuz took care of the general's pest in his inevitable manner. Now that we have their attention, we can proceed with phase two of our plan. First, we need to get this Zenti to Biomei for analysis. Are you up for going for a little ride?"

"Where to?" Crenshaw gazed at Territaff with eyes full of doubt and nerves.

"Let's keep that a surprise for now."

He nodded, his attention still fixed on the Zenti lying on his bedroom floor. Crenshaw realized he was looking at the face of the enemy. Even in an unconscious state, it was unsettling. He looked at Territaff, narrowed his eyes, and asked, "Whose Biomei?"

"Sorry, I thought I'd told you about her. Well, you'll meet her soon enough."

CHAPTER 37

Territaff brought up a map of the base on his cellphone and showed it to Crenshaw, "Do you know where this is?" he said, pointing to a circled area.

Crenshaw briefly studied it, then said, "That's the old rocket testing area. It's restricted and well-guarded."

"Yeah, but you know how to get there?"

He nodded.

"Good. Turn off everything in your apartment and lock up. You may be gone for a while."

"What's a while?" he asked.

Territaff shrugged. "I don't know. You can't stay here any longer, and you can't go back to the base. It's just not safe for you or General Dickerson." Crenshaw's expression took on a familiar quizzical look, and Territaff wanted to cut him off before the flood of questions began. "I'll explain everything on the way."

Crenshaw became confused. He didn't know what to do. He started for his closet, but Territaff clutched his arm and said, "Don't bother."

"I need a change of clothes, don't I?"

"Everything you'll need will be provided. All you need to do now is get your car keys, lock up, and drive us to that point on the map."

Crenshaw opened his mouth to speak.

Territaff shot his hand up. "No questions. Just do exactly as I say. Okay?"

A flutter -and then a sharp cramp rumbled in Crenshaw's stomach. "I have to go to the bathroom," he said, feeling self-conscious.

Territaff let out a sigh and mumbled, "Another nervous stomach. Go. Time's a luxury we can't afford. Where are your car keys?"

"They're on the small glass table by the front door."

"I'll put this Zenti in the trunk and meet you by your car."

Crenshaw nodded. He watched Territaff as he pulled up the unconscious alien by its arm and flung it over his shoulder like a sack of flour.

He gave Crenshaw a stern look and said, "Go already."

Crenshaw snapped to attention, then ran into the bathroom to relieve his spastic stomach.

* * *

For some inexplicable reason, Rob had gotten an odd notion that his father's spirit was next to him. It was a peculiar feeling that he wanted to dismiss as nonsense and tried pushing it out of his mind. Rob struggled with this intense emotion until they reached the outer fence of the testing base. I wish you could see me now, Dad, he thought.

Rob's attention shifted to a new situation. He saw General Dickerson waiting with two MPs standing on either side.

"Oh shit," Crenshaw said. "They got the general. They must be waiting for us. Turn around. There's a back gate we can try."

"Hold on a minute, Rob. It's okay. They're with the general."

Crenshaw recognized the impatient scowl on Dickerson's face. "Oh, I see that now. As usual, he's unhappy about something."

"You read your general pretty well. I've noticed how keenly you observe and read people and situations," Territaff said. "You're growing on me a little."

"Thanks." Rob's brow furrowed. "I think."

Territaff couldn't help smiling at the young man, whose value to the mission was growing in his eyes. He also worried that Crenshaw and General Dickerson would become targets and that additional resources would be required to protect them. Just what form and how those resources would be applied was becoming a cumbersome problem for Territaff. His first instinct would be to leave them aboard Biomei until this ugly mess was over. *That would be the prudent thing to do*. He also recognized they would strenuously object, and he needed their help. He reflected that such is the price of war that the innocent become expendable for the greater good of all. In this case, the so-called greater good involves multiple systems, with the Earth being the most vulnerable now.

Territaff watched Crenshaw as he went up to the general. Dickerson looked pleased and relieved to see him uninjured and his energetic self. They shook hands, and Crenshaw started an exciting depiction of his Zenti encounter. Territaff gave them a few minutes to relax in each other's company, retrieved the unconscious Zenti from Crenshaw's trunk, and transmitted a message for Cuz to pick them up at the pre-arranged coordinates.

After a few minutes, Territaff approached the two in conversation. They were exchanging their impressions of the Zenti attackers. From what Territaff could gather from their animated body language, they reacted with similar unsettling surprise and revulsion to their enemy's sudden appearance.

"Sorry to interrupt, General Dickerson, but you need to dismiss the guards now," Territaff said.

The general nodded, then told the guards to secure the gate and leave the area. Once the guards were nowhere in sight, Territaff gave the go-ahead to Cuz. Crenshaw gazed upward as soon as he heard the high-pitched whine overhead. The general eyed Crenshaw with a confused stare as he looked up to see what caught his subordinate's interest.

"What are you looking at?" the general asked.

"You can't hear that?" Crenshaw asked, still looking up at the empty sky.

Territaff looked on with interest at the differences in the two men's personalities and abilities. He was considering what each of them brought to the mission. With his sharp senses and inquisitive intellect, Crenshaw would bring a fresh perspective, and General Dickerson's years of experience in combat and politics could be invaluable.

Crenshaw also had another compelling quality. He shared some of the traits Kathy displayed before being transformed. He was weighing the justification for converting Crenshaw, but dismissed the thought when a myriad of potential problems flashed through his mind.

"Kathy is enough," Territaff mumbled. "*Disengage stealth mode, Cuz,*" he transmitted.

The small shuttlecraft became visible a hundred meters above their heads. The compact spacecraft didn't appear to be aerodynamic in form. It looked more like a 1960s-style Volkswagen Bus than a space shuttle. General Dickerson and Crenshaw looked on, impressed with how smoothly the small ship came down, almost like a leaf floating to the ground.

Crenshaw became infatuated with the shuttle's design. He walked around it, looking up and down while pointing out to no one in particular things that interested him.

"Are those solar panels built into the sides and rear?" he asked. "The high-pitched whine is from the air-breathing thrusters, but what's making the low humming sound? Wow, General, did you notice?" he said, pointing excitedly. "It's hovering a few inches above the ground. What's keeping it up?"

The airlock hissed open. Cuz came out to greet everyone. He motioned to the general to get into the shuttle as Territaff handed the Zenti to Cuz and then went after Crenshaw.

Territaff found Rob down on one knee, inspecting the rear engine assembly. "We need to go," he called to him.

"It looks like a simple design," he said, not looking up from the shuttle.

"Rob, we need to go now," Territaff insisted, gesturing with a sharp thumb jerk over his shoulder.

Crenshaw entered the shuttle's tight interior. He looked closely at the pilot's area as he sat beside the general. Dickerson looked preoccupied in thought. He surveyed the interior. "This ship looks more like a limousine than an alien ship," he said to the general, who nodded absently.

"How fast are we going to travel?" Rob asked as he strapped himself in.

"A little over 36.2 thousand kilometers per second," Cuz explained. "The shuttle can approach .42 of light speed, but we won't travel far enough to reach that velocity."

"Why that's... That's over eighty thousand miles per hour!" The general said with a surprising stutter.

"It's closer to eighty-two thousand, sir," Rob corrected. "And this small ship can travel up to over 126,000 kph?

"Will we feel the G-forces?" the general asked.

"Only slightly. The shuttle has a low-yield inertial dampening generator," Cuz explained as the shuttle glided upward.

The general didn't seem to share Crenshaw's enthusiasm. His expression looked more subdued, as though he was allowing the experience to pass over him. Crenshaw noticed his boss's contemplative gaze and didn't bother engaging him in conversation. Instead, he watched, fascinated, as Cuz maneuvered the shuttle straight up.

"What type of propulsion does the shuttle have?"

Cuz arched an eyebrow and smiled at Territaff.

"I know what you're thinking," Territaff said in a low voice. "He does sound a lot like Kathy." Territaff heaved a long sigh and sent Kathy a transmission, "*We're on our way with your male clone.*"

"*Huh?*" She responded.

Then he sent a message to Biomei, "*Permission to dock.*"

"*Permission granted. Proceed to aft docking bay-4.*"

"*Aft docking bay-4. Copy that.*" Territaff looked at Cuz and transmitted. "*I'm not sure I have enough energy to answer all his questions and handle Kathy, too. You'll handle Kathy for me, and I'll take the young inquisitor under my wing.*"

Cuz looked at Territaff with an amused grin and nodded.

"You guys talking about me?" Rob asked, his head craned

to the side, narrowing his gaze at Territaff.

"Yes," Territaff admitted. "We decided not to toss you out of an airlock before docking. But we may change our minds, depending on how annoying your questions become."

Rob and Territaff's eyes locked into an intense gaze until Rob laughed and said, "That was a joke... Right?"

"Maybe," Territaff said.

Rob swallowed down a nervous lump. He couldn't read through Territaff's unwavering stare. He looked at Cuz and got a similar feel from his stoic demeanor while busy at the shuttle's controls.

"Sometimes I can't tell when you guys are kidding."

"That's the idea, Rob. Now, sit back. We're about to maneuver tightly into Biomei's aft docking bay. The view out the portside will become most interesting in a few minutes."

Just as Territaff said, Cuz disabled the shuttle's solar guards on the view portals so they could see outside. To their surprise, Crenshaw and the general's eyes widened as Biomei's enormous grandeur filled their view. She looked majestically posed in a low orbit above the Earth.

Crenshaw looked down and saw the bright blues and whites of the Atlantic Ocean under thick circles of clouds, along with the entire northern hemisphere. It was a breathtaking view that Crenshaw often dreamed of but never thought he would see. It looked surreal and unimaginable that he was preparing to dock in low Earth orbit aboard a ship more massive than any ship he could have ever imagined.

"How big is that thing?" Rob asked.

"She's a magnificent-looking ship," General Dickerson said. He looked out and smiled in amazement. "What a wonderful sight," he murmured. "I never thought I'd live to see the day I would be in space. This is like a dream come true for me. I wish it were under different circumstances."

Dickerson leaned back in his seat, let out a low sigh, and returned to his brooding mood while staring out the portal.

"Good morning, gentleman," a feminine voice said.

Crenshaw and General Dickerson looked at each other in surprise.

"Did you hear something?" Rob said.

"Allow me to introduce myself," the voice continued. "My name is Biomei, an acronym for Biomechanically Engineered Entity. I know it doesn't quite match the spelling. It's a loose translation from Venubian, but close enough for Earth people." She let out a girlish giggle that startled both the general and Crenshaw.

"Biomei, I don't think they're in the mood for jokes," Cuz said, noticing the bemused expressions on their faces.

"You're a biomechanically engineered entity," Crenshaw repeated the acronym as if to let its meaning sink in. "Does that mean you're a sentient being?"

"Precisely, my astute young friend."

"I'm pleased to meet you, Biomei. My name is Rob Crenshaw."

"I know who you are, Rob and General Dickerson. I've been observing both of you from afar and must say you've comported yourselves admirably in the best traditions of your military and the country you serve." The compliment sounded sincere and friendly.

"That's a nice thing to say, Biomei," the general said.

"Okay, boys, we'll accelerate into a hard bank into Biomei's aft section. It will only be a few more seconds, then we'll be aboard," Territaff explained.

"Engaging maneuvering thrusters and decelerating to 12.5 meters per second," Cuz alerted them.

"Aren't you concerned about being visible to almost every major country and hacker with a telescope and computer?" General Dickerson stated that, with the sudden realization of Biomei's size and being positioned close to Earth,

"Under normal circumstances, I'd share your concern, General Dickerson," Territaff interjected, realizing he should have explained their positioning of Biomei to them earlier. "Biomei is in a blind spot right now. We have her in a stationary orbit before the sun's corona. We're using the sun's glare and a cloaking device, rendering her and us invisible to all orbiting devices and ground-based surveillance. However, this relative position will only be good for another quarter-hour, then we must get out of here."

The general nodded and said, "That's impressive. Whose idea was it?"

"It was mine, General," Biomei said.

General Dickerson cocked an eyebrow, looking at Territaff with a dumbfounded expression.

"She'll take a little time to get used to," Dickerson admitted to Territaff as the shuttle glided to a gentle stop.

"I've been told that I'm an acquired taste," Biomei added, "but like many unusual and new experiences, you only have to let yourself go with the flow."

The general didn't know how to respond to Biomei. She was as perplexing an anomaly as he had ever encountered. He looked at Territaff with his mouth pursed as if to ask a question, but didn't know what to ask.

Territaff smiled at him. "You know, General, my initial reaction to Biomei wasn't too different from yours."

"Really, what did you... I mean, how did you... Oh, never mind." He sneered disgruntledly at Territaff as he fumbled with his seatbelt.

Territaff leaned in and unbuckled the general from his seat. Dickerson stood, banged his head hard on the cabin's hull, then fell back into his seat.

"Are you okay?" Territaff asked, wincing.

"I'll live," Dickerson said, rubbing the sore spot on his head as he rose more carefully, then followed Territaff out of the shuttle.

"I should have warned you about the low ceiling. I've banged my head a few times. The shuttle was designed for

Venubians. Their average height is less than one and a half meters." Territaff placed a hand on the general's shoulder, "The secret to getting along with Biomei is first to accept her as part of the crew and not as the ship. Once you have mastered that, I strongly recommend heeding her advice and ignoring her attempts at humor."

"Ignore the latter, General, but follow the former," Biomei said, sounding congenial and surprisingly human.

"You'll take some getting used to," Dickerson said, then resumed his officer's bearing and walked to Crenshaw.

Crenshaw was almost in a daze of wonderment as he surveyed the docking bay. It was unlike anything he could have ever imagined. The bay was enormous, over two hundred meters deep and at least a hundred meters wide. He spied over twenty different shuttles parked on three levels along one side of the bay.

"Why do you have so many shuttles?" Rob asked.

"This is a transportation bay," Cuz explained as he walked to Crenshaw. "There are ten major and two secondary shuttle bays with various conveyances for specific jobs. There are five hundred shuttles and three-star cruisers for deep space exploration."

"Where's everybody? I feel as though there should be more people on board."

"Yes, there should be, but Biomei's original mission has been put on hold until the current crisis is resolved."

"Gentleman," Biomei called for their attention. "I would like to welcome you both aboard. You're permitted complete access to the entire ship, and all its facilities are at your disposal," she spoke in a warm tone but with an air of authority.

"By your tone, am I to assume you're in charge?" Dickerson asked.

"I am the ship," she declared, "but prefer you think of me more as your host than a captain. There is no military hierarchy onboard. However, Territaff is recognized as the primary facilitator and decision-maker. My function is to safeguard your lives while aboard me. In that regard, I have absolute authority. For everything else, it's Territaff's mission, and he's charged with executing a plan to defeat the Zenti while protecting you from harm."

"I see," the general acknowledged. "I guess that clarifies things." He aimed a narrow stare at Territaff. "We're awaiting your orders."

"Well, since you put it that way, I order us to decontamination."

"Will it hurt?" Rob asked.

"Only your pride." Territaff smiled.

CHAPTER 38

Territaff led them into the small turbo lift in the shuttle bay. He was so accustomed to decontamination by himself that he had forgotten the general and Crenshaw. They had to squeeze together to fit inside the small cylindrical car.

"Destination?" a soft, feminine voice asked.

"Decontamination," Territaff said. "Sorry about the tight fit. This lift is designed for Venubians."

The door closed with a quiet hiss, and the lift made a low whining sound as it flowed down the forty-four deck levels into the ship's bowels. There was no perceptible sensation of movement. Crenshaw wanted to ask about the unique ride, but the lift door opened before he could ask the question. The general and Crenshaw gazed with lined brows at the maze of translucent doors in front of them.

"Where are we?" Crenshaw said.

"We're in lower engineering, beneath the central core," Territaff explained. "Biomei has worked hard to minimize the decontamination process. My first one was quite an experience. It took over an hour to decontaminate me. My circumstances were different, though. Decontamination is a very critical process for protection against harmful microorganisms. Despite her size, Biomei is a confined environment; even the smallest contaminants can become a major problem. You can say I've been Biomei's guinea pig in perfecting the process. Come to think of it, I've been her guinea pig for just about everything on this ship."

"How often do we need to decontaminate?" General Dickerson asked.

"Every time you leave and return, you must go through decontamination. The first one is always the longest. The biofilters need to read your body's unique macro and microbiological signatures into a physiological map that will become a benchmark for all future scans. Subsequent scans will be shortened depending on what you bring back with you. I'll go first, then you two follow me. Questions?"

The general and Crenshaw shook their heads. Then, he watched with interest as Territaff stepped forward and waited for the system to recognize him.

"Good morning, Terri," a pleasant female voice said. "Please step forward onto the conveyor."

Territaff looked like he was floating in the air as he slowly moved through the first doorway. It took him into a small room that resembled a mantrap with doors on either side. They saw Territaff become enveloped with a fine, milk-like foam. The foam dissolved, and Territaff was standing naked as he floated through the next set of doors.

Crenshaw looked back at the general and asked, "Should I go next?"

General Dickerson gave him a stern look, and Crenshaw stiffened to attention, then stepped forward.

"Good morning, Rob," the voice acknowledged him.

The voice sounded as though it were right beside him. He glanced around but saw nothing that resembled a speaker or intercom. He felt nervous, realizing he would be naked in front of a strange, feminine-sounding thing.

"What will happen to my clothes?" Crenshaw timidly asked, hoping the general didn't hear him.

"They will be purified and sent to your quarters," the voice answered. "Please take another step forward."

"Won't they be dissolved?"

"Your clothes will be reassembled into their former molecular structure and feel and look brand new. Now, please take a step forward."

Crenshaw hesitated a moment. He imagined being gawked at by a room filled with strange aliens. His face flushed, and his heart pounded so hard that it worsened his headache.

"Any time now, Crenshaw," the general barked.

"Sorry, sir... I'm shy."

"You're what?"

"Shy."

"Shy about what?" Dickerson thought for a moment. "Oh, for Christ's sake, Crenshaw. Nobody gives a shit about what you look like."

"You're right, of course, sir." He took a step that felt like a leap off a high precipice onto the conveyor.

A smile broke across his face as he felt himself moving as though he were in a lucid dream. He could see himself moving, but his feet had no sensation of being on a solid surface. It felt more like floating than moving. He became curious about what type of technology could be at work.

"What an interesting sensation," he said, trying to calm his nerves.

Crenshaw started to look back at the general when the voice said, "Please keep your head forward and stay as still as possible."

The conveyor stopped as he entered the first set of doors, while a milky foam sprayed and covered him. He could feel a slight tingling sensation, but noticed nothing happening to his clothes. He stood in anticipation, then heard something like a rubber band snapping on paper. He felt a cool rush of air across his body. Crenshaw looked down and shivered at being naked. Cringing with a nervous shudder, he closed his eyes when the conveyor resumed.

He opened his eyes, one at a time, and saw Territaff's form through the translucent walls of the decontamination area as he progressed to the next stage. He heard a low-frequency hum when he entered the second set of doors. He looked up, and the humming sound stopped.

"Please keep your eyes straight ahead and stay as still as possible," the voice repeated.

The disembodied voice was irritating Crenshaw, but not as much as he was irritating the general. His motion stopped in the middle of being covered in foam.

"Crenshaw, if you don't stop moving around, I'm coming over there and kicking you in the ass," Dickerson growled. "Now, stand at attention and don't move a muscle."

Crenshaw snapped to attention and looked straight ahead. After a brief pause, the system resumed. When he approached the final set of doors, he felt his chest get heavy, and a sudden cold sweat chilled him to the bone. He didn't want to say anything, thinking it would exacerbate the general's irascible mood. Crenshaw took in a deep breath and tried hard to remain calm.

Somehow, the decontamination system recognized Crenshaw's condition as he entered the final section. Instead of a sonic shower, he felt a warm current of air surrounding him like a blanket. It calmed him. As soon as he relaxed, he found himself bathed in a cacophony of high and low-frequency sounds. He never felt so clean and revived as he did exiting the decontamination chamber.

"You gave the system a good workout," Territaff said to Crenshaw.

Territaff was already dressed in a colorful dark blue jumpsuit with broad silver stripes at the cuffs of the pants and sleeves.

"I'm sorry about that," Rob said, his face flushed. "I can't explain why I was so nervous, but—"

"No need to explain," Territaff interrupted. "You must learn not to be so hard on yourself. You should have seen me the first time through. I was so nervous I almost shit right on the deck."

Crenshaw laughed and said, "I was close to shitting a couple of times."

"I'm glad that's over," General Dickerson said as he joined them. "Are you all right?" he asked Crenshaw softly.

"I'm fine, sir. I just felt ill for a moment, but it passed."

"Gentleman, please step up onto the platform. We can get

you fixed up with the latest ship's attire," Territaff said, gesturing with his arm to a low platform in the center of the room. "General, please stand inside the circle on the far right, and Rob, take the one on the left. Stand upright and still while the scanner measures your body and metabolic rates. This will only take a few seconds. Once you're scanned, the system will produce a jumpsuit like the one I'm wearing. You can custom-design your suits whenever you want. However, there are specific suits that must be worn during missions."

"I can understand the custom fitting, but why metabolic rates?" Crenshaw said.

"The suits are intuitive and will adjust to changes in ambient and body temperatures. They can also protect you from exposure to harmful or hostile environments."

"I'd like to have what you're wearing, if that's all right?" Rob said.

"General, do you have a preference?" Territaff said.

"What you have is fine. No. On second thought, I've been in the army all my life. Give me something in a nice olive green."

"As you wish, General. Now, remember to stand still. It will only take a few seconds."

Territaff walked over to a small console on a pedestal. He pressed in a code, and the system activated with a high-pitched whirring sound. Two disc-shaped objects came from the ceiling and stopped centimeters above Dickerson's and Crenshaw's heads. Both men were wrapped in bands of colorful lights with a white ring running up and down their bodies. The lights had no noticeable effects. Within a few seconds, they turned off. A broader light appeared at the bottom of their feet a beat later. It moved up their legs. As the band of light moved upward, a material appeared on their bodies as it progressed. When the first band of light completed its run, they were clothed in dull white, form-fitted jumpsuits. Then, the second band of white light passed down their bodies, coloring the dull white material with their chosen designs and colors.

Crenshaw and the general looked at each other, dumbfounded. They inspected themselves by looking down at their legs and extending their arms outward.

"Don't you have a mirror?" Rob asked.

"Have something even better. Come over to the console." Territaff gestured for them to follow.

They gave him a confused look at not seeing a mirror.

"Just a second, gentlemen," Territaff said, noticing their confusion. "I need to create your virtual images. Biomei, give me a virtual reflecting image so our guests can view their new outfits."

"Imaging is ready on your request," Biomei said. "You both look handsome in your new uniforms," she complimented.

"Turn to your right," Territaff said.

When they turned, they looked in surprise at seeing three-dimensional images of themselves in front of them.

"Whoa," Rob said, almost giddy at seeing his double. "That's unbelievable imaging. Is it holographic?"

"Similar, but it's more of a virtual representation than a holographic one. Biomei can reproduce your images anywhere and in almost any medium. Over the next few weeks, you'll become more familiar with many new technologies. You both must be hungry, so let me take you to what I now call Biomei's Electronic Grill and Café."

"That sounds great. When you mentioned food, I realized how hungry I am," the general said, looking away from his image. He turned to Crenshaw and, out of the side of his mouth, said, "I don't mind telling you I find it a little creepy seeing your double right in front of you."

"I think it's fascinating." Rob grinned.

"You both look great," Territaff said. "Now, you're officially part of the crew."

"Oh crap," Crenshaw cried, clutching his chest. He felt a wave of nausea overtake him. His heart was pounding, and a sharp pain radiated down his left arm. "My heart…," Rob's voice sounded strained as he tried to gather himself from the sudden, unbearable pain. "My heart—it's beating too fast, and I feel lightheaded." His complexion turned chalky and clammy. His eyes closed in obvious distress as he clutched at his chest harder.

Territaff feared for Rob, seeing him in such great pain. He got to Rob and gathered him in his arms as his knees buckled.

"Rob, what's wrong?" the general said, looking pale.

"We need to get him to the med lab," Territaff said. "Biomei, give me a quick scan of Crenshaw's vitals."

"I was about to warn you that the decontamination scanner picked up a rise in his blood pressure during the procedure. The medical monitor detected a possible clot in Crenshaw's right aorta. He appears to be experiencing a myocardial infarction."

Crenshaw's body went limp in Territaff's arms. He laid him on the floor and placed his ear on his chest as Dickerson looked on, feeling helpless.

"Will he be all right?" the general asked.

"We caught it just in time, but I fear his heart is damaged."

"How could you know that?"

"I can hear the way it's beating."

"You can tell that by listening?"

"I have enhanced hearing and some basic medical knowledge. We only have a few minutes before there's irreparable brain damage." Territaff lifted Crenshaw in his arms and rushed to the primary turbo lift on the far side of the deck.

"I'm coming with you?" the general said.

Territaff nodded.

The turbo lift was much larger than the one they came in. It looked like an oversized service elevator that one would find in a typical office building.

As soon as they entered the lift, the doors closed. A

moment later, the doors reopened into the med lab. It was an enormous room, not too unlike a modern hospital ward. A row of beds with monitors above them was lined up on one wall. In the center of the room was an enormous couch with an array of monitors and a scanning device. A long, mechanical arm stood next to the scanner.

General Dickerson surveyed the room, thinking so much of what he had seen on Biomei was miraculous and yet surprisingly familiar.

"She's such a grand ship," he thought aloud. "Built to serve hundreds, maybe even thousands, and she feels so empty and underutilized."

"You're right, general," Territaff said as he laid Crenshaw on the couch. He stepped back, then spoke into the scanner's audible interface, "Begin scan with repair instrumentation."

Crenshaw's clothes dissolved as a thin, white material appeared, covering him up to his neck.

"What does that thing do?" Dickerson asked.

"It's the equivalent of having complete diagnostic and surgical teams at your side," Territaff explained. "The device in the center is a tunneling scanner that uses specialized neutrinos instead of magnets. It's like an fMRI, giving a real-time image of Crenshaw's internal organs.

"The mechanical arm is an automated surgical operator. It can perform various medical procedures on any biological form within its database with flawless precision. I've been a patient more than once on that couch and can tell you firsthand that it's a remarkable device." Territaff looked closely at the general and asked, "Are you squeamish?"

"I've seen more than my share of the insides of bodies. Most of the ones I've seen were either dead or in terrible shape." The general's expression turned reflective. "It's ironic that Crenshaw should be the one on that thing. I'm the one with the bad heart." He rubbed his forehead and looked at Territaff with a worried expression. "We can't afford to lose him. Please, Territaff. Rob's more than an aide… he's become," his voice choked up. He looked as surprised as Territaff by his unexpected display of emotion.

Territaff touched the general's shoulder and said, "I know how you feel. We can perform what seems like miracles with the technology on this ship. Don't worry. He'll be fine. If you don't mind me saying, sir, you look exhausted. Why don't you get some rest while we work on Crenshaw? You can use one of those beds."

"I don't think I could sleep."

"Get off your feet for a little while. I'll update you as soon as we know something."

He let out a long, heavy sigh while walking to one of the beds and lying down. He welcomed the comfort of the bed. As soon as he relaxed, the bed conformed to his body. It sensed the stress in his muscles, and he felt a subtle vibration moving up from his feet into his lower neck and shoulders. The foot end of the bed rose, and the head end lowered. The vibration changed to a soothing pulsing that felt as good as any massage he had ever experienced.

"I could get used to a bed like this," he mumbled.

It only took a few minutes before he fell into a deep sleep.

* * *

"*Terri,*" Biomei transmitted.

"*Yes, Biomei.*"

"*Sensors have detected a high-velocity projectile with a power signature identical to the one that attacked you. It's on an intersecting course. Cuz is running a real-time log. He believes he can capture it for analysis.*"

"*Careful, Biomei, it's unlike anything we've on record. It's advanced and has shown an intuitive ability to adjust to changes. Are you both sure about capture without detonation?*"

"*Cuz and I reviewed the data logs from your encounter and*

have determined we can disable its power drive with a precise discharge of high-velocity photons to disrupt its telemetry, forcing a shutdown of the projectile's propulsion. Once we disable its drive, we'll envelope it with our antigravity field and bring it into the lower engineering bay."

"That sounds good, but won't we disarm it before bringing it aboard?"

"Cuz says the risk is acceptable considering the potential reward."

"I don't know, Biomei. My experience with this device was pretty hairy. I'd be just as happy to blow the damn thing up."

"Unfortunately, it's too late. Cuz has informed me he has connected with the missile and is disabling its primary drive."

"Well, brace for impact just in case he screws up."

"Understood."

Territaff returned his focus to Crenshaw. The data display had a shortlist of proposed repairs waiting for Territaff's approval. He frowned when he saw that one procedure included a complete heart replacement. That means the bio lab will have to genetically engineer a new heart for Crenshaw.

"Give me an estimate of time for replacement and recovery?" Territaff said to the monitor.

"Using the patient's tissue and blood for genetic scaffolding, an organ replacement will take three ship-cycles. Rehabilitation of the surrounding tissue and arteries will require one ship cycle. Complete integration of biological replacement organs into cell memory, affecting patient recovery, will require two additional ship-cycles."

"Biomei, it looks like we'll be without Crenshaw for eight cycles," Territaff said. "I also think we should fix the general's problems while we have him here and hope we can get them both back simultaneously."

"I've been monitoring General Dickerson's metabolic rates. They're erratic. I concur. A cardiac episode is imminent."

"Let's do the procedure on him while he's resting."

"Don't you think he should be informed?"

"No, I don't want to waste the time arguing the merits of doing a lifesaving procedure. He'll only object out of some misplaced duty to complete the mission first. I'll explain it to him later."

"As you wish."

CHAPTER 39

"Terri, you need to see this thing. I don't believe it's an explosive device." Cuz transmitted.

Cuz's curiosity always gave Territaff a refreshing boost. Whenever he shared a moment of discovery with Cuz, he often felt like he was in the company of a precocious ten-year-old.

"The antigrav transfer was almost flawless," Cuz continued. *"It was remarkable the way the missile floated under control. The new antigravity field works well as a defensive mechanism and a retrieval conveyance. We should thank Karoft when he joins us.*

"The missile has no distinguishing marks or symbols of any kind. I perceive a low-frequency hum, but can't determine if it originates from the device or the force field we're generating. Terri, I could use assistance to discover how to open it. It's sealed, and there's no apparent access port or release."

"I'm almost finished prepping the general for surgery. Kathy is on her way to relieve me. She'll stay with our patients and monitor their procedures." He had a sudden thought. *"Cuz, do nothing until I get there."*

"Affirmative."

"Is it a coincidence that the transmission activity increased around the same time as the missile appeared?" he transmitted to Cuz, then thought, Am I getting too paranoid?

Territaff felt uneasy. The capture and retrieval of the mechanism seemed all too easy. He remembered his experience with the missile outside the Venubian corridor. He recalled how intuitive and elusive it was in countering all his evasive maneuvers and attempts to scan it.

"Oh, good, you're here," he said to Kathy as she entered the med lab. "I need to get to Cuz. The missile device he retrieved has me worried."

"Go," Kathy said. "Cuz had already briefed Karoft and me on it. For the record, Biomei also has reservations about tinkering with it. She resisted bringing it aboard, but Cuz made a convincing argument. She understands about gaining what information we can, but still would be as happy to see the damn thing destroyed."

"What's Karoft working on?"

"He's monitoring the various power signatures and radiation outputs from the Yucatan location. He told me he's pinpointed the location and is devising a plan of engagement. Also, he said he's identified a strange narrow-band carrier wave directed toward the moon."

"The moon? Interesting." Territaff pondered the new information. "It appears the Zenti has established a base on the moon. If you think about it, it makes sense. Strangely, nobody has picked up any of the transmissions besides us. They must be masking it somehow." Territaff shook his head and paced. "They're using some very sophisticated technology up there," he paused at the door for a second, then turned to Kathy. "I'll check on their progress when I finish with Cuz. We need to get Rob and the general working with Karoft as soon as possible."

Kathy nodded as she studied Crenshaw's monitor and said, "Just make sure our wonder boy doesn't do anything stupid."

Territaff smiled at the statement and said, "I thought I was the one who did the stupid stuff." Kathy grinned.

* * *

The first thing Territaff noticed was its size. It appeared to be at least a meter longer and slightly wider than the missile that had attacked his shuttle. It also lacked the degree of technological sophistication he was expecting. It appeared ordinary, much like a standard high-velocity torpedo.

"I agree with your assessment, Cuz. This isn't the same

missile, making it even more dangerous because we don't have a clue about it. What were you thinking, bringing something like this on board?" Territaff barked, realizing the full gravity of the situation.

Cuz regarded him with a quizzical gaze. "I'm confused by your displeasure, Terri. We used proper caution and employed all possible safeguards. I also enveloped it in an electromagnetic suspension field. Please, tell me what aspect of our process you disapprove of?"

Territaff didn't know what to say. Based on what Cuz explained, his concerns seemed unwarranted. Their precautions and retrieval execution were flawless. However, he still had reservations about the nature and purpose of this machine. The old proverb of the devil assuming a pleasing shape came to mind.

"I know you and Biomei deserve *a well done*," Territaff said as he circled the long, cylindrical instrument, scrutinizing every centimeter of its hull. "Have you done a micro-scan yet?"

"I was waiting for you to join me before starting," Cuz said.

Territaff looked up from his examination and nodded at Cuz. "Sorry for the grouchiness. It's just that... this thing's bothering me. Let's go slowly and carefully. Okay?"

"Don't I always?" Cuz said, going to a corner of the bay and getting a portable biomechanical scanner. "Biomei attempted to scan it with narrow-field telemetry before bringing it aboard."

"Let me tell you what she got. Nothing. Right?"

"Well, yes. However, we got a brief glimpse of its interior. There's something in there, but we couldn't determine whether it's biological or mechanical."

"So, what did you see?"

Cuz's expression turned impassive, and his body stiffened into his android persona. This sudden change surprised and concerned Territaff.

"What's up with you?" he said.

"One of my internal security sensors has enabled my

autonomic security protocol."

"Cuz, did the device cause it?

Cuz pondered him for a long moment, then said in a low monotone, "I'm running a quick self-diagnostic. Please stand by."

"So, what did you find?" Territaff said.

Cuz frowned and said, "Nothing. I couldn't determine which internal sensor tripped. Also, I didn't detect any residual traces of radiation in or around me. This is most perplexing."

"That's odd, Cuz. Something had to trip your security protocol."

"There must be something inside this manifold probing me," Cuz said, smiling at the revelation. "My linguistic library was just tapped. I believe the device is trying to communicate with me, but I can't establish a connection with it. It's attempting to tap my neural pathways for an interface."

"I don't think that's a good idea. We don't know this thing's origin or purpose."

"We must communicate with it. I sense no hostile intent. I'm allowing it to access my linguistic base and see if I can get it to link up."

"Well, go carefully and let the routine guide you." Territaff scratched the back of his head. "Maybe this is a good thing. Go with it."

"I've got an idea."

Cuz resumed setting up the scanner for analysis. As he brought the scanning arm over the head end of the cylindrical mechanism, a low-pitched hum emanated from it. He input a few standard programming settings into the scanner's controller. It made its usual high-pitched whine as it powered up. A narrow band of soft, white light appeared when fully charged. It started to flow down from the head-end of the tubular instrument. A green light lit up when the band of light progressed a few centimeters down. The top half of the machine popped open. A flash of bright amber light blinded them for an instant.

Cuz spied a shiny object through the glare. When their vision cleared, they looked at each other in surprise.

"Did you get a look at it?" Territaff asked.

"I'm trying to recall it from my short-term visual memory."

"I've already checked mine. All I got was a silver reflection with no details. Whoever planted this gave it a lot of thought."

"They also seem to know a good deal about us," Cuz said as he looked into the open device.

"Zohleemay didn't do this. He would have sent another explosive. This feels more like a test, but I don't understand by whom or why?"

Their attention was drawn to a wavering electrical hum in a far corner of the room. Cuz reached into his utility belt and pulled out his portable scanner. He opened it and pointed it at the humming sound.

"I've got a reading in the low EM-band," Cuz said, holding the scanner away from his body.

"So, what do you think?"

"It appears to be a mechanism cloaked in an infrared field."

Cuz jerked his arm to the right and left, keeping the scanner as far from his body as possible.

"Biomei, can you illuminate the object hovering in the corner of the bay?" Territaff said.

The bay took on a green-gray color. The object became visible for a moment, then disappeared.

"Biomei, did you get a read?" Territaff said.

"Yes," she said. "It's a mechanical device whose design, configuration, and materials are similar to Vultaran engineering."

"I concur," Cuz said, "and it's on the move."

"Don't let it out of the bay," Biomei cautioned. "I've confirmed its purpose. It's an information-gathering droid. The droid is attempting an electromagnetic survey of me. It has already gathered considerable data on Cuz and mine designs. Now it's trying to tap into my secondary systems, looking for a back way into my core memory."

"Information, huh? We'll see about that," Territaff said as he reached for a small hand pulse-phaser from his utility belt. "Cuz, give me a direction."

"Where did you get that?" he asked.

"It's a gift from Larzz," Territaff said. "I'll set it to its lowest power setting and hope I'll disrupt the cloaking field long enough for you to grab it."

"Just one thing," Cuz said, not taking his eyes from the scanner. "What if the droid has defensive mechanisms?"

"Then we'll know a little more about the damn thing."

"Oh." Cuz wrinkled his forehead. "Was that supposed to be reassuring or humorous?"

"Take your pick," Territaff said, raising the small phaser and firing it in the general direction of the droid's last position.

The phaser expelled a rapid pulse of pale yellow-green light that fanned outward into a small plume. Territaff fired again, making a wide pass across the rear of the bay.

"Terri, the droid appears to be anticipating you," Cuz instructed.

"What do you suggest?" Territaff transmitted, avoiding verbal communication.

"Try a more random pattern. I'll tell you when to fire. I'll let it make a few more moves to study its tactics. Up to this point, its movements have spontaneously responded to your actions. It appears to be well-programmed in evasive tactics."

Territaff nodded to Cuz that he was ready. Cuz moved in a small circle, trying to maintain a fix on the elusive droid with his scanner. Territaff watched him as he moved first to his right, stopped, moved back, turned to his left, and continued walking in a wide circle.

"You lost it, didn't you?" Territaff transmitted, noticing Cuz's jaw tighten.

"It appears the droid has changed the frequency of its cloaking mechanism. It's a remarkably adaptive device."

"Ya-think," Territaff transmitted, and changed the phaser to a more intense power setting on a higher frequency.

He fired the phaser in short, repetitive bursts as he slowly circled the bay's interior. The phaser's more powerful beam was scattering instruments and items all over the interior.

"I've got a lock on it. It's heading for the exit," Cuz alerted as he followed the droid with his scanner to the main corridor hatchway. "Fire now."

Territaff fired at the hatchway exit, and the silver mystery droid became visible as it fell to the floor.

"Biomei, what do you read from the droid?" Territaff said.

"It appears disabled... yet I'm getting several energy readings streaming from something inside. Please stand by while I investigate it more closely."

There was a brief pause while Biomei analyzed the energy patterns.

"It's transmitting an encrypted data stream. There's also an additional energy signature."

"Can you decipher it?" Territaff said.

"No. However, I've now detected two quantum data streams. It's a carrier signal directed toward the moon. The other is undecipherable and doesn't conform to any known energy signature."

"Cuz put the droid back into a suspension field and continued to analyze it. Biomei, prepare my shuttle, please."

"And where are you going?" Cuz said.

"To the moon. Karoft had discovered a narrow band transmission from the Yucatan, also directed at the moon."

"Do you think that's wise?"

"I don't know, Cuz. Whoever they are, they sent us a droid. It's only fair I return the favor and bring it back to them."

Cuz sighed and said, "You're looking for trouble. You may be going right into their trap."

"I appreciate your concern, but I need to know who sent us this droid. After all, they sent their invitation. We should take them up on it. Can you locate the droid's processing center for a little reprogramming?"

"Probably, with a little time to analyze its system configuration, but I'm also unfamiliar with its architecture."

"Come to think of it. All those frequencies we were chasing at Homestead were decoys."

"Yes, Terri. We already discussed this."

"No, we pondered on it but never made any conclusions when the Yucatan site became more interesting. I just realized that the energy pattern from this device was the same..." Territaff's voice trailed off as he rubbed his chin in thought.

Cuz recalled the energy's signature and analyzed its frequencies within his mind. His face rolled up into a pleasant smile with a surprised revelation. He came to the same conclusion.

"You are correct, Terri. It's the same energy wave. A very unique one. It has... a biological structure for an electromagnetic signature."

"It sounds like something in your batting range. It's complicated. Figure it out and then dumb it down to where I can understand it."

"I'm not sure I'm capable of such primitive standards, but we'll try," Cuz said with dripping sarcasm.

Territaff arched a thick, black eyebrow and said, "Get Karoft to help you. He's an expert on complicated systems. He may even have familiarity with Vultaran designs. How much time will you need?"

"At least a few ship hours. What do you have in mind, Terri?"

"I want you to reprogram our little friend to help us find its momma. Disable everything except its homing beacon, then give the coordinates to Hanc. I hope it was sent to get a good read on our systems, then return to its point of origin."

"What if the coordinates take you back to Vultaria?"

"Somehow, I doubt that. Someone sent that thing to us. My gut tells me whoever sent it wants us to find them. The moon is as good a place as any to start."

"As you wish, Terri."

"I'm going back to check on Crenshaw and the general. *Biomei, how are they doing?"* Territaff transmitted as he left for the shuttle bay.

"The general is in the final recovery phase. Crenshaw is stable. His preliminary procedure went well without complications, except for one interesting development."

Territaff stopped walking and frowned. *"You know, I worry whenever you say 'except'. What's the exception this time?"*

"It's about Rob. We discovered a high psi factor in him. His prefrontal cortex has an interesting density of neuron connectivity within the corpus callosum, showing a potential for both empathic and telepathic abilities and a rare form of what you call autism."

Territaff's face flushed, *"Biomei, please tell me you didn't do a transformation prep on him."* He picked up his pace.

"No, but I did a deep cortical survey and a complete brain scan. He's a perfect candidate for the new transformation procedure."

"No. Not now," Territaff snapped. *"There's too much going on. Let's first get a handle on our situation and a plan of attack before converting another person. I need everybody functional and at their best."*

There was a brief, irritating silence before Biomei added solemnly, *"There is something else."*

Territaff stopped walking again and sighed heavily. *"What?"*

"We removed the genetic defect for the potential personality disorder but left everything else alone."

"Need I ask why?"

"You already know. It was done in case a decision to proceed is given."

"Biomei, promise me you won't do any more tinkering with

Rob's brain and genetics."

"Will you, at least, discuss it with him?"

"Kathy is a better choice for that discussion, but not now."

"As you wish."

PART III

The Dark Sides of the Moon

CHAPTER 40

Territaff was reviewing Karoft's data on the signals transmitted to the moon. While Karoft couldn't decipher the transmissions, he found a common pattern in one of them. A repetitive signal was suggestive of a homing beacon. Just what he had hoped.

After glancing at his instruments, Territaff went through his preflight mental checklist. He stared at the six-centimeter square box for a second before pressing his thumb on the biometric switch, turning on the transmitter Cuz had installed.

"Got anything, Hanc?"

"You know that this is a two-way signal."

"Yes. I'm hoping it will lead us to its place of origin."

"Stand by. I am receiving a return ping."

Territaff was surprised at how fast the signal locked onto them.

"I have the coordinates," Hanc informed. "You were correct. It emanates from the moon's far side, outside the Pasture crater at 16.4 degrees south."

"Very good, Hanc. You know what to do."

"Initializing launch sequence." Hanc started the prelaunch routine.

As the shuttle's onboard systems powered up, Territaff contemplated what to do when he reached the moon. Once again, he found himself in a tenuous situation and improvising. It's a familiar routine of his chasing Zohleemay while always being on the defensive. Just once, *I would like to be on the offensive with that bastard*.

"Systems are enabled and nominal. Waiting for your signal to engage engines," Hanc said.

"Biomei, open bay doors for departure," Territaff requested.

The two large, curved doors at the stern shuttle bay glided

open, revealing the velvet blackness of space. In the distance, he could see a small cluster of restless asteroids floating in and out of light and shadow. While millions of asteroids orbit the sun, the average distances between them are vast.

"Engage inertial thrusters," Territaff commanded as he placed a Thailion crystal into the implanted sinus cavity in the back of his head.

Territaff's eyes grew momentarily brighter as the crystal initialized. While there was no real sensation related to the autonomic transfer, there was an awareness of his personality becoming less human and more robotic.

A discussion he once had with Cuz came to mind. They were comparing his autonomic state of being with that of an android. What was so interesting about the conversation was that Cuz stated that even when Territaff was in an autonomic state, Terri was still more human than he was. He remembered countering that remark by reminding Cuz that he's a humanoid of a different kind.

Then, he reflected on Kathy and her transformation. He had mixed feelings regarding her procedure, but she has adjusted quite beautifully up to this point. Territaff pondered Kathy's humanity, being so rich and compassionate that nothing could diminish those attributes in her. Now, he had to consider the possibility of transforming Rob. What would he become as a super-being? The thought disturbed him, even in his autonomic state.

The shuttle moved out of Biomei's belly, flowing into the black-draped, star-filled vastness of space. Territaff reflected on the exhilarating feeling he'd had the first time he piloted a shuttle into the immensity of outer space. Even with his human emotions suppressed, he still got a sense of the tranquil solitude that only being in the depths of the cosmos's bosom can provide. However, the feeling never lasted long.

The shuttle's two large plasma drives ignited and accelerated the mid-sized craft to point three of light speed in a few minutes.

"What's our ETA, Hanc?"

"Four hours, ten minutes, Earth-time."

"Okay, Hanc. Prepare for deployment of the environmental protection system at point-four of light-speed."

"Understood."

"Kathy, how are our patients doing?" Territaff called over his com, wanting to hear her voice more than a report.

"The general is in recovery and is doing well. He's alert, aware, and unhappy." She sighed heavily. "Crenshaw is a different story, though. His preliminary surgery was a complete success, but for some inexplicable reason, he has slipped into a coma-like state. Biomei and I are at a total loss about what happened. There's no medical reason for his condition. It just happened. Biomei is closely monitoring him, and she is encouraged... all his data is perfect except for his brain function."

"What about his brain function?"

"It's alarmingly low."

"Could this be a side effect of the genetic alteration to prepare for his new heart?"

"Biomei ruled that out. She believes the suddenness and severity of Crenshaw's arterial blockage must have overwhelmed him, and the coma is his body's recovery mechanism. We won't know for sure until we implant his new heart."

"Biomei." Territaff opened his com to include her.

"Yes, Terri."

"Why haven't you tried cortical stimulation?"

"I have, to no avail. He's not in a typical trauma-induced coma. All his vital signs and brain activity indicate a deep meditative state. He almost appears as if waiting for a specific stimulus. His condition has no medical precedent. All his major metabolic functions are nominal. As far as I can tell, he's in no immediate danger. I recommend we let nature take its course for a while and see what happens after we complete his heart transplant."

"Do you think it's wise to do a transplant while he's in this condition?"

"The risk is greater if we don't proceed as planned. The coma is a separate issue and will resolve itself regardless of what we do."

"Biomei, is there something you're not telling me?"

"There's another aspect to Crenshaw's condition that may be relevant."

"And that is?"

"The comatose condition started the moment the droid was released. I can't ascertain any energy that could cause Rob's physiological state from it. However, I'm picking up a narrow stream of varion particles, which are being directed toward the med lab. They also first appeared when the droid was released. I have Cuz and Karoft working on the problem. They're engaged in a close analysis of the droid's delivery system."

"Varion particles? Elaborate."

"They were once considered hypothetical. We know little about them. They're part of a group of negative elemental particles. Varions were first detected in the radioactive decay of tachyons. They were discovered when the Klaxons began analyzing the negative energies within the Corridors—another one of the many mysterious particles developed by the Ezdenians. An obscure part of their mythology posits that Varion particles are related to the subatomic elements that permitted the Ezdenians to travel as entangled energy. Of course, that's speculative mythology."

"You believe these varion particles somehow caused Crenshaw's coma?"

"It's too circumstantial for a viable theory. Suffice to call it a working hypothesis."

"Territaff, you feel and sound strange. Is everything okay?"

Kathy said.

"I'm in a special autonomic state."

"What do you mean?"

Kathy's inquiry reminded Territaff that she had never seen or communicated with him in his current condition. A part of him regretted the lapse in memory. Then, he wondered how he could have forgotten such an important detail. He made a mental note to do further analysis.

"It's an induced autonomic state that heightens my mental and physical senses. It's too complicated to explain now, but I'm sure Biomei can give you a fuller explanation."

"Sounds a little creepy."

"I'll update everyone when I arrive on the moon. Hanc has already transmitted the coordinates to Biomei."

"Wait a second," Kathy interjected. "Autonomic? I'm familiar with that. It was in my transformation procedure. A Thailion crystal induces a higher state of consciousness. I didn't like the sound of it. So, thankfully, Biomei didn't do that sinus cavity insertion thing. Didn't know you had it done. Terri, please try to keep the human state in one piece. And bring all of you back to us."

Territaff heard the uneasiness in her voice but couldn't respond meaningfully. He allowed the final remnant of his human side to subside back into the protected recesses of his mind. Hanc filled the shuttle's interior with a thick suspension liquid.

CHAPTER 41

The moon is a gray, desolate, and cold world—a perfect location for the Zenti to set up their primary base of operations. Territaff was impressed with how much the Zenti had accomplished in less than three years. They occupied much of the southwest quadrant of the far side and built an interconnected city above and below the moon's surface.

He transmitted what he was witnessing to Cuz. *"They've created a whole city with complete infrastructure. It covers over a hundred and twenty thousand square kilometers. There are domes everywhere. Interestingly, the dome's architecture is similar to the construction on Lunneziah. The topography is similar as well."*

"Territaff, do you think they still have Bylar slaves?" Cuz transmitted with great concern.

"It wouldn't surprise me. I'm sending you a data stream of the campus and will find a safe location to land and investigate. I'll communicate an update as soon as permitted. If you don't hear anything within thirty ship minutes, assume I'm either captured or incapacitated. Attempt no rescue."

"Understood. I'll be standing by for your next transmission."

Cuz could feel the difference in Territaff when he was in an autonomic state. While some of his personality would seep through, the perfunctory persona was most present. He also had no intention of leaving him on the moon under any circumstances.

Cuz joined Karoft at his workstation and said, "I received a transmission from Terri. He's finding a safe place to land and will investigate. He also confirmed what you and I suspected. The Zenti has established an operational base on the moon. Stand by for a moment. I'm receiving Terri's update. He has located the communications network. It's more advanced than expected."

Karoft's large eyes narrowed, and his high forehead lined

with concern, "Are you suggesting a global network?"

Cuz nodded affirmatively. "We need to find a back door into their system. Once in their network, Territaff can plant a low-frequency carrier signal, giving us a copy of all their communications. It has to be something innocuous and not easily discovered."

"Just a minute, Cuz," Karoft said, pulling on his chin in thought. "That's odd." He returned to his workstation and input data into the computer.

Cuz briefly watched him before asking, "What do you have?"

"I'm getting some strange data from the droid. Look at this, Cuz."

"Something inside the droid is trying to communicate with us."

"You're right. I got a clear message requesting one of us to retrieve it. What do you think it means?"

"I think you should do it. It may have been sent for a specific purpose. Let's find out."

Karoft's surprised expression turned into a long frown with a sudden thought. "What if its purpose is to gather as much information as possible and destroy us?"

"Now, you sound like a typical paranoid bureaucrat," Cuz said. "Somehow, I can't believe that's its purpose. That could've been accomplished without all the trouble. We're a sitting target now."

Karoft shrugged in agreement and went after whatever was inside the droid. After a few minutes, he returned, holding a little black box.

"You won't believe this, but this thing is giving me design instructions for a quantum splitter," Karoft said, holding the box between his thumb and forefinger for Cuz to see.

"Dare I ask?"

"It's a talkative little black box," Karoft said, looking as though he was listening.

"It's communicating with me in perfect Venubian, telepathically. I need to make some quick notes. Do we have a synthesizer?"

Cuz regarded the small black lacquered box and then Karoft with pursed lips. He took the box from Karoft, holding it between his thumb and forefinger.

"You seem to believe I should know what this is, but I'm unfamiliar. The synthesizer is over there." He pointed to a station on the other side of the bay.

Karoft grinned wide-eyed. "If what you're holding there, my young friend, is what I think it is... Well, it must be the strangest and most miraculous device I've ever heard of." He took it back from Cuz and went to the synthesizer station. "It told me it's a Vultaran Pougahr, an undifferentiated quantum synthesizer." Karoft looked at Cuz with his mouth gaping. "It just corrected me, it's of Ezdenian design."

Cuz became even more mystified and returned to his workstation to look for an explanation of what Karoft had described.

"Cuz, I see by your dubious expression you're having a problem grasping the essential elements of this mechanism."

"I understand what you had described is improbable, given that Ezden is more myth than reality. Evidence of its existence is unsubstantiated. One of the more popular theories posits that Venubia's red giant was their sun before it vaporized the Ezdenian system over twelve-thousand five-hundred annual planetary cycles ago. Since I know you wouldn't be joking at this critical juncture, I must assume that I have insufficient information to understand this black object and its Ezdenian design."

"I'm sorry, Cuz, for being so vague, but that's how this device is described. It's an undifferentiated quantum machine that can synthesize or replicate almost anything using inter-dimensional quantum structure. It reads your thoughts, extrapolates the problem, then creates an appropriate device to remedy it."

"So, you're saying that we transmit what we want, and the device somehow manufactures it." He frowned at the innocuous box. "Ezdenian design," he mumbled, recalling all the stories he had heard and read about the mythical Ezdenians. "Sounds more like Ezdenian wizardry than actual science."

"If you consider it, it adds to the myths about an ancient race of wizards who practice magic and could travel telepathically." Karoft playfully smiled. "Wait, a moment... It told me it can replicate itself remotely as a data stream of entangled particles using any quantum computer."

"That's remarkable." Cuz's eyes brightened with a sudden realization of an application for the device. "That's exactly what I was thinking." Cuz furrowed his forehead in wonder about the ten-by-ten centimeter cube. He was starting to believe in its validity. "Then we can replicate it and send it to Terri as a dual-band quantum splitter. He can use the one we gave him as the decoy and install the replicated one as the transmitter. If this thing works, the Zenti would never know."

"Precisely," Karoft said, looking around the engineering bay.

"What are you looking for?"

"I'm looking for a photon generator."

"We can use the wide-frequency laser. It can generate anything we need." Cuz walked over to a storage closet in a far corner of the bay and got the laser. He studied the unfamiliar machine for a moment, considering its older technology. *Why am I choosing this?* "Wait a second," he called to Karoft. "I never remember using this instrument." Cuz looked at the box, realizing the strange thing directed him to the laser's location. "Most odd," he whispered as he placed the laser on the end of his workstation and connected it to the computer's interface.

Karoft placed the little device on the synthesizer's transparent platform. They both worked in silence, following the instructions now being transmitted to them as conscious thoughts.

Karoft appeared excited by the workings of the mysterious gadget. Cuz, on the other hand, was inwardly struggling. He allowed an application from a seemingly miraculous mechanism of dubious origins and purpose to run freely inside his head. What was so confounding was instilling new knowledge in both Karoft and him with such ease. Cuz couldn't help wondering how this small piece of technology could achieve total integration simultaneously into a biological and artificial neural networks.

"Look at this thing work, Cuz," Karoft said with rising excitement.

Cuz walked around the laser to get a better look at the synthesizer. He watched, intrigued, as the little mystery cube created a quantum splitter atom-by-atom right before their eyes.

"Remarkable," Cuz admired as Karoft picked up and inspected the finished splitter.

"Perfect," Karoft beamed approvingly at the duplicate. "Now, let's get Territaff where he needs to be to receive this little beauty."

CHAPTER 42

The Zenti were very deliberate when establishing their base. It was well situated between highland areas to the east and surrounded by some of the deepest craters to the south. Territaff found a secure landing site inside a shallow crater only a few hundred meters from a large central dome.

Territaff took out a pair of field glasses and surveyed the area in full-spectrum and infrared lighting. The entire area was busy with heavy traffic of both guards and vehicles. Territaff frowned at seeing well-organized enemy forces using all the moon's resources. It looked like a staging area for an imminent invasion. He wondered how they were blind to all Earth-based technology.

He estimated that thousands of laborers in environmental suits worked outside the dome complexes. To his relief, he saw no Bylars among them. A well-organized workforce was conducting the labor. He could see a gathering of Zenti guards nearby, milling around the various vehicles and equipment rather than supervising the workers. This scene surprised and puzzled Territaff.

These are not the same Zenti who ran rampant over at least a dozen systems two decades ago. Who is behind this new Zenti threat?

Territaff, concealed in the shadow of a minor impact site, waited for the right opportunity to present itself. He studied the flow of traffic in search of a vehicle to commandeer. He didn't have to wait too long. A large tractor pulled to within a few meters of his position. He observed three Zentis getting out of the rear of the tractor's cab. There were two more still inside, busy working on the controls of the digging equipment. The tractor turned around, revealing a laser boring tool. The three Zenti outside the vehicle were setting up instruments. Territaff gave the instruments a closer look. They were for drilling cores for geological analysis.

The Zenti made a living by stealing and adapting technology and resources to fit their needs. Now, they were turning those well-honed skills toward the moon and Earth.

Territaff waited for the workers to separate before he made his move. The opportunity presented itself when the Zenti driver exited the cab to assist with the equipment setup. When the driver gestured to the worker inside the cab, Territaff made his move.

He pulled the knife from his utility belt and came straight at them. First, he took on the Zenti near the drill site. He came up from behind the now kneeling worker with a knife and cut the supply line to the worker's environmental suit. As the Zenti fell onto its side, struggling to reach the severed line, the Zenti closest to it went toward Territaff. With a quick move, Territaff was on top of the alien. With one thrust, he penetrated the thick protective material of its environmental suit. He smiled at the surprise and pain on the Zenti's face as it fell to the rugged surface. The third Zenti leaped toward Territaff, forgetting about the moon's low gravity. Territaff stepped aside from the air-borne Zenti and grabbed his utility belt as he passed. He flung it face down onto a sharp, jagged rock. The impact shattered the clear bubble helmet, and the razor tip of the rock penetrated the Zenti's forehead, killing him.

The tractor's driver had turned toward Territaff. His flat jaw dropped as he witnessed Territaff's swift and incredible power. The driver looked on in shock. A thin stream of green-blue blood bubbled up from his coworker's shattered helmet. The stunned Zenti ran for the tractor cab. Territaff could see the other Zenti inside, working frantically to bring the drilling laser up as he revved the electric engine. Territaff came around to the passenger's side of the cab. The Zenti became panicky, seeing Territaff's approach. The driver returned inside the cab, shoving the other Zenti out of the way. He jerked the tractor backward to dislodge the drilling rig from its hole. The drill snapped as Territaff was upon them. He first seized the Zenti at the controls, grabbing his arm and flinging him out of the cab like a rag doll.

The driver hissed and grunted in fear when Territaff slammed the door shut. He smiled sinisterly at the driver, terrorizing him into leaping out of the cab. Territaff jumped out in pursuit of the Zenti, skipping as fast as possible in the micro-gravity. In mid-leap, Territaff grasped its leg. All at once, the Zenti was spinning high into the moon's vacuous sky. Territaff watched as the Zenti flew straight into a wall of the crater. He bounced off a jagged outcrop of rock. His limp body sailed forward thirty meters and dropped. Territaff took a moment to survey all the fallen bodies to ensure they were dead.

Getting back into the cab, he paused in thought. He hoped that none of the Zenti workers had time to contact their base. Territaff concluded his presence was still unknown and headed to the communications control facility in the drilling tractor.

"I'm heading towards the communications center. Have you determined the signaling configuration for implantation of the device?" he transmitted to Cuz.

"Find their primary computer. It's in the same complex as the communications center... stand by," Cuz replied.

Territaff parked the tractor under the central dome and spied two guards outside the hatchway. He approached the guards nonchalantly as though he were supposed to be there. The guards raised their weapons, and one spoke to him in an unfamiliar Zenti dialect.

"Human," the guard growled. "Hands up, don't move," it said, pointing its weapon as the other guard ambled around to the back of Territaff.

Territaff gave the guard a friendly smile and said, "Your English is not bad."

As Territaff paid the compliment, the guard behind him poked him in the back with his weapon. On feeling it, Territaff turned to the side and simultaneously kicked the Zenti behind him in the midsection while grabbing the weapon from the other facing him. He turned the weapon and fired on the disarmed guard, then turned and fired at the other as he fell to the ground. The weapon was laser-based and fired effectively in the moon's vacuum.

Territaff examined the weapon and decided it was light and efficient enough to keep. He slung the laser rifle across his shoulders. He checked on both guards for any vital signs. They were dead. Territaff turned to the hatch and took another quick view of his surroundings. As far as he knew, he was still undetected by security. Territaff opened and peered into the hatchway. It led to a lift.

"Well, that didn't take you too long," a familiar voice greeted him as he stepped into the lift.

Territaff turned, grabbed the tall, feminine figure by the neck, and then moved behind her with the knife blade pressing against her carotid artery.

"Is that any way to treat someone who has come a long way to help you?" Her voice sounded even and undisturbed by Territaff's tight grip.

He checked the atmosphere composition and found it breathable. He turned her around to see her face and dropped his guard as he recognized the Vultaran's dark features.

"What are you doing here?" he asked, still holding the knife close to her, removing the helmet from his environmental suit.

"I will tell you as soon as you relax a little," she said, pushing Territaff's knife-holding hand to the side and moving away from him. "Now that is better. You remember me... Yes?" she said, giving Territaff a puzzled look.

"You didn't answer my question," he said, with a glaring stare.

"As I said, I am here to help you. You appear strange, Terri. Are you all right?"

Territaff recognized the Vultaran from Larzz's pub. He studied her face, suspecting her motives, and wondered how she could be there if she weren't working with the Zenti.

"I'm curious. How did you know I'd be here?" Before she could answer, he added, "The most logical answer is you're working with the Zenti." He pressed the knife tip to her neck, drawing a thin stream of blood, and in a low, menacing voice, said, "Convince me of your true intentions so I won't have to kill you."

Tehrarra had already gotten a glimpse of Territaff's violent capabilities. He had changed from the charming Terran she met at Larzz's. A nervous thread stirred in her as she contemplated her words. Territaff's eyes were narrowed and fixed like a beast's cold, penetrating gaze, ready to pounce at any move. She felt uncertain as she considered the shiny knife poised at her throat. For the first time in her life, Tehrarra was experiencing primal fear, and it was terrifying her.

"Who do you think sent the droid with the little black box to you? It was me," she pointed a finger at herself, trying not to show her fear. "I have secretly worked as a double agent with Vultaran and Venubian intelligence. I wanted to warn you at Larzz's, but I never got a chance. You left without saying goodbye." Tehrarra tried to read Territaff for any emotional response. All she sensed was intense and dark energy swirling inside him. "I have risked everything I have accomplished to get to you before the Zenti takes you to Zohleemay."

Territaff grasped her delicate neck and squeezed. "You have to do better than that, Tehrarra."

"You have to believe me." She gasped under his tightening grip. "Please! I cannot breathe," she pleaded in a choking rasp. "Terri, you can read my thoughts. Please... Please stop."

He stared with cold, dark eyes as her face brightened, and her lively eyes lost their luster under his powerful grip. Not until she nodded almost into unconsciousness did Territaff release her. She drew in a long, wheezing breath and coughed.

"What is wrong with you? You would have killed me?"

"I read your thoughts," he said, avoiding her question. "You're telling me the truth, but concealing a lot more. Tell me everything, or must I wring your neck again?"

She held her palm out for him to stop. "Let me catch my breath for a moment," she said, still gasping.

The young Vultaran impressed him with her strength and courage. He looked at her with impassive eyes and an emotionally detached demeanor that made her uneasy. She tried to reach out empathetically again, this time to soften his aggressiveness toward her. Her efforts went to no avail, as Territaff maintained his intense manner, waiting for her to speak.

"My people made a terrible mistake a while ago and helped the Zenti. We did not know of them. They were found on one of our moons, desperately trying to survive. They told us they were war refugees. We had no reason not to believe they were part of a dying race urgently needing our help.

"We heard about the war in the Venubian sector. However, my people are not aggressive by nature, and we had no interest in their war. Nor did we know who the Venubian and Kaydens were until we joined the Alliance. Therefore, we believed and helped the Zenti. As soon as they were strong enough, they turned on us, stole vital technology, and then took off with three of our starships. I believe you know the rest of the story.

"The only positive thing that came out of our mistake was joining the Alliance, at the cost of losing our naivety and indifference. We have become a new race in less than ten cycles. How strange and small our universe has become."

It was a familiar story for Territaff. He could sense the heaviness within her. Her regret and fears were genuine and well-founded. Territaff relaxed, brought her face close to his, and narrowed his dark eyes at her. Tehrarra tensed under the close, probing gaze.

"I'm sorry for hurting you," he said in a softer voice. "There's too much at stake. I had to be certain of your motives."

Tehrarra let out a long sigh as she tried to gather herself. Territaff noticed her trembling hands and took them in his. He was like an emotional chameleon to her. One moment, he was threatening her life, and the next, he was a calming influence.

"And I thought you were complicated when I met you at Larzz's," she said, relaxing under his warm and soothing touch.

Territaff forced a smile. He had difficulty maintaining his autonomic state, which was becoming a troubling dynamic in an already complicated situation. Usually, he gathered all the information he could from her, then sent her on her way. For some inexplicable reason, he believed he was better off with her than alone.

"We need to get up to the communications center," Tehrarra said suddenly. "We have little time. A shift of workers will come through here soon."

"Stand by, Tehrarra. I'm receiving a transmission."

Cuz transmitted an overview of the little black box they discovered in the droid and what they needed him to do. He studied Tehrarra as he listened to Cuz.

"That look again." A nervous flutter ran through her.

"Why didn't you tell me about the little black box?"

"I did tell you. I thought that was why you were here." Tehrarra looked surprised. "You took that long to discover the device?"

"Apparently," Territaff answered coolly.

"I have broken some of our most sacred laws in sending that Pougahr to you. I may face some serious charges and possible exile from Vultaria."

He pulled her hands against his chest and said warmly, "You'll always have a home with us." He kissed her gently on the lips.

She lifted her tearful eyes and smiled surprisedly at Territaff's sudden tenderness.

As Tehrarra studied his face, trying to understand his inconsistent actions, Territaff got a sudden flash before his eyes and an intense stabbing pain in the back of his head. Realizing it was from the Thailion crystal, he reached back and pulled it out. Tehrarra looked at it, then at Territaff. She noticed his eyes' retreating dark and sinister luster being replaced with the familiar deep, blue glow that first attracted her.

Territaff examined the crystal with disbelief. Its transparent amber luminosity had turned to a dingy, dark brown, and it looked drained of all its energy.

"That's impossible," he said, holding the crystal to the lift's light for a better look.

Tehrarra watched with interest. "Is that a Thailion crystal?"

Territaff nodded and said, "I've never heard of one of these doing anything like this. Something's happening to my physiology, and I'm having trouble staying focused. I'm worried, Tehrarra. So much is going wrong. I've no choice but to trust you, and I need you to stay close. We must locate a synthesizer or quantum computer with a dual-wave projector."

Tehrarra nodded and said, "What you are looking for is above us." She gave Territaff a wary frown and said, "What is it?"

His expression was filled with doubt and trepidation. "I've lost some of my abilities. But we can't do anything about that now. Let's get up to the communications center.

Her expression stiffened. "Can you still perform…? I mean, can you still carry out the mission?"

"Your concern is understandable. I'm still fully functional—only a little more human."

"Only a little more—" she stopped, noticing Territaff's solemn expression. "That is okay. I prefer your human side to whatever you were with that crystal in you." She started to smile, but something occurred to her, "I thought Thailion crystals were just used with computers and androids. You are the first humanoid I have ever seen with one implanted like that."

"It's a long story, and we need to get going. Remind me to tell you about it after we survive all the shit that's about to happen."

Tehrarra arched one of her thin eyebrows and said, "Something to look forward to—I think?"

"Communications," Territaff said.

The lift's power cell engaged with a slight jolt. The car rose smoothly for a few seconds, then stopped. The door slid open, revealing a large room full of cubicle workstations. Territaff peered into the room and saw a single Zenti technician busy at a workstation facing the lift. He gestured with his hand for Tehrarra to stay back as he moved toward the technician.

Without a sound, he came behind the Zenti and snapped its neck. He then lifted the limp body and placed it into an unoccupied workstation furthest from the lift.

Territaff jerked as a beeping tone sounded in another workstation. Tehrarra quickly went to its console to address the sound. A second beeping tone was heard. Tehrarra reached into the breast pocket of her environmental suit and pulled out a communicator.

"E'hh sho'caleh," she hissed in her native tongue.

"That doesn't sound good."

"Yes, it is not all bad, though."

"Oh?"

"It was the base commander." She smiled thinly. He wants me to come here and see what happened to the signal phase adjustment, which was what our now-dead technician was working on before you rudely interrupted him."

"So, fix it while I use the synthesizer and replicate your little black box."

"Yes, well, my understanding of Zenti is limited."

"You're familiar with their systems, aren't you?"

Tehrarra gave Territaff an annoyed look, then sat at the console and pondered the rows upon rows of Zenti pictograms.

"I have had my workstation programmed in Vultaran, so I would not have to interpret Zenti."

"Well, can you fix it, or should I get creative?"

Tehrarra didn't answer as she pondered the rolling rows of Zenti pictograms.

"You realize that the Zenti do not have a true language," she pointed out while transmitting keycodes into the virtual input display. "They have only been a verbal race for less than a few hundred cycles and never developed a written language of their own. They devised a mix of Venubian, Klaxon, and Kayden syntaxes and grammar, combined in these pictograms to represent their lexicon. It isn't very easy in the extreme. Please, give me a minute because it is only another form of mathematical symbols, and that is my specialty."

"Okay, I need to get the little black box replicated. Where's the synthesizer, and how do I use it?"

"It is a standard Venubian synthesizer we stole from Lunneziah. Thank Karoft for me when you see him."

"I didn't think you knew Karoft?"

"Only by reputation, but I took the synthesizer from his workstation. He is probably still looking for the culprit who stole it."

Territaff shook his head at the irony as he went to open the interior hatch to the main computer room. He gave the hatch's thick release handle a hard downward push. It was secured. Territaff contemplated the door, trying to remember how to approach the holographic combination pad next to the hatch.

What's wrong with me? He thought. His mind was blank, as if something came along and erased everything.

"Tehrarra," he called meekly.

She needed to finish the phase conversions and didn't want to look away from the multidimensional display.

Territaff watched her work for a moment, then, frustrated, he shouted, "I need your help."

"What?" she said, not looking up.

"My mind's a blank. I can't remember anything."

"Territaff, you have got to hold it together. I need you," Tehrarra encouraged, sensing his desperation and fear. "I am almost through, but concerned that the commander will call me in for one of his, to use an Earth colloquialism, grab-ass conferences. They are weirdly sexual, which makes them even more disgusting." She glanced at Territaff and noticed him staring at the hatch. "Terri, I need you. Get a grip!" Her voice rose with stress.

"*Biomei, help me,*" he transmitted. "*Something's very wrong. I'm disconnected and feel as though I have fallen into a horrible emptiness.*"

"*Remember your training, Terri. You need to reconnect with your inner voice,*" her transmission calmed his rising emotions.

Territaff took in a deep breath and let it out slowly, attempting to regain his focus. His mind seemed dull and adrift, as if he were drugged. Trying to fight off the effect, he sat on the floor, crossed his legs into a tight lotus position, and then breathed. With his eyes closed tightly, he allowed the meditative state to quell his troubled mind and dispel the emptiness that had enveloped him.

A stream of colors flowed past his mind's eye. For a moment, Territaff sensed his mind energized, and, at that moment, he seized the little thread of energy and let the light in. His head became lucid again as if his brain had thrown a switch that reconnected his senses. It seemed to him like he appeared out of a dark void and walked back into the light. He knew it was a tenuous fix, but he concentrated on his clarity and hoped it would last long enough to complete this task.

"Terri!" Tehrarra screamed.

Territaff opened his eyes and caught the arm of a Zenti who was just about to smash his skull in with the blunt end of his weapon.

"Not today, my nasty little friend," Territaff said as he crushed the Zenti's arm in his powerful grip. He caught the weapon as the Zenti dropped it. The Zenti soldier let out a hissing wail of agony as Territaff held it up by his shattered arm. Territaff stood and pinned the howling, wiry creature against a wall, pressing his forearm into the guard's neck. He leaned harder on the Zenti's neck and upper torso to increase the discomfort of his squirming captive. He glared at the Zenti's pain-laden face for a long moment. "Do you want the pain to stop?" Territaff asked, in a clumsy-sounding Zenti.

His captive stared back at Territaff, confused, struggling through his pain.

"Nod your head if you want the pain to stop," Territaff repeated, in a slow Zenti growl.

Tehrarra stood up and came next to Territaff. She gave the now terrorized soldier a sinister smile and shouted in a perfect Zenti dialect. "He will kill you. If you want to live, tell us the combination of this hatch. Do you understand?"

The soldier gave Tehrarra a pleading look and blinked his wide, swollen eyes.

"Let him go, Terri," she said.

Territaff allowed the Zenti to drop to the floor. The trembling soldier fell into a heap, cradling his crushed arm close to his side. He looked up at Tehrarra and hissed out the combination before passing out. She put in the combination, and the door release made several electronic beeps before disengaging. The heavy door cracked open with a hiss of its seal being broken, allowing some of the room's frigid atmosphere to escape.

"Crap," Tehrarra said, peering into the room. "I forgot, it's around four degrees Celsius in there, and our environmental suits are too bulky to work in that damn confined space."

"The cold won't bother me," Territaff said. "Tell me what to do."

She gave him an impressed grin, then sighed, "I can

handle it. I also have adaptive physiology and have been in worse environments. I hate the cold, though."

Territaff handed her the decoy and instructed her to find a location to conceal it, but she found it with a little effort.

Territaff went to the synthesizer and recognized its familiar design. It was identical to the one Larzz discovered while they were on Vexx, only much larger in scale. He flipped on the power, then transmitted to Cuz, *"Ready for quantum transmission."*

CHAPTER 43

Tehrarra was busy dismantling the layers of panels and boards to access the inner workings of the quantum transmitter while Territaff replicated the black box. He watched in amazement as the tiny box built a duplicate of itself on the synthesizer's platform. It assembled itself, starting as a minuscule black speck, and in a few seconds, it was completed. The assembly was unlike anything he had ever seen. Impressive, he thought, as he held it up in the room's soft lighting for a better look.

He took the tiny onyx cube to Tehrarra. She looked up from her work as he handed it to her.

"Fascinating," she smiled approvingly at the small apparatus. "We have little time," she cautioned. "I had to take the transmitter offline to reach the primary interferometers. They will send troops to see what happened."

Territaff nodded thoughtfully and stepped into the main work area for a quick look around. "It appears all clear," he said, looking through the transparent dome. "Where's everybody?" he wondered aloud as he gazed over the rows of empty workstations.

"They finished setting up the communications network and are now concentrating on mining operations. There is no need for personnel management. The system is almost completely automated."

"Raw materials for the carnage," Territaff whispered. "They appear to be executing a logical plan," he told Tehrarra as he watched her work. "Far too logical for the Zenti, which makes you wonder who's behind this?"

"I have a few ideas on that. When we get a chance, we can discuss it," Tehrarra said as she methodically worked through the multiple layers of circuits and power crystals. "This is so typically Zenti," she said, sounding frustrated. "It is a mess of cannibalized and re-engineered parts. Ah, thank the spirits, I am finally there."

Tehrarra placed the little black box deep inside the quantum transmitter's inner workings. She watched in awe as the box altered shape and merged into the primary laser's interferometer.

"I have never seen it work before," she said. "It is a miraculous tool. It seemed to have understood my intent and guided me to the right location. As soon as I positioned it at the precise location, it rebuilt itself into the transmitter array as though it belonged. They will never find it. We do not need the decoy."

"Are you sure?" Territaff questioned, still fighting the dark mood brewing in him.

"Look for yourself," she said as she stood and moved aside, allowing him to get into the tight space between a wall and the long optic tubing of the transmitter's photon generator.

Territaff bent down and peered into the open-access panel at the transmitter's laser array. It comprised a complex maze of small, shiny mirrors and multiple thin beams of colored lights. Looking through the lines of light running within the labyrinth of mirrors, he had to force himself to concentrate on what he saw. A short time ago, he could have looked at the complicated array and understood its workings. Now, he struggled to separate the lights from the mirrors. It all appeared to have merged into distorted images.

"I'll have to take your word for it. It's all a blur in there." Territaff's eyes looked glassy, and his face tightened with his debilitating condition.

"Something is wrong, Terri?" Tehrarra asked, sensing his conflicted emotions.

"We need to do a test to ensure it's working," he said.

"Good idea. Central control will assume I'm checking the phase alignment and may call off the dogs."

Tehrarra returned to the closest workstation and sent out a simple binary data string: Hello, goodbye.

"Did you get it?" Territaff transmitted to Biomei.

"Affirmative," she replied, then added. *"Terri, I scanned you…"* She hesitated to give him the bad news.

"It's space sickness," Territaff finished the thought for her.

"Yes, but it's in the early stage, and as you know, it can take days before it becomes acute."

"You should have seen what it did to my crystal. I can't recall any record that describes a Thailion crystal being depleted in that way. It appeared destroyed."

"Terri, remember your crystal is a hybrid designed for you. We're only beginning to understand their workings. Most likely, your crystal mitigated the initial onset of the illness and slowed the virus's progression through your nervous system. Remember that the disease affects different brain areas as it progresses, but never entire areas of brain function at one time.

"Also, you have built-in redundancies for this reason. When the disease presents itself, you can fight it off. Trust your enhancements. They'll protect and allow you to function until we get you back on board."

"Thanks, Biomei. Stay close."

"I'm always by your side. Fight the despair and depression. Remember that during any sudden manifestations, it's not real, and stay focused."

Territaff looked at Tehrarra's raised eyebrows and deep lines on her face. He forced a confident smile that appeared to have little effect. "Stop worrying. I'll be fine," he tried to reassure her. "You need to get out of here."

"I should stay with you," she said, moving closer to Territaff.

"It may be too late." He drew Tehrarra's attention outside the dome.

"To use one of your quaint Earth idioms, oh shit," she said, seeing a small detail of armed Zenti approaching.

* * *

Crenshaw's monitors alerted Biomei. His brainwaves had become dangerously erratic. She attempted a mind probe to better understand what was causing the sudden surge in activity. Her attempt was thwarted by a dense energy wave that acted as a protective barrier. The energy's pattern surprised her. It was composed of Zeta waves configured in alternating cycles. The pattern resembled basic information exchange but was configured with a simple baseline signal to hide additional energy signatures. Biomei surmised the energy was varion in structure. A strong premonition welled up in her as she studied the pattern. She transmitted for Cuz to join her in the med lab.

When Cuz entered, Biomei told him to go to the synthesizer station. There, he found a replicated little black box.

Cuz picked it up and said, "What do you have in mind?"

"Crenshaw's brain activity has become erratic, and his metabolic rate is much too high. We won't be able to implant his new heart unless we resolve this adverse activity. I have a strong impression that the box can help him." Biomei gave Cuz the impression she was acting more out of instinct than certainty.

"I understand you're not sure what this will do to him. Why are you suggesting this?"

"I know how this will sound, especially coming from me, but whatever energy is in the box can communicate with anyone it chooses. I'm convinced that mechanism is what Crenshaw needs right now. And I'm certain that this impression was sent from it."

"Intriguing," Cuz said, rotating the onyx cube in his hand. *This little device is as versatile as it is mysterious.*

While Cuz pondered the box, a strong impression hit him. He placed it on Crenshaw's forehead. He looked up at the monitor to see if it had any effect. What he saw was extraordinary. The cube appeared to sink into Crenshaw's forehead, exposing only a micro-thin layer of its surface. Crenshaw's brain activity returned to a normal sinus rhythm.

"Biomei, can you get a read on what's happening?"

"No. The cube is blocking any attempts to probe his thoughts. I hope we didn't jeopardize his recovery."

"All his vitals and brain activity have returned to normal," Cuz said, studying the monitor. "What's so strange is these readings are more indicative of a conscious state than an unconscious one."

"I noticed that as well. There's nothing more we can do at this juncture in his recovery. You should continue working with Kathy and Karoft on the Yucatan site."

Cuz glanced at Crenshaw's monitor readings one more time before leaving. He left thinking how strange human physiology can be. It was at moments such as these that he appreciated his android's simplicity.

* * *

Crenshaw's eyes focused on a scaled model of the space shuttle Enterprise. It was hanging on a thin wire over his head. He smiled at the familiar model from his childhood. A vivid memory of building it with his father flashed through his mind. It was a good memory. He stretched out his arms, letting out a long, heavy yawn. He felt as though he had awakened from the best sleep of his life. A moment later, the reality of where he was sank in with a jolt.

"I'm in..." He surveyed his surroundings. "In my childhood bedroom. How's that possible?"

He spoke aloud, hoping his voice would keep him grounded. He reflected for a moment and laughed. What reality? He thought. The revelation lingered and grew within his consciousness. Lying on his back, staring at the model, he hoped to fall asleep and end this strange illusion.

He lay back on the pillows and closed his eyes. A second later, he jerked up, realizing he must be awake and not dreaming. He could not recall falling asleep, only finding himself in his childhood bedroom. He got out of bed and walked to the full-length mirror on his closet door. Crenshaw studied his reflection in utter confusion, scrutinizing every aspect and feature, trying to rediscover his identity.

"Who am I?" he whispered, touching his face to reassure himself he was real.

"Hi, Rob," a voice spoke that sent a chill through him.

He turned toward the voice. A flood of memories surfaced as his father stood in the doorway to his room, smiling.

"Dad," he cried and ran into his father's arms.

The tight hug felt warm and reassuring. All that his father was to him rushed into a tide of emotions. Crenshaw could not stop himself from crying.

"Oh, Dad, I've missed you so much..." Reality struck him hard again. It knocked the wind out of him. "But you're dead," he gasped in shock. "This must be some kind of lucid dream because you're dead."

He gazed at the man who looked like his father when Crenshaw was only eight. He appeared a little older than Crenshaw was now, standing before him with an endearing smile. *How could my father be standing before me, looking as I remembered?*

"Rob, I'm only dead in a physical sense. I'm very much alive, for lack of an easier description, in a spiritual sense, or to be more precise, as an energetic presence."

"I don't understand. What's going on? This is too weird." He turned away from his father's image and shook his head, trying to shake the vision away. "I want to wake up," he shouted.

Seeing his father alive again overwhelmed Crenshaw. He trembled as he fell to his knees, holding his head between his hands, crying and shouting, "You're dead! You're dead... dead!" His sobs turned to anger. "Why is this happening?"

His head started to pound as his emotions grew more intense. He folded himself up into a tight ball on the floor to escape the pain and confusion tearing at his insides.

A warm hand touched his shoulder, but he didn't want to leave the shelter he had created for himself.

The hand gently squeezed his shoulder, and he heard his father say softly, "It's all right, son, you can cry. Get it all out. I'm sorry I had to leave you so suddenly. It wasn't my intent, but I'm here now for an important reason."

Crenshaw stopped crying and lifted his tearful face to look at the image again. He closely studied the man who claimed to be a replica of his father.

"Whatever you are can't be real," Crenshaw said. "I've always believed things happen for a reason." He wiped the tears from his eyes with the back of his hand. He shifted upright on the floor, then folded his legs under him. "Sometimes the reason isn't clear, but I've learned to accept a certain amount of improbability in life. That's the nature of things. However, you're beyond reason and unnatural. Therefore, I can only conclude one of two possibilities. I'm dead and rejoined with you, or I've lost my mind and am now in psychotherapy. Neither of these probabilities is appealing."

His father's image regarded Crenshaw with a patient gaze. The two studied each other for a long, silent moment as though one were waiting for the other to speak.

Crenshaw was about to utter his displeasure with the situation, but his father's replica cut him off, saying, "You're not dead, dreaming, or insane."

"Then what am I? Where am I?" he shouted in frustration. He took in a deep breath while studying the illusion that proclaimed to be his father. The more he studied the silent man, the more helpless he felt. What am I to make of this?" he pondered with a heavy sigh.

"Patience, Rob," the replicant said, breaking the uncomfortable silence, "it will all become clear soon if you suspend your disbelief for just a moment. You always overreacted to sudden changes, especially the stressful ones."

"What's that supposed to mean?"

"It means you jump to conclusions before carefully considering the situation. So, I'm asking you to give me a chance to explain."

He knew the replica was right. Sometimes, he reacted impulsively or excitedly to sudden changes. Crenshaw sensed whatever this copy of his father's purpose was; its intent seemed benign. He regarded the compelling form with conflicted emotions as he gestured for it to continue.

"Let me begin by addressing your questions." It walked to the bed and sat on the foot end.

"Join me," he motioned for Crenshaw to sit beside him.

Crenshaw hesitated, reflecting on all the times he had talked with his father like this at night before going to sleep. He remembered how much he loved those talks. His demeanor stiffened as he looked at the perfect replica. His eyes narrowed, and his brow tightened into an angry scowl.

"I loved those talks with you as a child," he mumbled half-aloud. "They became less frequent whenever you were between tours of duty." His voice became heated with anger. "Whenever you were home for extended periods, your focus was always on the next assignment, and we became a lower priority in your life." He noticed he had the apparition's full attention. "Why did you leave Mom and me so often? Why couldn't you give me a little more of yourself? You were always on a critical mission whenever I needed you during my teens. You missed my high school and college graduations! When we finally got closer, you went back and got yourself killed. Nice work, Dad!"

His father's image viewed Crenshaw with a sympathetic sigh, but he didn't react to his outburst.

"You haven't been there for me when I needed you in the past. So why do you think I need you now?" Crenshaw let out a long and heavy moan. "And you showed up as this... this...," he waved his hands at the manifestation, searching for the right word, "whatever the hell you are," he blurted. "Why am I talking to you?" He popped off the bed and paced, then stopped and shouted, "This is fucking crazy!"

"I understand your hostility, son."

"Stop calling me that!"

"Is Rob okay?" the replicant asked, seemingly undisturbed by his anger.

Crenshaw nodded.

"Let me explain what I am and why I'm here. That might clarify things for you."

Crenshaw came over and sat heavily on the head end of the bed. The replica looked pleased that he had joined him again.

"I'm a physical representation of your father created from the electromagnetic energy in your hippocampus combined with specific retrotransposon genes in your DNA."

"You're created from my memories and jumping genes," Crenshaw repeated the description, shaking his head incredulously. "If it weren't so crazy, it would be funny."

"Give it a chance to sink in. I know you're familiar with this phenomenon. You once published a speculative but accurate article on this possibility in college."

Crenshaw was surprised by the representation's knowledge of the article. He hadn't thought about it in years. With a sigh of resignation, he moved further up on the bed so his legs were off the floor. He leaned on his elbow and said, "Okay, you got my attention. Continue."

His father's replicant said, "Touch my hand and tell me what you feel."

Crenshaw considered the request for a moment while studying its face and gazing into its eyes. *He looks and sounds like my real father.* He took its hand, and its warmth calmed him.

"What do you feel?"

"A warm hand," he said in a quiet voice. "What does that prove?"

"Can you not trust your senses?" It asked as it squeezed his hand.

"You're like an avatar created from my mind. You're a creation from my psyche… an aberration…" Crenshaw's mind whirled with questions. "And yet you're a perfect replica of my father. This must be an elaborate form of holography, or you're somehow manipulating my senses."

"Now you're reaching, Rob." The replica looked impressed with his skepticism. Rob's father became silent, looking like he was gathering his thoughts. Then, in a soft, emphatic voice, he stated, "In all meaningful respects, I'm your father, Rob."

"Dad," Crenshaw whispered, wanting to believe. "Okay, I can't deny my senses, but I can doubt my reality. So, where am I?"

"You're still aboard Biomei, recovering from a surgical procedure to correct a congenital heart defect. Being on this magnificent ship saved your life. If left untreated, the defect would have killed you, then we never would have been able to meet like this."

"So, what you're telling me is I should be grateful to be alive? I'll grant you that, but that's not why you're here."

"In one respect, that would be correct. But as you're fond of saying, things happen for a reason."

The more Crenshaw engaged with the replica, the more real it became to him. After a few minutes of conversation, he accepted it. He forgot about his earlier skepticism and believed he was talking with his father. However, in his mind, he knew the man talking to him was a manifestation and not real. Knowing his mind produced such a complex illusion made the imitation compelling enough for him to accept its strange reality.

"Rob, I'm here because you need my help, and I need your trust. I'm your father—" Crenshaw opened his mouth to object, but the replica cut him off, "but I exist in an alternate reality."

"Alternate reality?" He wrinkled his brow into a puzzled

expression. "You mean like a parallel world?"

"No. Nothing like that," he answered as if understanding where Crenshaw was going. "Think of a reality formed from what you loosely refer to as dark energy. This energy is existential to your mind, and when incorporated into your consciousness, under special circumstances, it can be manifested into a corporeal form. In other words, I'm a physical duplicate of your father in a different energy configuration projected through your mind."

Crenshaw narrowed his gaze at the man and pondered what he had described.

"What you're describing is vague. Dark energy could be anything," Crenshaw rebutted. "I was getting used to the replica concept, and now you throw this wrench into the works?" He got off the bed and paced again. His father's replica watched him like he was waiting for an epiphany to strike. "So, what you're describing is you're my father's energy reborn into a corporeal state using a special form of dark energy? That's nuts!"

"No, Rob, it's not. You're not seeing the total picture. You've got to think a little outside the box, but still be logical. In your reality, your dad is dead, but all that he was is still alive in you. It's your imprinted energy of your father that makes me possible."

Crenshaw's jaw dropped with the stunning revelation. He stopped in front of the man and muttered mathematical expressions. Then he stopped and looked wide-eyed and full of questions at the man who claimed to be his father.

"What special circumstances?"

The man smiled and said, "I think you're getting the idea. Now let's discuss why I'm here and what you need to do."

CHAPTER 44

The Zenti stormed the communications center as Territaff and Tehrarra resealed the computer room. Tehrarra met the Zenti platoon leader, holding a weapon on Territaff. The platoon leader's large, bug-like eyes glared at them through the clear faceplate of his environmental helmet.

"I caught him trying to put this inside the transmitter," she explained, handing the decoy to the leader.

The Zenti took it from Tehrarra and glanced at the device before placing it into a pouch in his utility belt. The Zenti grunted something. Two troopers checked on the Zenti lying face down in front of the computer room. One of them knelt and turned the unconscious soldier over. He took out a scanner and did a quick run over the inert body, then looked up and hissed something unintelligible to the leader.

"They are speaking in an unfamiliar dialect," Tehrarra whispered to Territaff.

"Stay with the plan," he said.

The Zenti leader squawked out some orders to the other two soldiers. One of them moved behind Territaff. Pulling Territaff's arms behind his back, the Zenti placed a pair of magnetic hand restraints on his wrists. The other grabbed the weapon from Tehrarra's hands while leveling his weapon at her.

"You," the Zenti leader grumbled to Tehrarra in a wheezing Vultaran tongue, "come to the commander and talk." His Vultaran was choppy but understandable to Territaff's translator.

Tehrarra wasn't sure if she was also being taken as a prisoner along with Territaff. Although she wasn't handcuffed, she got the impression she was a suspect. She gave Territaff a worried glance as one of the Zenti handed her an environmental suit to put on.

The Zenti held up the backpack and tanks to Territaff's environmental suit and grunted angrily at him. Territaff knew what he wanted but wasn't in the mood to cooperate. Another Zenti came behind him and swung his weapon hard into the back of his legs. The blow would have brought the average man to his knees. Instead, the Zenti stepped back, looking incredulously at the broken stock of his weapon.

Territaff smirked at the stunned Zenti holding his environmental suit. He knew they would have to remove his restraints to get his suit on. The squad leader narrowed his bug eyes and grunted something. The other Zenti removed his restraints. Territaff kneeled enough for the nervous-looking soldier to strap the backpack on and place the helmet over his head. Territaff noticed how cautiously the frightened Zenti worked around him. He was pleased with the little demonstration, which he did for their benefit. Now he knew they'd concentrate on him and leave Tehrarra alone as they put the magnetic handcuffs back on.

"There are only four of them," Tehrarra said, in a low voice to Territaff.

He shook his head and gestured with his eyes for her to go along.

"I need to see Commander Hezvid," Tehrarra demanded in Zenti.

The squad leader flashed an annoyed glare and hissed in standard Zenti, "Good because Hezvid wants to see you. You have a lot to explain." He turned his gaze at Territaff, then hissed in Zenti, "The commander will enjoy himself with you." He wheezed out a laugh.

Territaff understood enough of what the leader said to know that Tehrarra had to come up with a plausible explanation. He studied their faces and smiled inwardly, convinced they were only following protocol with her, and she was most likely not in any immediate danger.

The squad leader held his weapon before Tehrarra and told her to wait.

Tehrarra gave Territaff an anxious look as a Zenti pushed

him into the lift. Territaff regarded the Zenti with a contemptuous sneer and was tempted to kick it in its midsection, but restrained himself. He looked at Tehrarra with a sly grin as the lift door closed.

* * *

"Come quickly," Cuz called to Kathy and Karoft.

"What's up?" Kathy said.

"Are you getting what I'm getting?"

"Yes. It's a disturbing communique from Hezvid to Zohleemay," Cuz explained, reviewing the message again to ensure he translated it correctly.

Kathy sensed that things were going wrong and nudged in closer to Cuz.

"My Zenti isn't very good. What does the message say?" she said, studying Cuz's blank expression.

"It's not in Zenti. It's Tungzi," Cuz corrected her, then looked up with a disturbed expression. "They got Terri and will transfer him to the Yucatan site."

"What could have happened?"

"They must have him in a sealed room because we haven't received transmissions from Terri. He's an hour overdue for a check-in."

Cuz went to the wide-beam transmitter and sent an encrypted message to Territaff, hoping to get a reply. After a few moments of anxious silence, Cuz frowned.

"You're wasting your time," Biomei said.

"Why?" Kathy asked.

"His last transmission informed me he was allowing himself to be captured, hoping to be brought to Zohleemay. He also insisted on no rescue attempt until he signals us. He was most emphatic about that, Cuz."

"I see. So, we should do what in the meantime?" Kathy said irritably.

"I suggest we devise a rescue plan for when Terri signals us," Biomei said.

"I agree, damn it. We need to stop all this damn analyzing and do something constructive, for Christ's sake!" Kathy was surprised at how loud her voice got.

"For Christ's sake?" Cuz repeated the expression with his eyes squinted. "Why wouldn't it be for Terri's sake?"

Kathy sighed, exasperated, and said, "It's an idiomatic expression. Check your linguistics files."

Cuz blinked, then smiled. "Interesting." He looked at Karoft and said, "She's correct, though. We need to formulate a plan based on two hypotheticals."

"What do you have in mind?" Karoft said, walking to Cuz's console.

Cuz asked, "Biomei, when was Territaff's last transmission?"

"18:20 hours Earth mean-time."

"Let's assume they're taking Territaff directly to Zohleemay. We now have the means to track their movements. All we need to do is wait for a shuttle with a Zenti power signature coming from the moon."

Cuz input a data profile for a navcom search and alert. He looked up at Kathy and Karoft and smiled confidently. "What's with the anxious expressions? He'll be fine. This is what Terri has been waiting for—an opportunity to get to Zohleemay. Now we have the exact location of his moon base and Zohleemay simultaneously."

Kathy pulled Cuz close to her and kissed him.

"That's why I love this man so. He's smart and handsome," she said, pinching his cheek.

"Kathy, please," Cuz's face reddened as he objected, "behave yourself." He gave her a shy grin.

"I believe the appropriate admonishment would be to tell you two to get a room, but there's no time for that now," Karoft said, frowning at their antics, but surprised and impressed with how humanoid Cuz was behaving. His emotions seem more genuine and not so emulated or mimicking humanoid behavior, he thought, and made a mental note to discuss Cuz's evolving personality with him later.

"There's something else you should know," Biomei said cautiously. "Terri is displaying the early stages of Zinfwa."

"He's got space sickness," Karoft said in surprise. "How bad is it?"

"It destroyed his Thailion crystal, but I believe the crystal may have helped suppress the immediate spread of the disease. Terri seems to be coping as well as possible."

"That was his worst fear," Kathy pointed out, looking as though her insides were aching with the thought.

"He has his enhancements and his training to help him through this. We must assume Territaff is not seriously incapacitated and will be ready when needed," Biomei reassured, addressing their immediate fears.

"What's your second hypothetical?" Karoft said to Cuz.

"The Zenti are keeping Terri prisoner for a possible negotiation. We won't know anything unless we verify Terri's disposition. I suggest that we split up into two teams. I'll go to the moon and investigate the situation. If Terri is still held captive, I'll devise an impromptu rescue plan. You two go to the Yucatan to find out if he's there. You should have an exact location locked in over the next few hours and report to Biomei what you find there. Don't attempt a rescue until I join you," Cuz hesitated, "regardless of Terri's condition."

Kathy and Karoft studied one another like they were taking in Cuz's plan with mutual displeasure.

"No. That plan stinks," Kathy stated.

"What do you suggest?" Cuz said as Karoft watched with interest as they interacted.

"We all go to the Yucatan. There's no reason to believe they'll keep Terri on the moon. He's too big a prize. They'll take him to Zohleemay. I'm sure of it. And that's what Terri wants."

"I agree with Kathy," Biomei said. "But I strongly suggest that the situation on the moon be investigated first. Cuz you'll take no action. All that's needed is to look, report, and return. I further recommend that Kathy and Karoft remain here until we clearly understand the situation in the Yucatan. We can't afford to risk all of you. We don't have enough information. Additionally, the general and Rob should be fully recovered by Cuz's return. They'll provide us with the needed numbers and enable us to devise a better plan."

"Very well," Cuz agreed, noticing Kathy's troubled expression.

"I don't want you to go alone," Kathy said. "Biomei, why does he have to go alone? Why not send the general with him?"

Kathy gently touched the side of Cuz's face and caressed him. With a smile, Cuz accepted the affectionate gesture, took her hand, and said, "Don't worry. I'll be fine and will join you directly." He kissed her hand and walked to the main turbo-lift.

"I have a bad feeling about this," Kathy shouted at Cuz. "The moon is too dangerous and no longer important. Territaff installed the device. It's working perfectly. You need not go." She became more agitated as the situation became more apparent in her mind. "Biomei, please don't send him."

"Sorry, Kathy, but we need to know the situation," Biomei said emphatically.

Kathy ran up to Cuz, kissed him again, then grabbed the collar of his jumpsuit and whispered, "You take care of yourself... and come back in one piece."

"I will, and you do the same." He leaned back in for another kiss, then got into the lift.

Kathy watched, chewing on her lower lip as the lift door closed on Cuz.

CHAPTER 45

Territaff lay on his back, staring at a softly lit opaque ceiling. His environmental suit was removed, and he wore an iridescent yellow jumpsuit. He stood, trying to gather his thoughts. He was locked in a large cube. The spacious cell had no visible conveniences, not a cot or a chair to sit on. The only sound was the rhythmic beating of Territaff's heart.

His head ached, and his body felt heavy with lethargy, as if he were drugged. Under normal circumstances, he could not have been drugged into unconsciousness. He worried that the disease was progressing more quickly, and it would keep him from completing the mission.

He went to each side of the cell and studied the area, trying to understand his surroundings better. He was in one of the thousands of cells built into the honeycomb pockets aligned horizontally and vertically in the prison walls. It was a typical Zenti confinement arrangement: Below the surface, in a dingy and dull-lighted hole. The Zenti preferred this arrangement over surface domes. Stinking hole lovers, it must be part of their insect DNA, Territaff thought.

He reasoned that the cell must be magnetically sealed and independent from all the others. Surveying the rows upon rows of dimly lit domes, he noticed half-domes interspersed between some of the cubes. As far as he could see, all the cells were empty.

Territaff turned his gaze downward and realized he was in the opening of an ancient lava tube. It became apparent that the network of cells and domes was built into the walls of a vast, ancient caldera left over from the moon's tumultuous beginnings.

With his mind, Territaff tried probing outside the transparent wall, but only sensed darkness rising in him. Then, for a moment, he sensed something. It seemed like a familiar presence, but he couldn't get a fix on it. Squinting his eyes, he strained to sense any presence near him. Nothing. He paced around his cell, stopping now and then to place an ear against a wall, intently listening for any sound from a close neighbor. Nothing. After several futile attempts, he concluded his cell was too insulated to sense anything outside it.

"Clever Zenti," he scoffed, "they sealed me in."

Territaff sighed, realizing his mental abilities were gone along with the rest of his enhancements. Once again, he found himself limited to his innate human abilities. His worst fears were becoming a reality and overshadowing his every thought.

I'm having an inner struggle with a powerful, dark energy for control of my conscious mind.

A mobile droid floated down to his cell, a narrow horizontal slot formed in the transparent wall. Territaff went to thrust his arm through the slot but was repelled by a heavy force field. A tray of yellow and green chunks in sealed containers and bottled water slid out from the droid's midsection. The tray and water stopped midway through for Territaff to take. He shook his numb hand from the force field while scrutinizing what looked like high-protein nourishment.

He said, "No thanks. I'm not planning on staying too long."

He tried pushing the tray back, but it wouldn't budge. The droid hovered for a few moments as though awaiting instructions. After a long pause, the tray was retrieved into the droid's midsection and floated away.

Territaff tried to follow the droid as it floated upward, but could only see it rise above his cell before disappearing from view.

Now, how in the hell do I get out of here? He pondered, feeling both physically and mentally exhausted.

As he contemplated his situation, his head and body ached again. The ache rose into a sharp, stabbing pain along with a hard throb like a pounding pulse inside his head. His deteriorating condition was alarming. Momentarily, he'd forgotten who he was and why he was sealed in a cube. Everything had merged into an excruciating blur.

He closed his eyes as he slid to the floor and crossed his legs into a tight lotus position, breathing in and out with slow, deep breaths. As he practiced his deep meditation techniques, a faint outline of a Venubian emerged. As he continued, the outline gradually formed into a beautiful female alien. He moaned sorrowfully at the image, remembering that his meditative breathing was a Venubian technique Nicki had taught him so long ago.

The alien's image grew clearer in his mind. It was Nicki, her sweet voice instructing him to stay focused. Territaff hung onto her voice like a life raft. His mind and body were responding as the pain subsided. He suddenly was at peace, sensing that an equilibrium had been reached. His mind and body were in balance once more.

"Terri," he heard Nicki's voice next to him. "Terri, open your eyes," she told him.

He opened his eyes and gazed at her lovely face, beaming at him.

"Oh, Nicki, I've missed you so," he said, his heart aching.

They embraced and kissed, the kiss lingering with passion. When they finished, he looked into Nicki's large, glowing eyes and wept.

"Terri, no tears, please, my love. I'm here for you." She held him against her chest and caressed the back of his head. "Why are you so emotional?"

Territaff lifted his head, studied the perfect image of his love, and said, "I'm crying because I know you're not real. And while every fiber of my being is filled with the joy of this illusion... But you're dead, and I must..."

Just as he leaned in close to give his imaginary Nicki a final kiss, her image vanished.

"Noooo," he cried, then looked around. "Get your act together, Territaff," he shouted into the deadened silence of his cell.

He heard a tonal alert in his cubicle. Then, a synthesized voice spoke in clear Venubian, stating that prisoners were being returned to their cells and all inmates were to step to the front of their unit during lockup. The message was repeated in Bylar and Tungzi, suggesting a diverse population.

The faint noise of heavy footsteps was heard. They became louder with lumbering feet above him. What he saw across the great chasm was disheartening. Legions of automatons and Zentis guided thousands of Bylars, Venubians, and many unfamiliar life-forms to their cells.

Territaff watched with interest as the automatons came into view. They looked strange to him. They were similar to Venubian Service Droids but lacked their humanoid characteristics in speech, movement, and form. Then, he scanned as much of the interior as he could see and was surprised by how the Zenti guards managed the vast population of prisoners. A diverse number of captives occupied every cell level. They controlled the population in a well-organized and efficient manner. This was uncharacteristic of the Zenti's behavior, he thought. Another interesting departure from the Zenti norm was that the prison population appeared well-nourished and in fair physical condition.

These are not your everyday variety of Zenti. Are the Zenti following a different drummer?

Then he saw something that gave him a glimmer of hope. There were turbo-lifts everywhere! *Great, a means of escape.*

* * *

Cuz was impressed by the clean and efficient design of the prisoner transport, which he flew behind wearing a small jetpack. The transport appeared to be automated. He observed four strategically stationed guards sitting in the front and rear of the long conveyance. Studying the prisoners' slumped postures and tilted helmets, he concluded that they must be returning to the prison complex. It was surprising how relaxed the guards appeared among the prisoners. A general impression of familiarity between the guards and captives puzzled Cuz.

While closely observing the transport, an idea presented itself. He decided to infiltrate the prisoner population, but needed a covert access point to board. He flew closer to the transport. It was moving swiftly a few meters above the moon's scarred surface. He checked his fuel supply and frowned. He had only a few more minutes at his present velocity. Noticing they were approaching an open straightaway, he took a calculated risk. Cuz pressed the pack's throttle to maximum, then flew to the rear end of the roof. He managed a light touchdown in the low gravity near a small service area. An eyebrow rose, noticing he had less than four-tenths of a second of fuel left. He removed the jetpack and tossed it.

Cuz walked cautiously around a domed skylight that ran down the entire center of the roof. Reaching the service hatch, he surveyed the car through the clear skylight. Two guards were facing each other right where Cuz wanted to land. The guards were sitting in a small compartment separated by hatchways on either side of them. One hatchway led into the main prisoner section, the other to the automated engineer's compartment. He considered the situation and planned an appropriate offensive maneuver as he opened the hatch.

To his surprise, the transport was pressurized as a rush of interior atmosphere pushed against him when he jumped into the compartment. He quickly assumed the atmosphere's lower oxygen and higher nitrogen levels must be for the Bylar population.

The guards' reactions were slow and uncoordinated, allowing Cuz to overtake them quickly. He struck the guard to his right with the butt-end of his laser rifle. He turned and kicked the guard on the left in the head, causing a spider-web crack to the darkly tinted faceplate. The left one slammed hard in his seat, but he was still aware enough to reach for his weapon. Cuz grabbed and lifted him off his seat, then threw the Zenti guard down before he got his weapon out. The Zenti's eyes were fixed in horror as Cuz lifted a foot and gave its chest a crushing blow.

Cuz checked the first guard to ensure he was unconscious, then took both of their weapons and tossed them out the open hatch. He closed the hatch, placed one of the guards on the seat, picked up the dead one, and leaned him upright in the opposite seat.

Cuz glanced through the large hatchway's portal to see if anyone was approaching before entering the automated compartment. To his surprise, two spare environmental suits with atmospheric conditioners were hanging inside the small compartment. He grabbed one of the atmosphere units and exchanged it for his empty one. Then, he checked the ambient environment. As Cuz hoped, it was set to universal supply and pressure. He adjusted his unit to those settings. Then he sat on the small jump seat inside the compartment, hoping to pass for a prisoner.

* * *

Commander Hezvid was not a typical Zenti. He stood erect as though he were trying to stretch his meter and a quarter frame into something taller. He spoke in Venubian in an almost clear voice. His Zenti still made a lot of hissing and guttural sounds whenever he shouted orders and directed his subordinates, but otherwise, he communicated well in both Venubian and Vultaran.

Hezvid's command style impressed Tehrarra. He maintained a well-organized, efficient operation that achieved all his objectives. Unlike his predecessors, he had a strong command presence and used it effectively. Hezvid believed that fair treatment of his captive workforce was more effective than harsh belligerence. His prisoners were treated more like POWs than like most of his colleagues preferred to treat their captives as slaves. His approach had yielded great dividends, exceeding all his superiors' expectations.

Despite all his accomplishments, Tehrarra still regarded him as a horrid-looking Zenti. Hezvid also had the ego of a strong leader, and any feminine species was fair game for his pleasure. His persistent pursuit of Tehrarra constantly irritated her, and she longed for the opportunity to dispose of this obnoxious Zenti.

However, Hezvid's interest was now focused on Tehrarra and the events leading to the capture of his prized prisoner, Territaff.

"You surprised him," he stated, narrowing his large eyes into an intense stare that Tehrarra tried to avoid. "You found the unconscious worker in a cubicle, then saw Territaff coming out of the transmitter room?" He curled his lipless mouth into a dubious smirk.

"Yes, Commander," she said, maintaining a passive expression before his expansive desk.

Hezvid regarded her with a silent intensity. Tehrarra tried occupying her mind by considering different ways of getting his fabulous desk. To her, it was a magnificent work of art. Its top was made of rare crystals from all the moons of Hezvid's tours. The crystals were embedded in a polished quartz slab and arranged into a beautiful mosaic of colors. Bone-white petrified wood and rocks formed its rectangular body. Solid ditanium legs, a precious and sturdy metal, supported the massive top. Tehrarra knew that ditanium only existed in the Celibran system and was one of the most precious metals the Zenti coveted. She figured the desk must weigh over 350 kilograms in standard ship gravity.

Hezvid relaxed his daunting stare and pointed to a seat before the luxurious desk. She sat and smiled back at the commander as he finished reading her report. He flipped the decoy splitter to her. She snatched it and placed it on her lap.

"What do you make of it?" Hezvid said.

"It's a multidimensional phase-splitter intended to intercept our transmissions. This one is not functional." She knew the commander already had the device analyzed and was telling him everything he wanted to hear. "I thoroughly checked the transmitter array and found no other device," she added flatly.

"Why would they plant a nonfunctioning device?"

"They were probably unaware of our array's configuration because the device is incompatible with ours," she said, looking at Hezvid with a cool and calm demeanor.

Tehrarra was uneasy with the direction the debriefing was taking. Hezvid's bulbous eyes fixed on her, his face tight with lines, looking unconvinced. She also worried about Territaff and how he was holding up.

"And what was the all-powerful Territaff doing during your thorough search?" Hezvid's tone had a disconcerting, sarcastic bite to it. It surprised her because Zentis aren't supposed to understand sarcasm. But it was a good question she hadn't considered in their hastily conceived plan.

"Oddly, I had to do little to control him." She was reluctant to divulge Territaff's deteriorating condition, but considered that a bit of truth would make her report more credible.

"Really?" He leaned a little closer over his large desk, then asked incredulously, "The great and powerful Territaff was so passive that you conducted a thorough investigation on one of the most complex instruments ever devised, and *he* made no move toward you? Not even one little jump to overpower you and escape? That is odd—very odd indeed."

Hezvid's skepticism was well-justified, and Tehrarra knew she had to be careful with her words.

"I understand your doubt, Commander." She crossed her long legs and gave him a soft, seductive smile, hoping to distract him. The commander reclined in his chair and let out a Zenti purr, a low hiss, and a gurgle. "But there is something wrong with Territaff," she continued. "He seemed preoccupied, as though he was having some mental crisis. It was most alarming how indifferent he acted toward me." She paused for effect, hoping Hezvid would prompt her to continue.

After a brief silence, the commander asked, "Indifferent? Indifferent how?"

The question told her she had his full attention and suggested he might be playing along with her. She took a risk and revealed everything she had omitted from the report.

"Commander Hezvid," she said, trying to gather her thoughts. "I left a few details out of the report because they were extraordinary. I feared it would have prejudiced the entire report as incredible."

Hezvid reclined a little more in his chair and steepled his long fingertips together into a thoughtful pose. His stare stayed fixed on her, making her a little less secure in her story.

"Incredulous," he said, with a slight upward turn of his mouth, "that describes your report precisely, my dear. Most incredulous."

"I understand your doubt, but we have both seen our share of strange events."

Hezvid nodded.

"When I entered the communications center," she suddenly thought, "I saw someone standing in front of the control room. He was wearing an unfamiliar environmental suit. At the time, I had no idea it was Territaff. He was standing with his back to me and not doing anything. Surprisingly, he made no move toward me, as though I weren't there. I surveyed the room and spied a boot sticking out of a workstation. As noted in my report, I rushed to the cubicle and found the unconscious guard. His weapon was beside him, so I took it and pointed it at the stranger. No response. Taking the opportunity, I quickly approached him and grabbed his weapon.

"After taking his weapon, I recognized him at once. He looked at me with vacant eyes. But he was not staring at me… it looked like he was looking through me, as though I was transparent. He appeared absorbed in thought, so I told him to sit on the floor. He passively complied and acted bizarrely. During my inspection, I found this." She held up the decoy. "There was no other device. As I stated in my report, I must have interrupted whatever he was attempting."

Hezvid said nothing at first. He stared up at the ceiling, pondering Tehrarra's story. After a long and tense moment, he sat upright in his chair and turned one side of his mouth into a cruel smile.

"That is a fascinating story," he said with a slight hiss. "How much of it is true? It is difficult for me to determine. If I were not so fond of you, I would have ordered your execution for telling such a ridiculous story." His voice broke into a hissing grunt, and his large pupils became small lasers, burrowing into her.

Tehrarra became fearful that Hezvid would do something unpleasant to her. She hoped he would only have her a little roughed up, then tossed into a cell. Maybe sexually abused, then thrown into a cell. Somehow, she believed he would not have her executed because she still had value. Then, it occurred to her that she should remind him of it.

"I told you it sounded ridiculous, but it is all true." Tehrarra studied the commander for a reaction. He sat very straight in his chair, gazing impassively. "Hezvid, you must believe me." Another thought struck her. "Commander, why not see him yourself? Bring Territaff here and interrogate him."

"That is interesting," he said, breaking his heavy stare. "I was thinking about doing exactly that." He leaned a little forward in his chair with a crooked smile. "I sure hope you were not reading my mind, he hissed, "You know, my dear, that would make me very unhappy."

Tehrarra gave him an injured look. "How could you suggest

such a thing?" She jerked from her chair and turned her back on Hezvid, completing her little drama. "I do not know how many times I have told you," she continued, looking out at the gray colors of the moon's rugged surface through the large, windowed wall of his spacious office. "I am empathic, not telepathic, and yes, I got a feeling you could see the logic in bringing Territaff in for questioning," she dramatically sighed. "You know how hard I have been working on this project. And you know how much it means to me—"

"You made your point," Hezvid interrupted in a low voice. "Get back in your chair," he commanded, then enabled the holographic keyboard on his desk and tapped in orders for Territaff to be brought to him.

Tehrarra smiled inwardly and faced him, maintaining her injured demeanor, as she sat back in the chair. While relieved about Territaff being brought to them, she was concerned that Hezvid may have something more in mind.

"You know you could offer a lady, especially one you insulted, a drink." She pouted to emphasize her point.

Hezvid gave her a distorted upturn of the corners of his narrow, lipless mouth. He closed his bulbous eyes and let out an ugly, wheezing sound that emulated laughter.

"You are always good for a laugh, Tehrarra," he said as he got up and walked over to the synthesizer.

"No. Not that awful, synthesized stuff." She wrinkled her button nose, then pointed to the credenza behind his desk. "Give me the good stuff, Hezzy." She used his nickname seductively, hoping to get him to relax toward her.

"I forgot," he said, trying to hold a smile, distorting his already repulsive features, "you know about the good stuff."

Hezvid went to the credenza and got a bottle of Klaxon brandy and two quartz goblets. He filled both goblets three-quarters full and handed one to Tehrarra.

She held her goblet up and said, "T'jahr." A Vultaran toast to success.

Hezvid tilted his goblet toward her, then drained it in one long swallow.

Tehrarra watched him for a moment, then smiled brightly and drained hers.

"Another?" he asked.

"Of course." Her forced warmth waned a bit, remembering that the little bastard could hold his liquor.

* * *

Territaff had resigned himself to the floor, where he sat meditatively, fighting with the inner demons rising in him. He squeezed his face into a grimace, struggling to focus his energy away from the dark images tearing at his mind. "Focus, dammit," he barked aloud.

When Territaff gained control over the horrific illusions, his cubicle moved forward. It moved out from its hole, then hovered over a long line of prisoners going to their cells. He got a good look at his prison. It was even bigger than he'd realized. Territaff watched as lines of prisoners shuffled their tired feet on the way to their cube-shaped units. Each one stopped in front of a cell, waiting for the door to open. They stood with their heads bowed. Some rocking side to side. Others appeared to stare unblinkingly outward under a weary brow. He gazed further down the long line and frowned at seeing a group of Bylars standing upright with their large, hawkish eyes closed. It was a heartbreaking scene for Territaff. It reminded him of everything he lost and what he must do.

* * *

Cuz watched as all the prisoners filed into a single line while disembarking the transport. Guards and prisoners alike walked at a heavy pace. Their tired feet and slumped backs were signs of their day's exhausting labors. He slipped between two Venubian prisoners a few bodies back from the front and glanced at the inmates next to him. Their faces were deeply lined with pain, and there was a loss of hope in their weary eyes. He wanted to reassure them that not all was lost or hopeless, but he couldn't risk exposing himself. Seeing Venubians as captives was disheartening for him. He had been told at the end of the last war that all the prisoners were exchanged as part of the Zenti surrender terms. In line with Zenti treachery, they held back hundreds of Venubians, Kaydens, and Bylars.

Those poor souls must have been enslaved since the Zenti-Venubian war. That's over thirty-five planetary cycles ago, Cuz reflected, a*nd how many cycles before that?*

They entered a narrow tunnel that forced Cuz to walk between the Venubians.

"You are a Venubian?" the prisoner behind him transmitted to Cuz.

"Yes, I am here to get a friend."

"Your friend is Venubian?"

"No. He's a Terran," Cuz hoped that he didn't know Uzil had become Territaff.

"Terran? Don't know of Terran," he transmitted with curiosity.

"Your silence may save our lives," Cuz transmitted emphatically.

He listened for a reply from the Venubian. He relaxed a little with the silence and refocused on locating Territaff.

When Cuz entered the cavernous area that housed the prison cells, he saw a few transparent cubes floating overhead. Cuz was drawn to a cube moving a few meters above him. "Intriguing," he murmured, seeing Territaff standing at a wall of the cube, staring outward.

Terri, he transmitted.

Cuz frowned when he didn't respond. He watched the cube float away, pondering how to get Territaff out.

* * *

Four armed guards led Territaff, shackled in magnetic locks, to Hezvid's office. Tehrarra restrained a gasp at seeing Territaff's deteriorated condition. His dark, shiny eyes were dulled, looking at her with a lifeless stare. With his sunken cheeks and gray complexion, he looked like death, waiting for a grave.

"He looks awful," Hezvid jeered, sounding pleased with Territaff's sickly appearance.

"He looks much worse than when I first found him," Tehrarra said, holding on tight to her stirring emotions. "That was only a short time ago," she whispered.

Hezvid motioned for the guards to leave as Tehrarra took Territaff by the arm and led him to a chair. He sat in the chair, maintaining an outward-looking stare. She gave him a glancing smile as if to say, 'Your act is working.'

"You are Territaff," Hezvid said, more a statement than a question.

Territaff ignored him.

"What did you hope to accomplish with this?" Tehrarra said, holding the quantum splitter close to his face.

He remained unresponsive.

Tehrarra arched an eyebrow and said, "I do not think we'll get much out of him in his present condition."

Hezvid returned to the bar and brought a decanter of Pido and a goblet. He filled the goblet halfway and offered it to Territaff. Territaff ignored the Pido with his unwavering, vacant stare. Tehrarra thought Hezvid's actions were crude and senseless.

"Odd, I thought you loved Pido," Hezvid smirked, swishing the thick, clear liquid under Territaff's nose. "Well, if you do not want Pido," he put the goblet on the credenza, "let us try something else."

Hezvid pressed a sequence of crystals on the top of his desk. The bottom drawer clicked open. He pulled out a thin cylinder forty-six centimeters long. Tehrarra gasped at recognizing the pain-inducing tool.

"You are not the squeamish type, my dear?" he asked Tehrarra.

"Is that necessary?" she said, trying to sound calm.

"Want to make sure he is not putting on an act."

"It is a waste of time on him," she said, "even if he were not in this debilitating condition."

"I am not so sure of that," Hezvid twisted his mouth into a sinister smile. "Let us see." He stood, slapping the device on his bony palm as he slowly approached Territaff. "Oh, I believe this is a good spot."

He shoved the device hard into Territaff's groin.

The pain inducer made a warbling sound as it touched him. Hezvid watched with evident disappointment as Territaff remained unaffected by the pain stick. Hezvid sneered at the shiny instrument, double-checked that the setting was on maximum, and then rubbed it against Territaff's side. The apparatus warbled louder. Territaff remained in his seat, looking unaffected by the insidious device, still staring outwardly. On Hezvid's third try, Territaff caught the devious instrument between his shackled hands and tore it out of Hezvid's grip.

He stood, holding the pain inducer between his constrained hands. Territaff placed it under Hezvid's chin. Hezvid's eyes grew wide with fear as Territaff picked up the Zenti with one hand while holding the pain inducer in the other. He held Hezvid by his stiff uniform collar, seething at him with all the pent-up hate he had for the Zenti.

"If you want to live, I suggest you remain silent," Territaff said through clenched teeth. "Now release the restraints."

"They can see you," Tehrarra warned. "You will never get out," she cautioned, acting like she was trying to talk Territaff out of his escape attempt.

Territaff saw the guards coming through the doorway with

their weapons drawn.

"You know what to do," he barked, tightening his grip around the commander's neck.

Territaff briefly regarded the pain inducer, then gave the commander a light brush across his face. The instrument made a higher-pitched sound as Hezvid's face contorted in pain.

"Stop," Hezvid cried in Zenti at the charging guards. "Go wait in the outer office," he ordered them.

"But Commander, we have a clear shot," one guard grunted back in Zenti.

Territaff lightly ran the pain-stick down Hezvid's back. He wailed in agony, causing the guards to back down.

"No. You wait." Territaff pointed at the lead guard. "Release these restraints."

The guard hissed to another guard, who rushed over to him. The Zenti's hand shook slightly as it observed the pain inducer while handing Territaff the release key.

Territaff glared at him and yelled in Zenti, "Do it."

The guard inserted the small, round key into the restraints on his wrists and ankles, allowing them to fall to the floor. He took a few paces back and stopped when Territaff shouted at him to drop his weapon and leave. The guard looked at Hezvid, sweat beading on his brow. Hezvid nodded, and the unsettled guard dropped his weapon by Territaff's feet and left.

"You there," Territaff said to Tehrarra, "give me that weapon."

Tehrarra did as instructed. He dropped Hezvid into a chair. Pointing the weapon at Hezvid's head, Territaff hollered in Zenti at the guards, "Toss your weapons to me." They stared at Hezvid in confusion. "Now, or I'll kill him," he barked.

Hezvid commanded them to do it. They threw their weapons to Territaff. He kicked them to the side. Tehrarra noticed a sinister expression on Territaff's face, which frightened her.

"You two are coming with me," Territaff demanded as he surveyed the room, trying to plan an escape route. At first, he considered taking Hezvid as a hostage, but the Zenti don't have strong feelings of loyalty for their officers and would have likely killed Hezvid to get to him. Then another thought came to mind.

He asked Tehrarra, "Is there a secret passage or private lift?" Tehrarra gave him a blank look. He walked back to Hezvid, grabbed the back of his neck, and lifted him off the chair again. "Where's your private lift?" He held the pain inducer close to Hezvid's face.

Hezvid rolled one eye at the awful device and the other at Territaff. The threatening instrument made a low-pitched moan as he passed it within millimeters of Hezvid's face. Lines of thin hair around his mouth and eyes stood up as perspiration ran down his forehead.

"One touch in the right spot and you're dead," Territaff whispered in his pointed ear.

"I do not—" Territaff choked off what he was about to say.

"Point to it."

Hezvid turned within Territaff's tight grip and pointed to the wall to the right of his desk. Territaff motioned with his head for Tehrarra to go first. She walked to the wall and studied the complex, circular patterns surrounding contorted figures, which the Zenti seemed to appreciate as art. She thought the irregular geometric shapes perfectly represented the Zenti's distorted minds. After studying the arrangements for a moment, she smiled at finding the embedded button and pressed it. The panel disappeared, revealing the lift's transparent doors.

"Tell them to stand down," Territaff ordered, seeing the guards slowly closing in on them.

Hezvid wheezed out the order, and the guards took a few steps back.

"Get in." Territaff gestured with his head to Tehrarra.

She got into the lift, expecting Territaff to join her. Instead, he made sure she was in, then placed the pain inducer across Hezvid's high and prominent frontal lobes. The Zenti commander let out an agonizing scream under the searing pain as Territaff fired at the guards. A cacophony of screams and hisses joined the quick puffing sounds of the sonic weapons. Small explosions of flying body parts, furniture, and shattered glass echoed throughout the spacious offices as Territaff killed everything in sight.

He pondered the contorted face of the commander's limp body, realizing he had held him by the neck the entire time. He let Hezvid drop to the floor, then regarded the hideous pain inducer for a moment before tossing it on the dead commander's body. He narrowed his eyes at the stunned guards who rushed into the office. They quickly recovered and fired at Territaff as he dashed into the lift.

Tehrarra felt unnerved by the depth of Territaff's violence. She forced herself to think about what she had witnessed. She thought this was not the Territaff I had come to admire. This is a demented killer.

Territaff was surprised by the fear he saw in her eyes. He wanted to tell her his sincere regret, but couldn't articulate it. *I'm trapped in this nightmare and powerless to do anything about it.*

"Was that necessary?" Tehrarra said with a slight tremor.

He didn't answer. He could only look at her with empty eyes.

They took the lift to the main prison level and were surprised by Cuz waiting for them outside. He greeted them with a relieved smile, wearing a stretched-out environmental suit and holding a small helmet.

"Cuz, what are you doing here?" Tehrarra said, giving the surprised biogenic android a tight hug.

"I was about to go to Hezvid to get you out. A guard told me you were going to his office for interrogation. It appears you beat me to it."

Territaff didn't seem to recognize Cuz or show any emotions. He stood silent like a Zombie, waiting for instructions.

"He is very sick," Tehrarra said. "The illness has progressed. He is really scary, Cuz. He is scary and ruthless. We need to get him back to Biomei." Her voice was full of apprehension.

Cuz scrutinized his friend for a moment, then transmitted, *"Terri, it's me, Cuz. I'm here for you."*

"Oh, Cuz, I'm not in control. I can't control my emotions. I... I did things... It's dark in here, Cuz. Bring me to the light."

"You must fight it, Terri. I'll attempt a T'al Shubajhr."

He grabbed Cuz's arm. *"No, Cuz. It's too dark, too dangerous. I can't..."* Territaff stopped his transmission and talked aloud. "The disease is contagious through telepathy," he said, sounding lucid. "It comes in waves. And... and..." His face contorted as if in pain for a second, then reverted to the impassive gaze he'd been fighting against.

Cuz sensed how hard his friend tried to hold on to the thought. Territaff's expression became tight, and his glassy eyes rolled back into his head as though he was struggling with intense pain. He looked at Cuz, then smiled like he just realized his friend was beside him.

"Cuz, it's as if the disease knows when I'm fighting it. It fights back with pain and uses my fears and horrible images. I can't get control..." His expression and demeanor became lifeless once more.

Cuz was shocked and disheartened by how fast the disease progressed. He looked at his friend's diminished state and felt deep sorrow. He'd seen him in many conditions, but nothing could have compared to the hollowed-out human standing before him.

"Terri, you must fight it," Cuz urged, looking intently into his friend's dulled eyes. "Try to focus."

"Let's get him to the surface," Tehrarra suggested. "There's too much electromagnetic interference here from the shields. We need to communicate with Biomei."

"We must release them," Territaff cried, looking back at the rows of enslaved prisoners coming and going to and from their cells.

"Not now," Cuz said, grabbing Territaff's arm. "We'll come back for them."

CHAPTER 46

"We'll need environmental suits if we have any hope of getting out of here," Tehrarra said as they hurried toward a bank of turbo-lifts.

"There's a pressurized tunnel that leads to a transportation hub," Cuz said. "I came in through there. There are environmental suits and a variety of conveyances we can use."

"That is great," Tehrarra said. "Now, we must survive long enough to get in one."

The turbo-lifts were only thirty meters in front of them. A large crowd of Venubian captives filed out as they approached the lifts. A detail of guards was talking among themselves as they trailed close behind. Cuz wore his helmet and acted as though he was escorting Tehrarra and Territaff to the lifts. One guard recognized Territaff and grunted something to Cuz.

"They're being transported to Zohleemay," Cuz said in his best Zenti impersonation.

The conversation didn't last too long. The Zenti guards surrounded them. Territaff's detached demeanor quickly turned into an aggressive posture as he grabbed the closest guard and snapped his neck. The other guards seemed stunned for a second, which was all Cuz and Tehrarra needed. With swift and precise movements, they rendered the guards nearest them unconscious.

Armed sentinels standing along the upper level of the facility saw their actions. Tehrarra shouted for them to duck down as the sentinels fired. Another group of guards came storming toward them, firing their laser weapons. The area exploded into a torrent of yellow laser discharges.

The Zenti sentinels were firing indiscriminately into the swollen mass of prisoners and emerging guards. Some of the shots were hitting their troops, along with any prisoners who crossed their line of fire. The scene erupted into deadly chaos as bodies were dropping, pierced, and dismembered by the heavy laser fire.

"You go for the lifts, and I'll cover you," Cuz called to them, pulling Territaff by the arm as he turned and fired on a leaping guard.

Tehrarra took Territaff by the arm and led him to the lifts while Cuz provided cover fire for them. She ran, ducking every few meters under the lethal lines of laser fire and hopping over fallen bodies. Territaff was walking upright, looking unconcerned about getting hit. Cuz followed right behind them when they reached the lifts.

"You are hit," she grimaced, noticing several laser penetrations on Cuz's face and suit.

"Don't worry, it looks worse than it is," he said, shoving them into the lift while firing at a group of advancing Zenti.

Cuz waited until the lift doors started to close before jumping in. He noticed Territaff was struck several times. A few of the wounds appeared serious.

"Are you all right?" Cuz said.

Territaff looked down at the cauterized holes, then back at his friend. "I'm okay, but you two must get out of here."

"I'm not leaving you behind," Cuz objected. "You're in no condition to do this alone. Zohleemay will kill you. Nothing is gained by you sacrificing yourself."

"It's too late for me, old friend," Territaff said, sounding surprisingly coherent. "You two must tell everyone what's happening here. Besides, Zohleemay wants me around for a while. He needs something from me, and he'll keep me alive until he gets it."

"Needs what?" Cuz asked.

Cuz noticed Territaff's eyes had lost their alert glow and were dimmed to a cold, empty gaze as if succumbing to the dark forces eating at his mind.

"I have seen this before," Tehrarra explained. "It has been the pattern of the disease. He would brighten for a few lucid moments, then recede into this almost catatonic state. It is a horrible and frightening sickness to watch."

The lift doors opened, surprising a group of guards. Cuz and Tehrarra fired on them before they could react.

"Most of the work details must be below by now," Cuz said. "Hopefully, they're only a few guards in the transportation area. Wait here with Terri while I check and see if the area's clear."

"No, Cuz," Tehrarra pleaded, as Territaff's head slumped to the side. She caught him right before he fell to the ground. "I must stay with him, and you must get back to Biomei."

"I don't understand." Cuz frowned. "Why must you stay? You can't help Terri. You'll only be surrendering yourself for no reason."

"I am duty-bound to protect and stay with him. He needs my help, even if it is only to provide comfort during his distress. I will not leave him. Bring help."

Three lifts opened as Cuz turned to go to the transportation area. He ducked into a service bay as a patrol of guards rushed out of the cars, surrounding Territaff and Tehrarra. His first instinct was to charge the guards, but he stopped, realizing he would probably only be captured. He looked back for a moment and saw the guards pushing Territaff and Tehrarra back into the lift. He waited for the platform to clear of Zenti before searching for a suitable vehicle.

* * *

Kathy sat alone in the small, dimly lit mess hall. She was staring into a cup of hot chocolate, which she thought would help her sleep. The ship had a hollow feel to it when Cuz wasn't there. She understood why he had to go, but knowing didn't make her feel better.

"Still no word," Kathy asked Biomei in a soft, dreamy tone.

"The last communications relayed that Cuz was in pursuit of Terri. However, I know Cuz is fine. It's Terri that concerns me."

"I know. Me too," Kathy said, propping her elbow on the table to rest her chin. "Something's wrong. I know it."

"Be patient, dear. You'll hear something soon." Biomei went silent for a long moment and then said, "One moment, I'm receiving an update."

Kathy sat upright in her chair, anxiously waiting for Biomei to speak.

"Well?" she said, trying to break the uneasy silence.

"Someone wants to speak to you," Biomei said.

"Cuz," she said, popping up.

"Yes," Cuz said.

Kathy turned and saw Cuz standing outside the mess. She ran and wrapped him in a tight bear hug. Cuz stood waiting for Kathy to release him so he could return her greeting.

"Oh my God, Cuz, I was so worried," she said, smothering him in kisses before he could answer.

"Kathy," Cuz said, pushing her back so he could look into her face. They stared at each other for a moment before kissing again with eager passion. When they finished, Kathy squinted at Cuz as if noticing the holes in his chest and the few gashes in his forehead and cheeks. One gash was deep enough to reveal Cuz's shiny superstructure.

"You're full of holes," Kathy complained as she examined Cuz's facial wounds. "That must have hurt."

"No. The wounds aren't painful, but I need a little medical attention."

"A little," Kathy replied, raising an eyebrow. "Biomei, did you scan Cuz's wounds?"

"Yes, but he insisted on seeing you first."

"Let's get you to the med lab. You're looking a little creepy." Kathy ran a finger lightly across the deep gash on Cuz's cheek. "Will there be any scars?"

"Don't worry, Kathy. He'll be as good as new," Biomei reassured.

Kathy turned to Cuz and said, "You're never leaving me like

that again."

"No. I already left more friends behind than I ever want to." Cuz frowned, reflecting on Territaff and Tehrarra.

"Is Terri on his way?" she asked as they walked to a turbo lift.

"No," Cuz answered solemnly.

"What happened?" Kathy said, staring wide-eyed.

"It would be better if I told everybody at once, but I'm fearful for their survival."

CHAPTER 47

General Dickerson woke from a troubled sleep. He sat up, heaving a sigh, noticing his bed sheets were soaked in sweat. His shiny, beet-red complexion glowed enough for Crenshaw to see him in the darkened room. The general clutched his chest, his heart pounding with a quick and heavy rhythm. He smiled at feeling no pain as he took a deep breath and let it out slowly with a sense of great relief. He thought for a moment, his face tightening with confusion.

"What the hell happened?" he mumbled.

The general's mind was covered in a sheer veil, letting in only spots of memory. His uncertainty lifted when he saw Rob's animated face, regarding him with a grave scowl.

"We need to get out of here and join the fight, sir," Crenshaw said emphatically.

Still trying to put everything together, the general ignored Rob at first.

"What a dream I had," the general blurted with a relieved expression. "It seemed so real—like I was there, Rob."

"You called me, Rob." His face beamed at hearing his name in that way.

"That's your name, isn't it?" the general said, giving him an irritated look.

"Yes, sir, that's my name," Rob said, still grinning.

Dickerson surveyed the med lab with a wrinkled brow. Rob looked at him, wondering why he looked so lost.

"What kind of hospital is this?"

"Sir, have you forgotten?" He looked closely at the general with concern. "We're on a ship named Biomei."

General Dickerson viewed Rob with a blank expression, then got off the bed. He stood a little wobbly. Rob rushed to the general and took his arm to steady him.

"General Dickerson, it's too early for you to get out of bed," Biomei said.

The general looked up at the ceiling and searched the room to see who spoke. He was surprised not to see anyone because the voice sounded in front of him.

"Who said that?"

"Biomei, he seems to have a lapse in memory. He doesn't know where he is, but he knows me."

"Who the hell is Biomei? And where the fuck am I?" the general snapped.

"Rob, please help the general back to bed so I can do a quick scan," Biomei said.

"Sir, please lie down, and everything will become clear shortly," Rob implored, tugging the general's arm to get him back into bed.

"I'm not doing anything until I'm told where I am and how in hell I got here!" He shouted, pulling away from Rob and walking toward the door.

"Sir, you may want to put on some clothes before you wander around the ship," Biomei said.

"Clothes?" He looked down at his nakedness and stopped. He turned and faced Rob, his face flushed with embarrassment.

"Sir, I promise if you get back in bed, I'll tell you everything," Rob said, gesturing toward the bed.

The general walked sheepishly back to his bed and pulled the covers up to his chin.

"You've got a lot of explaining to do," he demanded in a low voice, jutting his chin out to cover his embarrassment.

"That's better, General Dickerson," Biomei said. "Now, let's see what's going on in your head."

"Who's talking, and where is she?" the general whispered.

"Biomei, sir. She's the..." He had to think for a moment, wondering how to approach the subject. "For lack of a better description, she's..." He drew out his speech while observing the general's expression, "the... ship... we're on."

"Ship?" Dickerson thought for a moment. "What kind of

ship?" He clutched his bedcovers.

Rob swallowed down a nervous lump, worried whatever he'd say would exacerbate the general's irascible disposition. He gave him a meek smile and let out a long breath. As he was about to speak, the medical scanner floated down from the ceiling and hovered a few centimeters above the general's head.

"What's that!" Dickerson shouted, jerking his head up and banging it on the side of the scanner.

He fell back into the bed, holding his head. Uninterrupted by the jolt, the scanner continued to check down his body.

"Sir, may I suggest you lie still during this diagnostic scan? All your questions will be answered," Rob said, trying not to laugh at his antics. His expression filled with concern as he noticed the general appeared unconscious. "Sir...?" Rob studied him for a moment, then asked, "Biomei, did you knock him out?"

"I gave him a mild sedative."

"How? I didn't see you do it."

"I have my ways, young man."

"Yes, you do," Rob smiled. "So, what's wrong with him?"

"His amnesia is a normal side effect of the surgery. The damage to his heart was more extensive than first believed. He also lost a significant amount of blood, resulting in some minor brain damage. We cleaned up the damaged areas. Thankfully, there was no swelling, but short-term, selective memory loss is not uncommon in these cases. Don't worry. He should return to his normal, authoritative self in no time."

"That sounds more serious than you're letting on."

"To use an Earth expression: it sounds much worse than it is."

"I had that dream again. I know it was from the box." Rob relayed excitedly. "This time, I could see Territaff, Cuz, and an exotic-looking alien. They were all on the moon. I could see them struggling to get back to their shuttle, but they got caught by a Zenti patrol. They were being brought to Zohleemay. We all need to go to the Yucatan location and get them back. This Zohleemay, he's pure evil. I can sense his dark presence looming. He wants Territaff for some compelling reason. We can't let that happen. Biomei, we must destroy all his machines and his evil power source."

"You saw all that within the context of a dream? Rob, do you know where the box is now?"

He touched his forehead, "It's inside my head."

"Interesting," Biomei said. "It's an ancient device whose energy is both mysterious and miraculous. Rob, please be extra vigilant in guarding yourself against corruption. We know so little about that machine."

"Biomei, I know the box is here to help us. I'm not afraid, and you need not be concerned about me," he said, sounding most confident. "What's so strange is that it picked me. It also gave me a chance to make peace with my father. For that reason alone, I trust it."

"I'm pleased to hear that, but you must be careful. A moment. I'm receiving the telemetry from the scan."

Rob looked down at the general. He was tempted to give his hand a reassuring squeeze, but didn't, fearing it might be misunderstood.

"Rob, I want you to return to bed until I can scan you."

He nodded and climbed back into the bed next to Dickerson. He lay on his side, looking at the general, reflecting on his experience with his father's avatar. It helped him view his life in a new light, healed some deep emotional wounds, and gave him a sense of confidence he lacked. Rob smiled, realizing that, for the first time in his life, he liked himself.

He continued to gaze at the general, reflecting on their relationship. In the short time he worked for him, Rob had become fond of the general and felt close to him. General Dickerson had become a mentor and surrogate father. Rob sensed a strong emotional bond between them, but was unsure whether the general shared all of the same feelings.

Then a vision shocked Rob. His heart rate soared to a level the medical scanner picked up from across the room.

"Rob, what is it?" Biomei asked with alarm.

"They're torturing the alien. Her name is Tehrarra. Terri is watching and doing nothing. Oh, no… no—they're killing her!" Rob cried.

General Dickerson opened his eyes, hearing Rob's cries.

"Crenshaw, what's wrong?" the general asked in a dazed voice.

"Sir, I'm somehow connected to Terri. There's this beautiful alien who is being tortured to death and… and…" He tried to rein in his emotions as he spoke. "Terri is dispassionately looking on. There's something wrong with him. This is like a waking nightmare." He jumped to his feet and, in a forceful voice, said, "We must go to save them. They're in grave danger."

Rob's frantic expression became calm. He glanced at the general, then at the monitor above the bed.

"Looks like you're doing better, sir," he said.

Dickerson gazed at Rob, looking like he was gathering his wits. After a long moment, the general's expression turned bright, and he smiled broadly at Crenshaw.

"I feel marvelous. Never better." He looked around the room.

"What are you looking for?"

"My uniform," he answered. "Speaking of which, where the hell's yours?"

"Good question," Rob replied, realizing he was also naked. "Biomei, where are our uniforms?"

"Gentleman, one moment, please. I'm reviewing both of your bioscans." There was a brief pause before she continued, "You're both good to go. Your uniforms are stored in the replicator. Go over to the floor scanners at the rear of the lab. They're the same uniforms issued in the decontamination bay."

Rob looked to the rear of the lab and spotted four round discs on the floor.

"Come, sir. I found them."

The general got out of bed and followed Rob to the rear of the lab. They both stepped onto a disc and waited for the scanner to activate. Rob gazed at the general and realized how fit he looked. His musculature was well defined, and he had no apparent body fat. His posture was no longer slumped, and his shoulders were straight back and broad. He looked twenty years younger.

The real surprise for Rob came when he asked for a visual after coming off the replicator. His mouth gaped as he admired his new image. He smiled at seeing all his muscles prominent through the form-fitted suit.

"Shit, we look like superheroes," Rob laughed.

"Don't get crazy on me, Crenshaw," the general barked while still looking at his projected image.

"Sir, I liked it better when you called me Rob."

The general looked at him and blinked a few times, then, as if he suddenly remembered, he smiled. "Rob, it is."

CHAPTER 48

They all sat together in the small mess right off the crew's quarters, now called Kathy's Café. It was given the name because of Kathy's habit of eating large meals at all hours. When kidded about her voracious appetite by Cuz, she retorted that she was still recovering from the transformation process and needed the calories. The truth be told, Kathy ate whenever she was nervous or upset. Biomei altered the food synthesizer to produce low-calorie content whenever Kathy exceeded her required intake. Kathy considered it a woman's dream. Eat as much as you want and never get fat!

"Zohleemay used the Homestead base as an experimental lab for developing his Cyborg-Soldier," Cuz said.

"He wanted to create an army of indestructible force that could eliminate all human existence while leaving the basic infrastructure intact," Karoft added, taking a spoonful of Kathy's ice cream sundae. He nodded, pleasantly surprised.

Rob listened to the conversation, got up, and paced around the table.

"What's on your mind, Rob?" Kathy said.

"Why Earth? We have no advanced technology, and we're in an outer ring of our galaxy—kind of isolated from the worlds you described. Based on what I've learned about the Zenti, they prefer advanced civilizations near one another."

"If you look at the Zenti's strategy, Earth makes sense," Karoft explained. "It's the perfect planet for them. Their discovery of the Corridor made it possible for them to get to Earth virtually undetected. Earth being far enough away from other worlds is part of what makes it so appealing. Conquering this world will allow them to keep a low profile while still close enough to strike anywhere within the inner circle of the civilized worlds. To borrow a colloquial expression, Earth's a Goldilocks planet for the Zenti—an isolated, inhabitable world, set in an ideal orbit around a perfect star, away from everything. All that's left is to rid themselves of the meddlesome humans."

That struck a chord with both Rob and the general. They narrowed their eyes at Karoft.

"There are billions of lives at risk here," the general said in a low growl.

"There have been trillions of lives already lost, General," Karoft countered.

"I need more coffee," Kathy said as she got up from the table.

"While you're up, dear," Cuz said, "could you get me a protein shake? My biogenic system feels a little run down."

"Well, no wonder. You've been up for over fifty ship-cycles with little rest, not to mention riddled with laser fire, and almost killed. What you really need is some downtime."

"I'll rest when this is all over."

"Dr. DeZenti was about to perform the first series of tests on his new Cyborg-Soldier a few days before Terri and Cuz destroyed their factory," Rob said, retaking his seat at the table.

"What's so intriguing is that it was a well-conceived and brilliantly executed plan," Cuz said.

"What's your point?" the general grunted, sounding annoyed.

"It suggests that Zohleemay isn't the mastermind behind the projects. The level of sophistication is way beyond his capabilities."

"An interesting development concerning the mysterious Dr. DeZenti was intercepted in a communication between the Appropriations and the chairmen of the Armed Forces Committee," Karoft said, not realizing how important the information was.

"Why haven't you informed us?" Dickerson grumbled. "What did it say?"

"They're inquiring about Project CyberSword, and another called Iron Man," Karoft continued. "The chairman of the

Armed Services Committee was reported as being quite exercised over having nothing to show for all the billions they have shelled out to DeZenti. He has conveniently gone missing as he was subpoenaed to appear before the committee."

A smug smile spread across Rob's face. "It may have something to do with the well-placed e-mails and memos General Dickerson and I created?"

"Well done, by the way," the general complimented.

"Evidently, DeZenti's fictitious identity, along with all the payoffs and other illegal activities, was unraveled." Karoft was puzzled by the general's expression. He appeared most gratified by the news. Seeing how pleased everyone appeared, he regretted not telling them sooner. "His plan appears to have fallen apart."

"All of this should make for a scathing exposure of the depth and breadth of the government's incompetence and corruption. Which pleases me to no end," Dickerson added.

"It seems as though the potential scandal has already made it up the channels," Karoft said as he scanned an update on his portable monitor. "This should please you, Rob. It appears your e-mail has gone viral within the military community, to use an Earth expression."

"Rob made sure it went to the Secretary of Defense and the Joint Chiefs of Staff," the general added. "Unfortunately, the beautiful scandal will be squashed before it gets out to the media. This can't look too good for the present administration. Up to now, the President has been Mr. Teflon; nothing has stuck to him. He's a real slippery SOB. I hope they fry the bastard, anyway. If it hadn't caused such a disruption to so many other departments, I would have leaked it to the media hounds myself." He let out an exasperated sigh as he reclined in his chair.

"Zohleemay's plans weren't completely thwarted, though. While disrupting his primary goals, in reality, all we accomplished was to move up his timetable," Cuz said. "The thing that's bothering me is that Zohleemay and some of his staff had acquired morphing technology. Nickada explained that morphing required absolute mental concentration and great physical stamina to hold the altered condition. The Zenti is clever and resilient, but also narrow-minded and hasn't shown the complex thought processes and mental discipline required to create and maintain a morphed state. Yet, Zohleemay did and did it well. Also, a few of his staff had similar converting abilities. We've explored their extended morphing capabilities and can't explain it."

"I believed the Zenti have aligned themselves with an unidentified partner," Biomei interjected. "This mysterious partner must be advanced on many levels. They must have been assisting the Zenti with new technologies. They also organized the Zenti and trained them in plan implementation and execution skills. I've also given thought to the Zenti's morphing attributes. They appear to have perfected a different method for maintaining a morphed state that doesn't require the mental and physical discipline we're familiar with. It must involve specialized nanotechnology that alters their physiological makeup. It's the only hypothesis that fits all their enhancements."

"That makes sense, Biomei," the general said while thinking about all his interactions with Zohleemay. "Based on everything you have described, nothing else seems to explain how he could do it. We all agree that our priority must be to discover who's helping the Zenti, and why?"

"Our highest priority is to get Terri and Tehrarra back," Biomei said emphatically.

"She's right," Cuz said. "Let's synchronize our watches. At the mark, it will be 05:00 hours… ready… mark. Let's all meet at shuttle bay one for a 05:30 departure."

Cuz took a chance and used the multi-purpose shuttle to get them to the entrance of the Zenti's Yucatan base. It was a larger ship that was also a submersible and could dive to almost unlimited depths. General Dickerson wanted to coordinate a strike with a small group of Army Rangers, but Cuz was unsure how far the Zenti's infiltration was within the military. It took convincing, but the general finally agreed their best chance was to go alone.

CHAPTER 49

The Zenti were thorough with Tehrarra. They dumped her unconscious body next to Territaff, who sat on the floor in a deep meditative state. He ignored the guards. Nor did he respond to Tehrarra being treated so roughly. The heavy door made a dull thud, and the security lock clicked, sealing their prison cell.

One guard peered eagerly into the cell through the window cut into the thick metal door. He wanted to see what the great and mysterious Territaff would do. The other guard growled at the peering guard, who responded with an irritated wheeze and walked away.

When Territaff sensed the guards were gone, he turned to Tehrarra. He gently lifted her battered head onto his lap. Her beautiful, dark complexion was blackened and swollen from the brutal beating she had endured. Both of her eyes were swollen shut. Blue lines of blood were seeping down from her ears and the corners of her puffy, split lips. Her button nose was broken and bleeding new blood into the already dried blood. He carefully opened her tattered jumpsuit to inspect her injuries. Her ebony skin had burn lines from a pain inducer held too long against it.

Placing his hands on either side of her forehead, he was about to do a telemetry meld to help ease her pain. With a sudden realization, he pulled away. *I can't help you, my dear. My illness won't allow it.* His heart ached for her. *I can't even be supportive. All my mental energy is being used to fight this damn disease. Forgive me, Tehrarra.* Looking down at her battered body, he cried, "How can I help her? I can't even help myself. They're such brutal fools."

Territaff's insides churned in a slow-boiling rage as he continued to stare at her beaten and torn body. He leaned his head against a wall of the cell. Territaff couldn't fight his weariness any longer. So, he allowed himself to doze off, wondering when Zohleemay would come and gloat.

* * *

Tehrarra awakened Territaff with a kiss. He opened his eyes and discovered her lying next to him, appearing recovered from the brutal battering. Her eyes glowed with renewed energy. Looking back at her, dazed and bewildered, thinking she must be another disease-driven hallucination. He sat more upright against the wall, holding Tehrarra at arm's length.

"What's the matter?" she asked, looking concerned.

"How's this possible?" he said, running his hand down one side of her once swollen cheek.

"I woke up like this and thought you somehow did it."

"I can't even help myself, let alone perform a miraculous recovery on you."

"That's strange because I remember you placing my head between your hands, and I must have passed out."

Territaff stood, contemplating the situation. He gave Tehrarra a surprised look at realizing how clear his thoughts were. A slow smile lit up his face. He held out a hand to her and helped her up.

"You look different. I mean better," she said, staring into his eyes. "In fact, you appear well."

"I am," Territaff said thoughtfully and paced the small cell area. "Tehrarra, something happened to us. It makes little sense, but somehow we're recovered and ourselves again." His face screwed up in confusion. "The Zenti would never have done this, especially Zohleemay. He would've just as soon seen me rot as help. So, who... or what—

"Terri, stop," Tehrarra interrupted. "Do you sense a presence here?"

"What kind of presence?"

"It is..." she had to think of the right word, "spirits she stated, sounding certain, then paused for a beat, and then said with her eyes brightening, "No. It's energy. Powerful energy. I can feel it."

Territaff concentrated for a moment. He closed his eyes and reached out with his mind, trying to get a sense of what Tehrarra was describing. It only took a second before he found a strong energy source beside him.

"I just sensed it. It's not mechanical. Oddly, it's much like a biological entity. Similar to the energy that Biomei transmits, but there's something about it... It has a definite aura that fluctuates around us—as if..." Territaff lifted his head and turned to the side. His expression became pensive, as though he was listening absorbedly. "I believe it's trying to communicate with me." He drew Tehrarra close and said, "Remain still and try to blank out all thoughts and feelings. Let's see if I can draw whatever it is out with telepathy."

"Anything is worth a try," she said, closing her eyes.

Territaff heard a sound like a tight string being strummed under an incoherent voice. The voice sounded as though it was speaking backward. It took a concerted effort to isolate some of the sounds. Under the cacophony of resonances, he discerned a distinct voice speaking in a normal tone. The language was strange and incomprehensible.

"*I can't understand you. Do you understand English or Venubian?*" Territaff transmitted.

There was a brief silence, then a different language stream flowed into his mind. Tehrarra noticed a change in his eyes; they were fixed, giving him a mesmerized look.

"Terri, what is happening?"

He didn't respond and appeared to be straining. His face was tight, his mouth distorted, and he looked in need of help.

She got closer to him and asked, "Terri, what do you want me to do?"

Tehrarra became uneasy with his expression. His eyes had taken on a glassy, entranced gaze, and he appeared to be in distress.

"Terri—Terri," she shook him by the shoulders. "Terri, let it go. Listen... Let it go," she shouted, hoping to get through whatever had taken hold of him.

His eyes closed tightly, and his body trembled in pain as he fell to his knees. Tehrarra felt helpless as she knelt beside him and wrapped her arms around his broad shoulders. She tried to hold him close, hoping to provide some comfort. His body vibrated as if a strange current was running through him. She studied his face as it contorted under the mysterious force overwhelming him.

Tehrarra watched in horror as he held his head. Territaff let out a breathtaking scream.

"Terri, please tell me what is happening," she cried in frustration, "I want to help, but I do not know what to do."

Tehrarra concentrated, trying to get a read on him empathically. Having no telepathic ability, she had to rely on being able to read strong emotions. What she felt was shocking. His mind was in chaos. A myriad of emotions were coming in intense waves. Each sensation was coming right on the cusp of the prior one. She had to let go of the connection. It was too intense for her.

Suddenly, his body became still. He lifted his head and stood. Wiping the sweat from his forehead and face with the sleeve of his tattered jumpsuit, he let out a heavy sigh of relief.

"Are you all right?"

"Oh, Tehrarra, that was something I hope I'll never have to experience again," he breathed in deep through his nose and let it out slowly from his mouth. His body relaxed with a long exhale.

"You scared me to tears," she said, still staying close to him.

"Sorry. I can't find the words to describe what happened. The best explanation I can think of is that a noncorporeal entity overtook me. It was bizarre. It wanted to communicate, but it needed to take possession of me. Once it did, it overwhelmed me with information. When I got it to slow down, it explained that the entire body of Earth's linguistic tongues was one language. Therefore, it was speaking in thousands of languages and dialects simultaneously. It was most disconcerting. I can't go into the details because, at first, it bounced around my body, looking for a way to relay its information. Once I could direct it to my implanted compiler, it accomplished downloading all that it wanted to convey, then left me."

"That is remarkable. Can you give me a few details?"

Her eyes grew wide in anticipation. Territaff looked at her with a slight upturn of his mouth as he tried to recall any of the data from his compiler. There was a long silence as he concentrated before letting out a frustrated sigh.

"Would you believe it's encrypted in such a way I can't access it?" A sudden thought came to mind as Territaff continued to search for any retrievable information. "Wait a sec," he said. "Oh, it can't be that simple." He gave Tehrarra a surprised look.

"What is it?"

"Ask me how my day was."

"Huh?"

"Go on. Ask me how my day was."

She wrinkled her nose and said, "How was your day?"

The data was downloaded in a steady stream of concise information. Territaff sat back on the floor, crossed his legs, and meditated on the information.

"Zhrenzgrek," Tehrarra cursed in Vultaran. "What are you doing now?"

Tehrarra knew Territaff was almost inaccessible during deep meditation. She let out a long moan as she watched him sit on the floor, his eyes staring outward with an impassive expression.

* * *

"*Cuz*," Biomei transmitted.

"Yes, Biomei."

"I'm sensing Territaff but can't quite reach him. He's at the Yucatan location, approximately three hundred meters below the surface at the following coordinates."

A holographic image appeared between Kathy's and Cuz's couch on the shuttle. The image rotated and stopped at the intended coordinates, highlighting a virtual depiction of the area.

"That's wicked, Cuz," Rob said, seeing the holographic depiction of their destination. "It looks like a subterranean city."

"Indeed," Cuz agreed, studying the familiar Zenti architecture. "Hanc, position us at the following location, then hold for final landing instructions."

Cuz transmitted the coordinate numbers to Hanc. As he studied the holographic image, he thought about Terri. As he pondered the thousands of variations approaching the site, an idea presented itself.

He turned to Kathy and said, "Kathy, there's a microwave transmitter in the right-side compartment next to your seat."

At first, she saw nothing and was about to ask Cuz for help when a small compartment slid open.

Hanc asked Kathy in a perky synthesized voice, "Is this what you are looking for?"

Kathy was mildly amused and a little surprised by the computer's playfulness.

"Thanks, Hanc," she acknowledged as she searched the numerous objects in the deep compartment. "This looks like my kitchen junk drawer. What am I looking for?"

"A maser. It transmits microwaves that Terri can receive. It resembles a flashlight except it has a rounded head instead of a flat lens."

"This it?" she said, holding up a long, cylindrical device with a small dome-shaped head.

"Yes. Turn the back end up, and you'll see two dials."

She turned the back end toward her and spotted them. They were flat and had tiny symbols that encircled them.

"Okay, now what?"

"The left dial is frequency, and the right is intensity. Move the left dial three clicks clockwise and the right eight clicks counter-clockwise."

Kathy followed Cuz's instructions.

"All right, now what?"

"Please, hand it to me." Cuz took the transmitter and gave it a close inspection. "It's older technology, but it might do the trick," he explained.

Cuz pulled out what appeared to be a long power cord from the device's back end. He plugged it into an input receptacle to the left of the main pilot's console and concentrated on Territaff.

The general and Rob talked among themselves as they observed the enormous grandeur passing around them. Rob never thought he would ever live his dream of going into space. Now, he was once again traveling through space, seeing the Earth's beauty from a unique perspective. Being in the heavens far exceeded his expectations. Each venture was even more thrilling and more awe-inspiring than he could have ever imagined. However, he also discovered how scary it was, with uncertainty being the only sure thing.

* * *

Territaff's eyes became alert upon receiving Cuz's faint signal. As soon as he stood, the signal became stronger. The carrier wave was in an unfamiliar microwave bandwidth with a secondary transmission embedded. He concentrated for a moment on separating the embedded message from its carrier wave. A smile spread across his face as he deciphered Cuz's concise message: "We're on our way."

Territaff leaned over to Tehrarra, who had fallen asleep on the floor, and gently squeezed her shoulder. She opened her eyes with a startled jerk, then let out a relieved breath when she realized it was Territaff.

"What a dream I was having," she said as he helped her. She noticed an air of confidence about him she hadn't seen in some time. "You look like you know something."

Territaff raised his index finger to his lips, telling her not to speak, but the familiar Earth gesture confused her. Recognizing her confusion, he pulled her close and whispered, "Say nothing. Help is on the way."

Tehrarra's eyes grew large with the news, but she became nervous after a moment's thought.

"How will they get through that Zenti army?" she whispered.

"We also have help on the inside," he said and gently kissed her.

She smiled at being kissed and asked, "What... Who?"

"Not now. Stay calm and wait for my signal."

Tehrarra became confused. She worried that Territaff was having another illusion.

"What are you saying? I... I—"

He kissed her again. While keeping her close to his side, he said in a hushed voice, "Don't talk. Stay calm. I can't explain anything right now. They're listening and watching everything we do."

Tehrarra nodded, then pointed to the door. She saw Zohleemay staring through the small window in the door.

"Terri," she said in a low voice, "he has come for you."

"Perfect."

Territaff's expression became intense with hatred as he saw his nemesis enter the cell door.

"It's been a while, Phillip," Zohleemay hissed, a contemptuous smile growing on his broad, lipless face.

"I'm Territaff to you. You killed Phillip Mann, remember?"

He quickly moved toward Zohleemay but was stopped by two Zenti guards watching from inside the door. The guards pushed Territaff back with their weapons.

Zohleemay grunted something at them, and they stepped

back into the corridor. He regarded Tehrarra with a sneer and spoke to her in a slithering Zenti, "Tehrarra, we had such great hopes for you. Look what your treachery has wrought. Now you have forfeited your own life and jeopardized your world."

Tehrarra lunged toward him. Her long, razor-sharp nails extended, her needle canines showing a vicious ferocity that surprised Territaff. Zohleemay threw his arm outward with his palm open. It acted as a powerful force, throwing Tehrarra into the opposite wall of the cell. She fell hard to the floor. Territaff went to assist her, but she sprang to her feet. He caught her as she was about to go after Zohleemay again.

"Stop," he shouted at Zohleemay as he held Tehrarra back.

He turned to her and gave her a stern glare. She understood and relaxed her anger.

"I see you have met our Symbient friends," Zohleemay said smugly. "They are remarkable, would you not agree?"

"What do you want, Zohleemay?" Territaff said.

"You mean, after all this time, you still do not know?" He sounded surprised.

"Outside of stealing and killing everything, I'm clueless."

"Oh, Phil... I mean, Territaff. It is so simple—I want you. Or, to be more precise, I want what is up in there." He pointed a crooked finger at Territaff's head.

At first, he didn't understand what he meant. Then, a slow, defiant smile spread across Territaff's mouth with the revelation. "Of course, you want my compiler with all that wonderful data you've coveted for so long."

"Exactly." Zohleemay nodded and grunted something at the guards.

The two guards returned to the cell, their weapons pointed at Territaff. He looked back at Tehrarra and gestured with his eyes to the guard on her right.

"Wait," she shouted, "I want to say goodbye."

She went to Territaff and gave him a passionate kiss, and when she finished, she leered at Zohleemay. She tilted her head, signaling to Territaff that she was ready.

Territaff moved toward the guard on his left so fast he almost appeared as a blur of motion. He snapped the guard's neck like a twig and grabbed Zohleemay by the throat, as Tehrarra simultaneously thrust her sharp, talon-like finger into the other guard's neck, slicing it open. She jerked the guard's weapon from him as he fell to the floor. Dark blue blood squirted between its fingers, covering the gaping wound.

Zohleemay looked in disbelief, realizing his Symbient was gone. Now he was ordinary and defenseless, staring into Territaff's seething expression.

"Oh, don't look so frightened, my little bug. I won't kill you now. No. You're our ticket out of here."

"How do you plan to get out? There are over ten thousand troops between you and the surface," Zohleemay grunted, sounding confident.

"Walk," Territaff demanded, pushing Zohleemay out of the cell. He turned to Tehrarra. "You okay?"

"Never better," she said, smiling at Zohleemay's bulging eyes.

"The Symbients will stop you," Zohleemay said.

"We'll see about that," Territaff answered, picking up the dead guard's weapon and shoving Zohleemay in the back with it.

Tehrarra sensed a strange presence beside her as they walked down the corridor. She turned to her side, but nothing was there. As they continued, she recognized the alien force, before she could alert Territaff, it flowed into her.

"Terri," she shouted as a surge of energy grew inside her and then spread through her limbs.

Territaff grabbed Zohleemay's shoulder, stopping him. He faced Tehrarra. "Don't fight it. It won't harm you."

"But I saw what it did to you and..." Her voice trailed off as the entity made itself known. "Never mind, Terri. I understand, now," she said, looking pleased as if enjoying the entity's presence growing inside her. "Za-za-zee, she purred in Vultaran. That was great."

"Tehrarra, focus," Territaff said.

"Okay. It is only that—"

"I don't need the details, keep your mind on what we're doing." Territaff jammed the weapon in Zohleemay's back to make him move.

Whoever constructed the passageway had to cut through the rock wall of the sixty-five-million-year-old impact crater. The crater was formed by an asteroid impact credited with the extinction of all but a precious few species on Earth. Territaff didn't lose sight of the irony that the Zenti should select such a location for their planned Armageddon.

As they passed cell blocks, doors on both sides opened, releasing scores of prisoners to sudden freedom. Many could barely stand, but after a few moments of liberty, they all appeared to regain their strength. All their torn flesh, broken bones, and depleted spirits were miraculously healed. All were whole again and free! They followed behind Territaff and Tehrarra like an army of slaves unexpectedly given their lives back. They would have followed Territaff into perdition's flames if he had told them to.

The corridor led into a large opening that was environmentally sealed within a domed structure similar to the ones on the moon. By the time Territaff's group gathered in the cavernous area, it was already filled with thousands of captives from all over the massive facility.

Zenti troops flooded into the area, firing their weapons. The Zenti soldiers looked shocked as their weapons' energy discharges were instantaneously muted. The masses of enraged prisoners overran the soldiers.

All the color drained from Zohleemay's face as he watched, in horror, the carnage that was being inflicted on his now defenseless troops. The usually passive Bylars were ripping apart as many as four Zenti troops at a time. It was payback for generations of cruel and brutal captivity and servitude.

Territaff shouted, "Stop!" His voice rang out with incredible force, causing all but a few to cease their violent retribution.

His Symbient told him to go to the surface, where his friends awaited him. Zohleemay looked at Territaff with a distorted grin as though he knew something.

"You think you defeated me," he cried defiantly. "You're too late."

"Too late for what?"

"To save your world," he said, glancing at a small panel attached to his sleeve.

Territaff grabbed Zohleemay's arm and pulled it up for a closer look. The small display was in Zenti, but Territaff knew enough to recognize that the countdown was almost zero. An instant later, the sounds of heavy-lift rockets shook the cavern. It felt as though it was about to erupt.

"What have you done?" Territaff saw a turbo lift a few meters away and rushed to it.

"Where are you going?" Tehrarra shouted over the now almost deafening sounds of thousands of missiles launching under tremendous thrust.

The lift couldn't travel fast enough for Territaff. His heart pounded in his throat and chest as the car moved upward.

He walked onto the rocky surface under a crystal clear sky and warm night. Territaff looked up at the moonlit night and gasped. The sky was ablaze with the bright yellowish-white lines of the missile exhaust plumes. He looked behind and saw hundreds of missiles flying in all directions.

Territaff fell to his knees, screaming into the night, "How could this be? How could this happen? No! No! We're too late."

Territaff saw his crew rushing toward him. Cuz greeted him with a grave expression, pointing to the northwest as he helped his distraught friend to his feet. The velvet star-studded sky was filled with hundreds of troop carriers, trailing behind the missiles.

Tehrarra joined them on the surface, prodding a delighted Zohleemay with the muzzle of her weapon. She looked up in terrified awe at the ominous sky. It was a spectacular night, with a panorama that, under different circumstances, would cause one to ponder its beauty, but the pending annihilation that filled the sky instead scarred and distorted it.

"What a beautiful sight," Zohleemay rejoiced, seeing his planned destruction.

Territaff grabbed Zohleemay by the throat and, in a seething voice, said, "I refuse to let you gloat!"

He was about to snap his neck when he heard the voice of his Symbient say, *"Enough."*

Territaff's hand opened, releasing his grip on Zohleemay. "Let me kill him, please," he cried aloud.

"No," the Symbient answered. *"No more. We're done now. We understand and are sorry for all the pain we have caused. That was not our intention, but we will end it now."*

"What do you mean?"

"Look."

Territaff lifted his eyes and was stunned. The sky glowed with explosions. All the visible missiles detonated in mid-air, and hundreds of troop carriers dissipated like wisps of smoke into the night.

"Noooo!" Zohleemay fell to his knees, screaming hysterically. "You promised we would prevail. You promised... You promised," he kept repeating while banging his fist on the rough ground.

Territaff looked down at Zohleemay with conflicted emotions. His Symbient's presence was gone. All the hate and rage that had been a part of his consciousness for so many years had left him with a hollow feeling. He stared down at the vile creature that had caused so much misery to so many. Now, he appeared pathetic and unworthy of any consideration.

Zohleemay glared at Territaff with an expression full of vehement contempt. He stood with his bulbous eyes narrowed and fixed on Territaff. Straightening into a tense, upright stance, he watched the masses of freed Venubians and Bylars emerge from the cavern's depths. Looking at them, his face twisted with disdain, he grunted and hissed unintelligibly. He glanced at Territaff, then noticed Tehrarra approaching. Territaff turned from Zohleemay and greeted her with a warm smile. Zohleemay seized the opportunity and bolted back down the pathway into the cavern, screaming and ranting incoherently.

Territaff lifted his weapon and carefully aimed at Zohleemay, but hesitated to fire. He let out a long sigh and lowered his weapon.

"You are not going after him?" she asked, puzzled by his lack of action.

"I'm tired of chasing after him. He's no longer worth the effort. Besides, he has no place to go."

She nodded, understanding how Territaff felt, then gave him a thoughtful look and said, "Is your Symbient gone?"

Territaff nodded, still looking at Zohleemay, running like a madman against the flow of the freed captives.

"We've much work to do," he called to his approaching crew.

"That will be very hard to explain," General Dickerson said, pointing at the scores of aliens gathering along the cavern's edge.

"It won't be a problem," Territaff whispered. "The Symbients have taken care of that."

"What the hell is a Symbient?" the general asked as he joined Territaff and Tehrarra.

"Too hard to explain now. Trust me, it's all taken care of."

"They have that much power?" The thought filled Dickerson with a sense of astonishment.

Kathy and Cuz approached Territaff and placed their arms

around his waist. Kathy kissed him on the cheek. She smiled admiringly at him, then turned to Cuz and kissed him with tears in her eyes.

Cuz extended his hand to Territaff for a shake, but thought for a second, then grabbed and hugged him tightly.

"Okay, Cuz." Territaff laughed and patted his friend's back. "I love you, too."

Rob was mesmerized by the night sky. Living in the city with all its light pollution, he had never experienced such a sight. Now that the sky had cleared of all the menacing objects, he could appreciate the magnificence of the heavens. General Dickerson joined him in gazing at the incredible sight.

"It's incomprehensibly beautiful," Rob whispered. "I thought nothing could compare to our view of the stars from the observation lounge, but this is just as amazing. Do you think Venubia's sky will be as wondrous?"

"It certainly will be different," the general answered, squeezing Rob's shoulder. Rob turned and looked at him. "Well done, Rob," the general smiled while shaking his hand. "There are so many astonishing and wonderful things within the immensity of the universe," he murmured, appreciating the opportunity to share what Rob was seeing in the clear, starry night.

"Yes, sir," Rob nodded while maintaining his upward gaze. "I can't imagine what new and incredible experiences are ahead," he said dreamily, then added, "Thanks for believing in me, sir." He looked over his shoulder and noticed Cuz, Kathy, and Terri hugging and kissing each other.

He could feel the intimacy of their relationship. They were like family and hoped he'd share their closeness one day. Rob didn't realize that he was already part of the family.

Biomei's presence filled the sky a few thousand kilometers above them. They all looked up at her and marveled at her enormity. Everyone stared excitedly, knowing the long ordeal was finally over. Territaff thought of Nickada and made a sad smile that caught Kathy's attention.

"What is it, Terri?" she asked.

"I miss Nicki. She would've loved having such a full boat. Somehow, I believe she knows we prevailed."

431

CHAPTER 50

Biomei brimmed with passengers for the first time in her existence. It was a wondrous feeling to have all her systems in use. The Bylars presented significant problems, though. They were much too large for common quarters, and their diet and daily calorie requirements put a strain on the food synthesizers. However, these problems were quickly addressed by converting the available cargo bays into temporary dorms and implementing creative food management. In particular, Kathy had to limit her midnight food binges. To their credit, the Bylars seemed unconcerned with food, comfort, or amenities. They were accustomed to sparse living conditions and too preoccupied with going home to concern themselves with minor inconveniences.

Biomei satisfied the Bylar's varying ambient temperature and pressure requirements by installing voice-actuated controls in their dorms. Territaff and Rob volunteered to go into the individual bays and instruct the Bylars on how to set them. Territaff reviewed all the adjustments to the environmental systems in the lower cargo bays while Rob worked with the ones in the aft shuttle bays. The Bylars conveyed their appreciation to Territaff, telling him he and his crew members would be enshrined in the Bylarian verbal history log. "Songs will be sung in your honor," one of the older Bylars told him.

In the short time that Territaff had spent with them, he got a sense of the amenable side of their character. He saw them in a new light as both valued allies and trusted friends.

Rob informed Territaff he was starting on the primary shuttle bay's environmental systems, which had Territaff going to the secondary ones a few decks above. The process took much longer than expected due to all the additional greetings and expressions of gratitude given to Territaff as he entered each bay. At one point, he wished he could have a droid do the adjustments, but after a Bylar threw a droid across a bay, he decided against it. He was anxious to finish so he could debrief everybody. He also needed to review all the arrangements before departing for Bylaria and moving on to Venubia. He enlisted Karoft to take care of the storage and small shuttle bays spread throughout the mid-level decks to expedite this ever-growing and protracted amenity.

As Territaff made his way to the central turbo lift, he noticed that only the emergency floor lights were on. The winding corridor ahead was dark.

"Biomei, please illuminate central corridor B-24 through 27," Territaff said as he walked through the darkened passageway. Territaff stopped when Biomei didn't respond. "Biomei?" She didn't answer.

The silence was concerning.

"Biomei," he transmitted. No response.

Not hearing a response to his transmission put Territaff on high alert. For Biomei to be cut off from him, there had to be something wrong. He pulled out the compact field analyzer he was using to balance the environmental systems. He noticed a strong EM interference throughout the corridor. That explains why I can't communicate with Biomei, he thought. Now, what's generating it?

Territaff cautiously proceeded to the turbo lift. He stopped after a few steps. He turned his ear and listened to what sounded like labored breathing close behind him. He stood in the darkness, intently searching with all his senses probing the shadows. What they depicted seemed highly improbable until he saw the movements of a wiry figure with his augmented optics.

"Zohleemay," Territaff said in a hushed voice. "Why am I not surprised by your audacity?"

Zohleemay took a few steps toward him. His twisted form became visible in the shadowy lighting. He wheezed and hissed with each step, sounding like a wounded animal.

"You must pay," he cried in a heavy rasp. "You killed us and destroyed all our hope. We are enslaved again..." His words slurred into a long, whining shriek.

"You killed yourself and took your people with you," Territaff said calmly. "What do you want, Zohleemay? The Symbients will give you what you need. Your people have a chance for a long, viable existence, but that's not enough. So, what do you want? Revenge? You've taken your revenge on the whole quadrant. Don't you think it's time to try something else? Why not give your people an opportunity for a real life? A chance to be part of something productive."

"Making big promises is what you are good at, but in reality, you are only offering enslavement under a different master!" Zohleemay's voice rose into a shrill cry, and his face distorted into a contemptuous sneer.

Territaff shook his head and sighed. "I feel sorry for you, Zoh. You truly are a lost and tortured soul. All you understand is hate. Even after all you've done for all the worlds that have tried to help you, you still see nothing beyond your petty needs and distorted reality. You're so consumed with hatred, there's no room for anything else. Don't you understand that your true enemy is yourself? Let it go. It's destroying you and all you care about. Give your people a home and a chance for life."

Territaff approached Zohleemay with his arms open in a conciliatory gesture. "I'm not your enemy... I never was."

Zohleemay lifted a hand pulse-phaser at him and said, "First, I'll finish what I came for. Then I'll free my people from that vile force that took them. You're a meddling fool, Territaff the do-gooder. I'm sick of your human hypocrisy. You're worse than the Venubians and deserve to perish with them."

"Terri," A voice called out as the corridor lights came on.

Territaff sensed Rob jogging toward them. "Get down, Rob," Territaff shouted, then quickly moved toward Zohleemay.

Zohleemay's bulging eyes widened as he fired. Territaff was an instant too late with his swift and decisive kick to

Zohleemay's hand. Rob fell to the floor as the phaser flew onto the deck.

"You piece of shit," Territaff cried as he clenched his fist and gave Zohleemay a crushing blow to the side of his head. The blow sent Zohleemay crashing against a wall, falling hard to the deck.

Territaff rushed to Rob's side and turned him onto his back. The side of Rob's face had a long, nasty cauterized gash. He heaved a sigh of relief as Rob's eyes blinked open. Territaff held Rob's head to his chest and gave it an endearing hug.

"Thank the universe, you're okay," he whispered, almost in tears. "I don't know what I'd have done," his voice trailed off as he released Rob from his tight embrace and smiled.

"Geez, Terri. I didn't know you cared," Rob said, surprised by Territaff's affection.

"Are you kidding? I love you like the little brother I never had."

"Wow," Rob mumbled. "I already look up to you like a brother, but I think you know that." His eyes grew large as he yelled, "Terri, look out!"

Rob pulled his automatic out of its holster and fired.

Territaff turned in time to see Zohleemay fall backward, dark blue blood spraying onto the walls.

"Nice shot," Territaff said as he went to Zohleemay and observed the large, bleeding wound in his left shoulder. He also saw a long dagger lying next to him. Territaff picked it up and nodded approvingly at Rob. "Can you stand?"

Rob hesitated for a second to check how he felt. "Yeah. I've got a hell of a headache, and the side of my face is numb... but other than that, I think I'm okay." His hand shook a little, still holding the gun. "I always dreaded the thought of having to use this damn thing, until now." He frowned at the gun before placing it back into its holster.

Territaff helped him up, then gave him a close look over.

"You realize you saved my life."

Rob nodded, grinning. "Now, you owe me."

"Well, the good thing about getting hit by a pulse-phaser is that it leaves a bloodless wound. But they can do some damage if you get hit in the wrong spot. It'll get infected if not treated right away."

Rob started for the turbo lift, stopped, turned, and asked, "What will you do about him?"

"I hope he's dead," Territaff said, pulling on his ear. "But if he's still alive, I'll turn him over to the Symbients and let them deal with him." Gazing at Zohleemay's limp body, he added, "He's not worth any more of our time or consideration. I sure hope he's dead, though."

"Unfortunately, he's not," Biomei interjected.

"There you are," Territaff said. "What happened to you?"

"That little swond broke into one of my sub-junction interfaces and fused all the feeder circuits for lighting and communications and all the biometric sensors on three decks. I was able to reroute the lighting through a redundant circuit. Sent Rob to investigate what happened, and that's how he found you. Sorry, Rob, that unsavory little bug injured you. Please, come to the med lab so Aunty Biomei can care for you."

Rob grinned at Territaff and mouthed, 'Aunty Biomei' with a bemused expression. "Biomei, you feel all right?" Rob asked.

"Besides being upset about all the damaged circuits—I'm fine. Why'd you ask?"

"No reason. Just making sure everything's okay."

Territaff arched an eyebrow while trying to maintain a straight face. "Go. I'll meet you there after disposing of him." Territaff watched Rob as he got in the turbo lift, realizing how close his young friend had come to death. He looked at Zohleemay's unconscious body, wondering if he should do everybody a favor and toss him out of the closest airlock. He threw Zohleemay over his shoulder and started for the nearest hatchway, but halfway there, he reconsidered and took him to the med lab.

CHAPTER 51

Rob joined the crew at Biomei's Electronic Grill and Bar. A medicated mesh covered the side of his swollen face. He flopped exhausted in a chair and sighed as he put a leg on the empty chair beside him.

"You don't look so bad," Kathy said.

"Got the Bylars squared away?" Territaff asked.

Rob nodded, "That was worse than getting shot," he grunted. "What's up with their females, anyway?"

Territaff laughed, knowing what Rob meant. "It's all about male pheromones," he explained.

"Pheromones? I thought one of them would squeeze the life out of me. I don't know what would've happened if a male Bylar hadn't rescued me by batting her on the side of her enormous head."

"What can I say? They find human males irresistible, like cute little pets."

"Pets?" He shook his head slowly. "Anyway, they're really weird. Speaking of weird. Remember that mysterious device in my head? It resurfaced this morning, lying on my forehead. When I picked it up, it glowed momentarily, then evaporated. It was most strange."

"Interesting," Tehrarra blinked her large cat eyes. "I was uncertain how the energy inside the Pougahr would resolve itself after being integrated into a living organism. As far as I know, Rob, you are the first to have a Pougahr immerse its energy into a humanoid prefrontal cortex. With your permission, I would like to make a note of your experience in the Vultaran medical database."

Rob squinted at her and asked, "Will I be mentioned by name?"

"If you like," Tehrarra replied.

"If it's all the same to you, I'd prefer to remain anonymous."

"As you wish." She gave Rob an approving smile and added, "I should mention that you are already known to my people."

"You mean, I'm famous?" His expression beamed with pride. "Hey, that's neat. I'm famous on an alien world."

"Oh, Rob, my young friend, that's only the beginning," Territaff said. "Consider this for a moment, where you're heading, there are a hundred women for each man, and they're all beautiful, sexy, and affectionate."

"A hundred to one, hmmm. Now that sounds like a real Utopia."

"What will happen to the surviving Zenti?" Cuz said.

"The Symbients assured me they'll take them to an isolated planet similar to Earth, but with conditions more suitable to them," Territaff said. "What's so astonishing is that the Zenti's wrath was from a need to reproduce sexually. They didn't understand that all they had to do was ask for help. However, their childlike minds couldn't accept it was that simple. All they had to do was to say, 'we're dying and need your help'. Zohleemay didn't want to resolve their problem. He preferred his hate over finding a solution to his people's plight. That's what makes this whole damn struggle so maddening."

"You're telling me this whole atrocity was about sexuality?" Dickerson protested with an incredulous frown.

"In a real sense, it was, sir," Cuz said. "Their imminent extinction drove the Zenti's rage. That they had survived as long as they did was remarkable."

"I hope the Symbients don't make the same mistake as the Venubian androids and leave them to their resources," Kathy reflected. "They can't be trusted even if given what they want."

"I don't understand," Rob said. "What do androids have to do with it?"

"It's almost incomprehensible, Rob," Territaff said. "The Zenti was a biology experiment gone awry by a race of ancient androids. The Zenti's history is inseparable from the

Venubians. Biomei will give you the details as part of your orientation. The quick version is the androids who created the Zenti thought having sexuality would've, ironically, made them too aggressive. That nearsightedness of the androids is what escalated the Zenti's belligerence. Their android creators overlooked the ability for self-determination and natural evolutionary development. The Zenti experiment will make a perfect cautionary tale of the dangers of artificially creating intelligent biological life.

"When the androids decided the Zenti were not what they intended, they tossed them aside, believing they could deal with them later." Territaff let out a heavy sigh as a flood of painful memories surfaced. He closed his eyes for a moment to calm the rising tide of emotions. "So much could've been avoided," he resumed, "if only the androids had addressed the Zenti problem. It would've eliminated all that followed. However, there was disagreement among the androids on what to do with the Zenti. One faction was convinced the Zenti would have died off anyway and weren't worth the time and resources to eliminate them. Another group was curious how the Zenti would evolve and intended to use them as a resilient labor force if they survived."

"What you're describing is slave labor," Rob said.

"Precisely," Territaff said. "You have to keep in mind that the androids don't share our sense of morality. They have no moral compass. No right or wrong, only solutions to problems. The Zenti wasn't viewed as a real and viable life force. They were a failed experiment and nothing more.

"Because of how they were treated, the Zenti saw themselves as castoffs left to die. They got even more desperate once the Zenti realized their imminent extinction from a phenomenon known as Fade of Replication."

"Fade of Replication?" Rob repeated, looking confused. "I'm not familiar with that term."

"It's genetic cloning degradation. Something like making a

copy of a copy, with each successive copy becoming more faded until it's unrecognizable. The Zenti somehow developed cloning techniques without understanding the nuances of genetic engineering. Their DNA was no longer viable because it could not replicate without radical mutations in the code sequencing. After millennia of unsuccessful genetic adaptations, they faced extinction and became desperate."

"How'd the Symbients get involved in all of this?" the general asked. "I'm uncomfortable with the thought of something that powerful being so close to us."

"The Symbients, in simplified terms, are ascended beings. They must've evolved from corporeal to pure energy over millions of millennia. The Symbient that occupied me downloaded a detail of their origins and a little about their life form. It's a highly compressed file, still stored inside my internal compiler. It will require careful decompression to retrieve all the data. When time permits, I'll have Biomei upload it and make it available for everyone to review.

"The little I've retrieved is fascinating. They originated from a parallel universe, directly proving something I already suspected. We're part of an infinite multiverse. From what little I've gathered, their universe was extremely old and succumbing to entropy. New star production had long ceased, and everything was getting darker and colder. I'm still unclear on how they got into our universe. There was a reference to a black hole being a gateway, but the details weren't disclosed. They deliberately omitted that information. I guess they have their reasons. Nevertheless, they're a form of noncorporeal energy. Something they believe is unique to our galaxy. They've been wandering throughout our cosmos for millennia, feeding off any compatible energy.

"You all have seen what they can do. They can manipulate their energy to do whatever they desire. It's beyond comprehension." Territaff glanced at all the dulled eyes and smiled. "I can tell from your glazed-over expressions that this is getting a little too dense."

"I'm finding this fascinating," Rob said, now sitting upright and wide-eyed in his chair.

"You would," the general grumbled.

"Please continue," Cuz prompted.

"Anyway, they were about to leave our quadrant when they accidentally came upon the Zenti. At first, the Zenti intrigued them. Even though they were pure energy, the Symbients made what seemed like a human error in judgment. They perceived the Zenti as a developing species. However, compassion didn't initiate their involvement with them. It was pure scientific curiosity.

"The Symbients have no means of externally communicating or interacting with corporeal life. They must use a body as a host to communicate. I can tell you, being occupied by a Symbient is a profound experience. It's almost inexplicable what it means to be a host. However, the benefits are astounding." Territaff paused in thought for a moment. "I should preface by saying the Symbients have no emotions as we understand them. They've lost the concepts of good and evil long ago. Nevertheless, they understand energy, and the Zenti's conflicted minds and intriguing energy patterns fascinated them. Understand, the energy the Zenti produced with their underdeveloped psyches presented something novel for the Symbients to explore."

"You said the Symbients were bodiless... that they were made only of energy... negative energy. How's that possible?" Rob asked.

"Good question." Territaff reflected for a moment. "If you can picture this, they're a form of what we would refer to as dark energy. Most of our universe is made of weakly interacting particles. While these particles are still a mystery, there is growing evidence that they may be gravity leaking between the universes, and that's the reason gravity is so weak in our universe.

"Even Klaxons, among the oldest known species, are still unsure of the true nature of dark energy. While they've uncovered more than we have in some areas, they're not that far ahead of us in others. The universe is just as mysterious to them as it is to us. The Klaxons are also protective of their knowledge, maybe for the right reasons. They believe providing advanced data to a developing species could upset the natural course of development. After the Zenti experience, I can't blame them.

"The little knowledge I absorbed from hosting a Symbient, they can exist extra-dimensionally. What was inside of me was only a partial entity." Territaff closed his eyes, reflecting on the memory before continuing. "Even when it lived in me, it had no real presence. It was like a living thought within the framework of my mind. Something like being occupied by an ethereal spirit. Its presence existed for only a moment, then faded into something that had a dreamlike quality." Territaff looked at Tehrarra and asked, "How'd you describe it?"

Tehrarra made a thoughtful purr as though she was reliving the experience before describing it.

"It had no tangible form but manifested more like a vague notion of being inside of me. It was odd because it bounced around my body, stimulating different parts until it found its way into my mind. You had it right, Terri. It was more of an impression of its presence, which used my mind to communicate with me and my thoughts like an inner voice. However, its energy heals your body. After it left me, I felt rejuvenated. I was close to death in that cell. Terri, remember? It healed my body, and it healed your mind."

"That's true. I was a mess," Territaff said, "from space sickness. It appears Symbient's energy fixes anything perceived as a risk while present in a host. All I know is it cured me as soon as it occupied me. It also found my implanted compiler fascinating and stimulated it with unfortunate consequences. Mostly, it hurt like hell."

"So, what happened to the Zenti?" the general asked, showing a sudden keen interest.

"Once they occupied a few Zenti, they recognized their plight and gave a few of them sexual organs, as an experiment. The Symbients realized the Zenti were too biologically and psychologically immature, and the experiment regressed disastrously. Having sex for the first time drove them nuts. They became even more aggressive."

"You have no clue," Tehrarra said. "That miserable bastard, Hezvid, would drop his pants whenever we were alone in his office. He would chase me around the room until I was exhausted. I had to threaten him with bodily harm to get him to stop."

"That wasn't the only error the Symbients made," Territaff resumed. "They allowed themselves to be sucked into the Zenti dilemma. Zohleemay was experimenting with negative energy using zeta-particles. The anti-neutrino emissions are what attracted the Symbients."

"Zeta particles?" Rob questioned. "You mean like zeta-potential?"

"No, it's not quite the same thing," Cuz said. "A zeta particle, in this context, refers to the energy released in antimatter collisions. What Zohleemay was attempting, though, was dangerous and foolish."

"But it achieved in getting the Symbient's attention, Cuz," Territaff pointed out. "How Zohleemay manipulated the Symbients is still unclear. They were controlled, possibly through zeta-particles, but why they complied with the Zenti's wishes will remain a mystery. One thing was clear, though. They gave Zohleemay and his inner circle of cohorts the ability to maintain extended morphed states.

"The Symbients, despite all their power, acted naïvely. They seemed to go along with whatever the Zenti requested, purely out of scientific curiosity. Even to the extent of agreeing to occupy several key military and government positions.

Colonel Cameron and Captain Jason were among them, along with several key congressmen and military officials."

"Wow," the general bellowed through a long breath. "That explains a lot. No wonder," his voice trailed off as he reflected on some of the past events. "No wonder," he repeated, looking at Rob, who appeared almost dumbstruck by the revelation.

"Didn't they realize they were occupied?" Rob said.

"That's unclear. However, there's some evidence Captain Jason resisted."

"Why do you say that?" the general asked.

"My Symbient told me it had to adjust how it approached a human host. Jason may have been among the first to host one. The experience might have overwhelmed him and caused his tragic death."

"He was a good man," Rob said softly. "He was the first officer to take a real interest in me. I'll miss him."

"I'm sorry, Rob. His death was unfortunate for all of us, especially his family." The general's expression turned solemn as he reached out and squeezed Rob's shoulder. "There have been so many unnecessary losses. The real tragedy of war is that so many of our finest youth must die in them. Their potential is lost forever. As a military man, I was fighting to end aggression, but have come to realize the cost is far too great. The ends never justify the means in war."

"You're so right, General. War results from ignorance, intolerance to differences, and a failure to communicate," Territaff said, staring outwardly, reflecting on his own experiences.

"Didn't the Symbients realize what they were doing?" Kathy said, getting up and walking to the food synthesizer.

"They were clueless about the havoc the Zenti were raining down on us. I'm unsure if they could understand our situation or even care. It was all a grand experiment to them," Cuz said, sounding disturbed.

Territaff nodded. "I need a stiff drink."

Kathy turned and said, "Me too. How about you, General?"

"Got any scotch?"

"I have something even better, sir," Territaff said, jumping up and going to the synthesizer. "Who else wants a drink? Never mind. Drinks for everybody." Territaff returned carrying a silver tray with a crystal decanter filled with a clear liquid surrounded by tall cordial glasses. "Ladies and gentlemen, let me introduce you to my favorite drink: Pido." He served everyone. "To a lasting peace," Territaff toasted and drained his Pido.

"Wow," the general said, smacking his lips. "Now, that is what I call a drink. I'll have another."

"Help yourself," Territaff said, looking at Kathy, who held her empty glass up for a refill."

Cuz appeared to observe everyone with keen interest.

Dickerson said to Cuz. "I think there was more to the Zenti's craving for our planet than just our strategic location and resources."

"You would be correct in that assumption, " Cuz said. "When the Zenti discovered our planet had the exact balance of viable amino acids and the additional proteins for recombinant DNA strings, they went straight for us. What they didn't see was a need for humans. But they loved our planet. The sad thing about this is that they probably would have died out anyway. They're copper-based organisms, and our oxygen-rich atmosphere would've given them problems in the long run."

"Our planet's unique chemical makeup supports my carbon-based chauvinism. There's nothing better than carbon for building and sustaining organisms," Territaff interjected.

"Don't get too carried away," Cuz said, "there's a lot to be said for silicon."

"Cuz, I won't have this debate with you again. While we're on adaptation, you two have to return to the med lab and be adapted for alien environments and deep space travel,"

Territaff said, pointing to the general and Rob.

"Yeah, Biomei already informed us," Rob said, "And we don't have to go into hibernation, thank God. I dreaded that possibility."

"You've no idea how lucky you are that we can use the Venubian corridors now. It cuts a hundred and fifty years off the trip."

"I don't know about the rest of you," Kathy yawned, "I'm exhausted." She finished her Pido. "Cuz, let's go to bed. Oh, I almost forgot." Kathy squinted at Territaff. "Did you take care of Fred?"

"Oh yeah." He grinned.

"What we did to that poor man." Kathy shook her head, putting her hand out to Cuz. "Come on, baby, Momma needs a little loving."

Cuz popped up, gave everyone a goodnight wave, and took Kathy's hand in his. They walked out hand-in-hand, laughing, and bumping their butts as they walked.

"What an odd couple they make," the general said, watching them kiss as they entered the lift.

"You know, I'm tired as well. I'm going to sleep," Rob said, stretching his arms. "Hope you all have a good... whatever."

"Good night, Rob. And a job well done," Territaff said, then looked at the general's weary-looking face and said, "You look tired as well, sir."

"Yeah, I'm beat," he said, rubbing the back of his neck before standing. "Hope everyone sleeps well. See you in a few hours." The general took a few steps, then turned and said to Territaff, "We need to talk, but not now. I'm too tired and need to reflect on things."

"Whenever you're ready."

Karoft came in looking a little disheveled. His uniform was wrinkled, and his curly hair almost stood straight up.

"What happened to you?" Tehrarra said.

"Those Bylars are crazy. As I was checking the

environmental settings for the aft shuttle bay, one of the females tried to grab me. If it weren't for being close to the exit, she would have snatched me up in one of her menacing, sharp-clawed hands." Karoft was holding his hand in front of his face as he spoke. He groaned, sitting heavily in a chair.

"You might just be the first Venubian to have attracted a Bylar." Territaff patted his shoulder. "This is a historic moment. Biomei, please note that Administrator Karoft is the first recorded Venubian with Bylar-attracting pheromones."

"Noted," Biomei said.

"Thanks," Karoft sighed, looking more annoyed than amused, "Just what I always wanted on my permanent record." He stood, walked over to the drink synthesizer, ordered a Vultaran brandy, and left without saying goodnight.

"Well, it's just the two of us," Tehrarra said. "You know, I never had time to see your beautiful planet. I understand you have some very tall trees. We have nothing like that on Vultaria. Maybe one day we can return so you can show me your redwoods, tall pines, and oaks."

"You know, I can show you the next best thing." Territaff beamed.

"Yes?"

"There's an arboretum below the observation deck. There are a few modest oak trees there. There's also an impressive botanical garden," Territaff said, extending his hand out to her. "It's my favorite part of the ship."

"You know, Terri," Tehrarra said, wrapping her arm around his waist and pulling him close to her side. "This feels like the start of a beautiful friendship."

Territaff looked into her bright, smiling eyes and murmured, "Absolutely, my dear. Maybe even friends with benefits."

"Oh? And what benefits are you referring to?"

"Uh, let's see what presents itself."

They walked, holding hands, to the lift. Territaff whispered something in her ear that made her laugh as they entered. They embraced and kissed.

"You know, Terri," she purred, "You're one hell of a kisser."

EPILOGUE

The rain just started as Fred ran out to the mailbox. There was the usual stack of bills and advertising fliers. Fred grabbed them and ran back into the house. He threw the stack onto the kitchen table and poured himself another cup of coffee. He was tired and still had to shower and dress before starting his shift.

"Now, I've got to deal with the damn rain," he mumbled to himself.

As he was about to go to the bathroom, the corner of a plain brown envelope caught his eye.

He pulled the envelope out from the stack. There was no return address on it. Fred thought it was another solicitation, but as he held it, he got a funny feeling, and then tore it open.

"What's that?" His wife asked as she entered the kitchen.

Fred didn't answer as he saw the enclosed cashier's check from the accounting firm of Rosenberg and Jacobs. His eyes grew large, and his mouth fell open in surprise and disbelief.

"Oh, sweet Jesus," Fred said, half under his breath.

"What's wrong, dear?" his wife said, looking at her husband's sudden, shocked expression.

"You remember the crazy story I told you about the weird couple that robbed me?"

"Yeah?"

"Well, look at this." He pulled out his crucifix and gold chain, along with his wedding ring and watch.

"What kind of thief returns things?" His wife said, fingering his crucifix, her face tight with confusion.

"If you think that's something, take a look at this." He handed her the check.

She stared at it for a long moment, then screamed, "Is this for real?"

Fred nodded, laughing. He fell back into a kitchen chair as he read the enclosed note. It read: *Hope this makes things right. Thanks.* Signed- T.

"It's for real, Jo. We can send the kids to college, pay off the mortgage, and then take that Hawaiian vacation. Oh shit," Fred exclaimed, seeing the time on the kitchen clock. "I've got to get ready for work."

He ran out of the kitchen, then stopped outside his bedroom door, and thought for a second. He gave his wife a whimsical smile and shouted, "Fuck work! I'm selling the cab and retiring!"

* * *

It was a difficult decision for General Dickerson to let Rob go without first resigning from the military. However, the general knew in his heart that this was an opportunity of a lifetime for Rob. He also knew that after he explained Rob's heroic role in saving the planet, there would be no repercussions for him to face when or if he returned from Venubia. He smiled to himself every time he reflected on Rob going with Territaff and the crew to a new world. The general felt conflicted in his choice to stay. In hindsight, he knew it was the right choice and was glad he made it. Now, the whole story must be told. Regardless of the consequences, everything needed to be brought out into the hard light of truth.

* * *

3 Months Later: Meeting with the Joint Chiefs and Secretary of Defense

General Dickerson's report detailed how every level of both the military and government sectors was infiltrated. He held nothing back and described how naively high-ranking officials acted, often placing their ambitions above the people they were elected to serve. This was nothing new regarding politicians and factions of the military.

As the general progressed through the report, he could feel the conference room fill with the heightened emotions of military men being told they were unwitting victims of an extraterrestrial invasion. General Dickerson described a force so powerful it could have annihilated the Earth with a simple thought. After presenting the stunned group with absolute and unimpeachable evidence, their initial skepticism was abated.

"…In conclusion, we've been given a tremendous opportunity. The moon base described in my debriefing report is intact and can be used at our discretion. The base is fully functional and equipped with advanced technology that will give us the ability to study our universe in ways that exceed anything we could've accomplished with our present technology. The moon base was given to us as a peace gesture and must be shared by the entire planet. Not until we've mastered the technology and demonstrated that we're a productive, peaceful world will they contact us."

General Dickerson paused to give the now awe-struck audience a chance to take in what he had described. "If the events of the previous months teach us anything," he paused again, this time, to rein in his own emotions, "it should at least be a scathing reminder of how vulnerable we've become as a nation when we lose sight of our obligation to the people we're charged to protect and serve. The ultimate question of our very existence has finally been answered. We're not alone, and our galactic neighbors are observing us. As things stand, we have many challenges before us. It's how we face those challenges and grow as a species that will determine our place in the universe and our fate for the future."

The room became so quiet that the general feared he had overwhelmed them. He reached for the water pitcher and filled his glass almost to the brim. He had been talking for over an hour without interruption. His dry throat was not so much from his protracted report as from maintaining a passive demeanor while relating news he knew would change his world forever.

As he drank, he surveyed the room with his eyes. He noticed they were all gazing at him with similar dumbfounded expressions. Their reaction took him by surprise. He waited for the first cry of incredulous objection. Where are the expected fear-driven threats, he wondered? *I've told them that aliens are real and they're not all friendly.* Instead, he observed a room full of daunted minds, not knowing how to react.

"Thank you, ladies and gentlemen, for your attention. I'll take your questions now."

At first, the room remained eerily silent. After a few long seconds, the questions came in droves. Most of them are related to the obvious threat. Many questions went beyond the potential danger the Zenti and Symbients pose. A number were concerned with how we could maintain control of the moon base, and a surprising number were curious about the nature of the extraterrestrials. Those questions were the easiest for the general because they dealt more with the character of our new neighbors.

Dickerson proclaimed at one point, "The universe has just gotten a lot smaller."

Overall, the debriefing went well. The general believed, with guarded optimism, that the future looked full of promise. He was aware that the President would set a course of action and policies that best served his immediate political needs ahead of the interests of the planet. However, the top news came from the Secretary of Defense.

As Dickerson was on his way out of the conference room, the Secretary of Defense motioned to join him at the end of the long conference table. The Secretary was sitting next to the Chairman of the Joint Chiefs, Rear Admiral R. Jefferson Samuelson.

"You handled that well, Bill," the Secretary complimented.

"Thank you, sir."

"I think you know Jeff pretty well," the Secretary added.

General Dickerson gave the Admiral a firm handshake. "Yes, sir. We've served on a few committees together, and I remember a competitive round of golf a few years back," he reminisced with a smile.

"It wasn't competitive at all. You kicked my ass, and not just once, as I recall. You got me by six strokes the next day." The admiral smiled through a narrow gaze at the general.

"Home course advantage, sir," the general said.

"Bill, the reason I've asked you over is to tell you the President has requested me to relay an offer to you."

"An offer, sir? Should I be worried?" Dickerson smiled.

"Maybe... He wants you to head up the new Lunar Operations Initiative. It will be a joint civilian, military, and multinational operation. You're the best man for the job, and the President has every confidence in your abilities to ensure the operation will be well-organized and administered properly. It'll mean a promotion and reopen many doors that were closed to you," he let out a low sigh, "admittedly, for the wrong reasons. It's the President's way of making amends for many things. Also, his way of thanking you for a job well done."

"I'm honored, Mr. Secretary. If I considered the President's generous offer, I'd insist on some firm conditions."

"You'll have an opportunity to discuss all that with him. He wants a meeting to review the position and his vision of how the new moon base should evolve. It's a great break for you, Bill. If all goes well, you'll be able to write your ticket. I was pleased when he chose you."

The general could read right through the President's offer. He knew the President didn't want him hanging around with all that leverage over him. So, what better way to get rid of him than sending him to the moon? General Dickerson reflected on the assignment, feeling satisfied with his situation.

When he told Territaff of his decision to stay behind, Territaff had reservations. Dickerson explained that someone had to ensure the moon didn't get exploited and abused with political infighting and special interest money. He couldn't have positioned himself any better. As the administrator, he'll oversee the entire operation and will insist on complete autonomy in the various selection processes and mission directives. He knew the President was in no position to deny him anything he asked. Perfect, he thought, Territaff will be satisfied.

"Please give the President my sincere gratitude for the honor of taking part in such a historic event. Advise him that I'll give my decision right after I return from my honeymoon."

"Oh, that's right, Bill. You're getting married tomorrow. Congratulations. Please send my regards to Fran. I remember meeting her last year at the Geneva conference. She's a lovely woman. We wish you much happiness. I'll convey to the President to expect a decision within a few weeks."

"Make that a month, sir. We plan to do a little traveling before we settle down into our new life."

"Very well, Bill. I'll advise the President."

"Congratulations, Bill," Admiral Samuelson said, patting the general's shoulder while enthusiastically shaking his hand. "You're full of surprises today."

"If you think today was something, wait until our new neighbors contact us. That's when the real surprises will begin." Dickerson gave them a coy smile that made them pause in thought as he left the conference room.

THE END

The adventure continues with book three of the Territaff series: The Vultaran Dilemma, *coming next year.*

www.ingramcontent.com/pod-product-compliance
Lightning Source LLC
Chambersburg PA
CBHW051111300726
48981CB00001B/83